PROUD, COURAGEOUS, BEAUTIFUL—
THEY WERE THE McELIN WOMEN . . .

MARY—Hot-tempered, stubborn, only duty could uproot her from her beloved Scotland. With three half-grown sons, she crossed an ocean and a continent to seize a new life filled with passion, danger, and opportunity.

LUCY—Her refinement made her a rare jewel in her husband's eyes. Her delicacy made her unfit to share the harsh demands of his rugged life, the deep, intense needs of his proud highland heart.

JANETH—As mysterious as the mountains, she found warmth and shelter in her husband's arms. But the man who truly touched her untamed heart came too late and was forbidden her—forever.

CHRISTINA—Janeth's daughter. Born with a spirit as bold and free as the virgin land; rivalry, hardship, and loss threatened to destroy her. How long could she obstinately deny the solace, the salvation, of an enduring love?

RUTH—Christina's gentle, flaxen-haired daughter. She lived in the shadow of her dazzling twin until tragedy set her free and forced her to fight for what was truly her own.

THE MOUNTAINS OF EDEN

Also by Jaroldeen Edwards

WILDFLOWER

THE MOUNTAINS OF EDEN

Jaroldeen Edwards

A DELL BOOK

Published by
Dell Publishing Co., Inc.
1 Dag Hammarskjold Plaza
New York, New York 10017

Dell ® TM 681510, Dell Publishing Co., Inc.

ISBN: 0-440-15877-X

Printed in the United States of America

First printing—October 1984

... and so are we all pilgrims and strangers upon this earth, brothers and sisters, saints and sinners, seeking the mountains of Eden ...

Part One

THE HIGHLANDERS

1855–1870

Who hath measured the waters in the hollow of his hand, and meted out heaven with the span, and comprehended the dust of the earth in a measure, and weighed the mountains in scales and the hills in a balance?

Isaiah 40:12

Chapter One

Above the village of Kirkwall the cairns and bens of the Scottish Highlands stood like silent sentinels, their craggy heads silhouetted against the night sky, while at their feet soft, dark foothills huddled one against the other, like sleeping children. Ben Sinclair was the tallest of the mountains, with the Arles River hurtling downward from its mist-shrouded heights, gouging through rock, cascading, falling, leaping in its fury to reach the heart of the sleeping hills.

In the fertile soil of the foothills, the river, too headlong to slow its onward rush, cut a deep narrow gash for a valley and then raced on to the lowlands where it joined the estuaries of the River Clyde. Calmed at last upon the broad breast of the mighty waterway, the Arles finally emptied itself into the waiting sea.

Kirkwall village clung to the sides of the narrow valley on the lower slopes of Ben Sinclair. But to call Kirkwall a village was an exaggeration; it was little more than a small collection of winding cobblestone lanes, rock fences, thatched cottages, and small outlying farms. The only buildings of any eminence were the old graystone church and parish house beside the village green.

Above Kirkwall, on the brow of the hill, the black ungainly shape of a coal-shaft elevator was silhouetted against the night sky. A smoldering slag heap glowed with spontaneous combustion that smoked from its fiery depths, like a glimmer of hell itself.

For fourteen hours every day the valley shuddered with the rhythmic thump of the Newcombe steam engines pumping water from the mine, driving the shafts ever deeper. The sound echoed through the Arles Valley like an iron fist beating on a drum. It was the sound of servitude and commerce to the people of Kirkwall, all of whom were employed by the mine in one capacity or another. Only at night were the engines stilled.

In the silence of moonlight the sound of the church bell tolling

9

midnight could be heard clearly, but there were few awake to hear. All the cottages in the slumbering village were dark, except for one—a thatched, double-chimneyed home on the outskirts of town where a low candle burned in a small, unglazed window, casting a pale shaft of light across the stony road.

Inside the cottage, Mary McElin dozed in her rocking chair, but her baby's cry aroused her instantly. The infant's wail was scarcely as loud as the mewing of a lost kitten, but it was the very weakness of the sound that terrified Mary.

"Wee bairn!" she gasped huskily, her hands shaking with anxiety and exhaustion. "Wee Lucy, does it pain ye still?"

Mary picked up her swaddled baby and resumed her weary rocking, crooning a tuneless song as much to comfort herself as to comfort Lucy, but the baby continued to cry. It seemed to Mary that the sound of the baby's fretful sobs filled the gloomy cottage and mingled with the shadows of the dying fire as it flickered on the hearth and threw foreboding shapes onto the dark walls.

Mary was ashamed that she had fallen asleep, but she was exhausted from her efforts to feed her sick infant. Time and again she had brought the feverish baby to her milk-filled breasts, only to have the bairn turn her head and push weakly away, too sick to suck or swallow.

Mary looked across the hearth at her husband, Robert. His worn, leather-bound Bible was lying open in his lap with his thumb still marking the passage he had been reading. Robert's head was bowed in deep, exhausted sleep; the baby's cries had not awakened him.

"How young he looks in the firelight," Mary thought with sudden envy. Robert's features were ruddy in the glow from the embers and his thick black hair curled on his forehead without a trace of gray. Although he was not a big man—Highlanders seldom were— Robert was nobly proportioned and his face, in repose, had the strength and beauty of a clan chieftain.

"He does not look a day older than when he turned my head in Glasgow these many years ago." Mary sighed impatiently, focusing her tired eyes with a frown. "That is just how he looked when he came to my ribbon counter in Aunt Maude's notion shop!"

She was suddenly filled with an unreasoning anger toward her sleeping husband. In this exhausted state her emotions were like a weathervane blowing in a capricious storm, violent and erratic, and as she looked at him her fury mounted.

"Nae mark on him of all our children born!" she muttered

10

bitterly. "Look at him! Nae mark of the hard years of raising Margaret and the three boys! Nae mark on him of our two wee bairns, gone and buried! 'Tis written all over my ould face and my ould body—but nae, not one mark upon him!

" 'Tis a pact with the devil himself you must ha' made, Robbie McElin!" She flung the silent accusation at him across the hearth, and then her agitated glance caught sight of Robert's hands. As she saw the rough, blackened nails and the broken, permanently coal-grimed skin, her heart twisted with sharp pity and tears filled her eyes.

"Aye," she murmured, with a long sigh that sounded almost like a sob, "I may have lost my youth and beauty to our marriage, but you, my Rob, you have lost the joy and freedom of your highlands. Yours is the greater loss!"

Her anger spent, she nodded her head musingly and closed her eyes for a second. Years before, at her urging, Robert had left the rugged highlands of his inheritance for the employment and the schools for the children that the villages of the lowlands offered. For her he had given up the fresh sky, his high, windblown meadows, and the fierce and solitary independence of the clansman. How he hated the lowlands! He was like a hawk caged with chickens.

"Poor Robbie," she whispered softly. "Sleep on. Your mornings come too soon as it be."

For three days Mary had done nothing but tend her sick baby. She slept in snatches when the baby slept. In spite of all her care Mary could feel Death lurking in the cottage. When it came it was attended by untidiness and disarray. Around her she saw her unpolished copper and the half-filled peat baskets. The matted and rumpled straw sleeping ticks, the unswept hearth, and the musty look of dust and disuse mocked her. Her twenty-year-old daughter, Margaret, had done her best to manage the house while her mother cared for the dying baby. Each evening Margaret hurried home from her job in the village candle shop to set out boiling wash water and cold mutton pie for her father when he trudged home from the mines after dark. She had offered to care for her baby sister, begging her mother to rest, but Mary would not let anyone else touch the dying child—not even Margaret.

Mary sighed as she thought of her lovely, grown daughter sleeping peacefully upstairs in the loft and then, unbidden, the memory of her two other daughters came to her—babies forever, sleeping under their gravestones on the hill behind the cottage.

Mary clutched Lucy to her more tightly. "Nay!" she thought fiercely. "I'll not let myself think of dead bairns. I will think of my three bonnie boys, fine, strong sons, tending their flocks in the highlands right now and climbing to the sky itsel'! 'Tis only a few more weeks and they'll be coming home!" she murmured in her baby's ear.

Lucy stiffened abruptly and her tiny body became rigid, straining backward in an agonizing spasm.

"Robbie!" Mary screamed, waking her husband. "Quick! Run for the doctor and the Reverend Cameron! Ye must run! It's dying our Lucy is!"

Robert leaped up and saw his wife bent over the convulsing baby. His heart twisted with fear. He had always thought it a strange thing that a grown man should feel powerful emotions for something so unformed and tiny as an infant. Yet each time he watched Mary through her labor, when the midwife, after hours of Mary's agony, placed the squalling, red-faced newborn in his arms, he felt a painful constriction in his proud heart, and a piece of himself became inextricably tied to the tiny new being. In the short three months Lucy had been with them, this baby daughter had especially tangled him in her wee spell. Such a bonnie bairn she was! With a glimmer of red hair, like her mother's, and the sweetest little milky smile . . . when she curled her wee hand around his finger, he thought his heart would break with joy. Perhaps because he was growing older, her newness gave him a sense of renewal. Whatever the reason, he could not bear the thought of losing her!

In three strides he crossed the room and grabbed his coat from the peg beside the door. He spoke reassuringly. "Hold fast, Mary, and be of firm faith." He closed the door behind him with a hurried slam as a blast of cold air gusted through the cottage.

Working swiftly, Mary undressed the baby and prepared a basin of cool water. The child was still convulsing as Mary placed her gently in the water and began to lave her frail limbs with a soft cloth. As the water cooled the fever, the baby became limp and pliable once again. Mary wrapped her in a soft flannel towel and placed her own plaid shawl around her. Clutching the infant tightly, she began pacing the floor, praying for the swift return of her husband with the doctor and the minister.

When Robert returned, however, he had only the doctor with him. Dr. Sewell was a rumpled, fat, short-tempered man, with rough, filthy hands and a contempt for the coal miners and their families.

Since one miner's baby more or less seemed of little importance to him, he would have refused to make the visit altogether had he not feared the determination in Robert's eyes.

As Mary watched anxiously, Dr. Sewell made a cursory examination of the baby and then shook his head disgustedly. "She'll not make the morning light," he said coldly. "Abscess behind the ear. It's broken and spread infection through her entire body. Egad, woman! It's midnight! You don't need a doctor to see she's dying! You shouldn't have disturbed me for this."

It was more than Mary could abide. She flew to stand between the doctor and the door. He had been drinking, and she could smell the whiskey on his heavy breath.

"You drunken sot!" she cried. "How dare you stand there and judge who and what is worth saving! This is my daughter, do ye hear me? Every hair of her head, every whisper of her breath is worth more than the whole of your great sodden, filthy body and your miserable soul!"

The doctor was shocked by the woman's fury, and for a moment his alcohol haze dissipated enough for him to see her clearly.

She was small, as slender as a willow, with a mass of red hair falling around her face and shoulders. Her eyes, although ringed with weariness, blazed emerald green in the firelight. True, she was past the bloom of youth, but in her fiery state she was filled with a magnetic vitality that was more alluring than youth.

"My! Aren't you a pretty one!" the doctor mumbled appreciatively and reached out to touch her. Mary shrank back from his fat, filthy hand as Robert strode to the man's side and grabbed the scruff of his coat.

"You'd best leave!" Robert growled. "Before I throw you out!"

The doctor whirled and gave Robert an angry glare. How dare these people insult him!

"You ignorant people." The doctor spluttered. "You've no call to be rude to me. All your kind knows how to do is to make babies! Day in, day out I come to your filthy hovels. Like animals—that's how you live. Groveling in the earth for your wages, groveling in your beds for your pleasure . . . and these sickly infants are the result."

Robert took the doctor by his collar and lifted him up bodily. "You are a disgusting excuse for a man," Robert said to him. "I can hardly stand to soil my hands on ye!" He dragged the doctor to the door and threw him out into the night. "*You* are an animal!" he

13

shouted after the doctor. Robert slammed the door and turned back into the room breathing heavily from anger and exertion. He looked at Mary, who had placed the baby back on the table and was standing with her face buried in her hands. Her anger was spent, replaced by overwhelming sorrow.

"He is right, we are going to lose Lucy before morning. And I cannot bear it!" Her voice rose in desperation. "Did ye not bring the Reverend Cameron as I asked? Please, Robbie, tell me that you called for him!"

In agony, Mary rested her head gently upon her infant while her arms made a protecting circle around the little body. "Please, Robbie," she whispered softly, her voice filled with supplication, "let Lucinda be baptized before she dies. I must have the hope of seeing her again. I cannot bear the pain of losing her forever."

Robert's mountain-blue eyes were black with grief, but he turned a resolute face toward his sorrowing wife. "I called on the Reverend Cameron as ye asked. I thought he might give ye a word of comfort—and he is coming—but I will nae let ye have our wee one baptized! Sprinklin' is no true baptism and I'll not hae my children defiled by a false ordinance. Never ask me that again, Mary, for ye know I canna do it! 'Tis a matter of principle!"

"But Robbie." Mary wept. "She will go to her grave in unconsecrated ground like the others! Will ye not bend? Just this once!"

With a growl of pain Robbie turned from his wife's pleading eyes and walked to the fire. "Nowhere in the good book does it speak of sprinkling! I canna—I willna—accept it." Robbie leaned his head against the mantel, his back toward Mary, rigid as stone.

Hurt and anger flared in her eyes as she lifted Lucy and held her tightly. "Ye're a blind and stubborn man, Robert McElin! Nothing will change or soften ye once ye have made up your mind. How can I live so—with someone who thinks he is the only one who knows the will of God. You and your good book! You will kill me! That's what you will do. I shall die of grief."

Robert turned a ravaged face to his wife. "Nay, Mary. Ye do not understand. 'Tis not death I want to give you—but life."

A terrible silence fell in the room. The only sounds were the rustling of mice in the heavy thatch over their heads and the low hiss of the smoking peat fire.

Robert stared into the fire with despair. In only a few hours he would need to leave the cottage and walk up the rocky pathway to the mine. He would stand hunched in the meager dawn light with the other miners in their bulky clothes, black with coal dust, their cold lunch pails in their hands. The men would not speak, but stand silently, each dreading the moment when he would be shoved into the crowded elevator and dropped down into the depths of the mine shaft. There, sweating in the dim light from the lanterns, with the earth groaning and creaking around him and the thick black dust clogging his nostrils, he would pick and shovel, worm on his belly into narrow holes, shore timbers, and pray for the day to end.

Not until after dark would he return to the surface and plod his way home.

Robert's natural spirit rebelled against the physical confines of this dark, narrow life in the valley.

And how could he explain to Mary that, as much as he hated the physical confines of this daily existence, he had always hated in exactly the same way the confines of his spiritual existence? Even as a boy in the highlands he had rebelled against the superstition, ignorance, and pagan traditions that were so much a part of the "Old Faith" within the isolated orders of the clansmen. He had yearned, even in the open fields of the highlands, to find some essence of truth so that he could be as free in mind and spirit as his body was in the mountain air.

He had gone to Divinity School at the university in Glasgow and had studied the Reformation. With his proud and independent mind, he challenged everything he heard and he would not compromise. His professors turned from his dogged questioning with contempt or rage but he had continued his own frustrated search.

Finally, when Mary accepted his marriage proposal, he had withdrawn from the university and broken his ties with the Church. His religion had become what was written in the pages of the Bible. He and his family were unchurched and unbaptized. To Mary, this was the cause for shame and sorrow.

A new minister, the Reverend Donald Cameron, had recently moved to Kirkwall. He had made several visits to the McElins and genuinely seemed to enjoy discussing theology with Robert. For the first time Mary allowed herself to hope that Robert might relent and let his family belong to a church. Robert recognized Mary's hope in silent frustration. How could he explain that, though he gave up the freedom of his highlands for her, he could never return to spiritual servitude—not for her—nor for anything but truth?

In her arms Mary felt her baby give a terrible shudder, and she gently pulled back the blanket to look at the wee face. Lucy's delicate eyelids were closed, her sweet little mouth was still. For the first time in days Mary saw no trace of pain on her child's face.

" 'Tis of no matter anyway," Mary murmured dully. "She could not be baptized now, even if ye gave your consent. The minister will be coming to visit us in vain."

Without a word Robert stepped to Mary and took the little bundle from her listless arms. Too numb to think, Mary watched as he looked deeply into his daughter's lifeless face. Slow, silent tears filled his eyes. At that moment, Mary felt all the tears dry up inside of her, as though her heart had shriveled and died. She felt she would never cry again for there were no tears strong enough for her sorrow.

When the Reverend Cameron visited the bereaved parents the next morning, he offered to pray at the tiny gravesite Robert was digging for his infant daughter on the hill behind their cottage. By the fresh grave were two other small headstones.

With genuine respect, Robert thanked the minister. "I am grateful for your offer, but since we are unbaptized I think it more fitting if I read the words mysel'. We would be honored, though, if ye would come to stand wi' us."

In the chill and windy March morning the small group of mourners stood on the barren hillside—Mary, Margaret, and the young minister. They listened as Robert read, " 'I am the resurrection and the life; he that believeth in me, though he were dead, yet shall he live; and whosoever liveth and believeth in me, shall never die.' " Margaret shuddered as the first hard shovelfuls of dirt thudded on the tiny coffin, but her mother stood as unmoving as though she were made of iron.

When the brief service was over, Robert shook the Reverend Cameron's hand and thanked him for coming. The reverend pulled Robert out of earshot of Mary, who remained standing by the grave with dry eyes and a stony face.

"Mr. McElin, I am worried about your wife." The young pastor's voice was compassionate and his deep-set hazel eyes were troubled. "She does not seem to be herself."

"Aye," Robert acknowledged with a sigh. "Only six months ago we buried our wee Bess—and now Lucy—'tis more than she can accept. She is angered."

Puzzled, the tall, serious minister looked at Robert. "Surely you mean 'sorrowed'!" he corrected him.

"Nay," Robert replied. "Ye do not know my Mary! Hers is a

fierce and proud spirit. She has fought for her bairns and lost and it is anger she feels toward her adversary."

"And who is her adversary?" asked the young minister.

"I think she is quarreling with God," Robert answered. "She holds Him to account."

The wind was cold and the young minister shivered. "I must get back to the village. I wish I could offer more help, but you are a hard man to comfort, Robert McElin; you carry your own answers with you." Ruefully the pastor gestured toward the worn Bible in Robert's hands. Then the Reverend Cameron looked up the hill again where the bereaved mother still stood motionless. "But man! Your wife! That poor woman!—I should hate to be at a quarrel with God. How can she hope to win such a contest? The odds are mightily uneven!"

"Ah," Robert replied with a gentle smile, "but ye do not know my wife!"

For two days Mary kept her tearless watch on the hillside. She would return to the house long after sundown and retire wordlessly to her unmade bed. Robert, arriving home from the coal mines, would find a cheerless dwelling. If Margaret had not arrived before him, the fires would be unlit, and only cold ashes and a silent hearth would greet him.

On the third day Robert came home early and climbed the hill to where his wife kept her defiant vigil. "Mary!" he said firmly. "It is time for you to begin again. Come down wi' me now!"

Mary turned her small, set face toward him and he looked longingly at the woman who had captured his heart over two decades before. She had grown pale and lines of care and sorrow furrowed her forehead, but the firm, even features of her face were still lovely, and in her fiery green eyes Robert saw the shadow of the exquisite little shopgirl he had loved at first sight.

Mary did not move under her husband's scrutiny, and he knew from the set of her jaw and the intensity of her expression that she had reached some decision. "Has she ceased her quarrel with God," he wondered uneasily, "and moved it on to me?"

"Robbie," Mary said, "I have thought it through, and I know now that ours is the blame. We are being punished for the indecent joy we have taken in one another's bodies long after the time when such things are seemly in a marriage. We have been lustful all our wedded days, and God is punishing us because we have loved each other more than Him, more than our children, and more than our

17

proper duties in life. The doctor was right. We are ignorant and . . . like animals!''

Robert clenched his jaws with pain and fury, and he did not trust himself to speak. With cold finality, Mary continued.

''I shall be your wife, Robbie, and care for you always, but I shall never allow myself to carry another babe and bear it to pain and sorrow and death. I shall never lie with you again.'' Her words fell like stones on his heart.

''Ye canna mean this, Mary!'' Robert protested. ''It is only your sorrow speaking!''

''Nay!'' Mary replied. ''And is my sorrow not justified when ye will send all my wee daughters to unbaptized graves?''

''Ye still have a living daughter!'' Robert answered.

''Aye! One living daughter! Ye have three living sons!'' He heard the echo of her lonely highland years in her voice.

''Do ye think I loved these last bairns the less because they were daughters?'' Robbie cried. ''Ye do not know me well, my Mary, if ye think such a thing!'' He took a deep breath and spoke more quietly. ''I have loved my daughters more, God help me, because they were like you!'' Then he added with a faint smile, ''Except for Angus! There is no one in the world more like you than Angus!''

''Then you shall have to content yourself with what you have,'' Mary stated, ''for there shall be no more! I am done with birth and death—and sorrow!''

Mary turned on her heel and walked purposefully down the hill toward the house. Robert watched her go as a man would watch a dying lantern in the black mines. In his mind he again called up the vision of her as she had been behind the ribbon counter in her aunt's shop in Glasgow. He remembered the morning sunshine radiant on her unruly hair, her face vivid with youth and vitality. He saw her slender waist and her dainty ankles under swaying skirts. He remembered his first night with her and the sweetness of her mouth on his—the warm wisp of her body as it brushed against him.

He remembered their first year together in his beloved highlands where she, a city girl, had begun to learn the loneliness of the far mountains with their echoing rocks—the silent meadows, the straying, bleating sheep, and the incessant wailing of tree-strained winds. Unhappy as she had been, still, at night, in his arms, she had glowed like a candle and had come to him each time as the first time, filled with wonder and passion. Five years she had endured the highlands, and even after the birth of their first four children—Margaret and the three boys—she had continued to be joyful and abandoned in the dark, giving herself to him without reservation.

Then had followed the bad times. He remembered their first lost baby—born too soon—and Mary's long, hard recovery. In that year Mary had truly begun to hate the highlands, and even at night she had wept. He remembered watching as Mary and the children seemed to wane before his eyes. That year the lambing went badly as well. They lost lamb after lamb, and the ewes that survived fell prey to a wasting disease. The few sheep he had taken to market that terrible season had barely bought enough provisions to hold his family through the winter. The next summer the weather remained cold and wet, and he watched his flock dwindle even more.

It was Mary who suffered the most. Her loving eagerness disappeared, and even the children playing around her skirts could not rouse her smiles. Food was scarce, and she starved herself to feed the others. By midwinter Robert knew his wife could not live another year in the isolation and hardship of the highlands that he loved. With heavy heart he sold the remnants of his flock and the small parcel of land that had been in his family for generations. He moved his wife, daughter, and the three growing sons to Kirkwall. The village had been a bustling livestock center, but the mysterious sheep disease had decimated the local flocks as well, and the village was in a depression. The only work he could find was in the coal mines. Robert, the proud Highlander, who had lived his life under the open mountain skies, now entered the black holes and tunnels beneath the mountains. He hated the new life, but it had been worth the sacrifice for he had watched his Mary begin to revive.

As Mary settled into the cozy thatched cottage in the valley, protected from prevailing winds by the sheltering hills, she lived again among other women and could shop and visit. Slowly she returned to herself, and once again she had begun to respond to his aching need for her and once again her sweet body warmed his.

Sometimes Robert felt he could not force himself to go down into the mines one more day. However, at night, when he held Mary in his arms and once again felt the flame that lit in her at his touch, he knew he would pay any price for that joy. Three more children had been conceived in their newfound love and now all three were gone.

Mary meant what she had said, Robert knew. In all the years he had known his wife, she had never gone back on her word. He wondered now how he could continue to live in this wretched valley if he were to lose forever the touch, the smell, and the silent mystery of her body.

For a brief moment he looked through the gathering twilight at the lofty crests of the mountains that ringed the valley town. Those high peaks called to him and, for an instant, he felt a keening in his mind. The lure of the runic winds and the freedom of the summits begged him to come back and his heart was fully set for flight, but he wrenched his eyes from the beckoning highlands and stilled his yearning heart. With bent head and sagging shoulders, like a beaten man, he slowly walked down the hillside and entered the back door of the cottage.

Mary, true to her word, moved her bedding to the loft, and Robert lay awake that night in aching loneliness—sleeping alone for the first time since his marriage.

The three McElin brothers plodded across the high peat moor, with nineteen-year-old Angus in the lead. He paused and looked at the darkening sky with a practiced eye. The clouds had been massing all afternoon, scudding from behind the nearby peaks. Now the nearby summit of Cairn Sinclair had become invisible and a heavy mist was rolling down, filling the bowl of the high wild moor where they were traveling. The wind had grown colder, and it whipped the heavy tartans the brothers wore wrapped around their bodies. The Highlander's tartan was his life. It kept him warm in the wind, muffled his face against blizzards, served as a sling for carrying wounded lambs, held rations for a journey. At day's end it served as a makeshift tent or bedroll for the clansman as he slept outside under the low-slung stars. Angus wore the "hunting" plaid of the McElin clan, and Matty, his eighteen-year-old brother, wore the McElin "dress" plaid. Johnny, sixteen years old, wore the plaid of his grandmother's clan—the Russell tartan.

When Johnny had chosen the Russell tartan to wear as his own, Angus had looked at his youngest brother with affectionate exasperation. "Can ye no do anything the same as your elder brothers?" he had asked.

Now, as Angus thought of Johnny, an anxious frown crossed his face, and he turned from his position at the lead to watch as the boy stumbled several yards behind, hurrying to keep pace. "Shall we stop for a wee rest, Johnny?" Angus called.

"Nay!" Johnny called back, leaning heavily on his walking staff but moving steadily onward. Angus could see his brother's eyes sparkling with humor, as Johnny threw back his head in cocky defiance. "Dinna stop for me! I've no desire to spend the night in the drenchin' rain!"

Matty came abreast of Angus and spoke firmly. "The lad's all right. Let's keep moving until we reach the Glen of Arles. Maybe we can find some shelter there."

Another blast of cold wind roared down the slopes. Angus pulled his tartan more tightly through his belt and wrapped the loose end around his shoulder and face. He was the undisputed leader of the three. It was not Angus's age alone that made Matty and Johnny follow him, rather it was an elusive quality in him that the two younger boys would have been hard put to explain. In Angus they sensed a calmness in decison making and a fierceness of resolve that bred confidence and security.

The three McElin boys were as unalike in temperament as they were in appearance. Angus, like his father, was a true Highlander. He had vivid blue eyes and black curly hair and a beard. His features were aquiline, with a square, manly jaw, and his body was muscular and compactly built. Matthias, the second brother, called Matty, also had the coloring of a Highlander, but his face was narrower and his eyes more piercing and quick. He was much taller than either of his brothers, and, although he moved with an almost adolescent awkwardness, he had incredible physical endurance. He was a quiet young man who kept his own counsel and thought his own thoughts. Angus knew he could trust Matty with his life.

Johnny had been the baby in the McElin home for many years, and a more cheerful, joyous child had never been born. Through hard days and lean times the family had warmed themselves in the light of Johnny's mischievous laughter. He was slight and red-haired, like his mother, and often into trouble, but no one—not even his stern father—had the heart to reprimand him sharply. For all his lighthearted ways, Angus recognized that Johnny was dependable, gallant, and courageous.

Throughout their youth, the three brothers had learned to work as a team. Each one used his own particular strength to add to the whole—Angus, always the leader, Matty, strong and dependable, and Johnny, with his joyous heart.

Although the brothers had said nothing to one another, they each realized they were lost. Angus continued to tramp along, his head bowed against the rain-laden wind, but his eyes were ceaselessly

21

searching the surrounding rocks and crags hoping to see some sign of a mountain trail or pass.

Four days earlier the McElin brothers had been happily herding Laird Nevins's sheep in the remote summit of Cairn Sinclair. Lambing season had come early and their hard work was finished. When the spring herder had arrived from the village of Kirkwall, the brothers crowded around him for news of their family. The gnarled old herder squinted at the boys and told them about their baby sister's death, then gave them the message Robert had sent to his sons. "Well, lads," the herder said, "thee father says ye are to come home as swift as possible. Mary, thee mother, be in dire need of comfortin'. There's summat amiss down there, I tell ye—and ye'd best be on yer way home," he added in his rusty voice.

Angus had immediately hurried to speak to the foreman of the sheep crew. The flock they herded was owned by Laird Malcolm Nevins, but the man who employed them was the steward of the laird's estate and an old friend of their father's. Angus had begged his father not to send him to work in the mines, and so Robert had obtained the sheeptending job for Angus. Shepherding was a lonely, isolated way of life, but it was in the McElin blood, and, as each brother finished his schooling, he had chosen to join Angus in the mountains tending sheep rather than enter the mines. The boys knew it would be only a matter of time before they would leave the valleys and villages forever to live the rest of their lives in the harsh, heady freedom of the highlands. They also knew it was only their mother that kept their father from making the same decision.

Two weeks were left on the boys' sheepherding contract before they were due to leave for a visit home. When Angus asked the steward if the three brothers could leave immediately, the laird's man saw the boys' request as a chance to save some money.

"Aye, Angus," the steward said cannily, "ye and your brothers may go as ye wish. But if ye leave this two weeks early, I shall hae to dock ye for one month's wages—for breach of contract."

Angus frowned at the unfairness of the condition, but he felt an urgent need to answer his father's summons. The next morning, before the brothers left the sheep camp, Angus had gone to the steward to collect their wages. The shrewd sheepman counted out the pence with slow, meticulous care. As he laid out the last copper, Angus asked, "Is there not a faster way down the mountain to Kirkwall than the old Nevins path? I mind how ye once said ye could get down in one day rather than two."

"Aye," said the flock foreman. " 'Tis a more rugged way—and it is less well marked—but 'tis considerable faster."

Angus listened carefully while the steward had given him directions for the shortcut.

Anxious to get home and sure of their skills and strength, the three brothers had started off toward the rocky Glen of Arles that would then lead them to Kirkwall. On the second day of traveling, after a difficult rock climb, the brothers had lost sight of the long-unused trail. Retaining a sense of direction, because of their knowledge of the mountains and the position of the sun and stars, they had continued moving toward home. However, the obstacles in their path had become more and more difficult. This morning they had spent several hours in a blind canyon and finally had to retrace their steps to higher ground. The brothers knew the dangers of being lost in the mountains—the sheer cliffs, the treacherous high swamps, the impassable cascades, and the numbing cold rains that sapped the strength of even the hardiest traveler. They had brought oatcakes and dried mutton with them, but their food supplies were growing short and so, in the gathering gloom, they pressed on quickly across the mountain moor, anxious to reach the other side before darkness overtook them. Three days of hard traveling had seemingly brought them nowhere and they were tired and chilled.

Angus stoically forged ahead, but when he reached the rocky rim of the plateau and climbed through the opening in the rocks, his heart sank. Below him the earth fell sharply away in a series of shards, cliffs, and upthrust crags. Far below he could see the Arles cascade, bounding downward toward the valley. As he stood staring at the inhospitable sight, his two younger brothers scrambled through the rocks behind and joined him on the rim of the precipice.

"Is it hopeless?" Matty asked. "Will we need to turn back once agin?"

Exhausted, Johnny threw himself down on a boulder. "If ye need to turn back," he said, "ye shall simply have to leave me here to die in peace!"

Angus turned and frowned at his young brother. "Can ye nae be serious? This is no time for your wit!"

"Angus!" Matty exclaimed, pointing downward. "Before it gets any darker, have a look. See the ledge below us! Is that not a narrow trail leading down from it?"

In the poor light, Angus squinted at the rocks below. He could see the ledge Matty had pointed out—a fairly wide one about fifteen feet below them, and from the far side of it he saw a line that appeared to be a narrow trail leading downward.

"I dinna know, Matty," Angus said dubiously. "It could be! Here, lower me down so I can see."

"Nay!" Johnny cried, jumping up. "I'm lighter, let me down!"

The young men hooked their belts together and lowered Johnny to the ledge. "Aye!" Johnny called up. " 'Tis a trail indeed!"

Angus lowered Matty next, bracing himself against a rock until his brother reached the ledge.

For the third and last time he raised the belts, then looked around for an anchor. A sturdy, deep-rooted spruce grew out of the cleft of a rock. He tested the thick trunk and deemed it strong enough to carry his weight. After fastening the end of the belt to the pine, he carefully edged over the rim of the precipice and began lowering himself hand over hand. Suddenly a loud crack sounded above him, and the makeshift line broke loose from the shattered tree. In a shower of broken stones and branches, Angus hurtled down the cliff. His brothers caught him and pulled him to safety on the ledge.

They stood and watched in horror as the shower of small stones roared past them, dropping in a long, deadly free fall beneath them, until, far below, they crashed into the wild river. The belts, still attached to Angus's waist, dangled over the ledge, flapping in the wind.

A silence fell on the three young men as they realized that now there was no way to go back. Angus walked to the far edge and examined the trail. Johnny was right! For a short way the ledge remained barely wide enough for a man to traverse—if he could find adequate handholds above. But, as Angus stared, he realized what Johnny had not seen—the ledge petered out and became nothing but a crack in the face of the wall!

Rain began to fall in sheets, and below them they could hear the pounding of the river. Angus went back to his brothers. "There is no more to do tonight," he said with false cheer. "We must sleep and gather our strength."

The cliff overhang above them provided meager shelter. The three brothers huddled together against the back of the ledge. They put one tartan below them, and two over them, and with heads bowed against their knees they dozed fitfully through the night. The sound of rain and the thundering mountain stream below filled their dreams.

In the morning the two younger brothers awakened to find Angus at the far end of the ledge surveying the surrounding area.

"We must go on," he said without preamble. "I was hoping for sunshine to warm us, but 'twill be another rainy day. If we are to have the strength to succeed, we must start now!"

The three bound their tartans tightly to their bodies. Angus led the way. He inched along the ledge as it narrowed, fighting for hand-holds above him in the cold, slippery rock. Just before the rock ledge disappeared into the face of the cliff, he lowered himself slowly, his fingers clinging to the ledge and his feet braced against the sheer rock below. He continued to inch along as the ledge turned into a mere crack in the face of the cliff. His fingers were bleeding as he pried them into the crack, moving himself slowly toward a sharp upthrust of rock that stood parallel to the cliff. When he reached the rock pillar, he placed his foot against it and braced himself between the cliff and the crag of stone. Then, with his feet on the stone and his body against the cliff, he held himself in a wedge and began to chimney his way slowly down between the two rock faces.

His brothers followed him, duplicating his actions, and except for one terrible moment when Johnny's hand slipped and he hung, for what seemed like an eternity, by one arm above the jagged rocks before pulling himself up, they managed with surprising ease.

It took all morning, but by noon the brothers clustered, drenched with perspiration and rain, on a second ledge almost forty feet below the one on which they had spent the night. Twenty feet below them the mountain stream crashed between sheer walls of stone.

"Well, lads," Angus shouted above the water's roar, "we couldn't get wetter if we tried!" With that he took a deep breath, stepped out onto the ledge, and leaped downward into the raging stream.

The brothers saw him hit the water, and in a second they saw the bright swirl of his plaid being swept over the edge of a series of low cascades.

"S'truth!" Johnny exclaimed. "C'mon, Matty!" and he too plunged off the cliff. Matty watched Johnny's young body as it was swallowed up by the water and then bobbed to the surface.

With a resigned shrug, Matty followed. Before he knew it, the icy water had closed over his head and he felt his legs banging against hidden rocks. A swift current picked him up like a leaf, and he barely had time to gasp for air before he felt himself thrown over the cascades and plunged deep beneath the falls. He was hurled swiftly along under the water until he shot to the surface, fifty feet farther downstream. Another gasp for air, and he was dashed over the next cascade. He knew he was crashing and bumping against underwater rocks, but the swiftness of the stream made them feel like glancing blows. He wondered where his two brothers were and if perhaps they were floating dead or unconscious near him, but when he tried to grasp at a jutting rock to stay his furious passage, another undertow grabbed him, and once again he felt himself plunging over a cascade, down into the deep pool beneath him. This time when he bobbed to the surface the water loosened its grip on him and he found he could move more easily with the current. Looking around him, he saw the riverbanks had widened and a green meadow spread beside it.

With weary arms he swam toward the shore and dragged his body onto the weir. As he rolled over on his back, through bleary eyes and the blur of rain he saw a figure standing over him. "What kept ye, Matty?" Johnny's laughing voice asked. "We've been a'waitin'."

The three brothers found a small camp of sheepmen in the meadow, and after they had warmed themselves by the herders' fire and had eaten some of their hot mutton stew, they continued their journey.

Kirkwall village lay only twenty miles from the sheep camp, and the trail the sheepmen showed them wound easily through foothills and glen. Just after dark Angus, Matty, and Johnny saw the smoke of their own chimney, and their weary footsteps hurried down the last road.

As they opened the cottage door, they saw the familiar scene of home. Their mother was stitching a shirt in the old slatted rocker by the fireplace and their father was reading his Bible on the other side of the hearth. Margaret was spinning wool, seated on a low stool between them. Their older sister was humming a bit of a tune, but her young sweet face looked sad. At the sound of the door, their mother looked up, and when she caught sight of her three boys her eyes lighted with joy. The brothers were dripping wet, their faces bruised, and their eyes dark with exhaustion.

"Well," said Mary, "I dinna think ye could look worse! If I dinna know better I would think ye had been swimming!"

To her amazement the three boys broke into uproarious laughter.

The brothers had only been home a few days when it became apparent to Angus that something was very wrong in his family. He had caught a glimpse of some trouble his first night at home. After the boys had shared the tales of their adventures, their mother had set out straw ticks for them to sleep on. When bedtime came she bid them good night but, instead of going to the bedroom by the kitchen, she had gone upstairs to Margaret's loft. Angus's father had finished his reading, and, with a brief "Good night" to his sons, he had gone, alone, to the bed in the small anteroom by the kitchen that the parents had always shared. Nothing was said about the new sleeping arrangement, but, as Angus lay awake, unable to sleep because of the aching of his bruised body, he thought how all through his early life, each night, when the children were tucked in to bed, his mother and father had walked together to their own little room. He could remember hearing the murmur of their voices as they whispered and he thought of the years in which he had fallen asleep listening to the sweet sound of his mother and father together. Even as a child he had known, somewhere deep inside of him, that the sound of their quiet, private murmuring was the security and substance of his life. Now there was no murmuring in the night, only a cold, stiff silence.

There were other signs of change. Mary had not even bothered to set out the jonquils this spring. The bulbs rotted in the cellar, and, as spring came, the yard remained bleak and uncared-for. Inside the cottage Mary cleaned like a woman gone mad. She polished, scrubbed, whitewashed, and soaped until the boards of the floor were bleached. It was as if she wanted to wash away the memory of death. But nowhere in the house was there a single touch of beauty. She no longer placed blue bowls of heather on the tables, or gathered spring willows and sprigs of mountain columbine. Robert too had changed. Angus watched him leave for the mines as though he were going to his execution. In his father's face he saw anger and resentment. When Robert came home, he no longer washed himself clean, but gave his hands a cursory rinsing, growling, "What's the use! The filth will be back tomorrow!" Angus wanted to take his parents and shake them back to their senses.

Margaret also puzzled him. She seemed genuinely glad to have her brothers home but she was seldom there herself. In the mornings she left at dawn and sometimes did not return until long after supper. It was a symptom of the dissolution of the family that neither Mary nor Robert inquired where Margaret was spending her evenings.

Angus broached the subject one afternoon as he came in from the garden where he was planting early leeks. Mary was scrubbing the kitchen table.

"Mother," he said, "are ye not concerned for Margaret? Do ye even ask where she keeps herself these days?"

Mary, always quick to feel a slight, frowned at her son. "And are ye trying to tell me how to be a mother now, wee Angus?"

Angus, so like his mother in temperament, replied sharply, "Perhaps ye need reminding that there is still mothering to be done!" The moment he said the words he was sorry.

"Margaret is near a grown woman, Angus! She has no need for a keeper!" Mary returned to her harsh scrubbing and would not look at him.

Angus grabbed his mother's hand, which held the stiff-bristled brush, so that she could not continue her cleaning. "Look at me!" he pleaded. "Don't you see what you are doing? You are driving us away from you! We want to help—to care—but you willna let us try!"

Mary said not a word, but her hand trembled under his, and then she pulled it away and continued her vigorous soaping of the tabletop, scrubbing as though her life depended on removing the unseen stains.

One Saturday afternoon Margaret came home early from the candle shop. Since no one was about, she slipped into the kitchen, picked up a small basket, placed a few provisions in it, and hurried out the back door.

Angus, who had been up on the hill behind the house, caught sight of Margaret hurrying down the lane. His first impulse was to call out or run to her, but something in her furtive movements made him curious. He began to follow her at a discreet distance. At the crossroads, about a mile from the village, Margaret met a man in a dark suit. The two of them walked a way together and then she spread her shawl on the hillside. Angus saw them sit down side by side and begin eating. They talked as they ate with their heads close together in easy and familiar companionship. Angus watched for about an hour, and then the man stood up and helped Margaret to her feet. The couple walked back toward the crossroads, and then Margaret hurried toward home, alone, while the stranger took himself off in another direction.

Unable to contain himself, Angus ran down the sloping hill and intercepted Margaret as she turned a corner in the path.

"Aha! I have caught ye now, dear sister! Who is it ye are courting with, that ye need to hide it from yer kin? Is it a married man? Now tell me the truth, for if it be, I shall hide him—and ye, too! We've enough sorrow as it is!"

Margaret's brilliant red hair, blown by the wind, circled her fresh young face, and her cheeks, pink with the wind and embarrassment, gave her a rosy beauty. Her blue eyes, as clear and determined as Angus's own, stared back at him boldly.

" 'Tis not your permission I'm needing, Angus McElin! I can do as I please!"

"Oh, Maggie dearest!" Angus cried. "Can ye not see that I'm asking for your own good!"

Then Margaret started laughing. "Nay, you're not. You're asking for curiosity! That's what it is, wee Angus! Ye're dying of curiosity!"

Angus grinned sheepishly and dropped her arm. "Aye, that I am, Maggie. Will ye not tell me?"

"Oh, Angus!" Maggie said breathlessly. "I'm so glad you found out! I've been fair burstin' to tell someone, and I know you'll be so happy for me!"

The brother and sister sat down together on the stone wall by the roadside.

"After Lucinda died, it was like living in a house of the dead," Margaret told him. "Mother and Daddie hardly spoke and there was no life about the house at all. One day I was coming home, very slowly, not wanting to get there, and I saw the Reverend Cameron walking down the way. He asked how Mother and Father were doing and said he would like to come to visit them, but felt he was no comfort since Daddie was so opposed to the Church.

"Then I did a terrible thing, Angus! I said to him, 'I am not opposed to the Church. I think I need it very much.' And I told him everything, how Daddie was a Highlander who had abandoned the Auld Faith to come to Glasgow to study the teachings of Knox, and how he met Mother and returned to the highlands. I told him how Daddie had constructed his own faith directly from the Bible, how we had lived all our lives as outcasts because Daddie would not let us be baptized or join any church and folks thought us strange. Then I said to him, 'I'm tired of being an outsider! No matter what Daddie says, I want to be baptized!' I thought the minister would laugh at me or tell me I was too old, or maybe scold me for defying Daddie. Instead he said he would teach me himself and prepare me for communion!"

Angus stared at her. "Then that was the minister who was with you!"

"Aye!" Margaret answered. "We have been studying together in the kirk, but he had some calls in the country today, so I met him with a picnic. Oh, Angus, I am almost ready to be confirmed, he says!"

"Have ye thought about what this will mean to Daddie—to the family—Maggie? Ye'll be splittin' us asunder!"

"Oh, Angus!" Margaret's eyes clouded with tears. "I am so happy! I thought ye'd be happy for me! I must live my own life, don't ye see? I . . ."

She stood up and began to walk slowly toward the house. "Ye'll not tell on me?" she begged anxiously. "Even if ye don't approve? Ye'll not tell, will ye?"

Angus sighed. He felt himself surrounded by things he only half understood. "Nay," he said with a tired shrug. "I'll not tell. Besides, ye are just like Mother. Once your mind is made up, nothing will change ye!"

Angus and Margaret walked home together but their happy camaraderie was shattered. Angus had the feeling that Margaret had not told him everything, and on the next day his fears were confirmed.

It was the Sabbath. After the morning meal, the brothers accompanied their mother up to the little graveyard on the hill. When they came back into the cottage Robert was still reading his scriptures. Mary tied on her apron and began preparations for their simple lunch. Angus went outside to sit on the bench by the front door feeling restless and uneasy. As he looked down the lane, he saw a familiar figure striding toward the house. It was the same man who had met Margaret in the hills the day before. Angry, but curious, Angus sprang to his feet as the stranger turned in at the McElins' gate and walked toward him.

He was a tall, dignified young man, with deep-set hazel eyes in a serious face. "You must be Angus," he said. "I am Donald Cameron." The young minister reached out his hand and Angus reluctantly shook it.

"Cameron!" Angus exclaimed. "That's a Highlander's name!"

"Aye," replied the minister. "I am a clansman, but my calling has brought me away from the cairns. Kirkwall is my first ministry."

When Mary saw the Reverend Cameron enter the house followed by Angus, she had a presentiment of disaster. Robert looked up from his Bible with an inquiring glance. "Shouldn't you be out administering your apostate ordinances?" he asked the minister with heavy irony. "Our day of rest is surely your day of work!"

"I've not come to talk of religion today, Mr. McElin. I've come

30

to ask for your permission to bring Margaret into full communion in the Church and to take her as my wife."

A cry escaped Mary's lips and her glance flew to Margaret, who was sitting quietly peeling potatoes. Something in Margaret's posture told Mary all she needed to know. Margaret was in love.

Robert leaped to his feet. "Over my death!" he roared. "Ye shallna take my daughter into a faith that denies truth. Ye are a good man, Reverend Cameron, but your faith is false. Is this how you repay my friendship?"

"Mr. McElin," the minister replied earnestly, "I do not expect you to accept the Church—but why can you not accept your daughter's right to make her own decision? She has grown to love the Church and I have grown to love her."

"Oh, Daddie!" Margaret cried, unable to contain herself. "Please give us your blessing! We will be so happy!"

"What happiness is worth the price of your immortal soul?" Robert flung at her. He walked to the door and threw it open. "Ye shall leave my house now, Reverend Cameron!" he shouted. "And never enter it again! Ye have betrayed my respect for ye, and by enticing my daughter into yer false church ye have betrayed your own holy calling!"

"Nay," said the minister with dignity, "I have not enticed your daughter. I love her, and I would never encourage her to do anything that would not bring her happiness."

"Out!" Robert shouted. "Out of my house!"

Margaret ran to her loft, weeping, but later that night, as the family sat silently around the fire, she came down the ladder carrying a bundle.

She walked over to her father. "I am leaving now, Father," she said with quiet resolve. "I am going to be baptized and next Sunday the banns will be read for my marriage to Donald. I love him, Daddie, and I believe what he has taught me is true. If this pains ye, I am truly sorry, but I must go anyway."

Robert said not a word. He continued to stare into the fire with the Bible open on his knees and his head averted.

Margaret fell on her knees before him. "Oh, Daddie, please! I am still your wee Maggie! Let me go with your blessing!" Robert's hands did not move and he continued to look away. Wearily Margaret gathered up her bundle and went over to her mother, who sat dry-eyed in her rocker.

"I will be going, then, Mother," she said. "I will come for the rest of my things tomorrow."

"Where will ye go?" Mary whispered.

"Donald will find me a place," Margaret answered confidently, her chin rising. "I will let ye know."

Angus sprang up. "I'll walk with ye, Maggie! You canna go out into the night alone." He glanced apprehensively at his father, but Robert made no sign to stop him.

After Margaret and Angus left, Mary turned to Robert, who was staring into the fire. Mary knew how deeply he was wounded, but her own hurt was too great to contain.

"You and your God have robbed me of my last daughter, Robbie!"

In the following weeks the wedding banns were read while Margaret stayed at the home of friendly parishioners. At the end of the proper time a traveling minister from Glasgow came to the graystone church in Kirkwall and married the young couple with the whole of the Reverend Cameron's congregation serving as witness.

Robert McElin forbade any member of his family to attend the wedding. Angus and the other boys would have gone, if Margaret had not begged them to obey their father. "Ye see," she said, "I have sorrow enough from rifting the family, and if ye side with me now it will only make the break worse! I will always know ye wanted to come and that is enough!"

On the day after Margaret's wedding, Robert McElin rose at dawn from his lonely bed. He went to the kitchen, kindled a fire with soft coal, and upon the blaze he set the large copper wash kettle. When the water was boiling, he poured it into the zinc bathtub in the anteroom and added enough cool water to fill the bath. Lowering himself into the water, he scrubbed himself with a bar of strong lye soap and a hemp scourer, washing his ears, his neck, his elbows and ankles. He dug at the callouses and crevasses of his coal-blackened hands until they were red and raw and no trace of dust from the coal mine remained. After nearly an hour of soaking and scrubbing, he was satisfied and, wrapped in a heavy flannel sheet, he returned to his bedchamber. When he came out again he wore a clean white shirt and his one serviceable suit, and carried the old leather club bag, which he had brought to Glasgow as a young student over two decades before.

"Mary," he said quietly, "will ye walk a way wi' me?" Mary was sitting at the kitchen table with a puzzled frown on her face. Her three sons sat around her, eating oat porringer and buttermilk. Their faces registered concern as they stared silently at their father. It was apparent that the family had been discussing his peculiar behavior.

Robert put his bag on the kitchen floor, nodded to his sons, and turned to his wife. "Mary," he repeated calmly, with a note of command in his voice, "will ye come and walk a way wi' me?"

Mary snatched up her plaid shawl from beside the doorway and followed him out. They walked up the small hillside toward the graves of their children, but Robert put a restraining hand on Mary's arm and would not let her go farther. He did not want to say what he had to say with the tiny headstones listening.

Too distressed to wait for Robert's explanations, Mary whirled and faced him, her eyes flashing and her face twisted with angry grief. "Ye will have lost your job for your foolishness this morning! Are ye daft? Or are ye leaving me then, wee Robert?" she hurled the accusation bitterly. "Can ye not stay with me without my body in your bed? Is that all I have meant to ye?"

Her anger did not sting Robert; instead it dropped like another weight into the deep well of despair in his heart. With a heavy sigh, he took Mary's hands in his, hoping to quiet her enough so that she would understand his words.

"Nay, Mary. Will ye listen to me now, and hear what it is I have to say? I canna leave thee, not for the highlands, nor for my body's needs, not for anger or pain. I canna leave ye, for ye are my heart's beating, and it doesna matter what is wrong or right between us, for I canna live without ye. But I canna live with ye, either. Not like this. I can never go to the mines in the morning again. I could only go these many years because at night I gathered your strength as we lay together. I must leave this place of sorrow, and since ye canna be content in the highlands, I shall go to Glasgow and find a way to support ye there. When I have found work, I shall send for ye."

"But, Robbie, what shall we do with ye gone?" Mary's voice was shrill with fear and anxiety. "How shall we live?"

"Ye have three grown sons, Mary. They shall care for ye until I send word." Mary's volatile spirit raged and resisted her husband's words, but in his face she saw his indomitable spirit and she knew that nothing would sway him from his decision. For the first time since Lucinda's death Mary really looked at her husband. With dawning compassion she saw the deep furrows of pain and suffering and the hungering need in his eyes. He too had lost four daughters— three to death and one to his own proud stubbornness.

33

Hot tears sprang to her eyes, and Mary dashed them from her face with an impatient hand. "If ye must go, ye must go, Robbie. I'll not stand in your way!" Although her words were harsh, Robert heard behind them the whisper of understanding.

"Aye, I must go, Mary," he said softly. "I must find a way to save us—all of us. We must not lose any more! But ye must promise me ye willna speak to Margaret, nor heal the breach while I am gone. She has chosen her path away from us and we canna follow. Promise you willna speak to her when I am gone."

Mary, filled with the chasm of her many losses, did not argue but she made no gesture of acquiescence either.

Robert grasped his wife by her slender shoulders, pulled her close to him, and looked longingly into her face. Then, slowly, slowly, his arms went around her body, encircling her like a child, and he put his dark head on her shoulder and closed his eyes. As the wind blew down upon them from the highland slopes they stood locked in a tender and desperate embrace. Then Robert dropped his arms, and Mary, turning quickly so he would not see her tears, hurried back to the house.

Before leaving for Glasgow, Robert had a word with each of his sons. He spoke to Angus last of all, asking him to accompany him for a mile or two down the road. As father and son walked together, Robert charged Angus with the responsibility of caring for his mother and brothers, until such time as Robert would send for them. "Ye will have to work in the mines for a piece, Angus," his father said sadly, "but that will do ye no harm. You are young and ye'll have your years to return to the highlands afterward. Matty and Johnny will continue working the sheep contract, but I have arranged for them to come home every third week."

At the crossroads, Robert shook his oldest son's hand. "I will be writing as soon as I have myself set," he said. "I give ye my blessing."

Angus was almost speechless as he watched his father swing off down the road. Robert wore his tartan plaid over his coat and, with each step away from Kirkwall, Angus thought his father's stride became more powerful and free. Far down the road Angus could see his father in full stride, his head thrown back and his plaid swinging from his shoulder. In his father's powerful pace he saw the rhythm of the hardy Highlander—the clansman—and it was as though his father were walking to the unheard cadence of his own secret bagpipes playing deeply in the memory of his McElin blood.

Angus stood at the crossroads with a battle raging in his heart. No bagpipes cheered his soul! His father's command that he must care for the family filled Angus with deep resentment and frustration. As young as he was, Angus knew enough of pain and suffering to understand that Robert needed to leave to make a new beginning, or the family would not survive. "But why me?" Angus thought angrily. "Why should I be caught here, while he goes free?" The image of his father's springing steps would not leave Angus's mind, and his young spirit rankled as he turned and plodded back toward the village. At that moment he almost hated his father, and he yearned to walk away from the burden that had been placed on him.

Ever since Margaret's marriage Angus had felt a restless dissatisfaction stirring in his blood. He had visited Margaret and her new husband secretly, and although the young couple were circumspect and did not touch in his presence, still, when their eyes met Angus could feel a warm undercurrent of love that made him yearn to be part of something whole and beautiful. The happiness of the young couple, without their realizing it, made Angus feel like an outsider. He wondered if he would ever feel he belonged anywhere.

The quickening of spring on the hillsides drew him like a magnet, and he had begun counting the hours when his leave would be over and he could again return to Cairn Sinclair and the freedom of mountains and skies. Now his father had sentenced him to a year of slavery and toil in the mines! How could his father, who hated the mines so passionately himself, callously ask his son to turn to their cruel arms?

With bitter fury Angus kicked a stone on the path before him. His whole spirit raged against the obligations placed upon him by his parents' needs, and an intense longing burned in him to cut the family ties forever. All he had to do was to continue walking through Kirkwall, up into the foothills beyond the Glen of Arles, up the high mountain path! He would be his own man. Free and unfettered!

Then he remembered something he had seen that morning—his mother and father embracing on the hill, so close to one another they had looked like one creature. As he thought of that moment, he knew he would have to return to the cottage because his mother could never survive alone. She would crack like brittle china, or dry up and blow away like dust. Without his father, his mother was as vulnerable as a eweless lamb in a storm, and until his father sent for her, Angus would have to provide the shelter she needed. If he turned from this obligation his defection would haunt him all of his life, and he would never be free. He was driven by passions and hungers, but he realized he could never begin his own private search for peace until the breach between his mother and father was mended. Bowing to duty, like an old and weary man, Angus turned in at the path that led to his parents' cottage knowing, somehow, that he would never again think of this thatched, fieldstone cottage as his home. The ember of a hot and bitter anger toward his father glowed in his heart, and he knew that each day of enforced servitude would fan that resentment further. He held the heat of the anger close to him. It would provide the fuel to help him do what he had to do, so that one day he could turn his back forever on the father who had deserted him.

Chapter Two

Auld Tom McAlister, the postman, plodded up the rocky lane. It was one of those rare days in midsummer when the sun, unclouded and yellow as an egg yolk, beat down upon the green hills and bleached the gray rocks of the valley. Under his heavy tam-o'-shanter, perspiration dripped down onto Auld Tom's face, and the back of his heavy homespun jacket was dark with sweat.

He was muttering to himself as he moved slowly up the village street, his heavy leather bag over his shoulder.

" 'Tis going to be a day fit to fry toadstools. A man shouldna ha' to work on sich a day. I ought to be sittin' on me bench, soakin' in the warmth for the sake o' me auld rheumatism, but no, here I am, carryin' the notes o' folk who have naught better to do than sit themsel's down an' write!''

He came to the gate of the McElins' cottage and pulled a rumpled envelope from his bag. His damp, soiled hand smudged the letter as he walked to the front door.

"Mr. McAlister!" Mary exclaimed breathlessly as she opened the door. "Have ye something for me?"

"Aye!" Mr. McAlister said. "Here it be!" He handed her the envelope, and she looked at it with naked eagerness. Knowing it would be improper to open it in front of him, she restrained herself and asked, with natural courtesy, "Would ye care for a drink of water, or cold buttermilk, before ye go on yer way, Mr. McAlister?"

"Aye," Mr. McAlister answered. "Thank ye very much, Mrs. McElin."

It took all of Mary's self-control to wait patiently while the postman slowly drank his buttermilk. Finally he wiped his moustache with the back of his hand and turned reluctantly to walk back down the path. " 'Tis a right hot day, Missus McElin," he said, turning to face her.

"Yes, yes!" Mary said, trying to keep the impatience out of her voice. "I am sure it is, Mr. McAlister."

"This is no easy job, ye know!" he added.

"Aye!" Mary replied, yearning to shut the door. " 'Tis beholden to you we are!"

"Not many as appreciate it!" Auld Tom said, shaking his head, still standing on the doorstep, turned halfway to go and halfway to stay.

Mary could not stand waiting another moment, and so she grasped the handle of the door. "Thank ye, again, Mr. McAlister. I know ye must be going now." She closed the door firmly in the postman's astonished face and, leaning against the cool wood of the interior frame, tore open Robert's letter and began hungrily to read what he had to say.

"Dearest Wife," he began, "I have so much to tell that I scarce know where to begin. The first two days I spent in Glasgow were most disheartening. No sign of work, nor a place to bring you to stay. The third evening I was walking out of the city on the banks of the River Clyde and saw a most astonishing sight! Men and women dressed in white—the men in the water! I investigated and discovered that it was a baptism service—there, in the Clyde River! I knew then I had found what I had come to Glasgow to seek. Mary! It is the old religion restored and they baptize as Jesus was baptized in the New Testament!

"The next day I found work in a cabinet shop. The pay is not much, but it is light and cheerful in the workroom, and there is the smell of fresh wood. I live in a tiny room and am saving all my

37

wages. Each night I study with the elders, and they have taught me the Gospel of Jesus Christ. I am to be baptized next week.

"The following week I shall leave with these missionaries to go to America. We shall journey to the territory of Utah, and, as soon as I have built a place for us to live, and have saved enough money, I will send for all of you to join me there. I know it will be a hard year of separation, but the prize is worth the price. While I am gone I will send elders to you so that you can know what it is I have experienced.

"Tell my sons to care for you well. Within the year we shall all be reunited. Fear not." He signed the letter, "With loving affection, Your Husband Robert."

Feeling faintly sick, Mary walked over to the table with the letter clutched in her hand, then, with her face tight as a drum, she reread the entire letter, slowly, word by word, as though she had not comprehended it the first time.

When she had finished the second reading, she curled the paper up in her hand into a tight ball and threw it to the floor. Agitated and angry, she sprang to her feet and began pacing up and down. "Daft!" she muttered to herself. "The man has gone completely daft! America! Elders! Baptisms! Is his home nothing to him? His country? And what am I? Come when he says 'Come!' stay when he says 'Stay!' "

It was in this state that her son found her when he returned home from the mine that evening. He uncrumpled his father's letter and read the astonishing news.

Angus reacted to the letter with a blaze of fury. "You willna stand for this, Mother! You must write him and tell him so!" he shouted.

"Be calm, Angus!" Mary ordered. "Writing will do no good." She pointed to the date on the envelope. "This was mailed three weeks ago. Your father has already gone."

"What does he take us for?" Angus raged. "Some kind of chattel, to wait on his pleasure?"

"You are not a prisoner!" Mary snapped. "Nothing is holding you!"

"Nae!" Angus growled. " 'Tis duty holds me like a chain and I canna be free until our father returns to his rightful place—if he hasn't forgotten where and what that is!"

Mary's eyes burned with disapproval. "You willna speak of your father thus!" she warned her son with a ring of authority in her voice that Angus had not heard for months.

Her eyes softened and her voice took on a note of appeal. "Dinna be angry with your father because he is what he must be. Do not close your heart to those who love you. You make yourself so alone!"

"Alone!" Angus raged. "Alone! I am surrounded by my father's responsibilities!"

Mary shook her head impatiently. "You are so like me, Angus! Will ye not learn from my mistakes? But no, ye will go your headstrong way, I know, caring too much, wanting too much, expecting too much! Aye, the sins of the fathers—and the mothers— come down on your head. Dear laddie, will ye ever forgive us?"

"Then ye will listen to these missionaries he is sending? And go when he sends for you?" Angus said incredulously.

"Aye," Mary answered. "I do my duty as well."

"Then I will care for you and the boys until you are returned to Daddie and then I shall go my own way," Angus replied coldly.

"I shallna stop ye," Mary answered bravely. "If that is your wish." But in her heart she prayed, "Please Lord, don't let me lose another one!"

One balmy midsummer's night, there was a knock on the McElins' door. Matty opened it, and standing before him were two bearded men in frock coats. The formality of their attire and the aristocratic quality of their faces made the two men seem strange and foreign, as though the Laird Nevins himself had knocked at their cottage door.

"Your father has sent us," said the older of the two men, in an unfamiliar accent. "I am Elder Richards, and this is Elder Stover."

Without a word Matty stepped back and opened the door a little farther. "May we come in?" the man asked with grave courtesy. "We would like to speak with your mother if she is at home."

Looking tinier than usual beside her tall son, Mary came to the doorway. "Let the gentlemen come in, Matty," she said quietly. "We shall hear what it is they have to tell us."

The elders stayed at the McElin house for the rest of the month. They were men of education and distinction, and the McElins soon became accustomed to their unfamiliar American accents and manners.

Never idle for a moment, the two men mended furniture and windows, scythed meadow hay, and restocked the pens of Mary's domestic animals. They also gathered eggs, weeded and harvested the vegetable garden.

During the day the elders tramped in the countryside, distributing written tracts, leaflets, and books—teaching wherever they could. Most evenings they returned to the McElin home and discussed the things they had taught to Robert.

To Mary it was mostly a meaningless jumble. Religion was a simple thing to her way of thinking, and their talk of visions, angels, Zion, the millennium, the Plan of Salvation had little to do with her daily life of scrubbing, cleaning, and caring for her family.

One evening, after the elders had gone to bed, Mary was spinning by candlelight, when Johnny came softly to her side. He had been down from the sheep meadow for the week visiting at home.

"Why, wee Johnny!" she said, surprised. "I thought ye were sleeping!"

"I canna sleep, Mother," Johnny whispered. "I must speak with ye." He seemed uncomfortable, and paused.

"Well, go on!" Mary said impatiently. "What is it ye wish to say?"

"I want to be baptized, Mother. And so does Matty, only he's so quiet he willna tell thee—or anyone—what is on his mind."

"Baptized!" Mary exclaimed. "Like yer father! A grown man, walking down into the river and bein' dunked! Are ye sure, Johnny my lad? The village folk think we are strange enough already. The news will surely get to the herders and you'll take a fair drubbing from yer workmates."

"Aye," Johnny assented, "I know all that. But, Mother, somehow I know what these men have told us is true, and if we are to take our way across the ocean to this new territory, well . . . I . . . ."

"Yes, Johnny?" his mother urged.

"I want to really belong, Mother! Not like we are in Kirkwall—Highlanders with no church—outsiders to everyone we meet! Even in the highlands we are outsiders, for our parents live in the valleys, and we no longer have our own inheritance." Johnny's irrepressible humor got the best of him, and he grinned. "I thought I'd try a different way for a change and join the group."

"You're proposing a serious thing, Johnny," his mother said sharply. "See that ye do it for serious reasons."

His young face, so like her own, looked at her steadily. "Aye" was all he said. In a rare gesture of affection, she bent where he knelt and kissed his red curls.

"Very well." She sighed. "It is a man's decision, and you are a man, Johnny."

After Matty and Johnny were baptized, they returned to the highlands and Mary thought the missionaries would leave. The summer was beginning to wane, and often, toward evening, cold, damp winds blew down from the cairns with the promise of the cold season in them.

One evening Mary came out the back door and found Elder Richards working in the kitchen garden. He was harvesting potatoes and packing the hills for winter storage. She watched him work, the sleeves of his white shirt rolled up, his necktie in place, his beard neatly trimmed. He worked with precision and intelligence.

"Ye shouldna work so hard, Elder Richards!" Mary admonished. "Ye have had a hard day. Come in and have a bit of soup."

"I'll just finish up here," the missionary replied. "This doesn't seem like work to me. It eases my homesickness."

Mary was astonished, and she walked toward the garden to look into his face. "I never thought of ye having a home," she said with guilty compassion. "How long since ye have been there?"

"Which home?" he asked, his dark eyes smiling nostalgically.

"Why, the home ye be thinkin' of now, I guess," Mary answered, feeling out of her depth. "How many homes do ye have?"

Elder Richards paused in his work and leaned on the potato fork, his eyes watching the summit of Cairn Sinclair as it grew pink in the early sunset. He was a man in early middle age, tall, with a scholarly stoop and a thin, serious face. His beard made him look asutere and dignified. Without it Mary imagined he would have a very kind and gentle look.

"I was a minister in Ohio when I first heard of Joseph Smith," he mused. "But Ohio wasn't really my home. I was raised and educated outside Philadelphia. So I guess that's two homes to start with!"

The names were all foreign and unfamiliar to Mary, but she listened, fascinated by the man's account.

"My wife and I moved to Ohio. That is where I had my first garden. Perhaps it was that garden I was thinking of tonight."

"You must miss it," Mary inserted.

"Oh"—Elder Richards laughed—"I have been missing it for years! Once I was baptized, I left Ohio and joined the Prophet in Missouri. There I started another garden and didn't even get to harvest it! We were expelled from Missouri because of our antislavery vote."

"And your next garden?"

41

"In Nauvoo, Illinois. That was the finest one yet . . . and the little brick house . . . and Emily—that's my wife . . ."

"Is that where your garden is now?"

A look of pain flashed over the missionary's face. "No. They murdered the Prophet in Nauvoo, you know, and burned us out of our homes."

He stopped talking and Mary was afraid she might say the wrong thing, but she knew there was more to be said. Twilight was descending, and she whispered, "Where is your wife Emily now? Do you have children?"

Elder Richards drew a long breath and turned to face Mary. "My wife was barren, like Sarah, and then, like Sarah, after we had stopped hoping, she bore a child. The baby was born on the banks of the frozen Mississippi the night we were driven from our home. Across the ice of the river I watched Nauvoo burning as she gave birth. A little girl." His voice grew soft. "The baby didn't last the night. But Emily got well, and she is waiting for me now, in Utah. Next spring we will put in our garden together." He smiled ruefully. "Hopefully, that will be my last one."

Mary looked up at the three little gravestones silhouetted on the hills, and her heart swelled with anger and pity. "Much good your church has done for you! It seems to me you have lost everything but Emily. Even the little one you waited for so long! What good is it for you and Emily to be baptized, if your bairn is not? What hope of heaven can you see in that?"

The missionary turned a surprised face to Mary. "Mrs. McElin," he said slowly, "babies do not require baptism. Before the age of accountability—which is eight—no child can sin, and therefore, children—babies—automatically return to live with our Father in Heaven if they die. Infants are innocent of mortal sin! Our little girl will be with us on the morning of the resurrection."

The last glow of the sunset caught the missionary's face, and Mary could see in it a radiance and serenity she had never witnessed before. Suddenly she felt something give way within her, as though the bands of iron around her heart had broken and fallen away. She shuddered with joy. "I knew it!" she whispered, mulling the new thought in her mind like sweet wine. "I have always known it was so! And your church teaches this?" She turned to him with glowing eyes. "Will ye baptize me?" she asked.

The missionary turned a dumbfounded face to the tiny Scotswoman standing before him, her jaw set and determined.

"What . . . ?" he stammered. "What is it that makes you ask for baptism now? When we have worked so long and taught you so much and you refused?"

"Hope!" she exclaimed. Her chin lifted and her shoulders squared. "Baptism is a small price to pay for hope!"

After Mary's acceptance of the Church, Angus had become sullen and quiet. He did not discuss the baptisms of the rest of the family, and they found it difficult to understand him, or to explain their feelings. The missionaries left in the early autumn, and the winter set in, cold and dreary. In November two other traveling elders knocked on the door and stayed the night. They had recently arrived from America, and they brought with them a letter from Robert. He had arrived in the Salt Lake Valley and had worked on an irrigation crew until the winter snows had begun. He then found employment in a small cabinet shop and was busy making furniture from packing boxes, old wagons, and every other piece of wood available in the city of Salt Lake. The money was almost saved—and he asked Mary to sell the cottage as soon as possible so that she and the boys would be ready to leave as soon as he sent for them.

No one knew what Angus thought of all this, and Mary feared that perhaps when the time came to depart for America he would refuse to go. She did not think she could bear another loss, and so she avoided any confrontation on the subject.

Just before Christmas Robert's promised letter arrived with a banknote for their tickets and instructions to finish the sale of the house and their belongings, and book passage through Elder Richards to America.

Everything went well. The house and land brought more money than they had dreamed possible. After selling her domestic stock and furnishings, Mary had a tidy sum of money, most of which she converted into gold and silver coins. She sewed the coins carefully into the linings of her petticoats and into the boys' homespun jackets. The remaining banknotes she put in a soft purse that she wore secured to her body.

She and the boys packed tools, bedding, woolen fabric, and family keepsakes into the hampers, trunks, and baskets. The McElins crated everything they thought might be needed to start a new life in an uncivilized wilderness. The preparations went smoothly, and

43

Mary felt a lift in her spirits as she prepared to rejoin Robert. Only two things marred her leave taking.

One was her sorrow over Angus. Unlike Matty and Johnny, who had wholeheartedly embraced the venture, had been baptized, and were eagerly looking forward to the new life, Angus silently opposed the move. He had not attended the baptisms and, although he continued to give Mary his wages and had even overseen the successful sale of the family's belongings, he did his duties with a cold resentment that cast a pall over the rest of the family.

Mary could understand his anger. Until the last days before they left, she lived in constant fear that he would abandon the family to return to the highlands or, at best, escort them as far as Glasgow, see them onto the boat, and then refuse to accompany them farther.

As the time drew near for their departure, Mary knew her love for Angus was even greater than her need for him, and so she approached him late one night, as he sat packing the last box in the emptied cottage.

"Son," she said, "I know ye do not wish to come with us. Ye think it is a daft thing we are doing, and ye have no wish to leave your homeland."

Angus said nothing in reply, but continued tying his tools into waterproof oilskin packets. His face wore the same hard expression it had worn every day since his father had left. He seemed so alone and unapproachable—and so young to carry such a load!

Mary took a deep breath and prayed she would have the courage to say what must be said. "Angus, I release ye from your promise to your father. I mean it, son. We can make the journey without ye. Ye have already done all that a son should do, and I will not require ye to go halfway around the world against your will!"

Her voice broke, and she stopped speaking. Could she really let him stay?

Angus looked up at her, his eyes blazing with determination and stubborn pride, and said in a harsh voice, "I will fulfill my promise to Father! I will not leave ye until I have placed ye and the boys safely in his hands, and then I will be quit of all my obligations to him, and I will come back to Scotland without a backward look! I am a man of honor, Mother, and we will talk no more of this!" His face was like a thundercloud, but Mary's heart leaped with joy. She had gained him for another few months—and perhaps in that time something would happen—perhaps he would find a way to regain

44

his youthful enthusiasm and happiness. As long as he was with the family she could hope.

She needed every shred of hope she could gather, for with Margaret there was no hope at all, and this was the other sorrow she knew she would carry with her across the ocean and into her grave. Margaret—her only living daughter—the joy of her young motherhood. Margaret—as lost to her as her babies in their graves! Mary knew she must go to her daughter before the departure. Nothing, not even Robert's admonition, would deter her.

In the late autumn, Margaret had given birth to a baby boy. Mary yearned to see her first grandchild, but there had been no invitation from Margaret or the Reverend Cameron since their marriage. Mary cast about for a way to overcome the awkwardness of making the first overture, and on New Year's Eve came up with the perfect solution. At midnight she and her three sons ate the traditional lamb stew and cheered one another's health with a cup of noggin. Then Mary made her surprise announcement. "Now, boys. We are going first-footing in the village."

Although it was common practice for Scotsmen to go first-footing on New Year's Eve, the McElins, having few friends in the village, had never observed the custom.

"People will be glad to see ye, Johnny," Mary continued. "With that mop of red hair, ye will make a grand first-footer!" It was a widely held superstition that if the first person to cross one's threshold in the new year had red hair, the year would be filled with good luck. A black-haired guest who arrived first was said to bring bad luck in the coming year.

"Perhaps I should stay home!" Angus said dourly. Matty punched him on the shoulder.

"Come now, Angus!" Matty chided. "None of your angry looks and lone ways will do for tonight. We'll just shove Johnny in before us, and then folks won't mind our black hair, since we'll not be the first-footers!"

So Mary gathered the sweater she had knitted secretly for her unseen grandson, and she and the boys walked into the village carrying small lanterns. Happy townsfolk were thronging the midnight street singing "Auld Lang Syne" at opened doorways and greeting one another with happy shouts and best wishes. The windows of houses were alight, but Mary passed by one home after another and the boys began to look at her questioningly, until they

45

saw the gray church and the parish house looming in the night before them.

Johnny laughed and gave his mother a mighty hug. "It's Margaret!" he shouted exuberantly. "We're going to see our Margaret girl and the wee bairn!" Even Angus smiled in the dark, and the four of them walked hesitantly to the parish door. The boys had stood aside while Mary knocked, and as they waited Mary whispered, "Now, Johnny, mind ye, when they invite us in, be sure that ye go first, so as to bring them good luck!"

The door was opened by the Reverend Cameron. He was smiling as the butter-colored light from the lamps inside spilled out into the frosty grass of the dooryard, but when he saw who was standing on the steps his face grew stern.

"Mrs. McElin," he said formally, "what is it you want?"

It took all of Mary's strength to overcome her hurt at the coldness of his reception, but she pulled herself erect and looked at him with quiet dignity. "We have come to lay away the mistakes of yesteryear," she said quietly, "and to bid our farewells to you and Margaret and the babe."

The churchman stood in the doorway without moving. He opened the door no farther, and his body was rigid. "I am afraid that is not possible," he said. His face was grim. Only his eyes betrayed the sorrow and pain he felt. "There were many months when Margaret and I would have given our lives for this moment. We would have done anything in our power to heal the wound between our families, but now it cannot be. Not only have you rejected the teachings of the Church, but now you have entered into a covenant with the very church of the Devil and I, as a minister of God, cannot and will not allow you into my home. You have made your choice, and in so doing you give me no other choice!" Donald Cameron's voice shook with emotion, but Mary knew that he stood, as only a Scotsman can, on the unbending firmness of his convictions, just as her Robert had stood when Margaret had joined the minister's church. She and her daughter were parted forever by the rigid walls of men's stubborn principles and rigid beliefs.

The door closed and Mary and the boys turned miserably to leave. They could not speak, and Mary thought that as long as she lived she would hear the sound of the heavy parish door clanging closed. Just as the family reached the stone road, the door opened again and someone slipped out into the darkness and came hurrying toward them.

"Mother?" a soft voice called. Mary turned and saw Margaret, her head and shoulders covered with a woolen shawl, running toward her. "Mother!" she called again. Mary turned back and ran toward her daughter and they embraced. Under the shawl, Mary could feel the squirming of a baby.

"Angus!" she called softly. "Quickly, bring the lantern!" In the dim light, Margaret pulled the cloth back from the infant's face, and Mary gazed longingly at the sweet bairn, with his rosy cheeks and dark lashes.

"He is the image of thee father, Margaret!" Mary exclaimed. "Do ye not see the similarity?"

"Aye." Margaret smiled, but Mary could see the tears on her daughter's cheeks. "Donald is angry with me for coming after ye, but I had to see ye one last time. I want ye to know that I hold no ill toward ye or any of the family." The younger woman drew a shuddering breath and began to cry softly. "I cannot agree with what ye have done, but, Mother, I shall always remember ye, and Father, and my brothers." With that Margaret turned swiftly and put her free arm around each of her brothers in a quick, warm embrace. Then she turned to her mother one last time, and Mary wordlessly held her and her baby in her arms. The two sobbing women stood together for an instant, and then Margaret was gone as swiftly as she had come.

The stench, the crowds, and the noise of Liverpool's Dock Street were an assault to Mary McElin's senses. Mary recognized the odors of the street vendors' wares—steaming mussels, fish chowder, ale, fresh limes, and ginger—but they mingled with the reek of garbage, open sewage, unwashed, drunken humanity, as well as the salty tang of the vast ocean that lay upwind from the mouth of the Mersey River. The clamorous shouts of the vendors, the clatter of hooves and wagons on the cobblestones of the waterfront, the clamor of the grog houses and the incessant groaning of the heavy sailboats scraping at anchor were carried in the dull roar of the headland wind as it swept up the river from the sea.

Four days earlier the family had said their farewells to Scotland, leaving Glasgow by packet steamer, sailing southward out of the Firth of Clyde into the North Channel of the angry Irish Sea. They sailed past the Isle of Man down the coast heading for Blackpool, Birkenhead, and up the Mersey Channel to the protected harbor of Liverpool. Normally the trip took two days, but the winds had blown heavily in the rough seas and the steamer had developed engine trouble. During one long day the little boat was tossed on angry seas, adrift like flotsam. Passengers and crew had feared for their lives, and nearly everyone had been desperately seasick.

The McElins, although they had never been at sea, were not sickened by the motion, and Mary moved among the passengers, encouraging them to sip cold tea, holding their babies, bringing them damp cloths to wipe their faces and mouths. Johnny entertained the children by telling stories and inventing games to keep their minds off the wildly lurching boat, while Angus and Matty helped work the straining bilge pumps since some crew members were too ill to stand.

It was with great relief that the McElins finally sighted the open channel of the Mersey River. Their ship steamed to the docks of Liverpool where Mary and her sons disembarked, feeling wretched and exhausted. In the milling crowd on the quay they saw the familiar face of Elder Richards. He was scanning the passengers as they walked down the gangplank; when he caught sight of the McElins, he gave a shout of welcome and pressed forward to greet them.

The McElins followed Elder Richards, threading through the welter of humanity on the waterfront street. A drunken sailor, with a dirty beard and foul breath, fell against Mary, and she pushed him away.

A fish vendor's tray set her bonnet askew, and the whiff of the fresh fish made her stomach lurch, as it had not done on the high seas.

" 'Tis a fine place ye've brought us to, Elder Richards!" she said with asperity. "Can we nae find a quieter part o' the city?" she demanded. Elder Richards turned back to face her.

"I'm sorry for it, Sister McElin." He had to raise his voice so she could hear him over the din of the street noises. "You need to stay near the docks so you will be on hand when the boarding call comes."

"What are ye speakin' of?" she asked impatiently. "What boarding call?"

"I'll explain inside," Elder Richards shouted and turned into a foul-smelling hallway in one of the ancient brick buildings that lined the steets near the wharf. "This way!" he continued, indicating a cramped dark stairway at the end of the hall.

Mary followed him with ill-concealed reluctance, carrying her bundles. Her sons staggered up the narrow stairs with their loads of hampers and boxes.

The room they entered was small and mean, with a narrow unmade cot and unglazed, dirty window. Mary recoiled. "Can ye not find us a better place for lodgin'? I'm willing to pay, if that's the problem."

The middle-aged missionary fixed Mary with his tired and patient eyes. "I'll try to explain, Sister McElin," he said. His voice was kind, but weary and strained. "This room is literally worth its weight in gold. Dockside rooming is almost impossible to find because it's the best insurance for your passage money . . . especially now, when so many departures have been delayed because of the headwinds."

Mary pursed her lips in her quick, impatient way. "What are ye talking about, man?" she said. "A room such as this? We should be paid to stay in it, rather than the other way around!"

Johnny laughed. "Come on, Mother, give the man a chance to explain."

Elder Richards began again, but this time he addressed his remarks to Angus. "You see, ships can only sail out of Liverpool when the tide, wind, and harbor conditions are right. Departures are an inexact science at best, and, with the storm blowing up the channel these past two weeks, nothing has gotten out of the harbor. Once the scheduled departure time is past, all passengers are put on permanent notice. Your ship could sail at any time—but you can't board ship until the boarding call is given. Any passengers who don't arrive in time for the sailing are left behind. It's as simple as that! Sometimes passengers wait in Liverpool for weeks and then only have an hour to board!"

Mary looked at the elder with consternation. "But then, of course, they return the passage money? Or do they arrange for other passage?" Mary's thrifty Scots soul went straight to the heart of the matter.

"Neither! If you miss the ship you lose your passage money," Elder Richards replied soberly. "That's why you must remain close at hand, day and night.

"Angus," the churchman went on, "you come with me and we will supervise the transfer of your heavy gear from the steamer to the *Eliza III*—that's the ship on which you have been berthed. Most of our group—including myself—have been assigned to the *Canartic*, which is the sister ship. We will sail at the same time, but on different vessels."

Although a weak March sun was shining through the dirty window, the day was bitterly cold, and Mary could feel the dampness and chill seeping into her bones. The sea wind seemed to find every crack in the walls of the room.

"Mother," Matty said after Angus and Elder Richards had gone, "ye be tired from the journey. Best ye lie down here for a bit. I shall go find something warm for ye to eat, and Johnny will stay to guard ye."

"Aye!" Mary said, in an uncharacteristically acquiescent mood. "I am a mite tired. Perhaps I will rest until Angus returns." She looked with distaste at the filthy blanket on the bed, and with efficient hands she stripped the covers away and pulled out a woolen rug from one of her hampers. She placed the rug on the bed, then laid her heavy plaid shawl over it, and climbed, fully clothed, onto the bed. With cold fingers she grabbed the edges of her plaid and pulled it around her, so that she was wound like a tight cocoon in its familiar folds. She closed her eyes against the ugliness of the drab room. She could hear Johnny rustling in the baskets beside her and soon she heard his contented snore, but her anxious mind would not let her weary body sleep.

"Well, Robbie," she whispered, speaking to her absent husband without opening her eyes, "we are truly on our way!" She could scarcely believe that at any hour they could be called to board the three-masted ship and sail on it across an endless expanse of water, to an endless new land where her husband waited.

She felt that most of her life had been spent in weary vigil over those she had loved and lost. This voyage to the New World was something different—for the first time in many years she was preparing for a reunion, a homecoming. Something was to be added to her life rather than taken away, and she knew that was why she faced the journey with such a resolute and hope-filled heart.

"If only Angus will see the way!" she thought to herself. "If only we can keep him with us. . . ." On that thought she fell into a fitful doze, and by the time Angus and Elder Richards had returned from the docks, and Matty arrived with a newspaper filled with chips and fish, she was sleeping peacefully, curled in her woolen shawl like a child.

Several days passed. The sky was dark and lowering, but now scarcely a breeze rippled the waters of the Mersey River in the port of Liverpool, and the sailing vessels sat idly, with listless sails. During the days of waiting, while some of the Saints stood watch in case wind conditions changed and the captains decided to sail, most of the men combed the far markets of the city for provisions that would last without spoiling for the duration of the ocean voyage.

Elder Richards was returning to Salt Lake with the company and would be rejoining his wife in the valley. His mission was over and he had been given the assignment of organizing the convert Saints and instructing them on what they would need aboard ship. Since the only facilities provided would be their bunks and a common firebox on the open deck where all cooking had to be done, they were told to bring soap, cleaning aids, writing materials, cooking pots, medical supplies, bedding, clothing, and enough food to last six weeks for every member of their family.

On the third day of waiting an erratic wind began to blow, and the McElins, even though their food supplies were not quite complete, decided it would be safest to stay close to the docks in case the captain decided to sail. But by evening the wind died away altogether, and a damp, cold mist blew in from the water.

"I think I shall go back to our room to rest," Mary said. "Come with me, boys."

Matty shook his head. "Nay, Mother, I think I shall go cross town to bakers' row. They heat the ovens at night, and I can get us a supply of hardtack biscuit which will round out our rations. I won't be gone but two or three hours."

For some reason Mary felt uneasy about his suggestion, even though she knew the errand was necessary. They had barely enough food to last six weeks, and if the voyage was delayed by storm or adverse wind they could become hungry, or ill.

"I suppose ye must, Matty," she said. "But do ye not think Johnny or Angus should go wi' ye?"

"No need for more than one of us to lose our rest, Mother!" Matty replied cheerfully and sprinted off through the evening throng. He was soon lost from sight. Angus took his mother's arm and helped her through the horse-drawn traffic and past the busy street stalls. They reached their room just as the gloom of night began to fall.

It was much later when Mary was awakened by someone knocking frantically on their door. "Is it you, Matty?" she inquired.

"No!" came the quick response. "It is Elder Richards. They have called for the ships to sail. We must be at dockside within the hour!"

51

Mary flew to the door. "What do you mean?" she cried with alarm. "Has the wind risen?"

Elder Richards stepped inside, rubbing his hands against the cold. "No wind! They have decided to have the ships towed out into the river on the full tide. They are hoping they may catch a breeze coming up from the channel midriver. If not, the river's current will aid them out toward the sea. At any rate the captains are determined to delay no longer and we must board."

"But Matty!" Mary exclaimed in horror. "He has gone for more provisions and must have met with some delay. I canna leave him! We canna go!"

With swift sympathy Elder Richards took her hand in his. "I am sorry, Mary, but if you do not come with me now, you will lose all your passage money, and it would take you a lifetime to raise it again. I'll leave a message on the door for Matty to meet us at the boat."

The dockside was as dark as the tunnels of the mines, and Angus held his mother's arm firmly as they stumbled along the wharf through the clutter of crates, unloaded cargo, and the milling bodies of the confused passengers. Boarding was a nightmare. In the chill of the night, by only the weak light of a few shipboard lanterns, the frantic emigrants scrambled up the narrow gangway, shouting for friends and children in the dark and grasping at one another, desperately checking and rechecking the location of each member of their family group.

Angus, Mary, and Johnny followed Elder Richards toward the *Eliza III* where she bobbed at anchor a few docks removed from her sister ship, the *Canartic*. At the foot of the *Eliza*'s gangway a young officer was checking the names of those who were boarding, and when the McElins announced their name he informed them that they were to board the *Canartic* instead.

"For what reason?" Mary cried, agitated beyond all reason. "Our goods are loaded in the *Eliza*'s hold! My other son is joining us here! We must be berthed on the *Eliza*."

The officer, surrounded by shrill and frightened passengers, dismissed her with an indifferent glance. "If you want to get to America, you'll board the *Canartic*," he said, turning to the next passenger.

"But why?" Mary shouted at him. The ensign ignored her and continued his work.

"Come, Mother," Angus said. "We'll get nowhere with him.

'Tis best if we hurry to the *Canartic* and get aboard. We'll not lose our goods, for the ships will sail together, and we will retrieve our things in Boston.''

Mary stumbled reluctantly along beside her sons, more unhappy and confused than she had ever been in her life. "Where is Matty?" her mind kept asking. "We can't leave without him, but we can't afford to lose our passage money. What will we do?''

The *Canartic* was almost finished boarding when they arrived. The McElin brothers and Elder Richards were carrying the wicker trunks and crates that held their food, clothes, and provisions, and these they loaded efficiently onto the deck. The company of Saints was gathered in one section of the deck. They had lighted lanterns so that a warm orange glow was cast over the group, and in the midst of the confusion and shouting they seemed organized and serene. As soon as Elder Richards joined them, he began explaining the ship-board procedures and told them they need be in no hurry to go below deck; they could wait until dawn. Someone struck up a hymn, and there were several Welsh families in the group whose clear, melodious voices seemed to decorate the air. The confusion and shouting of the other passengers was stilled, and even the harried crew, preparing to cast off, seemed affected by the sweet sound of the music as it spun out across the deck. Only Mary was untouched by the sound. She ran frantically to the side of the boat and stood straining her eyes against the gloom. A slight silver cast in the sky gave promise of the coming of dawn, but the wharf was still cloaked in dark shadows, and it was almost impossible to distinguish one person from another among the stevedores, the relatives who were saying farewell, and the last, straggling passengers hurrying up the boarding planks.

With a lurch of her heart Mary saw the officer who had been checking the passenger list snap his manifest closed and turn to board the ship. "Oh, Matty!" she groaned, and turned to Angus. "I must get off the ship, Angus!" she cried. "I canna leave my Matty here alone.''

Angus's face was tight with conflicting emotions, but his voice was steady. "Nay, Mother, ye canna go after him. He is a grown man, and we will see to it that he gets another passage on a later ship. We can afford to buy one more passage—but never could we afford them for all of us! Matty can take care of himself, Mother, and it will not be long before he joins us.''

Logic said that Angus was right, but Mary's heart shook so

violently that she thought she would fall. Through a haze of agony she heard the captain giving orders to cast off, and she saw at the bow of the ship the longboat that was to tow them into the channel. The clank of the anchor chain sounded as the crew began to winch the heavy anchor from the harbor floor.

"Mother!" shouted Johnny, pointing toward the dock. "There he is! It's Matty!" Mary looked and saw her tall, thin son, running full tilt through the waving crowd toward the *Eliza III*. He was carrying a heavy basket and knocking people left and right as he ran toward them. "Matty!" she screamed. Johnny and Angus joined in the shouting, and when at last Matty spied them, he turned and ran toward the *Canartic*.

The gangplank was already pulled aboard, and Mary felt the boat move as the rowers engaged their oars and the bow began its slow swing away from the dock.

"Jump!" Angus shouted. "Jump, Matty, jump!"

A number of passengers had gathered beside them, and everyone stood with outstretched arms. With impulsive strength, Matty heaved the carton he was carrying across the foaming waters, into the outstretched arms of the passengers. Then, without a moment's delay, Matty gave himself four running strides and leaped out across the widening gap. He seemed to stand midstride suspended in air for a breathless moment as the crowd stared, and then his strong, mountaineer's hand grasped the railing. His body dangled precariously above the waves backwashing from the prow that was now cutting its way through the icy waters.

A dozen arms reached to haul him aboard, and Mary, weak with relief, turned her face so that no one could see her, and wept.

Johnny could not stop pounding his brother on the back, he was so proud and overjoyed at seeing him. Angus, his eyes shining and a smile showing on his bearded face for the first time in months, looked deep into his brother's eyes. "Ye're a strong, quick man, Matty McElin," Angus said with wonder and admiration.

"Aye!" Johnny added with a laugh. "And a daft one too!"

The day after they were towed from harbor a fierce storm began to blow upriver. The headwinds were so strong that no progress could be made against them. The ships rolled in the furious waves, battling for headway but finding it difficult just to hold their own. Finally, after two weeks, a strong and steady wind began to blow in a favorable direction, and that night, the two ships, still sailing on rough waters, plied swiftly through the channel toward the open sea.

When dark came, the *Canartic* took the lead. At eight bells the passengers and crew could see the running lights of the *Eliza III* close behind them. The captain noted the fact in his log. The next morning dawned bitterly cold, but with clear ice-blue skies and a calmed sea. Ahead of the ship the McElins could see an endless horizon of ocean and behind them the receding wide mouth of the Mersey, with the last view of the green coastline of England. Their eyes searched a full circle, but nowhere on the waters could they see the sails of the *Eliza III*.

Later that morning the captain called the crew and passengers on deck and announced that sometime during the night the *Eliza III* had vanished. He told them the watch had reported a clear night, no one had heard any cries of distress, and in the moonless dark the crew had seen nothing to alarm them. But with the dawn, it had become apparent the ship had disappeared during the night. "It is my assumption that the *Eliza* hit a submerged rock and that she has perished with all aboard. However, we have searched and found no evidence of shipwreck—no debris of any kind. In the absence of evidence that we can be of any assistance, and considering the already dangerous delays which have hampered this voyage, we ourselves shall proceed as scheduled."

The captain left the foredeck, and Mary and her three sons stood in stunned silence. Johnny was the first to put their thoughts into words. "We have lost all we own, then?" he said. "All except the things we have carried with us?" But it was Angus who gave it meaning. "Aye, wee Johnny, we have lost our possessions—but do ye not remember, *we* were to have been berthed on the *Eliza*!"

In the following days the McElins proved themselves invaluable aboard the ship. Mary helped organize the families below deck. Lice, fleas, and seasickness were ever-present problems. Illness fouled the air, but salt water was plentiful, and Mary encouraged the women and men to work hard to keep their crowded spaces clean.

Mary also assisted at two births in the first week of the journey and watched with happiness as two healthy boys joined the ship's company as nonpaying passengers. The thought amused her that someone had outsmarted the penny-pinching, heartless captain who had been so ready to leave her Matty behind!

The three brothers, as outdoorsmen, could not abide the smells and sounds of the cramped passenger quarters, and so arranged with the Petty Officer to remain above deck in return for helping the crew. They were given the lowliest of jobs, keeping the firebox burning, carrying bilge buckets, and repairing ropes, but the work was a relief from the tedium of the long days and the press of humanity belowdecks.

To Angus the sea was a puzzle. The ship seemed like a prison, and the deep, endless waters surrounding it were the bars of that prison. He longed for land, and yet, when he looked at the glorious expanse of sky above the ship, he sensed the openness and freedom some men found in the sea and began to half-understand the passion that drove sailors to this strange and isolated life.

Elder Richards was so busy keeping the company of immigrant Saints well and occupied that he scarcely had time to speak to Angus, let alone discuss the Gospel. The missionary's little group of convert families were his sheep, and he their shepherd. He started a school for the small children and organized Bible study groups for the adults. In the evenings the Mormon group frequently held short services, to which the passengers and crew were invited—although few others attended.

After the terrible weather at the beginning of the journey, the winds remained favorable. Although it was cold, and occasional chunks of ice were observed in the water, nonetheless the days were pleasant and a sense of well-being began to settle on the *Canartic*.

Three weeks out of Liverpool the captain, having passed successfully through the hazardous iceberg lanes, felt a celebration was in order. He called Elder Richards into his cabin and suggested he organize an evening of dancing, an idea enthusiastically endorsed by everyone aboard ship. For two days there was a flurry of preparation. Musicians and instruments were discovered among the passengers, and a program settled upon. Late on a cloudless afternoon the party began to assemble on the deck between the mizzen mast and the main mast. The passengers dressed in their finest clothes, and the sea air lent a sparkle to their eyes and color to their cheeks.

Elder Richards had taught the passengers American square dancing. He was calling a set, and even the children joined in and formed their own squares. There was much laughter. The ship's kettles were filled with warm fish chowder, made from salted fish, potatoes, and onions donated by the passengers. As the day drew to a close, some of the families began to drift away to put children to bed, but the young people remained on deck. As long as the music was still playing, they seemed reluctant to end the day.

Among the immigrants was a group of shopgirls who had saved their wages to come to America in search of a new life. Many of them had been friends in Glasgow and they were free and easy with one another—city-wise and tough. During the dancing they had managed to bring Johnny and Matty into their group, and now Angus heard a shout of laughter from them, as Matty's voice was raised. "Nay, you'll never get me to do it!" he exclaimed.

Angus stood apart from the laughing crowd and watched soberly. The habits of resentment and silence seemed to hold him in a vise, stifling his natural youthfulness, keeping him aloof from all personal associations. Johnny was dancing with one pretty girl after another, and even Matty had allowed himself to be led into the circle by a bold young woman. Angus yearned deeply to shed the heavy mantle of responsibility and early maturity his father had placed on him. He wished he could be like Johnny—lighthearted and gay.

Johnny hurried over to him, his voice breathless and excited. "Angus! There's a man here who plays the bagpipes and he says he's willing if we will do the dancing! Come on, Angus. What do you say? Let's show them what Highlanders can do!"

Angus's initial impulse was to say no, but the thought of hearing the pipes again—and how glorious they would sound wailing out over the vast sea—brought a pang of homesickness that robbed him of the will to resist. "All right," he said, "I be willing if Matty will too!" He thought perhaps his loneliness would be eased if he danced the old figures with his brothers and remembered happier times.

The evening took on a new excitement, as the brothers went to put on their tartans and kilts. When they came on deck again, they were astonished to see three of the shopgirls had also changed their clothes, and they too were wearing Highlander dress with shoulder tartans.

Two of the girls hung back shyly, but the third came up to Angus with a bold smile on her bright red lips. "May we dance wi' ye a bit?" she asked. Angus felt good with his tartan on his shoulders—more himself than he had been in months.

"Aye," he replied solemnly. The rest of the passengers stood back, and a heavyset man, with a square gray beard, stepped out onto the deck wearing a Douglas hunting tartan and carrying a set of pipes. With great squawks of sound echoing into the evening light, he primed the air bladder of the bagpipes and then blew until it filled and a steady keen rang out across the water. He put the pipe to his lips with his fingers ready at his side and began to play the ancient tunes of the mountain clans. At first with slow and steady dignity the six young people paced the steps of ancient patterned dances. Faces solemn, their arms raised, their feet light as thistledown, their bodies twisted and turned in the rose-tipped light of the ocean sunset.

Angus's young spirit was caught up in the sound of the bagpipes and the heady excitement of the dance. He could feel his muscles responding to the rhythm of the music and the traditional beauty of the steps. Suddenly he became aware of the girl who was his partner, as she moved lightly in and out of the shifting patterns created by the dancers. Her arm was curved over her head, her hand gracefully silhouetted, and her other arm placed saucily on her hip. Her lips were as red as berries and slightly parted. Although she moved with seemingly effortless ease, he could see a dew on her brow, and he was conscious of the quick rise and fall of her breathing. His heart raced as he caught sight of the pleasant roundness of her breast and the slender waist below. His handsome young face flamed in response.

The girl was performing a figure that caused her to move toward him. They slowly circled one another, their raised arms almost touching, their bodies bent toward each other. As he passed her he saw her eyes catch his. She smiled knowingly and then skipped away, to perform the same step with Johnny, as Johnny's partner moved to Angus. He scarcely saw the other girl; his eyes were on the saucy young woman, and he felt a peculiar twinge of jealousy as she held her face close to his brother's and then skipped away again as though borne on the air.

The dance was coming to an end, and, in its final moments, it increased in speed and in passion. The dancers began to whirl around each other, their tartans flying in the air. The girl's dark hair came loose and flew about her face, and the audience felt caught up in the passion and fury of the wild clans. Angus thought his heart would burst with the exhilaration of the dancing, and for the moment he forgot where he was, and why he was there. All that mattered was his ancient blood singing within him, and the call of the pipes, and the wild, glorious girl spinning beside him.

And then it was over. The last note was played. For a moment no one made a sound, except for the old piper, who took the air pipe from his lips and pressed his bag, so that the last air was expelled like a long mournful sigh. Night had fallen, the music was over, and the passengers broke into a roar of approval, stomping and applauding. The six dancers, unused to such attention, bowed awkwardly and moved out of the circle. They were breathless from exertion, and they walked as a group to the railings where they gulped in the cooling breeze of early evening.

In a few minutes the other passengers wandered away, and Angus found himself alone with his dancing partner. They still had not spoken, and Angus expected she would go off about her evening business as the others had done. He turned, walked over to an old storage box by the lateen sail, and sat down heavily, but instead of leaving the deck she came over and sat beside him.

" 'Tis a fine dancer ye are, Angus McElin!" she murmured in an oddly husky voice that he found disturbing. "I wish the dancing had never stopped!"

"Well," said Angus, his discomfort at her nearness making him sound more brusque than he meant to be, "I think I have danced my fill."

"Nay, but ye haven't!" the girl exclaimed in her breathless, intimate way. "Ye are hardly breathing fast at all! I think ye could go on for a whole night!" She bent her head and looked up at him sideways out of her dark, mysterious eyes. Her look made his head reel. Slowly she smiled, and it was the same knowing, seductive smile she had given him during the dance. "I think ye are a powerful and graceful man, Angus!"

He couldn't tell if she was laughing at him or flattering him. A part of him wanted to flee the narrow box where she sat so tantalizingly close in the twilight, but another part of him wanted to stay, wanted to move closer to her, to touch her, to drink in each mood and expression of her beguiling face.

"How is it ye know my name?" he asked gruffly.

"I know all about ye!" She laughed with cocky assurance. "I've been watching ye ever since the ship weighed anchor."

She was sitting very close to him now, and he could feel the damp heat of her body and the musky perfume of her wild black hair. Seated on the crate, they were almost the same height, and her face was so close to his it seemed to fill the universe.

Angus felt as though he had been drawn into a gulf of fire. His youthful passion was aroused and he was staggered by its power. Scarcely knowing what he was doing, he placed a trembling hand on hers.

"That's a good boy," she whispered, her voice seductive and filled with promise. She moved so that one soft breast pressed against his arm and he sat as still as death. Then she laughed and shook her head at him. "Oh, Angus!" she teased in that same husky whisper. "Your lips up close are even redder and softer than I imagined!" She raised her free hand and stroked his beard as lightly as the wingtips of a moth. He felt as though his beard were made of nerve fibers and every one was alive and aflame. Then she leaned her face to his, first darting a quick glance around the deck to make sure no one was watching, and in a practiced motion, she kissed him full on his lips. To his great astonishment, as their mouths met, he felt her swift warm tongue dart out and touch his lips lightly. But before he could respond, she slipped out of his grasp, laughing, jumped up from the storage crate, and was gone.

Angus sat trembling on the crate, his mind whirling with feelings and images and his whole body shaking with awakened desire. It was very dark on the water now, and the snap of the wind-filled sails, the hiss of the ship cutting through the waves, and the occasional call or cough of the watch were the only sounds on the silent deck. He walked to the railing and gulped in the bitterly cold air, striving to cool his emotions and to clear his head.

Angus was not ignorant about the ways of a man with a maid. However, in personal experience, he was as naive as a child. His only knowledge of women came from his proud and self-contained mother and sweet, modest Margaret. Nothing in life had prepared him for the seductive lure of an experienced woman. His lips burned where the girl's tongue had touched him and within him he felt an urge more lustful than anything he had ever experienced to hold and touch her. Angus realized that others thought him a cold, unfeeling man, but he alone knew how wrong they were. His heart was filled with passionate and powerful emotions. His fault was not that he felt too little, but that he felt too much.

It was because he feared the intensity of his emotions and knew they could betray him that he held himself in such careful control. His self-discipline had become a barrier, a mask to hide himself from others.

Torn by passion and longing, he stood by the railing and felt himself isolated from all the things he desired. Why couldn't he express the things he truly felt? His affection for his brothers, his anxious love of his mother, his joy in the highlands, his need for love and a sense of belonging. But if he dropped his guard to these emotions, what was to protect him from his others—the rage toward his father, the fury of his resentments, the slights to his towering pride? These were feelings that could do nothing but destroy.

Involuntarily he reached up and rubbed his mouth with his fingertips to erase the memory of the girl's lips. Why couldn't he be like Johnny, and laugh and steal a kiss, and go his own way? Because his heart would always feel too much, and so he must learn to live with too little—and if he was misunderstood, well, that would have to be the cost.

In the days of introspection following the night of dancing, Angus contemplated his complex problems and reached the absolute conclusion that if he did not want to roast in hell for all of eternity, he would have to find a wife. Angus knew that no man could live a lifetime with the agony he had suffered in the past days—that such intense physical desires could not long be denied. He knew he would not be able to resist the temptation of immorality and he feared for his soul.

Late one night as he stood by the railing of the ship, searching the western horizon for the promised sight of land, Elder Richards came to stand beside him. The two men had scarcely spoken during the voyage. The missionary, knowing Angus's deep resentment, had stopped trying to discuss the Gospel with him. He knew that conversion would only come from Angus's own heart. Although he could not guess the reason for Angus's mental struggle in the past few days, the young man's unrest and torment had not been lost on the churchman, and now that Elder Richards had almost finished his assignment of bringing the new Saints across the ocean, he had a few moments to pause in his labors to concentrate on Mary McElin's son.

"On to the last legs of our journey, Angus," Elder Richards said, walking across the rolling deck to stand beside Angus.

"Aye," Angus replied dully, not turning to look at him. "A far piece still to go, I'm thinking, even after we've touched land."

"Yes"—Elder Richards sighed—"but somehow it won't seem so far once we're on American soil. Already I'm feeling closer to the people I love."

Angus turned his head and looked at the gentle man. "You mean closer to your wife, don't you," he stated. "My mother told me you were married and left your wife in Salt Lake to come on this mission."

The missionary nodded. "Three years ago," he said softly. "An eternity."

Suddenly Angus could stand his anguish and puzzlement no longer. He turned on the churchman, his eyes blazing. "How can you stand it!" he cried. "How can you stand to be away from your wife for three years! Once you have known a woman, how could you bring yourself to leave her? How could you accept such a test?"

Then he looked away with cold bitterness. "And how could my father leave my mother?" He shook his head and all the fire went out of him. "What kind of church is it that you belong to, that can ask a man to make that kind of sacrifice—to give up all that is dearest, and best, and sweetest in his life? How can anyone love such a church?"

Elder Richards was shaken by the fury of Angus's emotions, and his heart wrung with compassion for the troubled young man before him. Wondering what to say to this proud, defiant man, Elder Richards cleared his throat and looked up to the sky.

To the west he caught the silver glimmer of light on the far horizon of the dark water, and he realized that he had just sighted the first landfall. The thought was like a talisman to him, and he knew what he had to say to Angus.

He put his hand on the younger man's shoulder, and his work-hardened palm was warm and firm. It seemed to Angus that the missionary's fatherly touch comforted him and defused the anger in his heart, and for a moment longer the two stood in companionable silence. Then Elder Richards took his hand away and said almost to himself, "In Utah there are mountains, taller and more majestic than any you have ever seen. The summits are white with snow, and the canyons are thick with quaking aspens and pines and golden birch. There are high basins of wildflowers and honeysuckle and wild berries and plums. Deer and ground squirrels, beaver and game birds populate the undergrowth, and hawks and eagles ride the sky. Mountains, Angus! Mountains like you cannot imagine! They are part of your blood, Angus, they call to you. Your soul reaches for the mountains like eagles reach for the sun.

"If you want to know why I love my church, Angus—this church which, as you have said, requires everything of me—if you ask me why I love it . . . I cannot explain it to you in words. But you will understand why if you can answer one question." The missionary paused, then took a deep breath and asked slowly, "Why do you love the mountains, Angus?" The question hung in the night air between the two men. Angus looked eastward across the vast ocean, and there his inward eye imagined the reach of the highlands over

62

three thousand miles away. He continued to stare into the night, his mind back on the cairns of home.

Angus did not hear the missionary leave his side, but he stood pondering the answer to Elder Richards's question. He loved the mountains because in their massive challenge they had the power to require everything of a man, to challenge him to the depths of his being, to ask of him everything he had. And because of the mountains' power to test man to his limit, they also had the power to give to him the ultimate triumph of man's spirit over desperate challenges, of self over mindless peril, the triumph of heart over certain defeat.

Suddenly Angus knew that if any church were true it would need to have that same power to require everything of a man. Only such a church could be worthy of a Highlander's heart! And it struck him then that, like his father, he had always been searching. "Perhaps in this new land I will find the place where I belong, after all!" Angus thought.

The silver-touched land on the dark, western horizon continued to glow, and Angus smiled as the *Canartic* charted its course toward a new continent through the dark and pathless seas, with only the bright light of the fixed stars to guide her home to port.

Chapter Three

After the passengers from the *Canartic* disembarked in Boston and were cleared through customs and immigration, most of them disappeared into the bustle of the thriving portside city. However, the group of converts under Elder Richards's direction remained together and traveled as a group by railroad car to Iowa City, where the tracks terminated. In Iowa, the McElins were amazed to see the efficiency and determination of the Church to which they now belonged. A corps of elders, returning missionaries and men who were just starting their years of service, were busy organizing the incoming streams of converts from New England and Europe who were about to begin the final, most challenging leg of their journey to the new Zion.

Mary was delighted to discover that, although she had lost most of her household goods, seeds, and tools in the mysterious disappearance of the *Eliza III*, the gold and silver coins she had sewn into her family's clothing were of greatly increased value in this new country where bartered goods were plentiful but coinage was at a premium. She was able to purchase all the essential provisions for the handcart journey to Salt Lake Valley, and she still had a comfortable number of coins left over.

The pioneer camp that the McElins joined bustled with activity day and night. There was, in the preparations, an anxious urgency that Mary did not understand but sensed went beyond the natural desire to simply "get on" with the journey. Because of the McElins' efficiency, they were among the first families to be prepared, and so they began to assist other families. Mary, in her quick, capable way, soon became a mainstay in the camp, caring for the sick, helping with the inevitable births, organizing the women's chores more effectively, and dispatching her sons to lift, pack, build, repair, wherever she saw the need.

As Mary became better acquainted with the company in which she was to travel west, she was overwhelmed with its diversity and courage. She saw families reared in the finest homes of England, dressed in silks, who had obviously never done a day's work in their lives, loading their carts with sets of china and linens. On top of their canvas bundles of food, cloth goods, farm implements, and furniture, one such family had tied a marble bust of Shakespeare. The sight of the poet's noble face, hanging sideways on the unevenly stacked cart, made Mary smile, but at the same time it pained her heart, for somehow the statue said to her, more poignantly than words, just how far from civilization they were going.

Some of the Saints were too ill from the ocean voyage to continue the journey. Lucy Patterson, a young Englishwoman whom Mary befriended, tried valiantly to keep pace with the preparations. One evening, though, she collapsed during the camp's devotional service. Angus carried her to the McElins' wagon and the next day Elder Richards came for her.

"We feel it's best if Sister Patterson rests in Iowa in the home of a good family. She will make the trip to the valley next year," he told Mary. In tears, Mary and Lucy parted.

A major problem in the camp, Mary quickly observed, was the

confusion of languages. Everywhere the babble of foreign tongues could be heard—Danish, German, Swedish, and many dialects of English. Mary thought the Tower of Babel must have sounded much the same as the pioneer camp, and yet the organizing elders, unperturbed, continued to direct the work so that, within two weeks, the immigrant group was ready to begin their trip.

The people in the camp were divided into two traveling companies. The McElins were assigned to Company A with a captain named William O. Edmonds. Elder Richards was assigned to the other company, so late in the evening before departure, Mary and her sons went over to say their farewells to him.

There were tears in Mary's eyes as she shook the missionary's hand and wished him a safe journey.

"I'm worried!" she confided in him. "It seems to me that our handcarts are made from green unseasoned wood, and I fear we will have trouble with them."

Elder Richards nodded his head solemnly. "Yes, we will. Wood was in short supply this year and we had to take what we could get. However, we are already nearly two weeks late in leaving, and it is better to take the chance of traveling with these carts than to be further delayed and face early snows in the passes of the Rockies."

Alarm widened Mary's eyes. "But surely there is no danger of that! We are leaving in late May . . ."

"I think you should know the truth, Mary, before you and your sons begin this trip." The missionary indicated that the McElins should sit on the ground by his campfire, and he sat down beside them. "I know your family will come through this experience very well. You are all healthy, and you have good equipment, but you must remember that the company can only travel as fast as its weakest members, and you will be forced to pace your mileage to the speed of the little children and the elderly. Because we'll be pulling or pushing the handcarts, only the smallest and most desperately sick can ever ride. The Church tries to screen the families who go west by handcart, but we cannot deny anyone the right to try it if they are determined to do it. Most are simply too poor to go any other way."

"So that is why we go by handcart! Money?" Angus asked. He had been puzzled at this odd means of locomotion chosen by the immigrant Saints. The handcarts they pulled were large boxlike frames mounted and balanced on two wheels of a circumference so large that the wheels reached higher than the side of the wagon. At the end of the wagon frame were two large pulling handles, and the wagon was balanced so that it rode fairly easily, even with a considerable load. The vehicle was pulled in front by two people walking, and, on inclines or rough ground, it was pushed from behind as well.

The pioneers, Angus included, would simply get up one morning, pack their carts, grab the handles, and walk to Utah, pulling their supplies behind them.

"We devised handcarts partly because of the money problem," Elder Richards answered, "but also for speed. Brigham Young figured that people walking, even pulling a load, could probably get to Utah faster than those who came by wagon train. Those heavy wagons move very slowly; there is much illness and injury to the horses and oxen that pull them, and many a family has been stranded by the death of their stock."

Mary felt a chill of apprehension. "We have come so far!" she whispered. "I felt we were through the worst, but I can see that it is still before us."

With a sigh, Elder Richards reached over and took her hand. "I have brought you this far, and I wish I could see you to the end. But I know we will meet again in the valley—and you shall get to know my Emily, and I shall meet your Robert again."

Mary brightened at the thought, but Johnny was still thinking about the long trek ahead. "How long will it take to get there?" he exclaimed. "If you say we must fear the snow, then I'm thinking we are in for a long trot!"

They all laughed, but a shadow of sadness crossed Elder Richards's face. "If all goes well it should take about three months, and you will be in the safety of the valley well before the early snows. Unexpected delay is our greatest enemy.

"Our first two handcart companies left here in July of 1857. They had a lot of trouble with their carts, and repairs and breakdowns delayed them seriously. They did not even arrive at the Missouri River, in Nebraska, until mid-August. There they refitted and forged ahead, but, as they approached the high passes of the mountains in Colorado, it was already September, with the promise of early snow in the air. In panic the pioneers began to unload their carts, caching food, clothes, and bedding along the way to lighten their loads so that they could move faster. However, the snows came, and without food or proper clothes, the hardship, misery, and death that resulted were terrible. Finally rescue teams from Salt Lake came up through the mountains from the other side, bringing food and transporting the survivors down into Salt Lake City where they were cared for. It was an agonizing lesson, but we have learned from it. Since that time many companies have traveled to Utah and their losses have been significantly less than those of people traveling by wagon train.''

Mary realized that Elder Richards had carried the burden of their needs for so long that he could only think of his fears and worries for them. What joy and relief he would feel when he could deliver his flock in safety.

She patted his hand and smiled at him. "You have been a friend to us, Elder Richards," she said awkwardly. Giving compliments always came hard to her. "The Lord has seen us this far, and He will see us the rest of the way."

With that she stood up briskly, afraid she had already shown more emotion than was seemly. She gestured to her sons, and they each shook hands with Elder Richards and thanked him for his kindness. Then the McElins returned to their own campsite. Each family had been assigned a place in the company, with Captain Edmonds taking the lead, one assistant in the center of the line, and the third bringing up the rear. Outriders would scout and carry communications. The cattle, except for some of the milk cows, would move in a loose herd behind the company, with the teenage boys taking turns moving them along. Captain Edmonds had been impressed by the McElin brothers and made Angus, Matty, and Johnny each responsible for a group of five families.

As Mary and her sons crawled into their bedrolls on the cold prairie ground, they were so engrossed in their own thoughts that they did not speak to one another. For a long time Angus lay in his hard bed, wondering if the others were awake as well. His mother was bedded under the protection of the cart, but he and his brothers were sleeping without so much as a tarp over their heads, and above him Angus could see the thick panoply of the black prairie night, singing with diamond stars. Was God somewhere in that infinite endless expanse, really thinking of them—caring for them—watching over them? All of these people who had left their warm, sweet homes, who had kissed beloved family and friends farewell forever, who had braved the fury of the mindless sea and had spent their last farthings on this incredible enterprise—did the God who dwelt somewhere in that glorious infinity really know and care about each one of them? Would they be spared devastating delays—or, if the delays came, would the Lord, in His watchful mercy, postpone the snows until they were through the mountains and into the safety of the Utah valleys?

Would his tiny mother, with her tough but frail little body, really be able to walk the trackless miles—and would a loving God count her footsteps and give her credit in his ledgers for every one?

Angus stared at the night, and he did not know if it would be so. But he did know that in his heart was an odd sense of purpose, and he felt as though it mattered—somewhere out there in the pulsing mystery of space, it mattered what he was doing. He could not explain it, but he knew what he was doing had meaning, and he felt a sense of rightness and of noble design. In him was the unspoken conviction that, in some way, tomorrow his family would be doing more than simply starting on a long walk. And for the first time in his young manhood, he felt, with a strange and inexplicable knowledge, that he was not alone.

For the first days the journey was halting. Feet became blistered, faces sunburned, muscles ached, and there was a general feeling of disorder and strain. In Company A there were two hundred and twenty-two individuals, one hundred handcarts, four horse-drawn wagons, twenty-four oxen, and twenty tents, as well as sundry milk cows, chickens, dogs, and mules. What astonished Mary the most was the noise they created as they moved across the vast prairie. The fresh, green wood of the new carts creaked and groaned with every inch. Their wheels could not be greased enough to stop the awful creaking, and every joint and plank of wood protested at each movement.

The racket was almost deafening. "If there are any Indians in the states of Iowa or Nebraska," Matty exclaimed, "it is certain that they know we are coming. They may even be hearing us in Salt Lake Valley!"

Morning, noon, and night the carts needed to be patched and greased. Wheels split, wagon beds cracked, hubs seized up, and the wagon tongues warped and splintered. Every man in the train was busy with hammer, wedge, plane, and vise. Johnny carried the grease bucket and ran up and down the line, daubing and doctoring the groaning axles, but somehow, in spite of it all, the company progressed.

Gradually, the disparate group of pioneers fell into a workable, companionable routine. Up each morning before five o'clock, the hardy band ate a cold breakfast from the leavings of the night before, packed their bedrolls, dressed, nursed and fed the children, and were on their way before dawn had broken. On days when the weather and terrain were cooperative, the company could travel as much as twenty miles. However, when it rained, or the sun was too hot, or the ground was rough or muddy, they were often slowed to as little as five miles in an entire day.

One day, just after the struggling group crossed the Des Moines River, they entered an area so thick with sandy soil that men, women, and children grunted and heaved to move the heavily laden carts that had sunk hub deep into the sand. The conditions lasted for several miles, and at the end of the day the pioneers had progressed less than two miles. That night most of the group did not even bother to unpack their bedrolls, they simply fell exhausted onto the ground and slept as they were. It took two more days of the same grueling effort before the carts were out of the sand beds and on to the hard plains again. "It's a good thing Lucy Patterson didn't come," Mary mused in her exhaustion. "She could never have survived this!"

Finally Company A entered Nebraska, and on an evening early in July they sighted the log cabins and welcome fires of the Church's waystation near Council Bluffs. Winter Quarters, as it was called, was built on the neck of land formed between the Platte River and the Missouri River as the Platte branched away and headed due west.

The Saints, by now travel-hardened and lean, entered the little settlement just before nightfall, to be greeted with warmth and generosity by the Church members living there. They were informed that Company B, with Elder Richards in it, had passed through about a week earlier and had seemed in good spirits with very little sickness, although they too had suffered from the carts breaking down.

That night the three McElin brothers were called into Captain Edmonds's tent. He looked at them with the intense and harried expression that seemed never to leave his face.

"Brothers McElin," he said, "it is imperative that we get our carts in better condition so that we can move with more dispatch. I am commissioning you to work with a group of men whose one duty will be to repair and repack every handcart in the company. We have two days in which to perform this task, and then we must be ready to leave. If we delay any more than that we will not reach the mountains before the first snow falls."

Angus did not need to have the seriousness of these words explained to him. He and his brothers were mountain men, and they knew that the weather could defeat a man, when the highest summit, the most impassable rock face could not.

In the next two days the men worked as if possessed. They did not sleep, and only stopped to eat or drink when the food was brought to them. The camp rang with the sounds of their labors, and, as the third day dawned, the company stood in readiness, with Captain Edmonds at its head, and everything in order for the last thousand miles.

Of the three brothers, Matty took the greatest interest in the territory they were covering. He had never seen anything like the great plains of North America, and, as they headed out along the Platte River, he passed each day in awe of the land which looked as endless as the ocean, the waving fields of prairie grass, with distant herds of buffalo and occasionally a clump of cottonwood or service berries. After asking Captain Edmonds if he could copy the company's maps, Matty began to spend his evenings studying the charts in the pale lamplight, on an overturned box. The names he read brought pictures to mind. The pioneers would travel along the Platte River through the prairies until the river forked, and then they would take the North Platte, past Chimney Rock, and on to Fort Laramie. Still following the North Platte, they would travel on past Red Buttes, and around Devil's Gate, entering the vast complex of western mountains they had heard so much about ever since leaving Scotland— the Rockies.

"You know . . ." Matty mused to his brother one night, as Angus lay in his bedroll trying to sleep, " 'tis not just a single chain of mountains we've been talking about! The Rockies are a whole network of mountain chains."

"Aye!" Angus grunted, turning over on the hard ground. "If we ever see the blasted things. I'm beginning to doubt they exist! I think this prairie goes on forever."

Matty gave a snort of laughter and then looked at the maps again. "Oh," he said softly, "ye'll be getting your mountains sure enough, Angus. About as much mountains as a man can take!"

And it was as Matty had predicted. The company, in the dead heat of August, moved through the desperate heat of Wyoming with red rocks shimmering in the sun, and the red dust clogging their nostrils and covering their hair, skin, and clothes until they lost all color but that of the red earth.

70

They dared not slow their pace. Those who were too ill to walk could ride in one of the few wagons, but even the children had grown so used to the daily march that they managed to keep up the grueling pace on their strong young legs. Only the smallest children were sometimes swung up on Johnny's or Matty's strong shoulders for a brief ride. Angus pulled the McElin cart most of the time, with the other brothers taking turns. Angus still felt the responsibility to deliver the family safely to his father, but now, instead of resenting the commission, he was driven by a desire to give his father a good accounting of his stewardship.

Late in August the handcart pioneers came to the Sweetwater River and began the tortuous journey into the Rockies. They headed north of the highest mountains, past Giant's Butte, and then dropped down to Fort Bridger, passing Redden's Cave and Pulpit Rock. Finally, as they approached the last ridges of the mountains, they let themselves believe for the first time that they were really going to make it all the way to Utah.

As they began climbing steadily, the Saints' excitement could almost be felt. So many pioneers had come this way before them that the passes were firm and smooth. Each company that moved west had tried to improve the trail for the ones that would follow. All along the way the members of Company A found evidence of other pioneers who had passed—messages written on rocks, campsites prepared with fire rings and beaten ground, caches of furniture or food, and often a small grave marked with a stone or a bare wooden cross. Mary would be silent for hours when she saw one of the little grave markers; it made her own grief seem fresh and real again.

Each day as the pioneers entered the mountains, they saw more evidence of people. Riders, wagons, and an occasional man on foot would pass them both coming and going. It made them feel even closer to their final destination. But as they reached the higher elevations, the nights grew bitterly cold. Freezing rain fell and one day they journeyed in a light whirl of snow and sleet. Fortunately, the next day dawned bright and clear so the snow soon melted from the trail. Above the high pass, on the towering summits, they could see evidence of new snow, and Angus stared in wonder at mountains that were so high that the snow never left them.

"Someday," Angus whispered to himself, "I shall visit that eternal snow!"

He felt himself coming alive. His body was even more hardened and strong than it had been in the highlands, and he drew new life from the sight of the majestic mountains, which were as glorious as Elder Richards had promised. Angus's soul rose to meet their challenge. He became an unacknowledged leader in the group, and even Captain Edmonds bowed to Angus's opinions on the most efficient and safe way to move the company over the difficult mountain roadway.

At the highest point the company slept for two nights in a sifting snow. The air became bitterly cold when the sun went down, but in the morning the temperatures warmed. Angus insisted that the company build fires and drink hot liquids for breakfast. He taught them how to make a quick gruel with wheat flour. The altitude made everyone weak, but Angus knew they must push on. A heavy blizzard could catch them at any time, and then, almost within sight of their objective, they could be defeated.

At last Company A began its descent into Parley's Canyon. They moved down the narrow defile with the cold winds from the mountains blowing at their backs.

The handcart company crossed the second ridge, the Wasatch Range, in good order on the well-smoothed trail and, at last, woke one morning to break camp with no more mountains in front of them, only a downward, twisting trail, and far below them the glint of water—the Great Salt Lake.

As they twisted in and out of the cottonwoods and aspens lining the trail, they caught glimpses of a mountain stream and heard the play of gentle water. Behind them the cold wind turned to a cooling breeze, and the air coming up from the valley was warm and sweet. They broke free from the constricting walls of the canyon and clustered on the brow of the hill, looking down at the place of which they had dreamed—Salt Lake Valley! They could see below them a small city, its streets laid out like a neat checkerboard, and busy roads leading toward it from every direction. On the city's outskirts the rejoicing company could see fields and orchards of green and gold, glowing in the sun, and from the mountainsides they saw irrigation ditches carrying life-giving water from the tops of the mountains, down to the valley floor.

Angus looked around him at the faces of those men, women, and children who had walked every step of the long way with him and his heart constricted with affection and admiration. He looked at his mother, Mary. She was as supple as a girl, but the sun had baked her skin and had aged her until she looked like a wrinkled brown apple. Still, to Angus she was beautiful. He looked at Matty and

Johnny who stood bursting with manhood, their skins bronzed by exposure to the elements, their shoulders wide and muscular and their bodies lean and powerful. "Have I changed as much as the rest of the family?" he wondered. It did not matter. They were there, safe and sound, and now he could turn them over to his father as he had promised. And then? Angus didn't know the answer to that question yet, but he did know that he would stay here, in the west, and find himself a wife. Somehow he doubted, though, that this pleasant valley would ever be his home. He saw on the faces of his family and friends as they looked joyfully at the valley an expression that said "I am here, at last. I have come home!" But Angus shook his head at the thought, and, with unconscious yearning, he turned his face away from the valley back to where they had been. When Matty looked at him, Angus was not staring at the thriving city lying below him, as was everyone else. He was looking upward and his eyes were fastened on the glorious, unattainable summits of the Rockies soaring above them against the high blue sky.

Robert heard the news of the arrival of the handcart company from one of his neighbors who had been trading at the Mercantile Center on State Street when the scouts had ridden into Salt Lake.

"I think it may be your family with them, Brother McElin," the gentle German told Robert. "The scouts mentioned that there were Scotsmen in the company, wearing their plaids."

"Aye," Robert replied, as he put down the plane with which he had been smoothing a window molding. "Elder Richards told me my boys would probably be in the next company to arrive. I thank you very much for your news, Brother Steiner."

Robert put his tools away with the studied movements of a craftsman and swept the golden curls of fresh wood into the corner pile. Then, having surveyed his cabinet-making room to be certain of its orderliness, he took one quick look into the other room in which he lived. He had built the small house of adobe brick soon after arriving in the valley and had immediately begun work, fashioning desperately needed furniture and wooden tools out of packing crates, old wagons, handcarts, and any cured wood he could find, barter, beg, or buy.

Since the only available trees grew on the high slopes of the surrounding mountains, the small milling companies could not keep up with the insatiable demands of the growing settlements for wood and lumber. Robert soon developed a reputation for being able to make quality furniture out of "kindling." Eventually Brigham Young had heard about the Scots cabinetmaker and had engaged Robert's services to build beds, desks, chairs, tables, and moldings for the Beehive and Lyon houses that the church leader was building next to the temple lot in downtown Salt Lake City. President Young had been a carpenter himself, and he took great delight in the smell of the workshop and the details of Robert's cabinetwork. President Young's descriptions and specifications on each job were very precise since he could both admire excellence and spot any flaws with the quick, appraising eye of a craftsman.

There was in Brigham Young the same graceful simplicity that existed in a fine piece of furniture—a practical, straightforward naturalness that belied the complexity and logic of the design. This was a man who was a doer, a dreamer of practical dreams, a man who saw the mortal and the spiritual existences as two parts of a whole and who was able to translate such abstract Christian mysteries as the love of God into something as simple as the gentleness with which a mother should wash her children's faces, "never with a harsh rag, or cold water, but with soft cloth and warmth." Here was a man acquainted with the Scriptures as though part of his own fiber, and yet who could relish the works of Shakespeare and the voice of Jenny Lind. A man who could take time from a brutal schedule of work and responsibility to ride in his carriage to the outskirts of the settlement simply to share his love of things well made with another craftsman. To Robert McElin such a man seemed the embodiment of the prophets of the Old Testament.

With the work and the challenge of building, Robert had watched the summer speed past, even though his heart was filled with a deep yearning to be reunited with Mary and his sons. Now that the time of that reunion was at hand, Robert found himself hesitating and strangely reluctant. "Will they be glad to see me?" he wondered. "Will we all have changed? Have they forgiven me?"

He snatched up his broad-brimmed hat and jammed it on his head and strode out into the street leading toward the canyons. A whole procession of people were hurrying in the same direction. The streets were broad and straight, running squarely east and west and north and south, broad enough to accommodate four spans of horses walking side by side. As Robert approached the hills at the foot of Parley's Canyon, he could see the first members of the handcart company threading their way through the narrow defile down onto the lower elevation and the roadway leading to the city. Robert's heart caught in his throat as he thought he saw the red gleam of a flying tartan on one of the striding figures at the front of the column.

To Mary and her sons, with their diffidence and unassuming ways, the entry into the valley was a source of both embarrassment and delight. The highway was lined on both sides with rejoicing people. Hands reached out to clasp them, shouts of joy were raised. Hymns were sung, gifts of food and clothing were pressed into their hands. Eager questions were called from the crowd. "Have you heard anything about Company C?" "Are the Lindstroms with you?" "Are the snows falling in Wyoming yet?" And over and over again there were inquiries about specific families. "Anyone named Barnes?" "Anyone from Holland? France? London?" Bewildered and touched, the McElins threaded through the thronging crowd, searching the faces for the one they longed to see.

Mary saw Robert first. He was pushing his way through a knot of people, and she knew he had seen them.

That morning her sons had come to Mary and had told her they planned to wear their dress tartans when they walked into the valley. Mary had agreed they should, and she herself had pulled out her plaid homespun shawl, given to her when she had gone to marry Robert. Her wedding day seemed long ago, and the bright, fine-woven plaid was faded and tattered. "It was your mother's," her aunt had whispered as she wrapped it around her shoulders. Mary hugged it around her now, and her heart began to beat so loudly she thought her sons would hear.

There was Robert hurrying toward her, his dark hair streaked with gray now, but his eyes as bright and his face as open and strong as it had been on the night he first bent to kiss her. "Oh, my Robbie!" she whispered under her breath. He came to her awkward with joy. "Well, Mary is it?" he breathed, and then reached out and pulled her to himself in a hungry embrace. His sons stood back, unsure and hesitant, and Robert turned to them and shook each of their hands.

"Let me pull the cart for ye!" Robert offered.

"Nay, Father," Angus replied, an edge of hardness still in his voice. "We have pulled it this far ourselves. We will finish the job."

"Verra well, then," Robert answered calmly. "I will show you the way to our home."

As they pulled away from the crowd, there was an uproar of

excitement, and the people around them surged forward toward an open carriage that had just arrived. "The Prophet!" Angus heard a woman next to him exclaim. He craned his neck to catch a glimpse of the great man.

Angus saw a stocky, powerful man dressed in a black suit with a gold watch chain and a white shirt gleaming brightly against the somber cloth. His face was handsome, with a well-trimmed beard and intent, compassionate eyes.

President Young alighted from the buggy and made his way through the crowd, stopping to speak to members of the handcart company, raising small children in his arms, shaking hands with the men, and congratulating the leaders who had brought the pioneers safely through. Suddenly the Prophet spied the McElins and he hurried toward them.

"Well, Brother McElin," he said, "I see your family has at last arrived, and safely. May I congratulate and commend you, Sister McElin, and your sons as well!"

Robert McElin introduced his wife and his three sons to the Prophet, and President Young shook hands with each of them warmly. When he met Angus, his eyes lingered on the young man's face with steady appraisal. "I have been told by the elders of your company about the help and support you have given them, both in keeping the carts in working order and in getting them through the mountains. After you and your brothers get settled I would like to have a word with all of you. Please call at the Beehive House at your earliest convenience."

The young men stared at one another in confusion and amazement, and stammered their acceptance. As quickly as he had come, President Young was gone, lost in the crowd for a few more minutes; then he mounted his carriage swiftly and rode back toward town with an entourage of carriages and outriders following after him.

Mary was delighted when she saw the snug sturdiness of Robert's little adobe home. She surveyed the fireplace and the polished hardwood floor—the one real luxury in the main room. Although she did not smile, Robert could sense her satisfaction with the size of the room, the beautiful sleigh bed in one corner, and the finely crafted chairs by the side of the hearth. The kitchen alcove was tiny, but efficiently arranged, and Mary immediately sent the boys outside to begin unpacking the handcart so that she could arrange her own utensils and household goods in their proper places.

After her tour of the main room, Mary opened the door into the workroom. The motes of sawdust were caught like specks of gold in the late-afternoon light, and her quick eye appraised the table and benches, the stacks of scrap wood, and the work in progress. She saw the neatly placed tools, the planes and saws, vises and levels, the stains, sanders, and emery, the glue pots and clamps, and smelled the fresh scents of the wood. She noted the wide deep windows that framed the mountains and the sky and let in the light and air. In her mind flashed the image of the dark, cramped mine tunnels.

Suddenly she was tired, more tired than she could remember in her life. She turned to Robert with a touch of her old asperity. "Well," she remarked, "I see ye have taken the best room for your workshop!"

Indignation rose in him, but then he caught the gleam in her eye, and realizing she was teasing him, he laughed. "Aye," he replied, " 'tis the privilege of the husband."

"Aye," she breathed and turned away from him, and walked over to the sleigh bed where she sank down onto the coverlet. The strain and the tension seemed to have vanished between them. Suddenly it was his Mary, tired and spent, and he could feel her weariness as though she were part of him again. Swiftly he went to her side and put his arms around her tenderly.

"Mary," he whispered, "I will never leave ye again. Never. I will care for ye for the rest of your life. Ye will never be tired again."

Mary looked at him, her face rosy-brown from the sun and her eyes as bright and green as the sea. "Nay, Rob. I will be tired again—but not alone. For bad or for good, whatever we have done to one another is in the past, and none of it can change the fact that we must be together. It is the thing which has brought me across the ocean—and has walked with me across this continent. Oh, Robbie, ye are nae an easy man to love!"

Suddenly Robert bent his head and kissed her hungrily. She sat quietly within his embrace. "I've missed ye so, Mary," he whispered against her neck. "My desire has been like a demon inside of me—and only my work to make me want to go on." He let go of her and stood up with his back toward her. His muscled hands were clenched at his sides. "There is only one bed. . . ."

Mary got up and walked in front of him. She raised her hands and placed them on his shoulders and standing on tiptoe put her mouth close to his ear.

"Rob, my childbearing years are over," she whispered. "The hard journey has taken care of that. We need never again fear that I will bear a child for the grave. I—I—" She took a deep breath and then rushed on, her breath soft against his ear. "I revoke my pledge never to lie with thee again."

Outside in the yard Angus, Matty, and Johnny were busy raising a tent so they could sleep in it that night. From inside the house they heard their father give a loud, joyous shout. Then there was silence. "Do you think we should go in and see if anything is wrong?" Johnny asked anxiously.

"Nay," Matty said, with a wide grin on his face, and he began to whistle as he pounded the tent pegs deeply into the soil.

Angus glared angrily at his two brothers, incensed beyond reason by their easy joy. They held no ill will toward their father! No blame for the year of misery! How could they forget and forgive so easily? Suddenly he felt lost and alone again. Could no one see as he saw? Without a word, he tramped out of the yard, making a beeline across the rough fields and open yards toward the mountains.

"What's wrong with him?" Johnny asked anxiously. "Do ye think we should go after him?"

Matty shook his head. "He needs to be alone for a while. It will take time before he and Dad can be together. Too much has passed between them."

It was almost dark when Angus returned from his long tramp. He came into the house without a word to anyone and sat down at the table where his mother had left some soda bread and milk for him. Without looking at anyone, he ate the food and then walked across the floor toward the outer door.

"Ye'll be sleeping in the tent, Angus?" his mother inquired from her chair near the fire. She was sorting piles of clothes and linens from one of the baskets. In the workroom beyond, Angus could hear his father and brothers laughing. There were sounds of heavy things being dragged across the floor.

"Aye," Angus replied. "Tomorrow I'll look for work."

Robert had entered the room and heard the last words. "President Young has asked to see the three of ye. Don't ye think that should be your first priority?" he remarked.

Angus turned his head slowly and stared at his father. His black brows were drawn together, and his jaw was set in a stubborn line. "I'll set my own priorities from now on, I've been thinking," he growled. With that he pulled open the door and hurled himself out into the night. Before he had taken four strides the door reopened and his father was beside him in the brisk night air.

"I know ye have been angry with me for a long time, Angus," Robert said. "But I have not asked of ye more than was my right to ask. Ye have brought the family here safely and ye have discharged your duties. I am proud of ye and grateful, but I will not apologize or feel that I have required more of ye than it was your duty to give. We are a family, and we are each responsible to the other. Now I wish ye would let me help ye."

"I don't want your help!" Angus growled. "I just want to be free to live my own life—to . . ."

"This is your life, son," Robert said softly.

"Nay!" Angus flung out. "That is just talk! Ye and Mother have each other, and I can see in your eyes—ye don't need anything else! It will be as much a relief for ye as for me when I am gone—aye, and the other boys too. Ye have all that ye need now—and I have brought it to ye. We are not a part of that—not any more—if we ever really were!"

Robert was silent for a minute. In the darkness he could hear his son's harsh breathing and feel the pent-up frustration and impatience that drove him. Robert didn't dare to touch his oldest son, for fear that he would fling his hand away, but his voice, when he spoke, reached out with affection and understanding.

"Ye are a passionate man, Angus my son. All your emotions are as harsh and strong as the rocks on Ben Sinclair—but ye are a strong man too. Passion can destroy as easily as it can build. It almost destroyed your mother and me, and, if ye do not learn to use it wisely, it could destroy those whom ye will love, as well. Even more important—it could destroy ye."

"Ye need not worry," Angus said bitterly. "I am a moral man!"

"Aye," Robert said equably. "I know ye are a moral man—but a moral man who needs a life of his own. Ye are right, Angus. The time has come for ye to look for your own way. Go to President Young, he will help ye find it! Go with my blessing and permission."

"I will go," Angus replied sullenly, "but I don't need either your blessing or permission."

"I know," Robert answered, and the ghost of a sad smile played on his lips, "but I give them to ye anyway." Before Angus could turn away, his father reached out and grasped his son's hand in a hard clasp. Reflexively, Angus yanked away, but his father would not release his grip, and, as the stars began to sprinkle the sky, the two men stood locked in a silent struggle, the older man holding tightly to his son's hand and the younger man pulling against his father's grasp with all his might. Neither one of them moved their feet. They were almost evenly matched in strength. Perspiration began to pour from their foreheads and the cords stood out on their muscular arms as they fought. In the pale light of the stars the older man's face looked noble, sad, and infinitely tired.

Almost unintentionally, Angus relaxed his resistance, and his father, caught off guard, lost his balance and slipped backward. With quick reflex, Angus grabbed his father's arm to prevent him from falling, and suddenly the two men were laughing, and Angus gripped his father's hand and held it in a warm, firm handshake. Still chuckling, Robert released his hand and held it gingerly, rubbing the reddened skin.

"Aye, Angus," he said, "I think you're right. Ye are no longer a boy-o!"

Angus laughed too, and the bitterness and harshness seemed to melt out of him like wax in the refiner's kiln. Oddly, he was left feeling empty and cold and he knew that even though the bitterness was gone, he would never return to the simple emotions of his childhood days.

"I'll be bedding down now," Angus said, walking toward the tent. "Send Matty and Johnny out soon, since we shall be getting up early for our visit to the Beehive House."

Early the next day the three brothers walked down State Street into the bustling heart of the new city of Salt Lake. Irrigation ditches bordered the street on either side. Log cabins, adobe-brick houses, and shops lined the thoroughfare, with kitchen gardens, root cellars, and tender young saplings in the yards. At the very center of the community stood the Brigham Young residences—the White House, which had been the Prophet's home; across from it, the almost completed Beehive House; and the excavation and framework for the larger Lion House. The cross street was called South Temple, and, looking down that road, the brothers could see the almost completed fence surrounding the large square designated for the tabernacle.

Brigham Young's office was adjacent to the Beehive House, and through its door a steady stream of visitors came and went. For a moment the young men hesitated, but Angus led the way and before they knew it, they were standing in President Young's office.

The room was imposing, with high narrow windows draped in

dark maroon and a carpet of the same color. The furniture was substantial and masculine, and the whole effect was one of solemn comfort and handsome utility. The genius of Brigham Young as a colonizer was his understanding of the uses of men and natural resources. No sooner had the Saints entered the Salt Lake Valley than he had begun to choose strong and gifted men to spread out and colonize promising areas in the surrounding territory. Peter Maughn and J. S. Wells were sent to Cache Valley, James Brown to Ogden, John Higbee south to Provo, Seth Taft and Charles Shumway southeast to Manti and Sanpete, Charles Rich across the mountains into California. Many others were sent to search out valleys, rivers, minerals, timberlands, and places for commerce and industry.

The president rose from behind his desk, shook hands with each of them, and indicated that they should be seated. Then Brigham Young fixed the three young men with his discerning eye. Though his face was stern, there was in him a profound good humor and optimism that made even his most solemn pronouncements seem warm and personal.

"I have judged you brethren," President Young said. "I have inquired about you among the men who have worked with you in the handcart company and from your father. I have judged you by your works, by your mettle, and by the spirit which I feel in you, and I believe that you are the men whom the Lord wishes to use in building up His kingdom in this place. It is my wish to call you to the work. Angus, I know that you have still not accepted the waters of baptism, but the Lord is calling you, along with your brothers."

Johnny's face lit up like a glowing sun, and Matty smiled his slow, winning smile, but Angus felt his heart plummet like lead. What was it the president wanted him to do? As a nonmember, he could not be called on a mission.

"For a long time," the president went on, "I have felt that we could raise the finest sheep in the world in this territory. What we have needed here are true sheepmen. Men who know and understand the animals, and who have a feel for the land in which they thrive. I believe you are just the men for that enterprise!"

Angus felt relief flood through him. Sheep! Flocks, and meadows and the highland, and the clean, fresh air! He stared at Brigham Young with wonder and he thought he saw, deep in the man's eyes, the glimmer of an understanding smile. "Can he know what I was thinking?" Angus asked himself, ashamed and amazed at the thought.

"I want you to explore the southeastern regions of the Rockies and see if you can discover an area that would be ideal for the raising of sheep. If you find such a location, I want you to return to Salt Lake Valley, gather family and friends who desire to assist you in this enterprise, and take them there to settle and develop a sheep-raising center that will supply both wool and mutton of a superior quality. My blessings upon you in this endeavor. Pray to the Lord for guidance, and report to me on your progress." As they turned to leave, Brigham Young shook Angus's hand and said, with a knowing smile, "I know you will find the thing for which you are searching, Brother McElin."

Overwhelmed, the brothers mumbled their thanks and earnest dedication to the assignment, and, before they knew it, they found they had been graciously ushered out of the building and were standing on the doorstep staring at the broad, busy street. "Well, I'll be . . ." Angus whispered. Matty was silent, but Johnny expressed what they were all thinking. With a wild whoop that startled the horses of a passing carriage, he bounded down the stairs, leaped into the air, and threw his cap as high as he could.

In the following winter, the three brothers became mountain men. They dressed in heavy, homespun wool and rough fur. Their beards grew full and they learned the ways of the wild animals and Indians who lived in the canyons, plateaus, and upper reaches of the Rockies. Through the bitter months of snow and blizzards, and into the mud and chill of spring, they searched. Through the heat of the summer they continued, returning to Salt Lake only for supplies and brief visits with their parents. It was during one of these visits home that Angus and Johnny discovered a secret Matty had been hiding.

During the long handcart journey the year before, Matty had courted and won a young woman from Connecticut named Zina Stillman. Although his brothers had noticed Matty talking to the young woman, it had never crossed their minds to imagine that Matty was serious about her. In all the months following the handcart trek Matty had never mentioned Zina's name to his brothers, but on a brief visit in the city, one balmy June evening, Angus and Johnny spied Matty and Zina walking hand in hand, and the look in the couple's eyes made it clear that their relationship was mutual and serious.

Caught red-handed, Matty sheepishly admitted that he and Zina had an "understanding" and that, as soon as the McElins discovered the spot for their new settlement, she would marry him and accompany him to their new home. "You know, my boy-os, you had better be finding yourselves candidates for wives as well, because once we settle in the mountains it's going to be a long, dry spell for young women."

Johnny responded enthusiastically and began attending every party and dance held in the valley. Before the brothers departed a month later on their further explorations, he had settled on a dimpled lass with chestnut hair and bright pink cheeks. Her name was Hester Blake. Her parents had joined the Church in Ohio and had entered Salt Lake Valley with one of the earliest wagon trains, when Hester was a little girl. Hester had a delicious laugh, and Johnny's antics filled her with delight. They seemed made for one another.

Angus alone seemed unable to play the suitor. He left Salt Lake with his desperate desires still locked in his heart and no girl who was even close to knowing him.

Many times during that long second winter of exploring, the brothers were tempted to stop searching and simply settle where they stood, not caring if the place had some imperfection—the soil too rocky, the streams meager, or the valley too narrow. Always, however, some inner drive for excellence kept them from compromising and pushed them onward. Finally, near the end of the winter, with supplies petered out and spirits exhausted, they topped the rise of a long stretch of unpromising mountains and saw below them the valley of the Virgin River, green and broad, with a wild plateau of meadows stretching above a second ridge of high mountains guarding the far side where the summits were white with snow. From the narrow gorge cut in the mountain wall by the restless river, they could see the rich, vibrant plunge of the Virgin's life-giving water pouring out onto the valley floor.

Their three hearts pounded as one, for this was the reincarnation of their Scottish home—the wild scenery, the jagged cliffs and rocks, the highland meadows, and the sweet, welcoming valley. The brothers knew they had at last found the place for themselves, for their sheep, and for their families. They could not contain their joy. They embraced and pounded exuberantly on each other's back. They shouted and hallooed across the open expanse to the silent mountains on the other side, and they heard their own voices shouting back in welcome.

That evening Angus spoke to his brothers around the campfire. "Tomorrow I have a favor to ask of ye."

"Ask away!" Matty said.

83

"I want ye to baptize me here, in our new valley."

"What!" his brothers exclaimed. "Are ye sure, man?"

"When I saw this valley today I knew the Lord had led me here. He has given me what I have desired and now I wish to return something to Him," Angus replied.

Matty was the first to recover from his astonishment.

"I shall be honored to baptize ye, and Brigham Young himself will confirm ye!" Matty declared.

Johnny, as usual, had the last word.

"Aye!" he said. "Any man who chooses to be baptized in a river as cold as this one has got to be a committed Saint!"

Matty and Johnny smiled at one another in the firelight and marveled at the look of peace and contentment they saw on their fiery older brother's face.

The McElin brothers returned to Salt Lake City and reported their find to Brigham Young, who was as pleased as they were. They spent the spring and summer gathering people, equipment, and livestock for the venture. Several families volunteered to accompany them—mostly men who had raised sheep in Scotland and New England. However, this would be sheep raising on a large scale. They knew there would be hardship and risk, but they welcomed the opportunity.

Matty and Johnny took wives immediately, but Angus was so busy preparing for the long journey and the coming winter that he scarcely had time to attend the weddings, much less think of his own unmarried state. His brothers were worried about Angus beginning the long years of work and isolation without a companion, but they could not entice him to join in any social activities where he might meet a suitable young woman.

It was Mary McElin, or, to be precise, her old plaid shawl that, in the end, resolved things for Angus. Toward the end of the summer word went out that a band of pioneers was stranded on the other side of Parley's Canyon. At church on Sunday morning the Saints were told by their bishops that this particular company had been hard hit by illness and early snows in the high elevations. A call went out for all able-bodied men to rush to the travelers' aid. Mary was away attending the birth of a child on a nearby farm, and so the men put together, as best they could, a bundle of food and clothing for the new arrivals, and set off to meet the incoming pioneers.

With their physical strength and knowledge of the mountains, the

McElins were among the first to reach the straggling handcart company. The makeshift camp was pathetic. Clothing too light for the freezing wind, gaunt faces, cold and hungry children. But soon the camp was filled with people from the valley bringing provisions. Fires were lit; the sick, young, and elderly were put on horses, or carried through the canyons and down into the waiting valley. In Salt Lake, the citizens opened their homes and prepared fresh beds to receive the ill and weary. The McElins made hot soup at the campsite and wrapped hands and feet in the woolens they had brought.

In the camp, the healthier pioneers continued to minister to the ill, and one young woman with pale blond hair and an English accent, so frail that one could scarcely believe she could stand, labored to prepare the sick for transport to the valley and encouraged the little children to sip the nourishing soup until it was their turn to leave. The young woman looked strangely familiar to Angus, but he could not place her.

He was moved by her selflessness, and he grabbed Mary's old plaid shawl, which he had brought, and placed it around the girl's shoulders. She gave him a sweet smile of gratitude and pulled the soft, warm cloth around her shoulders.

By nightfall the camp was emptied and the McElin men, along with others from the valley, gathered together the pitiful remnants of the group and piled them in the remaining carts to bring them down to the city.

Bone-weary, Robert and his sons returned home. As they entered the door, they saw Mary nodding in her chair by the fire. When she heard the door open she jumped to her feet. "Is everything all right?" she inquired. "I would have come to help too, but I have just returned from Sister Anders. She has a fine baby boy."

Robert sat down heavily and began to remove his boots. "Aye, all is well. All the members of the company are housed and provisioned for the night."

"Well, then," said Mary, "I must be back to Sister Anders. She may have need of me." Wearily Mary got up from her chair and walked toward the door. " 'Tis a mite chilly. I think I'll wear my plaid. Has anyone seen it?" She looked at the hook by the door where her shawl usually hung.

"Aye," said Robert. "We gave it to the new arrivals. A young English girl—she was nigh frozen and . . ."

Mary's expression caused him to stop speaking. Her eyes were flashing and her rage was like lightning. "Ye could have given her the house," she exclaimed, "or the cow, or the gold, but not my plaid!"

When Mary was in a temper, none of the men in her family dared speak back to her. For several moments she paced the floor, wringing her hands and raging. "Do ye not know what that plaid means to me? 'Twas woven by my own mother's hands! It has held all of my bairns, and warmed our bed! It has comforted me in the night and kept me from harm! How could ye take my plaid!"

"But, Mary!" Robert exclaimed. "It seemed old—scarcely more than a rag. . . ."

"A rag!" Mary spluttered. "A rag!"

"I'll buy ye a new one!" Robert exclaimed.

"Nae, ye'll not!" Mary replied. "Ye are to find her, Robert McElin. Give her a new shawl and return my own to me. I'll say no more about it!" And with that Mary threw an old coat over her shoulders and rushed out into the night.

Galvanized into motion, the McElins retied their boots and hurried into the street to locate the home where the young English girl was staying.

By midmorning the next day they had covered most of the homes in the neighborhood and still had been unable to find the young woman. Wearily, Angus knocked on the door of a small log home near the mouth of Parley's Canyon. Someone had told him that the last arrivals had been boarded there.

"Sister Parker," Angus said when the door was opened by a slender, gray-haired woman. "I understand ye have some guests from the handcart company—" As he spoke he saw the frail young woman walk slowly across the room inside the house. She was wearing his mother's shawl.

"There she is!" he exclaimed. "I must speak to her, Sister Parker!"

Astonished, Sister Parker motioned him inside. "Lucy," she said to the startled girl, "this young man says he must speak with you."

Angus stared into her face. In the confusion at the campsite the day before, he had scarcely glanced at her, but now, as he looked closely, he was struck by her pale beauty. Her light-brown hair was parted in the center and pulled into a smooth neat bun on her small delicate head. Her features were refined and her skin was pale and translucent. She seemed very fragile and small, and still weak from illness, but in the tilt of her head and the set of her jaw there was courage and determination.

"Lucy!" Angus exclaimed. "Lucy Patterson!" He remembered her from the Iowa camp.

"Yes," she said in a sweet, low voice. "What is it, Brother?"

"Don't ye remember me?" Angus asked. "I'm Angus McElin. Mary is my mother. I carried ye when ye fainted in Iowa!" He knew he sounded absurd.

"Yes!" the young woman said, her face lighting with recognition. "But why have you come to see me?"

With an effort Angus collected his thoughts. "It's my mother," he blurted out. "She wants to talk to ye. She'll be so happy to see ye! Would it be all right if I took ye to our home to visit with her for a few minutes?"

Sister Parker patted Lucy on the arm reassuringly. "The McElins live just down the road a piece, Lucy, and I'm sure you'd enjoy meeting their family. Sister McElin is one of the finest women in the valley. If you feel up to it, why don't you go?"

Embarrassed and awkward, Angus walked with Lucy toward his house. He couldn't think of any gracious way to explain to her about his mother's shawl, and so he walked along with scarcely a word. Lucy seemed at ease with his silence, however, and she walked slowly beside him, her calm, intelligent eyes drinking in the surroundings.

"There were times when I thought I would never see this valley," she whispered wonderingly. "And now, here I am!" She gave a profound sigh. Angus noticed that even the short walk seemed to drain her strength, and he wanted to turn and hold her.

Instead he replied, "I know. There were nights on the trail when I'd look at the tired and the sick, and the broken wagons, and I'd think . . . ."

She turned then, and their eyes met in a long solemn stare as though they had just recognized one another, and he felt somehow as though a weight had been lifted from his shoulders.

Mary McElin welcomed Lucy Patterson with open arms, and in no time at all she had the young Englishwoman sitting in the chair by the fire, eating a bowl of hot bread and milk, recounting the story of her conversion and subsequent disinheritance from her aristocratic English family and the long arduous journey that had brought her to Salt Lake Valley. Mary's practiced eye could tell that Lucy was not at all well. Only determination and a powerful will were keeping the young woman going. As the afternoon wore on, Mary still had said nothing about her shawl to Lucy, but she had reached a decision about the girl.

She beckoned Angus to step into the workroom with her for a moment. "Angus," she whispered, "ye are to run down to Sister Parker's and tell her that Lucy needs a good deal of nursing. Since I am not busy right now I will be happy to care for her here, if it's all right with Sister Parker. Pick up the girl's belongings and bring them here. I'm going to put her right to bed."

To Angus it seemed like a miracle. Within two hours his mother had fixed a pallet before the fire, and Lucy, dressed in a muslin nightgown, was tucked under the covers, with the old plaid shawl covering her and his mother's herb tea making her rosy and drowsy in the firelight.

His mother's wise care began to restore Lucy to health, and each day the family delighted in her progress. Angus was his mother's right hand in caring for the young Englishwoman. He lifted and carried her, for her strength had failed completely. As she grew stronger, he assisted her in short walks and brought her the nutritious food and treats with which his mother tempted her failing appetite.

Concurrently with Lucy's recovery, Angus oversaw the final preparations for the expedition to Virgin River, and so, after two weeks, Angus felt the time had come when he must speak to Lucy.

The McElin family had been conscious of Angus's captivation by the frail young woman. His brothers, who were thoroughly enjoying the privileges and delights of their new marriages, exchanged suggestive glances whenever they saw Angus and Lucy together. Robert noticed that the young woman's presence made his eldest son much gentler and more easygoing. Only Mary felt a pang of concern as she saw Angus's singleminded devotion to the girl. She knew Angus, perhaps better than anyone in the family, and she understood the depth and power of his emotions. When she looked at the pale, cool, self-contained Englishwoman, she found it hard to imagine that this quiet girl could ever match his intensity. Somehow she sensed that if he married this girl, a part of him would be forever empty and dissatisfied. But Mary had no words to express what she felt, only her mother's certainty that this was not the woman to satisfy her complex son.

Nonetheless, early in September, on an evening that gleamed golden and blue on the mountainsides, Angus knelt before Lucy in the prairie grass behind his home and asked for her hand in marriage, and she, bending with tender grace, kissed him on the forehead and said, "Yes, dear Angus, that would make me very happy." He scarcely dared embrace her, she looked so fragile and beautiful to him.

Angus and Lucy were married. One week later the three McElin brothers bid farewell to their parents. Robert and Mary had decided they were too old to start another new home. Robert's carpentry business in Salt Lake City was doing well and Mary had made a place for herself in the growing community. The parting was difficult for all because they knew their visits would be infrequent.

Mary and Robert accompanied the small company to the edge of the city and watched as they began their journey. The group consisted of some eighteen families of settlers, wagons, barn stock, mulch cows, a small flock of hardy sheep, outriders, and a year's provisions. The elder McElins watched as the company began its slow journey over two hundred miles of rugged terrain and mountain passes to the isolated valley that was to be their new home. When the travelers had moved out of sight, Mary and Robert turned back toward Salt Lake. "What is it that is frettin' ye, Mary?" Robert asked. " 'Tis more than just saying good-bye. I can tell."

Mary sighed. " 'Tis Angus and Lucy," she said. "Lucy is a fine, dear woman, but she is not the right wife for our Angus. I canna feel pleased about their marriage."

"What do ye mean?" Robert queried.

"There is something special, something larger than every day about our oldest son," Mary answered slowly, groping to express her apprehension. "It is the reason people turn to him for leadership. I canna find a word for it, but, whatever it is in him, it leaves an empty space inside, such a private, lonely space that only a woman could fill it."

"Aye," Robert answered gently. "I know." He smiled at Mary.

"But," she continued, "it will take more than an ordinary woman to fill Angus's needs. His heart is too large, too inaccessible and difficult. It will take a woman as large of spirit as our Angus. I don't know that such a woman exists." Mary sighed.

Robert took Mary's hand. "I suspect they shall be happy enough—and perhaps that is all Angus expects."

"Aye." Mary nodded unhappily. Then her emerald eyes flashed with the intensity of her fierce maternal love. "But just once I should like to see him shout for joy. I would like to see him filled to the brim and running over with happiness! Just once . . ."

Chapter Four

During the first two years in the Virgin Valley, the McElins and the other families lived in crudely built log huts, surrounded by a makeshift fort. The short growing season in the high altitude and the grinding cold and snow of the long winter limited their food supplies. They sent several expeditions across the mountains into Manti, Nephi, and Panguitch to buy foodstuffs, but even these short trips were arduous, and the settlers' money supply and goods for barter were limited since they had spent most of it on the original flock of sheep.

In the first week in the valley the three brothers met where the Virgin River, enlarged by other streams, flowed smoothly. They used their surveying equipment to lay out the spot where the two main streets of the proposed town of Pleasantview would cross. Each brother then drew a lot for one of the three corner lots at the intersection. They reserved the fourth corner for the Meeting House.

Other families then drew numbers for home lots along the proposed grid of streets, and in this way the dream town was surveyed and the building lots assigned. The actual building of the roads, homes, schools, and churches was delayed until the settlers could establish their flocks and farms and bring commerce into the community.

Their third winter was the cruelest of all. The Indians, who at first had been indifferent to the small group, and even tentatively kind, bringing them small gifts of dried meat and fur, suddenly became sullen and threatening. Several sheep were stolen, and Matty, who had become the interpreter and negotiator with the neighboring Indians, journeyed out to the Ute Camp and demanded that the animals be returned. The tension caused the settlers to reinforce the small fort in which they lived, and the few foraging parties that went out hunting or to Nephi were turned back by angry bands of warriors waiting silently in the snow.

Not wanting to risk open warfare, since they were badly outnumbered, the settlers brought their sheep into the valley and penned them in the low fields close by the fort. The enforced crowding in the rude fort, plus the cold and the inadequate food, began to wear on everyone's nerves.

Before the winter was over, several families had decided to return to the warmer climes and more advanced civilization of the Salt Lake Valley as soon as spring came. Contention, hunger, and despair had eroded the bright vision that had brought them to this desolate place.

It was during this terrible winter that Lucy finally became pregnant. Both she and Angus had almost given up hope that she would ever conceive, and so her pregnancy was a cause of rejoicing and hope. Shortly after Christmas, with a blizzard shrieking around the rough fort and a coldness in the air that not even the roaring fire in the stone hearth could dispel, Lucy went into labor. After many long hours of suffering that made even the most hardened pioneers blanch, with only a thin blanket hung to afford her privacy, she was delivered of a tiny premature boy. The child did not draw a single breath, and Lucy almost bled to death before the ministering women were able to staunch the flow of blood. After the tragic birth, Lucy never seemed to regain her strength. She developed a deep, harsh cough and walked in a stiff, painful way. Angus treated her with such sweet and tender respect that Hester, Johnny's wife, said it made tears come to her eyes just to see them together. The women watched Lucy and spoke in low voices.

". . . so badly torn—she'll never bear another child. . . ."

"Good thing too. Another child would be the death of her."

In early spring the battered settlers emerged from their cramped winter quarters in ragged clothes and boots, their thin white faces showing the strain of isolation and hunger. The Utes had already left for their summer hunting grounds, so the fears of the winter were largely past. The women went up into the high meadows where the men had taken the sheep. There they dug for the white roots of sego lilies and tender shoots of weeds and wild herbs to make teas and soups that could provide sustenance for their weakened children. Of course the settlers knew they would never starve to death for they could always eat the sheep, but if they did, they would be eating the hope of their future. Just as farmers, in the depth of hunger, cannot eat their seed corn, so the sheepherder must refrain from decimating his flock. Although hunger and despair had made it seem that the little colony could not survive the rigors of the highlands, the irony was that the sheep thrived!

After the lambing season in the spring, the McElin brothers culled their flocks for any sheep that could be sold. The ewes had been fertile. A healthy, robust crop of new lambs gamboled and foraged on the high grazing ground, and the cold mountain air had thickened the sheep's wool. At last the flocks were truly established and the McElins could afford to butcher the older sheep for mutton. As the settlers filled their stomachs, their resolve revived.

Angus, Matty, and Johnny herded a parcel of sheep over the mountains into the neighboring community of Manti where they traded the animals for generous food supplies. While there they contracted for a road to be cut through the mountains into the Virgin Valley so that Pleasantview could be joined to the nearby settlements on the north and south highway that led through the center of the Utah territory from Salt Lake to St. George. Pleasantview lay about thirty miles to the east of this main highway, with the Virgin River and the barrier of the mountains cutting them off from it. With the promise of a serviceable road out of the mountains, the brothers knew they would never again face a winter of such hardship as the one they had just survived.

As soon as the road was completed, the three brothers began building their town. They laid out the stakes for the broad streets of Pleasantview in the same pattern as those of Salt Lake City, squarely north and south, east and west, forming a checkerboard. Each block was one-quarter-mile long, so every residential lot had ample room for a garden, barn, and a small orchard for fruit and shade trees.

The pioneer families were encouraged to build their homes on the town lots rather than in outlying areas so that the women could enjoy one another's company as they did domestic chores and the children could easily attend church and school. The Mormon farmers and ranchers became the first commuters, traveling to their farms by day and returning to their homes in the town in the evening.

The three homes built by the McElin brothers were as different as the brothers themselves. Angus, who was the acknowledged leader of the new community, had developed into a handsome man. His hair was still as black as midnight, and he retained the fresh, ruddy look of a man who lived outdoors. His blue eyes were clear as the

Scottish skies he still remembered. His power and vigor were the foundation of the settlement and extended McElin family.

It was decided by common consent that Angus's house should be the largest since it would serve as a gathering place. Angus built his home plainly. It was large and square with a deep-gabled roof to discourage the accumulation of winter snows and a wide porch across the front to keep the house cool in summer. The house faced the eastern mountains and commanded a view of the Virgin River as it plunged out of the mountains. Even before the home was finished it was referred to by everyone in the valley as the Big House.

Through the years Matty McElin had retained his quiet grace, his loyalty and reserve. Even his wife, Zina, with her good-humored charm, did not seem to understand him completely. He had grown very close to the Indian people and spent many weeks each year visiting them. He would leave Pleasantview on his horse and ride into the mountains for days, often taking medicines and supplies to the nomadic tribes. He had mastered Indian dialects and often was called upon by other communities to serve as negotiator when problems with the Indians threatened.

Matty's house was compact and tight, of modest size, with many large windows that faced in all four directions so that every room provided an open vista of the outdoors. When the house was finished, Zina began to add decorations. It never seemed quite right to her, and each time Matty entered he could find a new piece of trim on the door, the eaves, or the roofline. She fenced in the property with a fanciful, ornate picket fence, and then added fluted columns and gingerbread to the front porch. As the years passed, the little house would seem to groan under the onslaught of Zina's fertile imagination.

Often a child would burst into Aunt Zina's front door to find among the plush velvet furniture and lace antimacassars a silent dark man with long braids and a beaded coat, sitting cross-legged on the living-room carpet. Frequently Indian families camped on Uncle Matty's lawn, and Aunt Zina fed them from her kitchen, sending them on their way with clothes her own children had outgrown.

It was Johnny's house, however, that came to stand like a friendly beacon in the middle of the growing town. While the two older McElin brothers were respected and admired, Johnny was loved. The bright red hair and volatile nature he had inherited from his tiny mother, as well as his innate charm and wit, were irresistible. He and Hester had already been blessed with two children, and a third was on the way. Wherever Johnny went laughter and affection followed.

His house was large—and it would end up being even larger. Originally he built a spacious two-story house, with a comfortable garret under the eaves. However, Johnny and Hester were prolific, and as the years passed and his family grew, he found himself adding rooms and wings to the original structure. In his happy, exuberant way, he planned the additions as they were needed and so he tacked on turrets, anterooms, lean-tos, and passageways with haphazard abandon. But somehow the results were pleasing to the eye, and the house developed a look of good cheer and a personality all its own. Apple and pear trees dotted his lawns, with swings hanging from sturdy branches. Aunt Hes's kitchen garden, as robust as the children who played near it, yielded green vines and tall corn. Uncle Johnny's front gate was always open, and the sound of laughter, music, and genial talk hovered in the air around it.

Through the years when the families were summoned to the Big House, they would wear their Sunday clothes and the children would walk with the quiet, serious demeanor they used in church. At Uncle Johnny's house, however, the cousins wore work jeans and school pinafores, and they could run, laugh, and eat clabbered milk with sugar on thick slices of white bread cut for them on the kitchen sideboard.

The town of Pleasantview thrived. The flocks multiplied and the years passed. Angus had resigned himself to his childlessness. He attributed Lucy's continued pain and ill health to the suffering and privations of the first winters in the valley, and he felt he could never repay her for what she had lost because of him.

Johnny had been called to live the law of plural marriage, and Aunt Hes had heartily agreed. The woman he married was a young widow from Nephi with a tiny baby. She was a hearty, cheerful girl named Min, and Hes and she became dear friends. Angus watched with admiration as Johnny's family now increased at an even greater speed. Angus was not at ease with children, and, as the years passed and his heavy responsibilities for the community grew, he became solemn and old beyond his years. The passions of his youth seemed buried beneath work, duty, and his tender, subdued love for Lucy.

Sometimes, when Lucy was having a "good spell," Angus would go to her room and she would touch the bed beside her. "Stay the night, Angus!" she would whisper timidly, eyes downcast and a deep blush on her pale brow.

Angus knew that these nights of intimacy were a great trial for Lucy, so he grasped her to him and swore that he would make it up to her by being kinder and more loving than ever. To Lucy, it was a great relief when she knew that she had done her marital duty and for a time could feel released from the strain of his needs and her own failures.

Lucy ran the Big House with quiet efficiency, and, though she spent a good deal of time in bed, she nonetheless was greatly loved in the community for her sweetness and bravery. She taught the children of the community music and elocution when she was feeling well, and her learning was a source of pride to Angus.

As the years slipped by the valley prospered. Isolated as they were, the people of Pleasantview maintained a thrifty, hard-working way of life, and their sheep multiplied upon the hills. Church leaders, visiting the valley on their regular circuits from Salt Lake, had nothing but praise for the McElin brothers and their settlement.

Often as the churchmen took their leave they would meet in private conference with Angus. More than once they closed their conversation with earnest encouragement to Angus to enter into the covenant of plural marriage.

"As leader of this community you have a spiritual responsibility to accept this grave stewardship, Brother McElin," they told him. "There are many unmarried sisters in need of care and protection. The Lord has given us this cross to bear and it is a mark of faith for those who do so."

Angus shook his head. "My wife is not strong enough to carry the burden of such a decision, and, as you know, I could not take a second wife without Lucy's consent."

The elder looked at him compassionately. "But surely your wife does not wish you to remain childless! I would recommend you go to her and ask. Her answer may surprise you."

A thin smile touched Angus's lips. "I doubt that Lucy's answer would be a surprise," he replied.

After this visit Angus felt compelled to speak to Lucy about the matter. The following evening as she lay stitching a linen collar, Angus looked up from the book he was reading and cleared his throat.

"I have been asked to live the eternal covenant, Lucy," he said without preamble. "I do not wish to take another wife, but I feel I should obey the Lord in this matter."

The delicate linen fluttered from Lucy's pale hand and she began to tremble. Twice she tried to speak but couldn't. Her head drooped back against the pillows.

Angus was at her side instantly. "Lucy!" he murmured. "I'm sorry!"

She shook her head, with tears in her eyes. "I can't do it!" she whispered. "I've known you would ask me someday and I've tried—I have truly tried—to have enough strength and faith to agree."

A sob escaped her and Angus put his arm gently around her shoulders.

"I am a selfish, foolish woman! How can I deny you the right to have children? But I cannot agree to a second wife! Not now, Angus—I'm not ready!"

"Hush!" Angus entreated. "It's all right. Don't upset yourself." He patted her shoulder soothingly.

"I pray for courage all the time, Angus," Lucy continued. "Perhaps the Lord will give me the strength to say 'yes' to you one day."

Her voice trailed away, and Angus knew he could not reopen the subject until Lucy came to him of her own choice and accepted it.

Chapter Five

In the spring of 1869 at Promontory, Utah, the golden spike was driven into the connecting rail between the Union Pacific Railway, brought from Omaha, Nebraska, and the Central Pacific Railroad, from San Francisco. Utah was forever changed in the final stroke of the hammer driving that single spike. No longer would the Mormon territory be able to function as a world unto itself—an island, self-contained and self-sustaining, in the middle of a boundless wilderness. Suddenly this forgotten tract of land surrounding a salt sea, which had been unwanted by the emerging nation of America and orphaned by the Mexican territories, became the crossroads of the west, the intermountain hub of a nation united by a railroad.

Whether Utah willed it or not, through it would flow commerce, tourists, politicians, armies, entertainers, and the great flux of humanity moving across the face of a nation that had at last fulfilled its manifest destiny and now stretched, unimpeded, from sea to shining sea.

Although the community of Pleasantview was far from the center of this historic event, the McElin brothers were well informed about what went on in the Territory of Utah. In the summer when the transcontinental railroad was completed at Promontory Point, the settlement of Pleasantview was fifteen years old, and Angus McElin was approaching his fortieth year.

Except for a few silver threads gleaming in his black hair and beard, Angus did not seem to have aged at all. However, the weight of the many years of ministering to the needs of his valley and its people had given his face a look of sober and profound seriousness. He was constantly searching for ways to improve the quality of life for the people in his community.

The transcontinental railroad struck Angus as the perfect means to expand the markets for the sheep and wool that were produced in the Virgin River Valley. Angus decided to journey back east to Omaha and St. Louis to try to set up purchasing contracts with the livestock associations as well as textile merchants there.

He was to journey by saddle horse to Nephi and by stagecoach from Nephi to Salt Lake. He would visit briefly with his mother, Mary, who had outlived his father, in the little adobe house to which Robert had brought her so many years ago.

Angus would travel on from Salt Lake by railroad. He planned to leave early in the morning. Since Lucy had been ill for several weeks, he slipped into her room and kissed her good-bye while she was still sleeping, not wishing to disturb her. He went on down to the stable then to saddle his horse.

As he was tightening the cinch he looked up with surprise to see Lucy standing in the doorway of the barn. She was wearing her white flannel nightdress with a heavy woolen shawl thrown over her shoulders, and she looked very pale and slender as a reed in the meager light of the dawn.

"Lucy!" Angus exclaimed. "You shouldn't have gotten out of bed. You are not strong enough, and this cold air will start your cough again!"

She stood with her hand propped against the frame of the barn door, as though she needed its support, but her smile was sweet and her deep-set eyes, darkly stained underneath with weariness, looked at him lovingly. "I could not let you leave without giving you my blessing once again. I shall miss you, Angus dear."

Angus nodded solemnly and, leaving the task of the saddle cinch, he walked to where she stood and embraced her. "I shall miss you too, Lucy, and I will worry about you. While I am gone you must take care of yourself. Sister Burton will live here at the Big House to care for you, but you must promise me . . . don't be foolish and overtax yourself!"

Lucy sighed, and he felt the fragile bones of her shoulders and back trembling with her breath. "I am so tired of being sick, Angus," she whispered. "You must not be angry if I try to fight against it."

He kissed the top of her head and his eyes were dark with patient sorrow. "Nay, Lucy, I could not be angry with you—ever! If you are ill, it is my doing. I should not have brought you to such a life."

His shoulders sagged and for a moment they clung together, husband and wife, and in his posture, Angus looked more ill and weary than Lucy. It was as though, for a moment, the pressure of all her sorrows and pain were his, and under the double weight of their burdens even his own mighty strength buckled. He raised his head, squared his shoulders, and his eyes flashed with determination.

"You must try your best, Lucy, as must I," he told her earnestly. "Do not fight the cure—fight the illness! You must try! For both of our sakes." His voice dropped to a murmur. "A man needs a wife." As soon as he said the words, Angus regretted them.

Lucy did not seem upset by his pointed remark. Instead she looked at him with a curiously ambiguous smile. "I promise you, you will be pleased when you return," she said.

"Come, dear," he urged tenderly. "I will help you back to your bed and then I must go."

"No, Angus," she answered softly. "There is one thing more I must say to you before you leave." Her hands trembled on his arms, and he felt a wave of protective love for her. "You asked me once if I would ever consider giving my consent for you to take a plural wife. I know you have refrained from asking again because you felt it would hurt me. But, Angus, I understand that a man needs a wife who can fulfill her responsibilities in the marriage bed, and it is painful to me to know that I have not been . . . valiant . . . in that role. Angus, when you return from the east, if you still feel the need to take another wife, I will not stand in your way." Lucy's clear glance wavered, and she swayed in his arms. A small sob filled her throat. "Angus, you must know that I want your happiness more than anything on the earth."

"Oh, Lucy!" he exclaimed, crushing her in a fierce embrace. "Oh, Lucy girl, you are the bravest and the best! We shall talk about it no more. It's off to bed for you, and off to the east for me—and when we are together again, let us hope that all is well with both of us!"

The journey to Salt Lake was uneventful. Angus paid his mother a visit and found her as sprightly and outspoken as ever. She was a great favorite of the people in Salt Lake, and it seemed to Angus that scarcely an hour went by that someone wasn't rapping on her door to ask for advice, to drop off a morsel of food, or simply to pass the time of day. Once again Angus encouraged his mother to come live with him and his brothers in Pleasantview, but she waved him off with an impatient hand.

"I'll not come to live where I'll be naught but an old lady rocking in the back bedroom. Here I have friends to care for, and my own wee house, and the comfort of familiar things—and I'm thinking I shall stay here until I join your father. It's not that I don't love you boys, Angus, it's just that if I came to live with you I couldn't be my own woman anymore—I'd just be your old ma."

Proud and defiant to the end! Angus understood his mother better than anyone, and the two of them sat staring silently into one another's eyes.

"Aye, Mother," Angus said at last. "Ye are right to stay! But if ye are ever in need, just send—"

"Wee Angus!" his mother interrupted. "I know that! I know you would come in a twinkling. But how is it with you—and Lucy? Are you happy, my son? Look at you! Only forty, and you have the look of a serious old man!"

Angus laughed mirthlessly. "That's not far off the mark, Mother!" he rejoined. "I *am* getting old. And Lucy continues to be very frail. If anything, I think she has been more ill these past few weeks than I can remember in many years. I was worried to leave her. I feel so responsible. . . ."

Mary gave a snort of impatience and wagged her finger at her son. "Angus! You've no cause to go around wearing a hair shirt over Lucy. You've treated her like a queen, walking around with the hang-dog look. You're not to blame for Lucy's illness, so stop acting like you are! She had the lung weakness before she ever married you. Probably brought it with her from England. Of course, the first years in the Virgin territory weren't the best thing for her—but they certainly didn't cause her sickness!"

"But the baby," Angus interjected. "If I had been willing to wait. No refined woman should have been expected to bear children in such circumstances!"

Completely disgusted, Mary shook her head. "Nonsense! Yours wasn't the first babe to die—nor will it be the last! Of course you should sorrow—but you can't wear it like a chain around your neck for the rest of your life. I should know, my boy. I tried it, and it doesn't work! And your guilt will end up eating you alive. You've lived so long with pity and remorse you've forgotten how to love— you've even forgotten what real love feels like. Don't let that happen to you, Angus, not while the blood still runs in your veins!"

Angus looked at the tiny, fierce woman who had borne him, flesh of her flesh, and felt the heat of her old banked emotions, the intensity of her wild, untrammeled spirit. It sent a spark deep into his own soul.

He laughed. "Ah, wee mother! Life has never succeeded in making you solemn or still. You will go, battling all the way, I'm thinking!"

"Aye, so I will, wee Angus, so I will! And you might do well to match me." There was a mischievous twinkle in her eyes—still the same bright green even though the tufted brows above them were white and the face was criss-crossed with a thousand tiny etchings of age.

When his train pulled out of Utah, Angus sat by the window watching the mountains recede in the distance. He thought of the long hard journey that had brought him to the valley so many years before, and he marveled at the ease with which he would cross the same land now. He also thought of his mother and wondered if he would ever see her again.

Chapter Six

In both Omaha and St. Louis, Angus's contract negotiations went well. He was aware, though, of mounting criticism and opposition to the Mormons in the Utah Territory, particularly since the practice of plural marriage had been openly acknowledged. Bills before Congress denounced the Mormons, and a measure had passed that restricted organizations in the territories from owning over fifty thousand dollars' worth of property. It was a punitive act obviously aimed directly at the Mormon Church and one that would certainly cause its impoverishment. The unconstitutionality of the law had prevented its enforcement, but, with the coming of the railroad and the loss of the Saints' self-imposed isolation, the old hatreds and suspicions of the outside world were heating up again. Though Angus had wondered whether he would find it difficult to establish business ties, he soon discovered that, in matters of money, people seemed to be willing to set aside personal prejudices.

In the end, Angus signed enough agreements and options to insure the prosperity of the sheep industry in Pleasantview, and he returned to his hotel in St. Louis with the satisfaction a man feels for work well done.

When Angus entered the hotel room, he was amazed to see a man lying on his bed. The man sprang up as Angus entered. "Brother McElin!" he exclaimed. "Forgive me for using your accommodations, but the clerk suggested that I wait for you here, and I guess I fell asleep."

Angus frowned in puzzlement. "Who are you?" he asked.

The man who faced Angus was of middle age with dark, tanned skin and eyes that had the look of faraway places. They were the eyes of an explorer, a trapper, or a scout. His body was lean and as lithe as a spring, and he wore trail clothes—clean and brushed, but obviously made for hard riding and the outdoors.

"I am Nathan Westville," the man answered, reaching out to shake Angus's hand. "Captain of the teamster train from Utah. We have been sent out from Salt Lake by Brigham Young to bring back a waiting company of immigrants here in St. Louis."

Angus nodded. He had heard of the program in which the Church was sending teams of wagons and supplies to meet the incoming European, eastern, and southern Saints who were gathering to come to Utah. The roads by now were well worn, but the trip was still filled with hazard. The wagon trains acted as ferries between Salt Lake and the eastern outposts of the Church, as rail travel was still too expensive for most families.

"Well, Brother Westville, have you just arrived from Utah?" Angus asked.

"We arrived at the immigrant camp outside of St. Louis about four days ago, Brother McElin, and we are now preparing for the return journey. This group is larger than we had expected. Fortunately, several families have purchased their own wagons, so we are going to be adequately supplied, but we are lacking leadership. President Young told me I might run into you on this trip, and he suggested that you might be willing to act as my co-captain on the wagon train going back to Salt Lake."

Angus smiled. "There are few things that miss President Young's notice."

Nathan Westville smiled in return. "Yes. He is a mighty man for knowing and for caring. Have you concluded your business in this place, Brother McElin? Would you be free to assist us?"

Angus nodded.

"Then would you accept the call to help lead this group of wanderers back to Zion?" Nathan grinned.

Thinking with dismay of how long this would delay his journey home, Angus raised his hands in a gesture of resigned acceptance. "I will," he said reluctantly.

The days following were filled with frenzied preparations. Angus bought trail supplies for himself and an excellent saddle horse. He would share wagon accommodations with Brother Westville and two of the outriders who accompanied them. The administrative details were endless, and he and the other camp leaders inspected wagons and supplies and organized equipment trials and instruction sessions, which had to be translated into German, Swedish, Danish, and Dutch. The leaders assigned each wagon to its place in the train and selected leaders to care for the needs of each group of ten families.

On a soggy April morning, the company was at last ready to move out. The train spread out in an extended, halting line along the rutted trail and finally pitched camp that first night scarcely five miles from its starting point.

With the encouragement and guidance of Nathan and Angus, the pioneers improved in efficiency as the week progressed, and by the Sabbath, they were entirely comfortable with the daily program of their journey: up before dawn, harnessing the teams, milking the cows, gathering the scattered herd, and eating a cold breakfast left over from the night before. Children were roused, dressed, and fed, and everything was made secure for the day's travel, which began at sunrise. The train traveled until noon, when there was a short stop for rest, assessment of problems with equipment or animals, a brief lunch, and watering of the animals. Late in the afternoon a bugle call sounded the making of camp, and the wagons were positioned in a circle, fires built, and grazing areas found for the stock. The women would prepare great quantities of food, bake bread, wash clothes, and teach brief school lessons to the children.

Music, dancing, conversation, and children's needs filled the evenings around the campfire. At a last reveille of the bugles, the Saints would prepare to retire for the night.

There were, of course, disagreements, quarrels, disputes, and complications, but each day the operation became smoother, and Angus found that, even though he was so tired he nearly fell into his bedroll at night, he was nonetheless really enjoying himself. In some ways, he felt more alive than he had for years!

He and Nathan had developed an easy working relationship. Nathan respected Angus's insight into organizational and human problems, and Angus was amazed at the knowledge Nathan displayed of animals, equipment, and the rigors of the trail.

That first Sunday night, after the camp was bedded down, a light rain began to fall. By midnight, the air was slashed with lightning, and great drums of thunder percussed the night air. Livestock bolted in fear, and the sound of aroused animals, crying children, and shouting adults filled the air as men and women raced to and fro in the darkness trying to protect their possessions from the onslaught of the storm. Canvas tents and wagon tops flapped in the high winds and Angus and Nathan seemed to be everywhere, with rope and rawhide, lashing down tarps and pounding tent pegs more deeply into the muddy earth. By morning the rain had not eased, and, on the trail, the deep ruts had turned to muddy rivers. For two days the group pushed forward into the face of the storm. Progress was measured by inches. Men strained with poles against the mired wheels, and the wet, miserable animals pulled stolidly against the wagon tongues. Everyone was wet, cold, muddy, tired, and discouraged. Finally, on Saturday morning, a pale sun peeked through a tear in the clouds, and by midday the sky was clear.

Nathan sounded the call to make camp early that afternoon, and the exhausted travelers pulled their wagons into the large circle and began to assess the damage. They boiled water and washed their mud-caked clothes and bedding. The children huddled around the fires for warmth, and their wet shoes and clothes steamed as the fire heated them, so that they were surrounded in an eerie mist and the campfires looked like haloes of celestial light glowing through the vapors.

As the leaders surveyed the damage, one fact became clear. In the camp were several single women—three of them were widows, two with teenage children, and one with a family of small children. There was also a group of unmarried single women who had joined the Church and were traveling alone, because they either had no family or had been disowned when they were baptized.

The widows were hardest hit by the disaster. Even under the most favorable conditions, the women were slower and had more problems than the other travelers, but under the grueling experience of the past week, their situation worsened.

The single girls were having problems of their own. Since they had no means of transportation, they were assigned to travel with other families. They earned their passage by working for the families with whom they were traveling—helping with the children, the laundry, and the cooking. The wagon train's accommodations were very crowded, and even the most generous of the families found it hard to accommodate an extra adult. During the worst of the storm, Nathan had discovered three of the unmarried women huddled under a cowhide, since the shelter under the wagons was already filled with children, wives, and the elderly.

All during the next week Nathan became more convinced that a better way had to be found to care for the women. Finally he gathered together the leaders of the camp and proposed that if any of them felt inspired to do so, he felt they should consider taking some of these women as plural wives under the covenant of the Church.

"You know, brethren," Nathan said, "they are going into a society where it is almost impossible for a woman to survive alone.

If they do not marry, in our wilderness society they are doomed to lives of servitude and incredible hardship."

Angus was moved by the plight of the widows and concerned for the single girls as well, who had left home and family to cast themselves into this great venture, friendless and alone. The fact was that in the Territory of Utah there were few single men and too many women. Without plural marriage, most of these faithful women would be denied the opportunity to marry, bear children, and establish homes of their own.

For several nights Angus struggled with his natural reluctance, but finally, after the camp was settled on the plains of Iowa, he approached Nathan, who was already lying in his sleeping pallet under the lead wagon.

"Nathan," Angus whispered, "I'd like a word of counsel and advice with you, if I may."

Nathan sat up immediately. "What is it, Angus?"

"Before I left the Virgin Valley, several months ago, I spoke with my wife, Lucy, and she told me that when I concluded my business in the east she would consent to my taking a second wife. I feel called to do this now because of our present circumstances, Brother Westville. I believe it is the Lord's will that I should take the responsibility of caring for one of these poor widows and her family both for the rest of the journey and for the rest of their lives. I am willing to do so."

Nathan stretched out his hand and shook Angus's hand warmly. "You are right to do this, Brother McElin. I commend you for the decision. With the power given to me by President Young, I grant you permission to choose whomever you will."

"Nay!" Angus replied. "I think you, as the leader of the company, should choose which of the women is most in need of care."

There was a moment of silence as Nathan thought, and then he spoke. "I think the young Widow Green with those three small children. Even with all the extra help that others have given her, she has scarcely been able to keep up with the company."

"I will speak to her tomorrow," Angus said solemnly. The weight of his decision was like lead in his heart. He returned to his blankets but could not sleep.

On the following day he rode next to Sister Green's wagon. He harnessed her team, milked her cow, carried the youngest boy on his saddle in front of him, and helped her secure her supplies. He built a roaring fire for her when the camp finally came to a standstill.

With natural good humor and grace, the young woman invited him to join her and her children for supper. After the meal, he sat watching the children frolicking in the firelight with a gentle smile.

"Is there going to be square dancing tonight, Brother McElin?" Helen Green asked, her eyes sparkling. She was a sturdily built young woman with gray eyes and golden hair that curled around her plump, good-natured face. She had a casual way with her children and her belongings, doing all the necessary things but with a cheerful lack of attention to detail. Even with the hardships of the journey she still laughed a lot and found time to play with her little ones. She cooked with a liberal hand and did not seem to worry about waste, as though she lived with a happy confidence that tomorrow would provide for itself. He knew she was well liked, and, even though the pioneers were sometimes impatient with wagons that consistently slowed down the progress of the group, he had never heard anyone complain about her delays.

"I do not know, Sister Green, but I wonder if I might ask you to take a brief walk with me, over by the river. We can ask Sister Palmer to watch your children for a few minutes."

Somewhat surprised, Sister Green made the arrangements and then accompanied Angus down through the budding cottonwoods and willows along the bank of the creek near which they had camped.

Never before in his life had Angus felt so at a loss for words. "Sister Green," he began, his voice solemn and severe, "I am married to a fine woman in Utah. We have no children. She is a faithful member of the Church and a woman who understands the plan of the Lord for the establishment of Zion. She has already sacrificed much, and now she has accepted the need for us to live the law of plural marriage."

Helen Green made a little noise that sounded almost like a squeak in the dark, and Angus hastened on.

He cleared his throat. "Both Brother Westville and I have noted how much you seem to need the support of a husband in order to make the rest of this journey and to survive in the rigors of the pioneer community in Utah. Therefore, I am willing to enter into the covenant of plural marriage with you and to accept the responsibility of caring for you and your children—"

Before he could say another word, Helen Green reached out and placed her hand on his arm. In the pale light of the moon he could see her merry face, and he could tell that she was struggling not to burst into laughter.

"Oh, Brother McElin!" she exclaimed, her voice brimming with humor. "How good you are! And how kind! And I know that you feel it was the Lord who inspired this suggestion." She could not hold it any longer, and a silver laugh pealed forth from her lips.

"I am flattered! Truly I am! You are a wonderful man—important and successful—and any woman would be blessed to be your wife. But I was married to someone whom I loved and who loved me very much. Of course I'll marry again—I know I shall have to! Maybe it will even be in a plural marriage—but, don't you see, I've known what love is, and I can't settle for anything else. I can't marry just to be taken care of—or for ease!

"Besides—" She moved closer to him, and he could feel the heat from her woman's body and the fresh scents of baked bread and laundry soap and sage. Her face was tender now, and the laughter was gone. "You would never be able to live with my slipshod ways, my rowdy children, and my need for laughter," she said. "I'm sorry I laughed. It's just that you took me by surprise. I know you were serious, and I am very serious too, when I tell you that I would drive you mad if you married me. It just wouldn't work, Angus. But I thank you for asking me."

She slipped away from him quickly and he saw her shadow as she hurried toward the circled camp. In the distance he could hear the sounds of fiddles being tuned.

He tramped slowly back toward his wagon. He didn't want to see anyone just yet. He wasn't even sure what he was feeling—pain? relief? surprise? shame? anger? amusement? Perhaps a little of each. It was going to be awkward to tell Nathan what had happened.

As the days passed, Angus could not let the matter alone in his own mind. His masculine pride had been stung by her laughter and rejection, and he felt frustrated that what he had taken for a righteous action had caused him embarrassment and a sense of failure.

He found himself questioning his own motives and wondering if he had not, in truth, found the prospect of Helen Green's warmth and laughter more appealing than he would care to admit. Was he really grasping for something he had long closed away in his heart—a desire for love and robust, vibrant emotion?

Angus found himself avoiding the Widow Green and taking every assignment that took him away from the camp—he rode as a scout and made foraging trips for provisions in communities along the way.

Nathan suspected what had happened, and he was understanding in giving Angus, his proud, dignified friend, time to assimilate the experience.

As the days passed, the prairie spread before the pioneers like a greening blanket. The stock thrived on the lush grass of early summer, and the air hummed with hundreds of freshly hatched insects. Occasionally the travelers would see herds of buffalo ranging in the distance, but these were nothing like the vast herds of the shaggy beasts the first wagon trains had seen. Those herds had stretched for miles across the face of the untouched wilderness, and the thunder and dust of their motion could fill the inverted bowl of the sky until the sun itself seemed blotted out.

The pioneers feasted on buffalo meat, rabbit, and occasionally an elk or deer. The days had settled into routine—challenging and physically demanding—but the strength of the men, women, and children had increased enormously and they did their tasks with relative ease.

One evening as the company gathered around the campfire to sing, several pioneers began to ask Nathan and Angus about the Salt Lake Valley.

"Is it true that the streets are bordered with streams of water, and the valley has blossomed like a rose?" asked a sinewy New England farmer.

"Aye," Angus replied, "but not without a deal of work. The soil is rich, and irrigation has made it fertile, but the grasshoppers and crickets are still a problem, and you'll battle for every bushel of wheat and corn. The fruit trees flourish, though, and the cherries, peaches, and pears are the finest you'll ever taste!"

"Will we enter the valley through the same canyon that Brigham Young used?" asked a sweet, young mother with a sleeping baby in her arms.

Nathan smiled at her. "Close to the very spot!" he assured her.

"Ah!" she replied. "Can you imagine what it must have been like to be in that first company! Or even worse—to have been with one of the handcart companies!" She clucked her tongue with wonder and sympathy.

"Well"—Nathan laughed—"you don't need to wonder. We have a man here who knows all about the handcart trip. Brother McElin, why don't you tell them about your first journey to the valley?"

At first with reluctance, but then with conviction as the memories came tumbling back, Angus recounted the story of his long-ago trek across the trackless wilderness with the valiant pioneers of his handcart company.

As he talked the company around the campfire grew still. He looked at their faces and could see that already the first pioneers were becoming a legend to this tide of new immigrants. The thought made him feel old, and more than a little weary.

Throughout his storytelling, Angus had been conscious of a young woman sitting near the fire. He recognized her as one of the unmarried women—Danish—probably in her early twenties—with jet-black hair hanging in a single braid down her back. She was a silent woman, and it was assumed she did not speak English. Quiet and efficient, she had been a great help to several of the Danish families, gathering wood and water, tending their children, organizing and packing their wagons with spare orderliness.

There was an impassive look to her that deterred others, and although they were kind to her, no one had really come to consider her a friend. It did not seem to Angus that the girl minded her solitary condition. She simply did whatever she was asked or could see needed to be done and then went her quiet way.

Tonight, as he spoke, Angus could not keep his eyes from hers. She was looking up at him with the same calm expression on her face that she always wore, but her black eyes, in the firelight, were alive. They seemed to burn into him, to search his face, his mind, his very soul. Never in his life had he felt anyone regard him so intently, and it made him uncomfortable. Drawing his narrative to a hasty conclusion, he excused himself and left the bright circle of the fire. As he walked to his wagon he could see the gleam of her ebony hair in the firelight. She had not moved, but her head was bowed and she seemed deep in thought.

Two days later Angus was out riding patrol several miles ahead of the wagon column. There had been reports of Indians, and, although they were not the threat they used to be, a prudent wagonmaster made it his business to know where the Indians were and what they were doing. Thievery was one of the main problems. The Indians retaliated for the invasion of their land by rustling any stray stock and pilfering small items from unattended wagons. Brigham Young had always recommended that the Saints be generous with the Indians. "Feed them, don't fight them!" was his admonition. Nathan, nonetheless, still felt it wise to keep his scouts on the lookout for any possible trouble.

As Angus rode he saw a cloud of dust coming from the direction of the wagon train—a single rider, traveling at breakneck speed. The horse's head and tail were stretched out and it was striding across the prairie with powerful thrusts of its muscled legs. The rider was crouched close to the horse's neck, and for a moment Angus tried to see who it could be. Possibly some Indian trick! Then he saw something billowing around the rider's legs, and he realized the rider was a woman wearing a dress. In a few more yards he could divine the features of the woman—it was the dark-haired Danish girl, Janeth Rasmussen. Astounded, he drew his horse to a halt and waited for her to reach him. "Is anything wrong?" he shouted as she approached.

"No!" she said, drawing her horse to a sudden halt, causing it to rear and prance restlessly beside Angus's mount. "I was just out for a ride, and I saw you and decided to catch up."

She spoke the sentence in a deep, rich voice with a strong Danish accent. There was no laughter or coquetry in the tone; it was a quiet statement of fact.

"I didn't know you spoke English!" Angus said in surprise.

"Yes," she replied. "I have been mostly with the Danish families so I usually speak my native tongue, and no one else has asked."

Suddenly he had a vivid image of what it must be like for her in the wagon train. To go from place to place making herself useful, depending on the generosity of others. How easy for everyone to assume she was someone else's responsibility . . . to take no interest in her!

He looked at her intently in the bright summer sun. Her sunbonnet had fallen off her head, and her forehead was streaked with dust and perspiration. She did not have a beautiful face—it was too strong and enigmatic for a man to be comfortable with. Her dark brows, the black, penetrating eyes, the high cheekbones, firm jaw, and closed lips made her seem as unapproachable as a statue.

"Well," he growled, "of course people haven't asked you! They think you want to be alone. You never smile." As he said it, he realized how absurd the accusation sounded.

"My—er—my employer used to say the same thing to me. 'Janeth,' he would say, 'you must learn to smile and be happy.' 'I am happy,' I would say to him, 'I am just not smiling-happy.' You see, I cannot pretend to smile—that would be a lie. Besides, you do not smile much either, Brother McElin. In all the weeks of our travels I have only seen you smile once, and that was when you spoke of your brother Johnny!"

Angus, caught off guard by her accusation, exclaimed, "Johnny!"

"You see!" she said triumphantly. "You just said his name and you are smiling."

He looked at her, and she was smiling too, her white even teeth gleaming and her dark eyes sparkling.

"Now you see!" Angus said. "If you would smile like that more often, there isn't a person on the train who wouldn't want to get to know you. You have to try to look like you want to belong. For example—your clothes!"

Janeth flushed a deep crimson and nodded her head. "I know," she whispered. "They look . . . how do you say it? . . . ridiculous!"

While all the other women of the train dressed in homespun or linsey wool, or simple linens and cottons in dark colors, Janeth's dresses were of formal design, with tucks and ruffles, made from poplin, silk, and brocade. As the journey had continued her dresses had become travel-stained and torn and were a source of private merriment and casual gossip among the pioneers.

"They are all I have," she murmured. "I would trade all of them for one simple calico dress."

"Why didn't you ask?" Angus was incredulous. "Surely some of the women could have . . . ?"

She raised her head and her dark eyes flashed. "I would rather look ridiculous than be reduced to begging!"

Angus shook his head and stared at the young woman. She sat astride her horse like a man, with her skirts tucked around her legs. Her carriage was tall and straight in the saddle, like that of a trained horsewoman. Everything about her was mysterious, except her eyes, which were as straight, honest, and uncompromising as any he had ever seen. Suddenly he was reminded of his mother—Mary had the same proud, fiercely honest look.

"Who are you, Janeth Rasmussen?" he mused aloud. "And how come you to be here?"

As they rode together she told him her story. Janeth had been born the daughter of the household steward of a minor member of Danish royalty. The manor house was one of great wealth and culture, and Janeth, in her early years, had been raised in the nursery with the children of the house. She had eaten with them and learned to speak three languages before she was ten. She was an apt student, and the imperious baron was fond of her, as were his young daughters. It was when she turned ten that Janeth became achingly aware of the fact that she was not, however, one of the baron's children. At that time the baron's daughters were moved out of the nursery into their own sumptuous rooms, and they began a series of lessons in the skills that were essential to royalty at that time—dancing, music, riding, and the endless etiquette of the court. Janeth became a personal maid to the youngest daughter. In the next few years all vestiges of their friendship vanished, and she became a genuine servant to the girl, who treated her with the same casual disregard with which she treated all the household staff.

It was at this time that Janeth's father died, and the baron called her into his private rooms to tell her the tragic news. By then Janeth was grown into her teens, a tall, graceful girl with a strong, unreadable face. The baron, perhaps moved by the memory of his affection for her as a child, asked if there was anything he could do to help improve her lot. The baron's oldest daughter was preparing to marry within the month, and Janeth was emboldened to make a request. "When you have grandchildren, and the nursery is reopened, may I work there, as governess?"

The baron was astonished at this request, but, after a moment's thought, he gave his promise. Within the year a child was born, and Janeth was returned to the one place where she had been happy. Caring for one infant, however, could not completely fill her energetic need to be useful. The quiet hours in the nursery lay heavily on her hands. It was at this time that she had asked an elderly woman, who had been a friend of her father's, if she would teach her how to weave.

Janeth proved to be a gifted pupil and very quickly became a skilled craftswoman. Before long the baron moved a fine loom into a room adjacent to the nursery where Janeth could spin and weave with the door open, listening for the child. Her linens and wools were the finest in the city. Another child was added to the nursery the following year, and the baron added a nursemaid to the nursery staff. By the third year, Janeth remained living in the nursery but she performed only two tasks—weaving and tutoring the older child in languages.

It was about this time that Janeth heard the missionaries speak at a sidewalk meeting when she visited the city on her day off. Something about the two elders touched her, and she began attending their instruction classes. In two months Janeth was baptized, feeling that finally she had taken a step that could give her life meaning and value. Everything would have been fine—if Janeth had remained silent. The baron rarely inquired about her activities; his daughters visited the nursery as seldom as possible and scarcely spoke to their former childhood friend. However, in Janeth's zeal for the new Gospel and cherishing in her heart a misplaced feeling of love and filial bond to the baron, she went to him one evening in his elaborate chambers to tell him of her momentous decision. Innocently believing that she was giving him something that would become the most precious thing in his life, she handed him a copy of The Book of Mormon.

The baron recoiled from the gift, and his face became as closed and haughty as a mask. In confusion Janeth quickly left the room, but the next evening the baron sent for her and told her without preamble he was horrified to discover such a wayward and apostate soul in his own home. Without a trace of warmth or avuncular concern, he addressed her as if she were a disobedient lackey. "You will either forswear this mad religion and promise that you will have nothing more to do with it or its members, or you will leave my employ at once and never return!"

Pride, bitterness, and betrayal rose in her throat with the sharpness of a knife, and she turned on her heel and left the room. For years, as governess and artisan, she had worn not the standard uniform of a maid but the cast-off day dresses of her mistresses. These dresses were the only clothing she had, and she packed them up, kissed the babies good-bye, ran her hand lovingly over her loom one last time, and left the graystone manor house where she had lived all her life. She walked through the stable yard where she had ridden with the young baronesses, slipped through the rose arbor, and hurried past the formal gardens and out into the dark streets of the city. By midnight she had found the door of the elders' lodgings and had presented herself to them with the simple statement, "I wish to go to Zion!"

A fund had been set up by the Church to help destitute converts make the journey to Salt Lake, and, although the money was meager, the elders were able to book passage for Janeth and attach her to a small group of Danish Saints who were also making the journey.

Shyness and the stamp of being "different" from the other humble converts had made Janeth an outsider in the little group, but she had continued on the journey with faith that when she entered the land of the New Jerusalem she would at last find the place where she belonged.

Janeth told Angus the story in a soft, unemotional voice, but Angus could imagine the hundreds of small slights, the loneliness and frustration of the young woman's life, and he was disturbed and moved by her.

For the next two days Angus cast about for some way to help Janeth without causing gossip. Helen Green had exercised discretion in not talking about his rejected proposal with others, and so, somewhat hesitantly, he went to her. He told her briefly about Janeth and asked if she might be able to help the young woman by finding her more appropriate clothing and by trying to include her in group activities.

Helen's eyes were filled with quick sympathy, and Angus thought that perhaps he had underestimated her. She was certainly not the shallow, careless woman he had tried to convince himself she was. Within the week he noticed that Janeth was dressed in a sturdy brown dress made of hopsacking. The dress was a little too small for her, and emphasized her bosom and broad shoulders, but the style was serviceable and the fabric clean and durable. Several of the pioneer families seemed to be paying her more attention, and at supper one evening Nathan informed Angus that Helen Green and some of the other women had set up a school program for all children of school age and had asked Janeth to teach each evening after supper.

It pleased Angus to know that Janeth's skills were being utilized. One day he saw her walking by one of the wagons carrying a drop spindle. Several little girls were walking with her, and she was explaining the spindle's use as she spun a fine thread from a patch of fleece. He paused beside the group and watched with fascination as her fine, slender hands, with strong, adept motions, twirled the swinging bobbin and fed the thread onto it. Her motions were so swift and skilled that it was almost impossible to follow them. "What remarkably capable hands that woman has!" he thought.

Of course, Janeth's personality did not change. She was still formal and withdrawn, and, although the children respected and minded her, they were not drawn to her by affection. As soon as lessons were over they ran off to more jovial company, and she was still alone a great deal of the time.

Angus tried very hard to be discreet about his interest in the young woman. Indeed, he did not understand his attraction to her himself. She was enigmatic and complex, and he scarcely knew her, yet he found himself worrying about her and making absurd arrangements to cross her path during the course of the day.

She too, with a straightforward simplicity that embarrassed him, sought him out. When Angus was gathering water at the river in the evening, or tethering and grooming the horses, he would often look up to see her standing nearby, and they would talk for a few moments before she slipped away. In as close a community as the wagon train, their mutual interest could not pass without notice.

One night while making his rounds, Angus passed Helen Green's wagon. The children were tucked in for the night, and Helen had just finished hanging out a wash on the wagon tongue. She looked weary, and Angus dismounted. "Let me empty the wash pails for you," he said, "and I'll bank the fire as well."

"Thank you, Angus," she said gratefully and sat down on an upturned crate. "It has been a long day."

When Angus finished the chores he came to say good night. "Thank you for helping Sister Rasmussen," he added. He turned to mount his horse, but Helen's voice stopped him.

"Why don't you marry her, Angus?" Helen's voice was like a challenge. He turned and looked at her in disbelief.

"Don't look so astonished, Angus!" Helen laughed. "I declare! You told me yourself that you had been called to live the covenant of plural marriage, and just because I wasn't the right one doesn't mean your calling wasn't true!

"That poor girl is going to need a husband. Anyone with a face that strong and intelligent . . . it's going to take a powerful man to be interested, let alone willing to take on all that intensity! Mind you, I like her, Angus—but she's not the kind of girl that makes men comfortable.

"Mark my words. She doesn't know a hill of beans about how to make friends or meet people. She'll be lost in Salt Lake—lost among strangers, and the chances are she'll end up being someone's hired girl or an old-maid schoolteacher, just as sure as my name's Helen Green. Believe me, Angus, that would be a terrible waste! There's a lot of woman in there."

Angus's face flamed scarlet as he listened to Helen's onslaught, and he could scarcely find his voice. "I—I—would never consider marrying a second wife who was so young. . . . I would take a second wife only for her need."

"I know that," Helen replied seriously. "I know that even better than you know it yourself. You are one of the most honorable men I have ever met, Angus McElin. I know you do not love Janeth—not yet—but she does need you!"

Helen rose with a sigh and put her hands on her back, palms down and stretched, throwing her head back to ease the strain. "I am tired!'' She moaned, with another little laugh. ''My mind's befuddled and I'm talking too much! Don't listen to me, Angus. Go talk to Nathan.''

Nathan agreed with everything Helen had said to him, and Angus, confused and uneasy, tossed sleeplessly through the night.

After a mighty wrestle with his soul, and much prayer, Angus felt Nathan and Helen were right. It was his responsibility to provide a home and family for Janeth Rasmussen, and he informed Nathan of his decision.

When he proposed to Janeth, she was absolutely silent. Her face became even paler than usual, and, for an awful moment, Angus was convinced he was about to be refused again, but she raised her eyes to meet his and, still wordless and unsmiling, she nodded her head. They were married that evening in a simple ceremony performed by Nathan and witnessed by Helen Green and the Danish families who had been providing for Janeth. Janeth would move into the supply wagon with Angus, and they would have a tent for their use. Nathan had arranged to sleep in the scout's quarters.

For the wedding, Janeth brought a dress out of her basket that she had not worn before. It was a dark-blue satin, with a white lace fichu at the neck and small, satin-covered buttons that reached from the top of the high collar down the back far below her waist. The bodice fit like a glove, and the skirt was a miracle of drapes and pleats. Janeth had gathered her dark hair into a bun and somewhere on the prairie had found some little yellow flowers that she had woven into her tresses. In the firelight her face looked softer, prettier, but the expression in her eyes revealed nothing to the pioneers gathered to witness the nuptials. They marveled at her calmness.

Angus had pitched their tent by the stream in a small clearing, a piece away from the others. They would be close enough to hear any alarm, but far enough away for privacy. The summer night was full of the sound of insects, and a warm breeze played in the leaves of the bushes around them. The newlyweds bid a dignified farewell to their wedding guests, thanked Nathan, and finally, for the first time since their horseback ride, they were absolutely alone together.

''I came after you that day on the prairie, you know,'' Janeth whispered, as they walked through the brush to their tent. ''I begged Nathan to let me borrow his horse and tell me where you were—and he did.''

''Why?'' Angus asked, made awkward by the revelation.

"Oh, Angus!" Her voice seemed faint and strained in the dark. "Can't you guess?"

Angus scarcely heard her question, he was in such a torment of thought. Janeth could not have imagined the guilt and self-doubt with which he was struggling. He had never known a woman except Lucy, his valiant, faithful first wife. All the years of his life he had lived with restraint and self-control, with only a few brief periods of physical intimacy when Lucy was well enough to welcome him. He had been gone from home now for several months, and the image of Lucy had faded somewhat, but tonight he felt her presence vividly and he wondered if she really would approve of this marriage as she had promised. He had never intended this wedding to be more than a covenant to take care of this poor, misplaced girl, but now, as they moved together toward their marriage bed, he knew he was obliged to fulfill every obligation of a husband—including the responsibility to give this mysterious woman beside him warmth, love—and, if possible, children.

He held aside the tent flap. Janeth entered wordlessly and knelt down on the ground since the tent was not tall enough for her to stand. Angus stood by the tent opening and lit a small lantern, then he too entered. Janeth was kneeling beside the bedroll on the ground, her back toward him, and she was struggling to reach the long row of buttons.

"This is why I never wear this dress," she explained. "I can't reach the buttons! Sister Green buttoned me in, but I'm afraid you will have to button me out."

Reluctantly, Angus knelt behind her and tentatively reached for the top button. His rough, work-hardened hands fumbled with the tiny loops, but slowly he began to get the knack of it, and, in the dim, flickering light from the lantern, he undid each one carefully.

Neither of them spoke. She knelt before him, her head bowed, so that he could get a clear view of the buttons. At first he was intent on his task, but, as the first several buttons were undone, her dress fell open slightly, and he saw the creamy nape of her neck, tender and graceful before him. She seemed so defenseless! Something stirred in him, and his hands trembled as he continued unfastening the small satin buttons. As he reached the waist button, she shifted her weight as though tired of kneeling in the same spot, and as she moved, the dress, now gaping open in the back, fell from her shoulder. Angus stared at the soft, pearllike skin of her back and shoulder, smooth and round, gleaming in the golden lamplight. It

117

was the first time in his life that he had seen a woman's body—even this much of it—unclothed and revealed. Lucy always wore a white, voluminous flannel gown that covered her modestly even when they made love, which was always in the dark. Now he looked at Janeth's shimmering back and thought he had never seen anything so lovely.

Janeth, not understanding why he had stopped, murmured, "Perhaps I can reach the rest of them myself, Angus. Thank you for helping me."

Angus, filled with a desire so intense that it shamed him, whispered hoarsely, "Would you like me to wait outside?"

Suddenly she turned to face him fiercely. "Oh, no, Angus!" she cried. "I do not want you to leave me! Not even for a minute!"

With a cry that was almost like a moan, she threw her arms around him, and he, heady with her emotion, embraced her, pulling her toward him, and his hands sought the opening in the back of her dress and he stroked her glorious smoothness.

Without another word he turned and extinguished the lantern. In the darkness he could hear her rustling and struggling out of her clothes, and then the bedcovers were thrown back and he could hear the sound of her lying down. Like a blind man reaching for a guide, he held out his hand, and, miraculously, her hand was there to meet his, and she gently pulled him toward her. He followed her hand to find the wonderful mysteries of her love and the well of joy he had never known before.

In the next weeks, as the wagon train continued its dusty, weary way toward the mountains, through the hot cruelty of a Wyoming summer, Angus felt he had been seized by some glorious madness. He was spellbound by Janeth. His mind was filled with her, and his days seemed endless until they could come together once again in the sultry warmth of the tent, where the heat of his desire was more impetuous and intense than the heat of ten desert suns.

Often during the day he castigated himself, feeling that such passion and joy could have no place in a righteous man's life. Somehow he felt he would be condemned for loving a woman's body with such abandon. But at night he could not withhold himself, and all the years of self-control melted before the heat of Janeth's passion and beauty.

On one hot day Angus and Janeth had gone scouting together. The red Wyoming dust filled their nostrils and their hair, until they looked like ochre statues on ochre horses. As they turned to ride back to the camp, they came upon a small stream, feeding into a rock-lined pool. Scrub pine and surrounding bluffs hid the spot from view.

"I'm going in!" Janeth declared. She put her mount to graze near the stream, pulled off the dusty shirt and heavy skirt she was wearing, yanked off her boots, and waded into the cool water. She was wearing only a light cotton chemise, and Angus, watching her, was thrilled at the lovely curves and secret places of her body revealed in the wet, clinging fabric.

"Come in!" she beckoned. For a while more he watched her, and then, removing his outer clothes, he joined her. They splashed in the water like children, and then he brought her to the bank of the stream, laid her on the spread-out skirt, and there, in the broad daylight, he made tender, passionate love to this young, mysterious woman who, by some miracle, had become his wife.

Late that afternoon as they rode into camp she pulled her horse close beside his. In the rosy patch of the sunset her face shined up at his. "I will never forget today, Angus," she whispered. "When I am an old and gray woman, with scarcely a tooth in my head, I shall remember this day and be glad!"

He looked at her. "You're smiling!" he said.

A few days before the wagon train's final descent into the Salt Lake Valley, messengers from the city rode into camp with supplies and mail. Included in the letters was a note to Angus from Matty, telling him that Mary had passed away while he was gone. Matty and Johnny had sold the home and her belongings and had settled the family's affairs in Salt Lake City. "Hundreds of people attended her funeral service, from miles around. She had been an angel of mercy in this valley, and I hope she and Father are at last at rest with one another," Matty wrote.

The two brothers had bought a new flock of sheep and were on their way back to Pleasantview. "We are trying for an even stronger hybrid. We cannot wait until you get home to tell us your adventures," Johnny added at the end of the letter.

Another letter was from Lucy. It was short and sweet, saying little else than that she was feeling much better and could not wait for his return. Seeing Lucy's handwriting smote Angus's heart, and he felt again a rush of guilt and concern. Perhaps he should have found a way to warn Lucy about Janeth. But no, he felt certain she would

119

understand better if he could explain it to her in person. He was convinced that once she met Janeth and knew the circumstances of the marriage, she would be pleased with his decision. "Eventually," he told himself, "Lucy will rejoice in this! Janeth will be such a support and a help to her—and the two will grow to love one another like sisters!" Calming his apprehensions, and buoyed up by his determined optimism, Angus saw the wagon train to the end of the trail, bid farewell to his traveling companions, urged Nathan Westville to consider coming to Pleasantview for a visit—and, if he wished, to make his permanent home in the Virgin Valley.

Angus and Janeth spent a few days in Salt Lake City in a fine, clean boardinghouse with white linen sheets and lace curtains. They indulged themselves with delicious foods—chicken, roast beef, sauces, honeycakes, raised bread, cheese, fresh fruits, and compotes. They attended a play at the newly completed Salt Lake Theater where Janeth wore the blue satin dress in which she had been married and drew many an admiring eye. The McElins saw Brigham Young, newly returned from his summer residence in St. George, sitting in his box. He nodded to Angus and Janeth during the intermission, and his smile was like a benediction on their marriage. Janeth glowed in the recognition.

Angus realized that they could not prolong their stay. He purchased some sturdy, practical clothes for Janeth, bought a lovely carnelian brooch for Lucy, and the two of them boarded the stage for Manti.

A week later Angus and Janeth rode over the crest of the mountains on the western ridge of the Virgin Valley and, for the first time, Janeth saw the scene that had greeted the McElin brothers years earlier. Even with the neat houses and farms of Pleasantview nestling in the bowl of the valley, the scene was still one of magnificent, wild, exuberant nature. The fierceness of the river cascade, the mighty upthrust of the rocky summits, the windswept beauty of the high meadows overwhelmed her, and tears came to her eyes.

"It is the most beautiful spot on the earth, Angus!" Janeth exclaimed. "Thank you for marrying me and bringing me here."

Looking at her, Angus knew that he had at last found a woman who was a match for the challenge of his mountains. "Oh, Lucy," he prayed silently, "please give her a chance!"

As they rode down the trail into town, Janeth took a small

notebook out of her pocket and began writing. Once she dismounted and picked a cluster of small red berries.

"What are you doing, Janeth?" Angus enquired.

Janeth blushed and handed him the book. He glanced through the pages where she had identified and drawn specimens of all the plants she had seen on the trip across the country. He was amazed at the specific detail and minute observations about each specimen—its qualities and habitat. The book was a treasury of botanical information and scientific observation. "This is a wonderful achievement, Janeth!" Angus exclaimed.

She beamed, unaccustomed to the praise, and put the book back into her pocket with a small, happy smile.

As the couple entered the town of Pleasantview, Angus pointed up the wide street to the center of town where the three white houses graced their respective corners and the church raised its steeple on the other. "See!" he directed her glance. "The Big House with the wide porch. That is . . . our home." He could not say more, because the joy of being back in his own place had filled him with strong emotion. Without meaning to, he urged his horse forward, and Janeth trailed slowly behind him up the street. With a joyful shout he leaped out of his saddle onto the front steps and shouted into the Big House. "Lucy! I'm home!"

Janeth, feeling suddenly shy and awkward, remained on her horse in the street. She saw the front door of the big, white house burst open, and a middle-aged woman, slender and erect, hurry out onto the porch. The woman's pale hair was pulled back into a sleek knot, and the bone structure of her delicate face showed through her fine, white skin. She looked as fragile as china, and yet there was something imposing in her carriage.

"Angus!" the woman exclaimed, her voice filled with trembling joy. "You are home at last, my dear!"

In two bounds Angus was up the stairs and had enfolded Lucy in a tender, careful, almost worshipful embrace. Janeth noted with a wrench of triumphant jealousy that there was nothing of the fierce abandon with which he embraced her. This was an embrace reserved for an object of reverence and inestimable value.

The two stood together for a moment on the porch, and then Angus gently disengaged his arms. "Lucy," he said. "You look wonderfully well! Far better than when I left. You must have taken good care of yourself."

Lucy gave a small, enigmatic smile. "I am feeling better, Angus. And I have a wonderful surprise for you."

With a start Angus remembered Janeth, still sitting on her horse in front of the house, uncertain what else to do.

"No, Lucy," he exclaimed. "First I have a surprise for you. I think you will feel this one is wonderful too."

Again Lucy smiled her secretive smile. "Not nearly so wonderful as mine, Angus! Wait here."

Angus stood on the porch uncertainly for a moment, and then, just as he was about to turn to go help Janeth dismount, Lucy came back out of the house holding a tiny bundle in her arms. For a moment Angus could hardly breathe.

"Lucy!" he cried softly, incredulously. "Is this . . . ? What are you telling me? A baby?"

With a silver laugh of pure happiness, Lucy smiled up at him. "Yes, Angus. Our baby! Yours and mine. A little girl only three weeks old. I have called her Mary after your mother."

Angus could not speak. He walked over beside Lucy and gently pulled down the white shawl. Inside was a tiny infant with dark hair like his own and a delicate face with features that were a miniature version of Lucy.

"Oh, Lucy! How could you keep such a thing secret? Are you all right? I should have been here!" His thoughts came tumbling out of him, and his wife put her hand on his arm.

"I didn't want to tell you because if I did, I knew you would refuse to make the trip east. Besides, I was afraid . . . I thought . . . I didn't want you to have to go through it if I lost this one as well. But I didn't! And she is here for us to love and care for. And now you are home . . . Oh, Angus! I am so happy!"

"I too, Lucy!" Angus replied. "You are so brave and fine."

"Now show me your surprise!" Lucy said gaily. "Have you brought me a gift?"

"In a way," Angus replied. "Lucy, I would like you to meet Janeth."

Lucy looked up as Janeth dismounted from her horse and began to walk slowly up the path to the porch. As Janeth came closer the smile on Lucy's face faded and first puzzlement, then horrified comprehension twisted her expression.

For a moment Lucy swayed like a straw in the wind, then Angus caught her and the baby together and lifted them into his arms. Carrying the double burden, he entered the house. Janeth stood shivering in the warm summer breeze, alone on the porch steps.

The next days were nightmarish for all three of them. Lucy, devastated by the shock, returned to her bed. She refused to speak about the second marriage to Angus, and the midwife recommended that he should wait until Lucy was stronger before he discussed it with her.

Janeth was sent to stay with Johnny, Hester, and Min. She saw the warmth and love in their household, and wondered how Johnny and his two wives had achieved such a felicitous arrangement. In her heart she knew that nothing like it would ever be possible with Lucy and Angus in the Big House.

For three days Angus did not come to see her or speak to her. On the third day he knocked at Johnny's door and asked to visit with Janeth. The two of them sat like strangers across from each other in the formal parlor.

Angus explained to Janeth in a painfully controlled voice that Lucy was very weak since the baby's birth. He told her what he had learned from the midwife of the agonizing delivery, after months of bedridden pregnancy. The baby had been small and weak, and Lucy, unable to nurse, had found a woman in the valley who had just given birth. The woman nursed Mary along with her own child and the baby was doing well, but Lucy was still very delicate.

"I cannot tell you how I feel, Janeth. I feel I have betrayed Lucy, and you as well." Angus's eyes were dark with pain and exhaustion.

"You haven't been sleeping well, have you, Angus?" Janeth asked with concern. "It's all right. I understand. Johnny and Hester and Min are treating me very well, and I think I'm a help with the children. I'm sure I can stay here until Lucy is feeling better."

Angus shook his head. "You don't understand," he said sadly. "I don't think she will ever feel better—at least not about our marriage. Janeth, I know it will be impossible for Lucy ever to share her home with you. I can't ask her! I have given orders for a house to be built on the acre behind the Big House where the kitchen garden is. As soon as that house is finished, it will be yours. You can move in there and I promise you, Janeth, that I will fulfill my promise to take care of you for the rest of your life, but . . . Lucy is my first wife—we have a little daughter now. You will have to recognize that I can do nothing to jeopardize their well-being!"

123

Janeth sat staring at the hands she held clenched in her lap. She had no words to touch him, and he stood to leave. "Oh, Janeth!" Angus groaned as he looked at her. "I think of her here, carrying my child, bearing it alone when she knew she was risking her life—for me! And all the time you and I were . . ."

Janeth's eyes flashed. "Lucy has her child, hasn't she? That would be worth all the suffering a woman could endure. You have given her a daughter—can't you see that? You have nothing to feel guilty about—there was nothing shameful in our love! I won't let your guilt and sense of duty rob me of those memories. . . ."

Angus's eyes flared with anger. "I will not allow you to demean Lucy or her sacrifice! You'll have to bear my decisions, Janeth. We cannot build happiness on another's sorrow. I know you are a strong woman, and you will be able to adjust. You must understand how much Lucy needs me."

With blazing eyes, Janeth faced him. "But what of me, Angus? I have needs too. Surely Lucy would not begrudge the love I can give you in our marriage bed!"

Angus's face was strained. "I cannot speak of this further, Janeth. I cannot undo what has been done. You must forgive me—and forget."

"I cannot forget, Angus!" Janeth exclaimed. "Neither can you. Our love will haunt us! Angus, I want so little. Only to make you happy. . . ."

Angus put his arms around Janeth in a grim, impassioned embrace. "We must learn to live with this—you and I," he said hoarsely. "Do not make it any harder than it has to be." With that he turned and left the parlor.

In the ensuing weeks, as Janeth's house was built on the garden lot behind the Big House, the family and the people of the valley came to accept the strained situation.

Janeth was included in family gatherings at the Big House, and Lucy, when she was well enough to attend, spoke to her in tones of cool civility. Angus visited Janeth formally once a week at Johnny's home and took her to see the progress of the Garden House. He encouraged her to make any suggestions she wished, but Janeth looked at the progress of the narrow, two-story frame house and registered no sign of interest. Angus treated her with gentle courtesy. He saw her every need was cared for, but he did not kiss her, or hold her, or give any indication that there would ever again be any intimacy in their relationship.

Finally, the Garden House was completed. Angus furnished the house with items from the Big House and extra family furniture. It smelled of fresh pine and paint. The windows were uncurtained, and the floors rugless, but the house was liveable. The McElin relations came to see Janeth and help her settle in. Later she walked through the clean, impersonal rooms in silence with Angus by her side.

"It isn't a prison, you know!" Angus whispered to her fiercely. "It's a warm, sturdy house. Most women would be thrilled to own such a home."

She looked at him from under her dark brows. "I did not marry you for a house, Angus," she replied softly.

She saw his shoulders sag, but he continued to escort her through the rooms. They finally came to the main bedroom. It was large and airy, on the second floor, with back stairs leading into it from the kitchen entryway. With a look of pain Janeth observed the narrow single bed in the middle of the polished wood floor. Angus crossed the room without comment and opened a door on the far side that led to a small anteroom Janeth had assumed to be a small dressing room, or sewing chamber.

"You may want to look at this," Angus said, his voice edged with disappointment.

She walked across to the open door and glanced through. There, in the middle of the small room, was a beautiful loom. It was meticulously made and crafted in such a way that she knew that it must have been very expensive. It was made of seasoned hardwood—unavailable anywhere around Pleasantview, so Angus must have sent to Salt Lake City or even had the loom shipped from the east as a surprise for her. She wanted to thank him, to tell him that she knew how much he was suffering and how hard he was trying to make it up to her, but nothing would assuage the agonizing hurt and humiliation she had experienced in the weeks since she had come to Pleasantview, and her fierce pride made her lash out at him.

"If all I had wanted was a loom, I could have stayed in Denmark," she flung at him bitterly as she walked from the room. Angus slammed the door to the weaving room and hurried after her down the stairs. In the kitchen Johnny had started the stove, and Hes had put on a pot of hot broth. As Angus and Janeth entered the kitchen, Min poured warm cups of the soup and brought it to them. They raised their cups to Janeth.

"May there be joy within these walls," Johnny said with a false and hearty cheeriness. Hes hugged Janeth and told her she would miss her. But the atmosphere was strained, and the others soon left, leaving Janeth and Angus together in the bare, new kitchen.

Janeth was sorry she had been so difficult, and yet she could not bring herself to apologize or tell Angus that she was grateful for the house and the loom. He had said it was not a prison, but she knew, for her, that was just what it would become. She understood that Angus would never share this house with her, so she would live there, alone, and no one would dare to befriend her because they would fear Lucy's displeasure. Angus stood up to leave. The harsh silence between them filled him with pain and he wanted to be quit of the whole situation for a while.

Suddenly Janeth was terrified to have him go, and she reached for his sleeve, wanting to do something—anything—to delay his going.

"Angus!" She did not know how to say it, but she felt she had to give him something to take away from this bleak house, something that would make him want to return, if not as her lover and husband, at least as a friend.

"It will be homelike," she said quietly, "that is, if a child can make a home."

Involuntarily, Angus's eyes raked Janeth's body, and he noted the new fullness in her breasts and the touch of heaviness at her waist.

"Oh, Janeth!" He groaned and walked over to her and put his arms around her in a long, hard embrace. "My poor girl!"

"No!" she exclaimed, springing back from him. "It is the one thing you have given me which I shall value all my life! Don't call me a poor girl—and don't pity me ever. I shall bear you a daughter, one as rich and full of life as our love for each other was! She will be as glorious as your mountains, Angus! And I shall love her, and care for her, and teach her how to be happy and strong! She will never live in the shadow of the Big House. I will teach her to be free!"

As though the outburst had spent her strength, Janeth fell into an old rocking chair by the fire and her shoulders slumped. Angus stood looking at her helplessly, and then with a long sigh he bent and kissed her on the top of her bent head. "Be well, Janeth," he murmured and walked out of the room.

Janeth did not add much to the house. She did make curtains for the windows, and put a rag rug on the kitchen floor, but her wants were simple, and through the autumn, while she was still able, she spent her days tramping in the hills identifying plants, herbs, and shrubs that grew in the valley. Angus admonished her to take care, but the fresh air and the vigorous tramping seemed to add to her robust health.

Late in November, Sarah Gill, the sister of one of the valley's farmers, came to live in Pleasantview. She had lost her husband in a logging accident, and she had two young boys. Her brother scarcely had room in his house for his own family, and he inquired of Angus if there was anyone in the valley who might have room to board his sister and her family in return for her cooking and housekeeping. Angus asked Janeth if she would like the help and company of the other woman, and Janeth accepted. Relieved of the need to cook or do housework, Janeth began to spend more and more time at her loom.

Soon after Janeth moved to the valley she had discovered the beautiful, long staple of the wool from the McElin sheep. She had access to as much of the fleece as she desired and so she began weaving in earnest.

She also intensified her interest in native plants and began experimenting with natural dyes to create bold, beautiful effects in the increasingly daring creations that came from her active loom. It was as though she were pouring all her pent-up passion and creativity into the glowing wool.

Angus was always considerate and concerned for her welfare. He visited her regularly and often accompanied her on long walks. Because they both understood the need to avoid personal conversation, Angus gradually found himself talking to Janeth about the business and administrative problems that piled upon him. He was astounded at her ability and, without realizing it, came to rely upon her judgment. And though he could not have verbalized it, he knew that with her he felt a peace he felt nowhere else. Lucy accepted the time spent visiting Janeth, as long as Angus did not stay the night with her, and his visits were openly observed. She knew Janeth was expecting a baby, but she could not bring herself to discuss it, or ask any questions of Angus, and so she did not know when the child was due.

As the year came to an end, tense equilibrium had been established. Only once was the fragile balance threatened. On a cold day in December, Angus came to check the fires at the Garden House. Janeth was alone, since Sarah and her boys were visiting her brother. The kitchen was cozy in the firelight, just before the lamps were lighted, and Janeth asked Angus if he would stay and eat supper with her. He was tired, and the warmth of the room regaled him into accepting her offer. They ate a delicious stew flavored with the fresh herbs Janeth had gathered and dried.

Angus asked her about her weaving, and she invited him up to look at a new method she had just developed. "The idea," she said enthusiastically as she held up the lamp to light his way up the narrow steps, "is to make the weave very loose, and leave the lift of the wool, like gossamer, to give it a softness and a hazy look."

They opened the door to her workroom and he examined the lovely fabric that lay like a dewy spider web in the moonlight.

"It's beautiful," he said, shaking his head in wonder. "Your hands are wondrous!" Without thinking, he took her slender, strong hand in his and kissed the palm. She moved into his arms as naturally as though they had never been apart and he kissed her hungrily, until his heart beat like thunder in his ears. Scarcely realizing what he was doing, he led her slowly to the chaste and narrow bed. At that moment the kitchen door slammed below and they heard the thump of the Gill children's feet on the floor, and Sarah calling, "Now mind you don't get mud on this clean floor!" Angus sprang away from Janeth and turned to the stairs. "If it helps you to know it," he said in a broken whisper, "I never stop missing you!" And then he was gone.

"Not now!" Janeth whispered, sitting down as tears spilled into her lap. "But soon. Soon you will stop missing me, and this new, barren love will be all you remember between us."

On a bitterly cold night in February, with a ferocious wind blowing down from the summits and the cascades of the Virgin River frozen like a witch's hair on the face of the mountain, Janeth sent for the midwife, and, with Sarah and Sister Burton in attendance, she gave birth in the early hours of a cold and brilliant morning to a vigorous baby girl with bright red hair and strong, fine limbs.

When Angus hurried over from the Big House to see the new arrival, he kicked the snow off his boots and rushed upstairs to the bedroom where Janeth lay with her baby in a cradle at her side.

Tenderly Angus reached down and picked up the baby. She seemed to look into his eyes for a moment, intensely and honestly like her mother, but then she screwed up her wrinkled, newborn face, and began to scream, outraged at the man who had taken her out of the soft fleecy blankets in the cradle and exposed her to the cold air and the indignity of his scrutiny. The baby cried with a wild, lusty, carefree wail and kicked her strong little legs against her father's hands.

Angus threw back his head and laughed at the squalling, red-haired, furious infant. "I'm thinking that this is the child who should have been named Mary! She reminds me exactly of my mother!" he said.

Janeth laughed too and reached up for the child. Angus tucked the little one in beside her mother, and the baby calmed down. "I think I would like to call her Christina, after my father," Janeth said. "His name was Christian."

At this moment there was nothing that Angus would deny this woman who had endured so much. "It will be as you say, Janeth," Angus agreed softly. "Christina McElin—my second daughter!" He smiled down at the baby with pride.

THE VIRGIN LAND

1886–1898

. . . and the wilderness shall blossom as the rose and the barren desert become a verdant field . . .

Chapter Seven

The Virgin River plunges like a knife through the heart of the Rocky Mountains. It is a raging, heedless force that has cut its own prison more deeply with each succeeding eon.

Poor mad, wild river, forced to run southward between towering canyon cliffs. "Westward!" the river screams, whipping itself into a fury of white, seething rapids, treacherous whirlpools, and cruel undercurrents. "Freedom!" Headlong it crashes against the red and gold walls of its own self-made chasm, relentlessly searching for a crack or weakness in the shadowed depths of its canyon. The river is like a range mare brought to corral. Unbroken and furious, she batters her hooves against the wooden stall that holds her until, at last, the weakest board breaks and the victorious creature smashes her way to freedom.

The Virgin is not a kind river, yet, where it cascades at last unrestrained into the high empty foothills above Pleasantview, it brings with it a glorious touch of its own wild beauty and sweet, life-giving water.

In March the wind that follows the Virgin River through its narrow defile is as violent and cold as the river itself. It always amazed Christina that a wind so cold could melt the snow, but from where she stood she could see rivulets of black, melting water, cold as ice, running down from the high pastures into the turbulent river.

On this brilliant windswept day Christina was exultant to be back in the highlands after the long winter with the sheep foraging in the lower pastures of the valley. The week before, the men had moved the flocks from their winter pastures up into the higher elevations, and the sheep, which had stripped the lower fields bare, were now happily foraging on the higher ground, discovering the first tender shoots of grass under the edges of the melting snow. In a week or two Angus and the other men would start repairing the lambing sheds. The thought made Christina smile, because, for her, the lambing sheds were the sign that spring had truly come, even though the weather was still cold. She strode across the hills expertly checking the sheep and making note of their number. The animals were gray, heavy, and matted from the cold winter, and they moved slowly.

Angus had been amazed when four years ago Christina, then twelve, had begged to take the afternoon watches in the sheep field. He had given his permission reluctantly, only because her cousin Jeremy, Johnny's son, had the grippe, leaving them shorthanded. When Angus realized that Christina did as good a job as any of the boys, and that, unlike them, she never complained about the chore, he had begun to rely upon her. Through the intervening years he had even occasionally boasted of her ability with the animals.

Whenever a guest expressed astonishment over such a young slip of a girl taking responsibility for herding the flock alone, her father would say, "Aye, Christina's a worker! That she is!" Christina flushed at his words. It embarrassed her to have Angus think she tended the sheep because she was a willing worker. "If Papa only knew the truth!" she thought to herself. The truth was that she tended the sheep because she loved the wild, open fields. She delighted in racing with the wind and running with the sheepdogs. It was freedom she craved—freedom, privacy, and the majestic silence of the mountain crags.

One other thing made her love tending the sheep. When her father tramped with her in the fields, on the rare occasions he praised her skills with the flocks and dogs, she felt that she finally had earned his undivided attention and regard. She treasured those brief moments with him and would gladly have spent her life tending the flocks alone for the joy of those precious minutes and affectionate words.

Christina knew her aunts clucked in alarm at her behavior. "She is the willful, impudent daughter of a strangely independent mother," they concluded. "Janeth simply lets her run wild, and Angus has been too burdened with Lucy's illness to take her in hand. Heaven knows what will happen to the child when she grows up! And now Angus is letting her handle the sheep, alone . . . what kind of a way is that to raise a girl!" The aunts would shake their heads and go on with their quilting.

"I don't care!" Christina shouted across the empty field into the knife-sharp wind. "Do you hear me, world? I don't care what anyone thinks!'' She laughed and tore her bonnet from her head, breathing deeply the fresh, cold air.

''I am a wild thing!'' she thought. ''I am never so whole as when I am alone with the wind and the river and my own mad joy!'' Christina laughed aloud again at the thought of having escaped the musty schoolroom for the afternoon, and she ran, slipping on the rough, icy ground until her young body tingled. ''I won't ever be prim and proper like Mary, living like a quiet princess in the Big House! And I won't be kept like a backyard prisoner in the little Garden House with the dreary sound of Mama's loom and the dingy smells of Aunt Sarah's soap making either!''

A year after Sarah Gill had moved into the Garden House to keep Janeth company, Angus had decided that it was his duty to accept responsibility for Sarah and for the raising of her two sons. He had married Sarah, in name only, and had accepted the task of educating her boys. This marriage had given Sarah a secure home and a sense of well-being. Sarah had become a permanent part of Christina's childhood, but there was little affection between the two of them, and Sarah's two sons had left the valley to go on missions while Christina was still a little girl. It had always puzzled Christina, as a child, why she and her mama lived in the Garden House with Aunt Sarah instead of in the Big House with Papa.

''But if Papa is my father, just like he is Mary's, and if you are his wife, like Aunt Lucy, then why do we have to live in the Garden House? Why can't we live in the Big House too?'' she would ask. ''Or why doesn't Papa live with us? Doesn't he like us as much?'' Her mother, without pausing in the rhythm of her weaving, would answer in her uninflected voice that always sounded so impersonal and calm, ''Because the Big House is your father's home, and the Garden House is ours!''

''This is a plain house!'' Christina burst out. ''I don't want to live in the backyard!''

Janeth turned to look at her impassioned daughter, and Christina found her temper fading under her mother's intense eyes. Janeth's eyes always unsettled Christina because she could not tell anything from them. They were so dark it was difficult to see the black pupils, and so her emotions were hard to read. Whenever she could no longer support her mother's steady gaze, Christina would shift her eyes to Janeth's hands. They were capable and beautiful, made soft and white by the lanolin in the wool. Sometimes Christina

135

thought her mother's hands were the only part of her that was truly alive and warm.

"Papa has done the best for you that he can," Janeth said evenly. "You must learn to control yourself, Christina, and accept your life as it is—not as you wish it to be!"

But Christina could not control her strong spirit. Why did these passions shake her like a tempest? Why was she driven by so many unnameable longings? She knew the family was anxious about her since it had become clear she would not outgrow her impetuous, independent ways. Lucy had attempted to teach her knitting, and Hes tried to develop her skills in cooking or caring for children, but the more the aunts tried to change her, the more stubbornly Christina clung to her freedom. She continued to plait her hair in two long, plain braids, instead of wearing it up, as most girls of sixteen did, and she refused to lengthen her ankle skirts or to wear a boned camisole. She would never let them make her grow up to be like all the others—not as long as she could escape to the high meadow and the sheep!

Christina walked along the rock-strewn bank of the river. Its waters were black with cold, and the river churned through its ice-rimmed boulders. Turning from the icy spray at the river's edge, Christina climbed up a low hill that gave her a good vantage point for watching the sheep. The sun was staining the sky with the promise of an early sunset, and the wind, sensing the encroaching night, had increased in vigor.

She leaned against the wind, her body cushioned against its force, and as she felt it rush against her she almost felt she could hear the keening of ancient bagpipes. She stood on tiptoe, her face raised to the mountains, her arms upflung while her clothes whipped against her slender body and her long, auburn hair, torn from its braids, streamed behind her. She felt the wind mingle with her body, and its coldness etched the image of each nerve ending upon her brain, until she could imagine herself a cold, naked statue vibrating in the air. Oh, the glory of it! A primitive goddess worshipping the primal force!

Jeremy had approached the meadow by the back trail. He was breathless when he topped the pasture rim and caught sight of Christina standing on the rise. Her face was turned away from him toward the mountains, and she was standing right where the full blast of the evening wind rushed down from the snow-bound peaks.

"Idiot girl!" Jeremy thought with exasperation. "She'll catch her death! She doesn't have as much sense as the poor dumb animals she's supposed to be tending!'' He walked a few steps farther, but Christina still did not move. ''What in tarnation is she doing on that hill anyway?'' he wondered. ''You'd think she'd be watching somewhat so's she could at least meet me halfway!''

''Christina!'' he yelled, but the wind snatched his voice away and his cousin did not move or respond.

He plodded on, conscious of the chill seeping into his wet feet.

''I'll probably be up here past dark!'' he muttered to himself. ''Prayer meeting is bound to go on longer than usual because of Aunt Lucy being so sick. And when I get home Aunt Hes will probably be mean as hen water because here I come tracking in mud on her clean floor long past suppertime! Probably nobody will save anything hot for me anyway, and Ma's bound to be over at the Big House tending Aunt Lucy. Don't see why Christina couldn't just as well have stayed up here as me! She sure don't seem to mind being here.'' Then he chuckled at a humorous thought. ''She don't seem to mind the sheep either. What is that fool girl doing anyway! If her pa could see her now I don't suppose he'd be so fast to tell all the rest of us what a hard worker she is.''

Jeremy had reached the foot of the hill on which Christina was standing, and he looked up expectantly, thinking she would surely see him now and come down. As he walked closer he was annoyed to observe that her eyes were closed. Her rosy, wind-swept face had a strange glow. Unconsciously, Jeremy stopped moving and stared at his strange cousin. The setting sun, reflecting off the peaks, bathed her in a wash of pure golden light that highlighted the grace and perfection of her slender body. Her forehead, firm and clear, the dark thrust of eyebrows, and the long sweep of black lashes that lay above her high, strong cheekbones, made a sharp contrast to the alabaster skin, the deep red lips, and the firm square chin.

Christina and Jeremy, both children of second wives, had grown up more like brother and sister than cousins. She was as familiar to him as his old worn work boots and he had never even thought of her as pretty or not. To him she was simply Christina. So why, all of a sudden, did he feel such a funny wrench inside of himself as he stood staring at her, and why did his mouth feel dry and that oddly pleasant clutch come to his throat? He felt he was looking at a stranger, a woman whose clothes were molded against her curving body, and he felt both angry and excited, as though Christina were playing some teasing joke. To shrug off the uneasy feeling, he began to run, swiftly and silently, up the hill. When he reached the top he was behind Christina, and he realized she still had not heard his approach, so, on impulse, he grabbed her from behind around the waist and shouted, "Caught ya!"

Christina, lost in the sound of the wind, was taken completely off guard. She screamed in a reflex of fear and fury and brought her arm backward to strike her unseen attacker. Not expecting such a powerful reaction, Jeremy lost his footing on the slippery mud. Still holding Christina tightly around her waist, he fell to the ground, and the cousins rolled, locked together, down the side of the hill. Christina was pounding and flailing and Jeremy held on to her for dear life. Skirts, petticoats, boots, coattails, lunch pail, gloves, and scarves tangled together and scattered as the two of them stopped with a thump at the bottom of the hill. Christina sat up, her eyes blazing, her hair blowing across her face, and her dress and jacket streaked with mud. "Jem!" she yelled, pounding him. "What do you think you're doing? You nit! You . . . !"

Jeremy grabbed her arm and shielded his face from her blows. "I'm sorry!" he shouted, half laughing, half angry. She pulled herself from his grasp and was preparing to hit him again when she caught his eyes looking at her with a grim challenge. "Just try it!" Jeremy growled. "Hit me one more time, and I'll forget you're a girl!" Her face was streaked with dirt, her jaw squared and menacing, and her tiny fist was clenched, but as he looked at her, the sight was too much for him, and he started to laugh. His clear-blue eyes filled with merriment and he rolled onto his back and gave himself up to laughing.

Christina continued to glare at him, but in a few seconds his humor infected her, and she too fell backward laughing with him. The sheep drifted near them to stand in a quiet circle, staring blankly at the two young people rolling on the ground in helpless amusement. The sheep's bland expressions added to the absurdity of the situation, and the cousins laughed until the tears ran down their faces.

"What do you suppose those poor dumb sheep are thinking?" Christina gasped.

"They probably think we're the ones who need tending!" he answered, wiping his eyes with a muddy fist and sitting up. "I tell you, Christina, if what you were doing when I got here was tending sheep, they might as well tend themselves!"

Christina blushed furiously and jumped to her feet. "I thought I was alone!" she hissed. "You had no call to come spying!" She began shaking and brushing her muddy skirts. "Why don't you grow up, Jem!" She was angry again. "That was such a fool thing to do—sneaking up on me. I'll never get clean, and Mama is going to be so—"

"Oh, my gosh!" Jeremy leaped up abruptly. "Your mama! I clean forgot what I came for! Your mama says you are to hurry home as fast as butter to help Aunt Sarah finish the laundry. You best hurry if you want to get down off the mountain before dark."

"Why do they need me?" Christina protested. "Mama's there to help Aunt Sarah."

"It's Aunt Lucy," Jeremy answered, his eyes solemn. "She's taken a turn for the worse. Your mama will be nursing at the Big House tonight."

"Oh, Jem!" Christina exclaimed, snatching her trampled shawl off the ground and throwing it around her head. "Why didn't you tell me right off? I shall be late, and Mama will be angry! Poor Aunt Lucy!" As Christina talked she dashed about picking up her scattered belongings, and then, with a final shake of her heavy woolen skirt, she tore headlong down the path leading back to town. She was still scolding Jeremy as she hurried away, her skirts flapping and her small, boot-shod feet stepping surely across the rugged field. "Boys!" was the last word Jeremy could hear distinctly, and she said it with such disgust that he grinned and scratched his head in wonder at the fierceness of his unpredictable cousin.

The sheep were restless, and Jeremy decided he would start a small fire and watch them from the top of the hill where Christina had been standing. The first blue light of twilight was obscuring the mountains. Jeremy suddenly thought of Christina as he had seen her standing in the wind, and he smiled at the jumbled memory of her in his arms as they rolled down the hill. Giving a wild, Indian whoop of joy, he bounded across the field, scattering the placid sheep before him like white cotton tumbleweed.

It was dark when Christina pulled open the back door of the Garden House and stepped onto the mud porch. She pulled off her shawl and jacket quickly and took off her mud-stained boots. The night air blew through the cracks in the floorboards and made her shiver. With a last despairing look at her skirt, she drew a deep breath and opened the door that led into the lamplit kitchen.

The kitchen was moist and steamy, as it often was, since Sarah made soap for all the McElin families. Occasionally Sarah also did the laundry for the other families, especially in the winter when much of the drying had to be done indoors. Today the kitchen was hung with criss-crossed lines on which diapers and flannel shirts were drying. A clotheshorse in front of the open oven held heavy work pants, and on the black iron stove the hot copper wash kettle glowed, still boiling white blouses, aprons, and baby linens. On the table, Christina could see stacks of freshly ironed sheets. Flat irons were heating on the side of the stove, and starched blouses and petticoats were rolled up in a basket waiting to be ironed.

Sarah, with her weary, pinched face, was standing by the stove stirring a small stew pot. Looking at her, Christina could not help thinking how old she appeared. Christina knew that Sarah was about the same age as her mother, Janeth, and yet Sarah looked at least ten years older.

Janeth was just entering the kitchen from the back stairs. She was wearing a dark homespun cloak and carrying her medicine bag. Christina's mother was not one to make a fuss over other people. She did not like to go visiting, or entertain, but let someone become ill—adult or child—and Janeth, quietly and efficiently, would appear at the bedside. As soon as Janeth appeared, the sufferer would feel a sense of calm relief. Janeth had a quiet, authoritative way in the sickroom. With never a wasted motion she would firm the sheets, clean and dress the patient, diagnose the illness, and, from her store of precious herbs and medicinal preparations, she would administer healing and pain-relieving potions.

Janeth scarcely glanced at her, but Christina knew that in that quick glance her mother had taken in the mud-stained skirt, the wild hair, and wind-reddened cheeks. However, her mother asked no questions. It was not her way to scold or get angry, any more than it was her way to smile or to give praise.

"Is Aunt Lucy really bad, Mama?" Christina asked, her voice trembling. "Is she going to . . . ?" She couldn't say the word "die" so she stumbled on. "Jeremy said the priesthood is holding a special prayer meeting for all the men tonight. Will Papa stay with Aunt Lucy or go to the meeting?"

Without answering immediately, Janeth walked over to the kitchen door and put on her outside boots, which were warming by the stove. "I've been sent for," she said. "That is all I can say."

As Janeth moved toward the outside door, Sarah spoke. "Give Lucy my love, Janeth," she said softly.

"I will," Janeth replied. "You try to get some rest, Sarah. You

140

have put in a long day. Christina is here now, and she can take care of finishing up. I have confidence in her.''

Christina could scarcely believe her ears. Had her mother really said those words? Talked about her as though she were a grown woman? If Janeth told Sarah she could trust Christina, then Janeth meant it—because she never said anything she didn't mean. Maybe she did approve of her after all. Christina's heart sang as she picked up the flat iron and set to work on Sarah's Sunday blouse.

It was colder outside than Janeth had expected as she tramped across the frozen mud between the Garden House and the Big House. She could see the shadow of the Big House in front of her, with only a few lights shining in the downstairs windows. From down the street, on the icy wind, the sound of the men's voices was carried from the church as they sang an opening hymn. In the darkness Janeth switched the medicine bag to her other hand and thought how ironic it was that Lucy had sent for her—had begged her to come—after all the years of bitter jealousy and painful stress between them.

In the darkness, Janeth felt the years roll away, and she remembered with fresh pain the moment when Lucy had discovered the news of her and Angus's marriage. For a minute, all the hard-won accommodations and adjustments, the iron control and numbed pain, were swept away, and Janeth felt again the old sharp pity for Lucy and her own tearing anguish as she saw Angus turn away from her in remorse and guilt.

Unable to give Janeth love, or the warmth of a true marriage, Angus had expiated his guilt by sending for the finest textbooks for her botanical studies. She had begun her search for plants because of her interest in dyes and in concocting preparations for the cleansing of wool, the hutching of flax, or the bleaching of cotton. As she searched her books, however, she began to take an interest in the medicinal purposes of the plants she'd collected. Almost without conscious thought, she began to collect. . . .

In the summer when Christina was seven, the little girl had begged to stay at Johnny's house for the summer. Hes had been willing, so Janeth had spent that entire summer studying the medicinal herbs. That was also the summer when, high in the mountains above the Virgin Cascade, on a plant-gathering foray, she had met Gabriel Martin. Janeth supposed that if she had not met Gabe, she would not have been called to nurse Lucy tonight. ''Strange,''

Janeth thought, "how life goes in circles and patterns, one inside of the other!"

"Gabriel—Gabe!—another name from the past, and what emotions does that name bring?" She could not think of it, not now! Besides, it was all so long ago. All of it . . . so long ago . . . and Lucy was waiting . . . perhaps in pain. Janeth prayed she would be able to help. She had caused Lucy enough pain for one lifetime. It would be a great blessing if now she might be able to relieve some of it for her. With that thought Janeth hurried into the Big House to see what could be done for the dying woman.

Later that night Janeth wearily settled herself in the armchair beside Lucy's daybed in the parlor of the Big House. Angus had brought Lucy to lie in the front room to save those who were nursing her the climb up the steep steps from the kitchen to the bedroom. The Franklin stove in the parlor kept the room warm and, even though the night was chill, Janeth had removed her woolen shawl and put on a white, starched apron. She had fixed Lucy's sheets and had administered a soothing syrup that had calmed Lucy's racking cough and had made her drowsy. Now, as the night pressed on, Janeth sat like a silent sentinel warding off death. Tonight she knew that all she could do was watch and care as the shadowed wings across Lucy seemed to hover and deepen. The Messenger, more silent even than she, would come this time to claim his own.

Still Janeth would not give in, and she sat, untiringly watching for the smallest flicker of hope. Lucy coughed and Janeth heard the heavy fluid that filled the sick woman's lungs. There was the sound of uneven, labored breathing, a weak moan, and Lucy's eyes fluttered open while her hand trembled weakly, groping on the white coverlet. Janeth reached forward and took Lucy's wasted, birdlike hand in her own.

"It's you, Janeth," Lucy whispered, without looking at her. "I could tell, I feel better."

"I just tidied you up a bit," Janeth whispered. "That's all."

Another coughing fit seized Lucy and Janeth put an arm behind her to raise her until the paroxysm passed. Lucy's face contorted with pain, but she did not cry out.

Janeth turned to the small bedside table and poured some liquid from a vial. "Sip this," she murmured. "It will ease the hurt."

Obediently, Lucy swallowed the draught, and then sank back against the pillows and closed her eyes. She was not asleep, and, in a minute she began talking, her words slurred and vague. Janeth leaned forward. "Hush!" she whispered. "You must not waste your strength."

A ghost of a smile touched Lucy's pale face. "Nothing to save it for!" she whispered, but her voice became a little stronger. "I only have one thing left to do to prepare to meet my Maker." Lucy took a long shuddering breath. "I need to repent of you, Janeth."

Janeth said nothing, but her black eyes clouded and she looked quickly away from Lucy's face, as though she did not want to hear more.

"I hated you at first." Lucy's eyes were closed and beads of perspiration gathered on her brow from the exertion of remembering and speaking of her old emotions. Janeth bent over the bed and straightened the covers.

"No more talk," she said firmly. "Sleep!"

"No!" whispered Lucy fiercely. "You must let me say these things!" Her breathing became quicker and more shallow. "I hated you, I wanted you dead—or at least I wanted you not to exist. Then, since I knew you had to stay, I pretended as though you didn't exist—in my own mind, you see—I pretended you weren't real. You were so quiet and it was easy to shut you out! I did it—we all did it—we shut you out—except when we needed you—and then you were always there. The cloth you made, the herbs you gathered, the sick you tended." Lucy's lips were trembling and tears hung on her lashes. "We took it all—everything you gave us—but never you, Janeth. And now, too late, I repent of that with all my heart."

Janeth rinsed a cloth in a warm bowl of water and gently wiped Lucy's brow. "No more!" she admonished. "Those are all old things now. I don't carry them in my heart—and you must not let them weigh on yours. Please, Lucy, rest. Rest and forget! Angus is asleep in the next room. Would you like him to be here with you? I'll go wake him. . . ."

"No!" Lucy said peevishly. "Stay with me, Janeth! Nobody else makes me comfortable. Min was here all day, but she's no use in a sickroom! 'Clumsy' and 'cheerful' makes the worst nurse in the world!" Lucy gave a dry chuckle, but it turned into another coughing spell. When she finished the spasm, Janeth could see that Lucy was noticeably weaker.

"I think I will get Angus, anyway," Janeth said, and gently extricated her hand from Lucy's. This time Lucy made no protest and, as Janeth moved toward the door she heard Lucy, half delirious, muttering to herself.

"But the covenant wasn't easy! The hardest thing the Lord ever asked of a woman. I wasn't prepared, you see. Angus should have told me. I was so happy to see him after all those months! And then you were there . . ." She trailed off into senseless syllables. "Never easy. I tried—no, I didn't try!" As Janeth reached the door the dying woman's voice raised in a wail. "I didn't want to try." She drew a long, hard, rasping breath. "That's what the Lord knows—I didn't want to even try!" She began to weep, and Janeth flung open the connecting door to the family parlor.

"Angus!" she called. "You had best come quickly!"

In the dark room, Angus jumped up from a deep couch and sprang to the door. Without a word he brushed past Janeth and rushed to Lucy's bed. He knelt beside the bed and put his arms around the weak, hysterical woman.

"What is it?" he asked, looking at Janeth anxiously. "What's wrong with her?"

"She needs comfort," Janeth said simply. "The end is very close."

Angus turned to Lucy and tenderly stroked her hair, holding her closely in his arms. " 'Tis all right, Lucy. 'Tis all right," he whispered. "The Lord is your shepherd, you shall not want."

Angus's tender, solemn voice was the only sound in the darkened room. He finished the verse but remained kneeling beside the bed, cradling Lucy's body in his arms. Janeth had not moved from where she stood in the shadows by the parlor door, but, watching, she detected the very moment when the fragile body grew still in his arms. He gently placed Lucy back on the snow-white pillowcase and looked at her face for a moment, then carefully closed her eyes. He raised himself slowly to his feet, and, although his back remained straight, he bowed his head. Janeth knew he was praying, and she bowed her own head in silent prayer.

When she had finished her prayer, Janeth opened her eyes. She yearned to go to Angus, to put her strong arms around his shoulders and to hold his grieving head upon her breast, but she knew he would not accept her comfort and so she remained silently by the door waiting for him to speak. Angus was looking at Lucy's face, which was sweet and almost young-looking in death. "She was a good woman, Janeth," he said.

"Shall I call the others?" Janeth asked softly.

"Nay," Angus replied without turning to look at her. "Leave me alone with Lucy for half an hour. Then you and Min can prepare the body. I will wake wee Mary myself to tell her about her mother's passing. Do not wake Sarah. She is not well herself and needs her sleep. The morning will suffice."

With one last look at Angus's stern, sorrowing figure, Janeth left the room to do his bidding.

On the day in early April when Lucy McElin was buried, the sky was blue and cloudless and the majestic mountains seemed so close that they could be touched by a reach of the hand. The valley was filled with the pleasant sounds of trickling water and rushing streams, as the snow melted from the highlands and the fields around the town of Pleasantville blushed green beneath the warming sun.

Since early morning a steady stream of buckboards, wagons, carriages, and horsemen had been moving slowly toward the center of Pleasantview from the settlements surrounding the valley. Erastus Peterson had come from Salt Lake City to speak at Lucy's funeral and to represent the officers of the Church. The local church leaders were sitting in their stiff black suits behind the podium, their shirt fronts so startling white that their faces stood out in bold relief, like painted portraits.

Music from the old pump organ swelled out as Jeremy and his brothers and sisters followed his father, Johnny, his father's first wife, Hes, and his own mother, Min, into the meeting house and up the aisle to their seats. Across from Jem, on the opposite bench, were Zina and Matty, who had just arrived from St. George where they were building a winter home. With them were their oldest son, Samuel, and his new wife Anna. On the front row Angus McElin sat with his daughter Mary, who had come home from school in Salt Lake when she heard her mother was dying. Mary wore a small black bonnet that hid her profile, and her black-gloved hands were clenched in her lap holding a crumpled handkerchief.

In the front row on the opposite side, Janeth, Christina, and Sarah sat together. Christina had pinned her hair up in a neat bun, and the style made her look older.

Just then the opening hymn began. Christina loved the slow, sad melody and joined in with her sweet young voice. She loved the last verse: "Truth is reason, Truth eternal, tells me I've a mother there." She wondered if her heavenly mother would be anything like her Aunt Lucy, and, at the thought, she remembered, as vividly as

145

though Lucy were standing beside her, the sweet dignified smile, the light fragrance of lavender soap, and Lucy's cultivated English voice as she read from Dickens or Shakespeare on the long winter nights when the families gathered in the Big House. Christina wanted to cry, but she knew Mary would be angry if she did because it was Mary's mother's funeral, and Mary wouldn't think Christina had any right to be sad. Mary didn't think Christina had a right to any part of her life. She got to live in the Big House with Angus, and she acted as though their father was hers and hers alone.

Sometimes it seemed to Christina that she and Mary could not love one another because they were both so afraid. Each of them struggled desperately to prove who Angus loved best. If Christina forced herself to think fairly and unemotionally, she had to admit that he always tried to be impartial. He never gave one of his daughters a gift without giving the other one something as well. It wasn't his fault that no matter what gift he gave Mary, it immediately became the one Christina wanted.

Once, at some imagined slight, Christina had run home to the Garden House and slammed the door in fury. Her mother was sitting at the loom weaving, and Christina had stood in front of her in a storm of weeping.

"I hate Papa!" she had shouted. "He is never fair! Never!"

In all of her life that was the only time Christina had ever seen her mother angry. Janeth strode from the loom and snatched Christina up onto a high chair so that their faces were even. She had gripped Christina's arm firmly, and, looking full in her face, she exclaimed in a voice shaking with intensity, "You are never to speak of your father like that, do you hear me, Christina! He is your father, and he loves and cares for you, and if I ever hear you speak of him disrespectfully again I shall . . ." Janeth was trembling with anger, but she took a deep breath and loosened her grip on Christina's arm. "I shall hear my heart break," she whispered, finishing the sentence. Then she returned to the loom and began throwing the shuttle again with controlled rhythm.

The incident had surprised Christina because it was so unlike her mother. She was silent for a moment, but then her indignation got the best of her and she muttered sullenly, "Well, he isn't fair!"

Janeth looked up, her face calm and composed once again. "If life were 'fair,' Christina, we should all have to be identical—we would have to wear the same clothes, eat the same foods, live in the same houses. Everyone would have to think, feel, and look like everyone else. 'Fair' is just a fancy word for 'same.' The Lord gave us the opportunity to be ourselves. You are smart enough to know that, while some of the things you have are not as nice as other children's, you also have many things which others would envy. 'Fair' would have to take both away—not just the things you want that others have, but the things you have that others might want. Do you understand what I am saying? Do not waste your time worrying about 'fair.' And do not compare your life to the lives of others.''

Christina was fascinated by her mother's long speech. In Christina's memory, never before had Janeth said so much at one time, and she was stunned and puzzled by the strange ideas and the unexpected burst of words.

Now with a sideward glance Christina looked up at her mother, who was sitting beside her in the chapel, her dark head bowed and her face solemn with sorrow. They both looked up as the visitor from Salt Lake, Elder Peterson, began to speak, and Christina's mind returned to the present.

"I bring the love and concern of all the brethren in Salt Lake to you, my dear brothers and sisters," Elder Peterson began, "President John Taylor," he continued, "as you know, remains in hiding during this period of cruel persecution. Throughout Utah the leaders of the Church are being hunted by marshals and arrested for plural marriage. However, the president is in constant touch with the organization of the Church and all is well. I will assure you over and over again," Elder Peterson reiterated, "all is well!"

He turned his compassionate eyes toward Angus, who was sitting straight and dignified on the front pew. "And to you, Brother McElin, I bring the same message. Sister McElin is not dead, but sleeping. All is well. She has been removed from those who love her but for a short time, and right now she is with those who have gone before us. You, my dear brother, are called to continue your work here upon this earth until the Lord, in His own wisdom, calls you and you will be reunited for time and all eternity with this good and gracious woman. All is well!" Elder Peterson's voice thundered across the chapel, and Christina felt her spirits lift.

After the funeral and the procession to the small cemetery plot on the hills outside Pleasantview, Angus and his two brothers met with Elder Peterson for a few minutes in the parlor of the Big House.

Matty put his arm around Angus's shoulder. "It's good to be back in Pleasantview, Angus," he said. "I am just sorry such a sad occasion brought me here.''

"Aye," Angus responded. "We miss you in the winter, Matty, but you have a mighty work to do among the Indians and you are needed in St. George. You have trained young Samuel well, and he is doing a fine job of caring for your property and the sheep while you are away."

Elder Peterson was standing in the parlor dressed in his traveling clothes, preparing to take his leave. "I have a long journey today, gentlemen. Brother Parker, my traveling companion, and I are going to Manti to see about furthering the work of the temple building there. Within two years we hope to dedicate the Manti Temple!"

" 'Tis a miracle!" Uncle Johnny exclaimed. "When I think of the emptiness of this land when we first saw it—and now . . . we may need to worry that it will become too crowded!"

"But it is filled with the children of Zion," Angus said, half smiling at his younger brother. "There can never be too many of them."

"No! Not all children of Zion!" Elder Peterson responded soberly. "That is what I must speak to you about. In Salt Lake more and more we are threatened by those who wish to destroy us. We have fled so far to escape persecution, but our enemies will not let us rest. As you know, Congress has passed the Edmunds Bill, which disenfranchises every member who practices plural marriage. We have challenged the bill in the courts, and poor Brother Reynolds, who volunteered to stand for the trial, has now been sentenced to hard labor and a crippling fine, even though he was acquitted by the first court. The federal marshals are tracking down every influential member of the Church hoping to trap them with evidence of plural marriage. We struggle to live within the law, taking our grievance to the proper courts and legislatures, but all we meet is a wall of prejudice and hate."

Angus's face clouded. "It was a hard day for the Church when the Lord gave us the covenant of plural marriage. Does the world not know that only a small percentage of the Church is called to practice the law—and then only if there is a divine purpose?"

"You can't explain to people who live in cities what it is like to live in an isolated wilderness. We are wilderness people among whom the marriageable women have always outnumbered the marriageable men. Plural marriage was God's solution, but how can you tell that to men sitting in the marble comforts of Washington?" Elder Peterson thundered.

"How will it end?" Matty asked. "We are a law-abiding people.

148

It puts us in an impossible position when we must choose between the law of the land and the law of God.''

Elder Peterson shook his head sadly. "There is no solution, and only the Lord can tell us what to do. And I'm afraid I bring two further pieces of bad news. President Taylor is not well. The terrible strains of staying in hiding and the physical discomforts of being pursued are beginning to tax him. The other thing that causes us disquiet is the proposal of a new bill in Congress that stipulates that all organizations practicing polygamy—which is as much as to specify the Church—will be unable to own property or have any legal rights whatsoever.''

"You mean," Johnny exclaimed, "they will confiscate all of our churches, our temples, meeting houses, businesses, the Immigration Funds—everything that is owned by the Church! What will we do?''

Elder Peterson sighed, and his face showed the strains of his years of service to the Lord. "The Lord will provide the answers, brethren,'' he said. "But only, I am afraid, after the most bitter trials of our faith.'' He smiled then, and, for a moment, he looked like an Old Testament prophet. "The irony is that we continue to grow. The more they persecute us, the more the converts flood into the valleys. Our troubles seem to nurture growth, and Zion is flourishing!''

The women had prepared a sumptuous buffet. After their conference the men ate heartily, but quickly, and then walked out to see Elder Peterson and his companion on their way.

"May you go in safety," Angus said. "On behalf of my family, I thank you for coming today.''

Elder Peterson put his hand on Angus's elbow and led him out of the earshot of the others. "Brother McElin, before I go, I must give you a private warning. Your isolation in this valley will not save you from the federal marshals. They are scouring every corner of the territory, and you, as the leader of this community, are known to have more than one wife. They will arrest your wives and daughters, and, if they will not testify against you in open court, they will be put in prison as well. If they do testify, you will be placed in a federal penitentiary, possibly for the remainder of your life.''

Angus's proud, strong face darkened with rage. "How can they do such a thing? My marriages were not against American law when I contracted them.'' He took a deep breath and muttered, "It is a rank injustice, but we shall prepare for it.''

Elder Peterson mounted his horse, and the men clasped hands in a warm gesture of farewell. The elder and his companion galloped off over the rough road toward the western pass.

Angus walked back toward the house grappling with the shock of the news. His mind leaped ahead and searched for solutions and contingency plans for his coming flight. As he mounted the stairs he stopped, sighed, and shook his head. "Not even time for mourning!" he thought sadly.

Chapter Eight

Matty and Zina left for St. George soon after the funeral, and things began to return to normal. The spring lamb crop was abundant and the pastures were luxuriant with new growth. The women of Pleasantview busied themselves in their kitchen gardens and set out flowerbeds around their houses. At recess time voices from the schoolyard sprinkled the air with laughter as the children played and ran in the newly minted sun.

Above the town, on the high sheep trail, Christina and Mary walked toward the mountain pasture. Min had asked them to take a lunch pail up to Jeremy, who was tending the flock, and the half-sisters had seized the opportunity to spend the morning in the mountains instead of working with their aunts. To Mary the Big House, without her mother's presence, seemed gloomy and empty, and although she felt great sorrow at her mother's death and pity for her lonely father, she nonetheless was chafing to get back to Salt Lake City and the excitement of her music school and friends. In comparison, Pleasantview seemed like a muddy, backward village, and now that she had seen the gracious, elegant mansions on South Temple Street in Salt Lake, the Big House, which had once given her so much pride, seemed scarcely more than a large farmhouse. Thinking such thoughts made Mary feel disloyal and ungrateful, but it also gave her an exhilarating feeling of superiority over the other members of her family who had never been outside the Virgin

Valley, particularly Christina, whom she considered an unpolished, countrified girl.

Mary had always been secretly jealous of Christina. It seemed to her that everything had come easily for Christina, even music lessons! When Lucy could entice Christina to sit at the piano, the girl would accomplish more in a few minutes than Mary could learn in hours of practice. Many a time Mary had heard her mother say to Angus, "If Christina could only be taught some discipline she could be a brilliant student—and an excellent musician. Janeth is too lenient with her, and so are you, Angus!"

Mary could still remember the sick feeling it gave her when her mother and father said nice things about Christina, and she wanted to shout, "Don't talk about her! Talk about me! Say that I am brilliant!"

But Lucy and Angus said other things about Mary: "What a good girl you are, Mary!" "Such a hard worker!" "Such a good example!"

Mary had always known that in some strange and undefined way, Christina was a threat to her. She both feared and admired her younger sister. Christina was like a sore tooth. Mary could not ignore her but had to keep probing and prodding her feelings for her, no matter how much it hurt, aware that, in some way, the fact of Christina's existence touched everything in her own life.

As Mary plodded up the hill she looked at her sister: Christina's brown homespun dress was too short above her boot-tops and her wild mass of red hair curled down her back, blowing wantonly in the wind. Suddenly Mary saw Christina clearly as someone she would be ashamed to know in the stately drawing rooms of Salt Lake society. The thought gave Mary secret pleasure and let her feel a tiny rush of pity and love for Christina.

"So what's it like in Salt Lake, Mary?" Christina shouted over her shoulder as she scrambled up the rocky path. "How do you like it?"

"Slow down, Christina!" Mary puffed. "You needn't show off how much faster you can climb than I! I have no desire to compete!"

Christina flushed with quick anger. "I wasn't trying to compete!" she answered indignantly. "Why don't you lead the way then? You can set whatever pace suits you!"

Christina stood aside on the narrow trail and Mary squeezed past her. "Very well," Mary said serenely, "I shall be glad to lead."

Christina fought down a sudden flush of anger that darkened her cheeks and forced herself to plod silently behind Mary. "Keep remembering that Mary is leaving soon!'' she told herself. ''She's only here for a short visit! Don't spoil it!'' With all her heart Christina wished she could find a way to establish a better relationship with her sister.

It was getting hot on the mountain trail, and Christina, impatient at the slow pace set by Mary, stared at her sister's back. ''She walks just like her mother!'' Christina thought. Mary's back was as straight as a ramrod; her high-held head and thin body were stiff as her feet took small, brisk steps. After a few minutes Christina, who had walked off her temper, could tell that Mary, out of pride, had set a pace faster than she could maintain. She felt sorry for her tiring sister and so she called out, ''Could we stop to rest for a minute, Mary? I think I've got a stone in my boot.''

Without a word, Mary left the path and sat down primly under a small pine tree. ''Very well!'' she said breathily, her thin chest heaving. There was a dew of perspiration on Mary's brow, and her dark hair had blown loose from its tight bun. ''She almost looks human!'' Christina thought with a hidden smile.

Mary gave her sister a surreptitious glance and then smiled too. ''Sorry I've been such a cross companion. This is more of a climb than I remembered,'' she admitted awkwardly.

Christina shrugged good-naturedly and threw herself down on the grass beside Mary. ''So, answer my question! How is Salt Lake? Don't you get dreadfully homesick?''

''Oh, no!'' Mary answered eagerly. ''I mean, it isn't that I don't love home and Pleasantview, it's just that . . . oh, Christina, Salt Lake is so wonderful! All the concerts, the beautiful clothes, the parties and dances and visitors from all around the world. You can't imagine what it is like to walk through the mercantile store and see the furniture from England, clothes from New York, shoes from London. It's . . . well, you just can't know unless you've seen it!''

Without meaning to, Mary had allowed a note of superiority to creep into her voice, and Christina could feel her face burning. There was a moment of strained silence as Mary became aware of the insensitivity of her comments. ''How—how has school been this year?'' she asked, trying hard to sound natural.

''Oh, all right,'' Christina answered reluctantly. ''Pretty much the same as when you left, I reckon.''

''Well, you'll graduate this year,'' Mary said with false cheer. ''What does Papa say you are to do then?''

''Nothing,'' Christina answered dully. ''He probably hasn't even thought about it. Your mama was sick for so long and we were all so worried—Papa hasn't thought about much else all year." Christina struggled to change the conversation. "How are your music studies coming?" she asked.

Mary was off again, talking about her choir, the organ lessons, and music theory. Her professors, as she described them, were all brilliant and handsome and her friends were clever and gifted. As she talked Christina watched her, noticing the unconscious manner-isms of refinement and big-city sophistication Mary had picked up. No one watching would have guessed that the two girls were sisters. Mary with her jet-black, smooth hair and her narrow face with straight clear-cut features would have been quite beautiful except that her dark-brown eyes were set a trifle too close; they gave her face a pinched, serious look. She was tall and slender, and with her erect carriage and striking coloring she attracted a great deal of admiration.

Christina envied her sister's commanding presence. Christina had inherited the vivid blue eyes of her father and her Grandmother McElin's dark-red, naturally curly hair. Her skin was rosy and fair, but, as she was forever losing her sunbonnet, the long hours in the sheep fields had tanned her face and brought bright color to her cheeks. She was smaller than Mary, shorter, with a tiny waist and budding bosom, but her body was lithe and fit. Sometimes she wondered if she would ever be able to school her quick, impulsive feet to walk slowly and gracefully as a lady should.

Mary was humming in the afternoon air, and Christina lay back, half listening, watching the clouds playing near the summit of the nearest mountain.

". . . he is just the best-looking man in the whole city!" Mary was saying.

"Who is?" Christina asked lazily, bringing her wandering mind back to Mary.

"Oh! You haven't heard a word I've said!" Mary exclaimed petulantly.

"Yes, I have, honest!" Christina replied. "I just dozed off for a moment. It's so warm here, and I was tired from the walk. Please tell me! Who's the best-looking man—"

"Peter! Peter Saunderson. I told you he danced with me twice at Aunt Hattie's social last month." Aunt Hattie was Hes's younger sister. She had married a well-to-do store owner in Salt Lake City and had raised her family there. When Mary turned sixteen Hattie

153

had invited her to come spend the winter in Salt Lake City and to attend the music academy there. Lucy, knowing she was not well, had felt it a great blessing for her daughter to be cared for during that difficult winter.

"Peter Saunderson?" Christina drawled out the name. "He doesn't sound handsome! He doesn't even sound Mormon!"

"That's all you know, Christina!" Mary retorted hotly. "His folks were converted and came to Utah from Sweden even before our family got here. Peter was born in the Utah Territory same as us! As a matter of fact, his people live over in Nephi!"

"Then what's he doing in Salt Lake?" Christina asked.

"Well!" Mary's voice dropped conspiratorially. "He hasn't been there very long, really. He's been working in Uncle Seth's store while he decides what he wants to do. His folks want him to enroll in the university. He lives with his uncle who's a doctor in Salt Lake—"

"You sure seem to know a lot about this young man," Christina exclaimed with a touch of raillery in her voice.

"He's so exciting to listen to," Mary went on, oblivious to her sister's teasing. "He's done more things than you could imagine! Two years ago he went with a sheep-shearing crew all the way up to the Canadian border. He even spent two weeks in a Blackfoot Indian camp! I declare, I don't think he's afraid of anything!"

"So he woos you with tales of adventure, does he?" Christina asked, rolling over on her stomach and chewing a long blade of barley grass.

"As a matter of fact, Peter doesn't talk very much about himself," she went on. "I've learned most of the things I know about him from listening to Aunt Hattie and Uncle Seth talk. I gather his parents are a little worried about him. He's over twenty, and he doesn't seem to want to settle down. I guess he's considered, oh, you know, a little—wild. But I think it's just because he wants to enjoy himself, and when the right person comes along . . ." Mary bowed her head, and a little pink flush tinged her pale ivory skin. "I think the right person would be able to make him settle down.

"Oh, Christina!" Mary turned to her sister with her eyes glowing. "He is so handsome! Tall, blond, with the whitest, straightest teeth and the bluest eyes!"

"Yuck!" Christina groaned. "That is the worst description I have ever heard. It sounds like something you read in a novel!"

154

"That does it!" Mary scrambled to her feet. "I won't talk about him to you anymore! What do you know about such things anyway!"

With a flounce of her black mourning skirt, Mary set off at a brisk pace up the hill, and Christina, half sorry but chuckling over her sister's discomfiture, followed quickly behind.

Two weeks later Angus called a family council in the parlor of the Big House. Mary had not yet returned to Salt Lake, and Janeth, Christina, and Sarah were all present.

"I have been informed that the federal marshal entered Manti yesterday and is in the process of arresting several Church officials there. We must move to protect ourselves. Since we will not break the law, nor perjure ourselves, we must avoid the possibility of arrest."

The women looked at one another apprehensively. "I have made the following arrangements," Angus continued. "Mary will leave for Salt Lake immediately. Sarah, I have talked to your brother and he will be happy to have you come to live with him."

Angus turned his eyes to Janeth, and Christina saw a look pass between her father and mother that puzzled and touched her. It was a look of pain and longing. His voice became softer, almost gentle.

"Janeth, you will have to go too. The Taggerts over in Nephi have invited you to stay with them until this terrible time is over. I will escort you there, and then I will go into hiding until the marshal grows weary of his search."

"And Christina?" Janeth asked anxiously.

Angus turned to look at Christina with fondness and concern. "Christina will go to Matty's. Jeremy and Sam will ride with her as far as Manti and then she will take the stagecoach to St. George.

"Christina!" Angus said, speaking to her directly, as though the rest of the family were absent from the room. "I have been giving your future much thought lately. You have become a young woman— and it is time now for you to become a young lady. You need to further your education and your experience. Matty and Zina have extended a most warm invitation to you, and I know there are many fine things to be learned in their home. See that you do so!"

Even though Angus's speech was stern, Christina felt a happy glow. "He's been thinking about me!" she thought to herself. "He didn't forget! He was planning for me all along!"

*   *   *

The next day the men of Pleasantview set off an explosive charge in the hills above the only road through the mountain pass. Heavy boulders cascaded down and closed the pass. Only a few men knew the narrow, hidden trails that were now the only link between the Virgin Valley and the rest of the world.

"That should slow down the marshal," Angus told his brother Johnny. "You needn't fear arrest. I'm told they only have a warrant for me, but, if you do get worried, send Hes and Min to stay with neighbors. Apparently I'm the target, and, if I'm gone, they may leave the rest of you alone.

"Wee Johnny, you will need to run our Church and business affairs while I am gone. I will see that you know where to contact me as soon as I am safely hidden. I am leaving tomorrow to take Janeth to Nephi."

Johnny's compassionate eyes searched his brother's face. Angus seemed to have aged ten years in the past few months. "Angus, would that I could go into hiding for ye, but I will care for your affairs here and nought will suffer if I can help it."

Angus smiled at his brother and plodded away to continue his preparations. Mary had left with two families who were traveling to Salt Lake City shortly before the pass had been closed. The rest of the family would be prepared to leave by the next day, Christina traveling the southward trail over the mountains to Manti and he and Janeth taking the one to the north. After Janeth was safely settled in Nephi, he planned to return in secret to the valley and live in hiding in the mountains surrounding his beloved valley until the marshal and his men gave up their hunt. Then he would bring Janeth home again, and they could live together at last as man and wife.

Christina and Jeremy were in Johnny's barn packing saddlebags for the next day's journey. The luggage was ready for the packhorse, and Hes and Min were finishing up the provisions in the kitchen. Christina knew she should be feeling sad at the thought of leaving her mother and father and the only home she had ever known. Although she did feel a deep vein of sorrow and apprehension, nonetheless, threaded through it was an eager thrill of excitement and joy. The journey tomorrow marked the opening of some unknown door in her life.

"Remember that book by Mr. Dickens that Aunt Lucy read to us last winter, Jem?" Christina asked.

"Umm!" Jeremy grunted, nodding his head but not taking his eyes from the knot he was tying.

"That's just how I feel!" Christina whispered. "It's the 'best of times and the worst of times.' I mean, it's awful to have to leave when everything is so topsy-turvy, and Papa is in danger, and poor Mama and Aunt Sarah have been turned out of house and home. . . . But, oh! Jeremy! It will be such fun at Uncle Matty's and Aunt Zina's! There will be dances and parties, and visits to Indian caves, and the weather in St. George so warm and pleasant. Oh, Jem! I am going to see the world at last!"

"Hmph!" He snorted with derision. "If you call St. George the world, it's a sure sign of how much you don't know. Besides, it seems to me a body should be content with their own home."

"Oh, you're just jealous!" Christina threw at him.

"Am not!" Jeremy answered, his face turning red with anger.

"Are too!" Christina shouted back, making a face.

With an enraged growl he lunged at his cousin, and she, quick as a hare, slipped through the barn door and was halfway across the chicken yard before he began to run. Laughing, she sped across the lawn, past Hes's apple trees and the swing Johnny had built. As light as thistledown, she leaped over the fence and sped across the street. Jeremy followed her but his heart was not in the chase, and he stopped when he reached the fence.

Christina continued running until she reached the back door of the Garden House. She opened the door breathlessly and entered the utility porch; her eyes were sparkling, a mischievous smile on her face. As she entered the porch she noticed an earthenware bowl of buttermilk sitting on the stone-topped dairy table. Christina grabbed an old enamel drinking cup and scooped it into the bowl. She took a long drink and then her neat pink tongue licked the white moustache from her upper lip. She took another long swallow and sat down at the kitchen table. The house seemed different—empty and lifeless. Everything was neat and clean because Sarah and Janeth had scrubbed, dusted, and emptied the cupboards and closets. The huge black stove was cold, and dust motes filtered in the shaft of sunlight that beamed through the crack in the closed gingham curtains.

Christina's smile faded as she realized she was truly saying goodbye to this home, to her childhood, and to her mother and father. Suddenly fear and hurt gripped her and she leaped to her feet and moved lightly toward the back stairs, which led to her mother's room. She didn't know exactly what she wanted, but she felt the need to see her mother, hear her voice, touch her hand, look into her calm, dark eyes.

Christina was almost to the top of the stairs before she realized someone was in the upstairs room with her mother. She paused on the landing and was surprised to hear her father's voice, speaking in a tone so soft it was almost unrecognizable.

"Nay, Janeth, I cannot spend the night here with you. It would not seem right to others—so soon after Lucy's death. It would only create ugly and idle gossip." Her father's voice sounded choked and unnatural. "We must wait at least until we leave the valley." Christina was so shocked and surprised that she stood frozen on the landing. Then another voice, her mother's, but so unlike her mother that she could scarcely believe her ears, spoke on the far side of the room.

"What is not seemly, Angus, is the years that I have waited for you to come here to sleep with me. The nights that I have lain in this bed alone, aching for you—for the sight, the touch, the smell of you. Angus!" Her mother's voice was broken and harsh, filled with a sound of pleading and passion that had no place in Christina's memory. How could her mother—so self-sufficient, controlled, quiet, strong—speak this way? Christina shuddered, not wanting to hear more and yet riveted to the spot.

Her mother was crying now, but the sobs were hard and torn, as though she did not know how to cry and the sounds were ripped from her breast by force. "Is there any love left for us? I have waited these many years and hoped that you were waiting too. Tell me that you still have something left to fill this awful emptiness!"

Her father's voice was stiff with pain. "I do not know what is left. The years have passed. We have fallen into other patterns. I am no longer young."

"Nor am I!" Janeth's voice rose with a furious intensity. "Is that it then? My skin is no longer soft and pink. My hair is touched with gray and my body is heavy with years of labor. Have I nothing left that draws you to me? Nothing but my mind?" She said the last word with a bitter laugh. "My mind does not need you, Angus. It is my body that does."

"Do not say such things!" Angus's voice was a harsh whisper. "It is not right nor womanly, Janeth!"

"Not womanly?" Janeth laughed a low, throaty laugh that shook Christina more than the sound of her mother's sobs. "Is passion not a womanly thing, dear husband? When we lay together under the stars, you did not chide me for being unwomanly then. You drank in my passion, you warmed yourself in the heat of my body, you gloried in the fire of my needs. Oh, Angus, you cannot have forgotten! There must be some remnant left in you of our love! Give me something, if only a crumb . . . before I must leave!'' Again her mother sobbed, and Christina wanted to scream, ''Stop! Stop this ugliness! You are old and my mother!''

But no sound would come to Christina's lips, and in an agony of shame she heard her father walk swiftly across the wooden floor to the side of the room where her mother was standing. In Christina's sickened and heightened perception she could hear every rustle, every nuance of sound, even the whisper and crush of clothing as they embraced. The floorboards creaked beneath them as they rocked in the power of their embrace and then she heard her father's voice, muffled and thick with emotion. ''Janeth! Janeth!'' was all he said. She heard the bedsprings shriek beneath their double weight, as they moved to the bed, and Christina, livid with shock, crept like a thief down the stairs, burst out the back door, and ran into the empty barn, where she threw herself into a straw-filled stall. How could her mother behave in such a way so soon after Aunt Lucy's death? What kind of a woman was she? All Christina knew was that she never wanted to be like her. ''Never!'' she cried to herself over and over again.

Upstairs in Janeth's bedroom, Angus and Janeth sat on the side of the bed. Angus's hand stroked Janeth's hair as she wept against his coat.

''Forgive me, Angus!'' she whispered. ''I think my fear and sorrow have unsettled me. We will be together tomorrow, and after all these years, what is another day?''

Angus held her closely. ''We shall have the time together on the trail, but you cannot turn back the years. You must remember who we are now, Janeth.'' His voice was weary.

''Oh, Angus!'' She turned a tearstained face toward him, and in it he saw the vivid beauty that had touched him so many years ago. ''I have waited so long!'' she whispered, her voice filled with pleading.

He stooped and kissed her brow. ''Finish your packing, and then I will expect you and Christina to join me at the Big House for supper tonight. Tomorrow we will leave at dawn.''

Janeth walked to the window and watched him as he emerged from the door and strode purposefully across the lush lawn to the back porch of the Big House. He still walked with the same powerful grace that she remembered from his younger days. She remained by the window for some time thinking, and then she returned to her baggage and resumed her careful packing.

It was soon twilight, and the quietness of the house made Janeth aware that she had not seen Christina since early afternoon. With a frown of concern, Janeth hurried down the back stairs and out into the yard. All the domestic animals had been removed to Johnny's outbuildings and so the barns and sheds were enveloped in the same eerie silence as the empty house. She felt an unaccountable shiver of apprehension, and with a shade of anxiety in her voice, and much more loudly than she had expected, she shouted, "Christina!" There was no answer, and once again she called.

Just as she turned to hurry across to Johnny's house to see if the girl was there, Janeth heard the door of the stable creak, and Christina came slowly out of the deserted building. Her hair was a tangled mess and straw clung to her rumpled clothing. Her face was white and expressionless and her eyes were pools of ice.

Janeth looked at her daughter but her face betrayed none of her surprise. In her characteristically even voice Janeth murmured, "You had best wash up. We are expected for dinner at the Big House tonight." Christina's eyes flashed for an instant with what—anger? hurt? defiance? Janeth could not tell. Then the eyes became controlled and cold again, and, without a word, Christina brushed past her mother and went into the house.

That night Christina lay on her bed, fully clothed, her thoughts in a furious turmoil. What could have possessed them? In the broad daylight to be talking of such things . . . to be doing such things! What little education Christina had about the relationships of men and women she had learned in church with the thundering and terrifying "Thou shalt nots." Her only other knowledge of sex came from working with animals, from the boys behind the barns smirking and telling awful stories and the older women whispering.

How could her mother desire such things? And her father—so righteous, so unassailable and dignified—how could he be lured into such acts? At some level, she knew the marriage act was necessary. It was the way babies came into the world. But wasn't it a thing to be ashamed of—something to be done in the dark, neatly, quietly, secretly? She wished she could wash the things she had heard out of her mind. Feeling hot and faintly sick, she rolled over and lay face down on the bed, praying for sleep.

Upstairs Janeth moved the last bags from her bed and slowly

160

removed her clothing. The summer air was cool now that the sun had gone down, and she rummaged in her packed cases for a flannel sleeping gown. She slipped the fine-spun garment over her head and, as she was tying the ribbons at her throat, walked over by the window to blow out the lantern. As the room fell dark she glanced out into the night. The rising moon had cast a bright gleam on the face of the tallest mountain that thrust its snow-laden peak above the valley floor. For a moment her gaze was riveted on the shining summit. She did not know whether it was because of her awakened passions, or simply the pain and nostalgia of her impending farewell to this valley, but as she looked at the mountains, thoughts of Gabe came flooding into her mind, and she sank down onto the floor, rested her arm across the windowsill, and leaned her head against the pane. For the first time in many years she let herself think of him. "No harm in remembering now," she thought. "Tomorrow I will be gone from this place forever. Perhaps Angus will never desire me again. Perhaps that part of my life is over. For tonight—just this one more time—I will think of Gabe . . . Gabriel Martin."

Looking across the valley silvered in moonlight, she gave a long sigh and whispered, "Oh, Gabe, where are you now?" Her eyes searched the night, but the dark, mysterious heights of the mountains gave her no answer.

In the summer of Christina's seventh year, Janeth had just begun her study of medicinal botany. She had read extensively in the volumes Angus bought for her, and she recognized an instinctive feeling for plants and for healing within her. Christina had begged to spend that summer at Johnny's. "I will come to see you every day, Mama! But they have such fun at Uncle Johnny's—playing games and laughing in bed at night! Please, Mama, can't I go? Aunt Hes says I will be very welcome!"

Seeing Christina's yearning face—hungry for life, warmth, and the vitality of Johnny's rollicking family—Janeth could not refuse her daughter's request, and so Christina's bags were packed and she had moved into one of the little bedroom wings under the eaves of Johnny's home. Janeth had faced the summer feeling more alone than she could ever remember.

With Spartan determination, Janeth began daily forays into the meadows and mountains. She packed food and a collection box, strapped them over her shoulder, and, with a notebook in her spacious apron pocket, heavy boots to protect her feet, and an old straw, wide-brimmed hat tied under her chin, she tramped the surrounding wilderness, searching for every variety of wild plant. She tasted, tested, boiled, dried, dissected, and catalogued each new discovery—bloodroot, Indian turnip, wild columbine, turtlehead, blue-eyed grass, evening primrose, lupine, cinquefoil, wild rose and strawberry, yellow toadflax, lungwort, harebell, lilium philadelphicum, tawny hawkweed, gentian, sego lily, and honey mesquite.

She learned to find the bulbs and tubers, the delicate pollens, the crushed leaves of the mature flowers, the hard-cased seeds—and from each she learned. Medicinal, pain-killing teas from roots, lily sap for disinfectant, foxglove as a stimulant, monkshood as a powerful opiate, camomile for stomach pain.

Often the night would overtake Janeth as she worked with the day's harvest. If she was too far from home to return in the dark, she would simply unwrap her heavy shawl and build herself a bed of boughs. She had lived a solitary life for so long that few things frightened her, and the iron control she had imposed upon her feelings had made her a woman who accepted the circumstances of each moment without alarm. Angus, however, was concerned about her wanderings. "Why do you not take one of the young boys with you when you go?" he asked with combined irritation and anxiety. "If you feel you must continue your study, then surely you can find one of the young cousins to accompany you!"

Janeth smiled her slow, reasonable smile and in a low, humorous voice replied, "I think perhaps I am better able to take care of myself than a young child could—even if he were a boy, Angus. I am a grown woman, strong and well in command of myself. The Indians have left for their summer camps up north. What do I have to fear?"

Reluctantly, Angus refrained from making any further objections, and Janeth found herself venturing farther into the mountains as the summer progressed. High above the treeline she began to experience the strange spell the high reaches of the Rockies cast upon all who venture into their loftiest peaks. On the windswept meadows, with nothing but blue sky, an occasional crystal cold lake, and the last impassable peaks between her and heaven, she found carpets of wildflowers, untouched since the Lord's hand had scattered them upon the breast of the earth and Adam and Eve had tended them.

Some days, in the thin, cold air, Janeth would stand alone, feeling that she was on the roof of the world and knowing that she had never been so free—never so gloriously her own person.

She almost became a creature of nature. Her hair grew long and sleek, and she wore it in a single braid down her back. Her face became a burnished brown, her eyes clear and sparkling and her body as strong and supple as a sapling bow.

It was on a hot day near the end of June when Janeth first met Gabriel Martin.

She had been climbing in one of the upper canyons of a mountain the Indians called Tokewamna. It was a small mountain, wedged between two massive peaks, but she had often had good luck on its lower slopes where a number of lively streams ran down from a silvery waterfall. Today she had followed a tributary that led her higher into the mountain than she had ever gone before. At the head of the stream she discovered a small jewel of a lake, brimming in a tiny canyon, as though trapped in an emerald cup. Its water spilled over the ledge and trickled down into the rocky stream below. She climbed over the boulders that guarded the access to the tiny plateau on which the lake rested.

All morning she moved happily from one plant to another, sketching, cataloguing, and then, with her specimen fork, lifting the plant, root and all, into her box. About midday she walked down to the edge of the lake and stretched out full length. Hot and thirsty, she plunged her face and hands into the icy cold and drank deeply. Then she propped her chin on her hands and peered into the clear water.

The mountain lake was very deep with no gradual incline into its blue mystery. She could see trout, as clearly as though in a glass, their mottled backs gliding beneath the surface, but underneath them she could see no rocks, no moss, no lake bed, only the water growing bluer and deeper. "The lake must fill a deep crevasse or hole in the face of the mountain caused by some violent eruption from the heart of the planet itself," she thought. Mystified and intrigued, Janeth continued to stare into the water, feeling the awe of someone who has glimpsed powers and forces beyond their ken. The sunwarmed earth beneath her body seemed almost like a living thing, and the breeze that skipped across the surface of the lake cooled her face. She cradled her head on her arms and closed her eyes for an instant.

Although she had not heard a sound Janeth suddenly opened her eyes and, without moving or seeing anything, could tell that she was no longer alone. Very slowly, she raised her head. About five yards from her a man was squatting on his heels, as still as a stag. No hair nor muscle moved, only his eyes, watching her with solemn intensity. It was his likeness to a mountain deer that calmed her fear. When she saw deer she understood she was an intruder, and somehow, as she looked at this man, she again had the feeling that this was more his mountain than hers.

Moving slowly, she got to her feet, her eyes never leaving his face, and he rose as well, so that they stood, separated by the uneven ground but joined by their silent stare.

Afterward Janeth wondered why she had known immediately that he was not an Indian. He was wearing a fringed deerskin shirt, pants and moccasins, his hair was long and black, and his skin was the color of mahogany. On his back was a bow, and in his belt a hunting knife. A long-barreled rifle rested carelessly in the crook of his arm. Still, Janeth did not think for one minute that he was Indian. Somewhere, on some unconscious level of her mind, she must have noted at first sight that his eyes were blue—as blue and clear as the water of the lake.

The intensity of their stare became unnerving, but Janeth still had no idea what to do, so she did nothing. Finally the man broke the silence. He threw back his head and gave a loud bark of laughter. "You aren't a squaw!" he exclaimed in an astounded shout. "No squaw at all. When I first saw you I was convinced you were—that hair, those eyes. But you aren't an Indian woman—there's the smell of civilization about you." He laughed again. "Although I swear I never did see a civilized woman with skin as dark as yours!"

Janeth's face flamed and she snatched her straw hat up from her back where it had slipped and jammed it back onto her head. "My hat keeps falling off!" she exclaimed, her eyes snapping.

"No offense intended, ma'am," the strange man said. "It's been some piece since I've talked to someone from civilization. I reckon I've forgotten how."

He began to walk toward her, and Janeth instinctively drew back. He stopped and faced her, his expression showing that he understood her apprehension. "My name is Gabe. Gabriel Martin. I hope I haven't upset you, ma'am. But I have to say you've given me quite a start myself. I've been coming here for five summers, and you are the first person I have ever seen on this part of the mountain. You aren't in any difficulty are you, ma'am?"

Five years! And no one from the valley had ever seen him or heard of him. Now she understood. Gabriel Martin must be one of the mountain men she had heard Angus and his brothers talk about.

A man who left the civilized world and lived in the wilderness of the vast mountain range. These mountain men existed by hunting and trapping, and they knew the secrets of hidden places as well as the deer and the mountain lions knew their own territory. Sometimes the mountain men married Indian women and took them to live in hidden valleys where their half-breed children played in happy isolation. "What would cause a man to seek such a life?" Janeth wondered. And yet, sometimes when she roamed the high meadows, wasn't she almost willing to forget who and what she was?

Janeth found it hard to catch her voice. "I followed the stream up the canyon," she explained. "I am a plant gatherer—a medicine woman—a . . ." She was speaking slowly, carefully, as though the man were deaf or simple.

Gabriel Martin put back his head and laughed again. "I may look like an Indian, but you don't need to talk to me like one!"

Again Janeth flushed. "I'm sorry," she murmured. "It's just that you are so . . . unexpected . . . and I think I am frightened."

Immediately she felt ridiculous. What kind of a thing was that to say to a total stranger? If he meant her harm such an admission certainly didn't give her any control over the situation.

"I'm from Pleasantview," she stammered, "down in the valley. I was just going to leave to return home. My family is waiting for me. If I am not back soon they will come up the canyon looking for me. As a matter of fact they are probably on their way to join me now."

The man's clear-blue eyes looked through her. "You needn't be afraid" was all he said, but something in his voice, some deep integrity, touched her heart, and she knew his words were true. The fear left her with a rush, and she felt light and clean.

Without speaking, she nodded her head. He turned away from her and went down by the lake. From his pocket he drew a string and hook, which he baited and then dropped into the water. Immobile, he waited, crouching on a rock beside the lake. Suddenly there was a silver splash and the man drew a spangled trout out of the water and threw it on the grass. Five times he repeated the process until there were six shining speckled fish lying beside him.

He cleaned the trout with his knife. Janeth, fascinated, watched as he built a small fire on a flat rock near the lakeshore. With swift hands he fashioned saplings into pointed sticks that he thrust into the ground. He bent the other end of the saplings over the fire with the filets of the trout bound to them.

After a while Gabe beckoned to Janeth, and she picked up her collecting box and lunch sack and moved closer to the fire. Pulling one of the sticks from the ground, he handed it to her. The trout meat was golden brown, flaking and white when she bit into it. She thought she had never tasted anything so delicious!

Words seemed out of place, so she simply smiled her thanks. Gabe did not smile in return, but his glance told her he acknowledged her gratitude. Janeth reached into her lunch sack and brought out the loaf of fresh-ground wheat bread. She broke the loaf and handed it to him, and he took it from her hands and began to devour the bread as though he were starving. She gave him a thick slab of ham and cheese and the heavy rhubarb pie Sarah had added. Each offering was taken from her hands without a word and eaten with fierce concentration.

Gabe handed Janeth another stick and she ate the second trout with the same delight with which she had eaten the first. By now Gabe had finished the pie, and, with a huge belch, he wiped the sleeve of his shirt across his mouth and lay back on the ground and closed his eyes. Within seconds Janeth was astonished to realize the mountain man was really asleep—as simply and quietly as a child.

With a sigh, Janeth opened her collection box and spread a white cloth on the ground. Carefully and swiftly, she spread out the plants she had gathered in the morning and began to work. From her apron she took her plant journal to record the number and varieties of plants. Anything she could not identify she drew, with careful attention to detail. She would track them down like a detective until she knew their classification and variety.

She gathered wet moss from the sides of the rocks and prepared to repack her box so the plants would remain fresh during her long walk home. As she carried the moss back to her plants she felt a sudden chill. Looking up, she realized that the sun was moving behind the nearest peak. "It must be later than I realized!" she thought, and began to scurry to gather up her things so she could begin her long descent before darkness could overtake her.

The mountain man had not moved, but as she glanced at him she saw that his eyes were open and he was watching her as she carefully lifted her plants.

He stood up in one swift fluid motion and came over to her.

"You have a good hand for this!" he said, examining the plants. "They are scarcely bruised." He bent and picked up a deep-rooted specimen of lungwort. Slowly he peeled back the root and took from inside it a white slippery tuber. "Bitter," he said, pinching it between his fingers, "but good for stomach pain." He then took a cluster of wild rose and broke off some dried hips. "For scurvy in the winter," he said.

Suddenly Janeth was excited. "What is this?" she asked, pointing to the slender flower, delicately blue, with dark-blue pointed petals. "I do not recognize it."

"The Indians call it 'shooting star,' " he answered. He plucked the petals and rubbed them between his fingers. They stained his hand a dark purple. "Excellent for dye," he said.

With sparkling eyes, Janeth eagerly began to ask questions about the other unfamiliar plants. He answered her carefully, showing her the secret of each one. She discovered things she had not known, things she had overlooked or observed incorrectly, and, once or twice, she was able to show him a plant she had found useful and could tell him of her discovery.

Unheeded, the sun slipped below the mountaintop, and it was not until the light began to fade that Janeth again became aware of her precarious position.

Swiftly she gathered up the remaining specimens and threw her box over her shoulder. "I must be going," she cried and started down over the lip of the basin, knocking rocks loose with her feet.

"How will you find your way in the dark?" the dark man called.

"I will follow the sound of the stream!" Janeth replied.

"No," he said, "I will show you!"

Moving in his smooth, silent way, Gabe Martin stepped in front of Janeth and began to lead her down the mountain. He was much faster than she, and his moccasin-clad feet were sure-footed on the rough boulders beside the cascading stream. Janeth stumbled along behind him, her awkward collection box banging against her side. When he got too far ahead he would stop and wait until she caught up, and then he would move ahead once more. They were less than halfway down the mountain when the sun went down, and the darkness became so thick that Janeth felt as though she were blindfolded.

Suddenly Gabe was at her side. "We will sit and rest until the moon rises," he said simply. She knew he was right. In the pitch black of the night a misstep could be fatal. The two waited in a strangely companionable silence, until slowly the mists of night seemed to clear, stars spangled the sky, and, at last, the moon, not full, but with a strong gleam, climbed into place. Once again they started on their way, but this time Gabe reached out and took her wrist firmly in his hand. He moved at her pace, and his arm was like iron. She discovered, even in the darkness, that with his help she was moving quickly and surely down the rough canyon. Over boulders, broken tree trunks, and once through the furious stream itself, he threaded their way without hesitation. At the base of the mountain, in the dark meadow, he let go of her hand. The field was bathed in moonlight and the long grass waved in the night wind like a dimly shining ocean.

Far off to the southwest she could see the flickering lights of Pleasantview. "It is too far to go tonight," Gabe said. "What will you do?"

"My husband's flock is just over that long hill," Janeth said, gesturing to a tall foothill on the left. "I will go and spend the night in the sheep camp and continue down tomorrow."

Again Gabe led the way, hurrying across the high meadow and up the smooth incline of the foothill. As they crested the hill together, they could see below the small campfire and the dark shape of the sheep.

"If you want to know about mushrooms, meet me at the mouth of the canyon. I will show you," he said.

"But when?" she asked. "Which canyon?" He had melted into the darkness and she could no longer see him. "How will I find you?" she called.

"I will find you," his voice answered from below her, and then he was gone as silently and mysteriously as he had come.

For the rest of the week Janeth remained at home in the Garden House, sorting and cataloguing the plants she had gathered on the upper meadow of Tokewamna. The information Gabriel Martin had given her was invaluable. She found herself aflame with curiosity about the mountain man. Who was he? How did he know so much about native herbs? What more did he have to teach her?

Monday morning, early, she packed carefully, anticipating that she might not return the same evening, and prepared to return to Mount Tokewamna, determined to find the strange man who could shorten her quest for knowledge. She rode a horse up to the sheep camp and left the animal with the man who was tending the flocks. "I am going to the Tokewamna area," she told him. "I have found some excellent fields of plants there. I expect to be back by evening, but if not, there is a protected area there where I will camp. Don't be concerned—I'll pick up the horse on my way back."

The young sheepherder, a recent immigrant who had come to the valley to work for the McElins, accepted her plan without argument.

True to his word, Gabriel Martin found Janeth. She spent the morning on a lower slope of the mountain, near the mouth of the canyon where she had first met Gabe, and at midday he suddenly appeared, as silently and mysteriously as before. Without a word he walked over to see the plants she had collected, but she shrugged her shoulders and said, "Nothing new. I'm not having much luck today."

He beckoned to her and she followed him, past Mount Tokewamna and through a rock-filled upper valley. By early afternoon she saw that they had circled behind the mountain and were approaching Mount Ouray from its eastern face. They toiled up the lower slope through tangled underbrush and thickets of scrub pine and aspen. A slide area of shale and small rocks impeded their progress, and Janeth slowly inched across, watching the loose stones hurtle downward and praying she would not follow.

On the other side of the rockslide, Gabriel found an old Indian trail, barely visible, but winding surely through the trees, affording occasional glimpses of lower peaks and the distant thread of the Virgin River far below.

Suddenly the trees began to thin, and Janeth knew they were approaching the timberline. The air was thin and crisp, warmed by the summer sun. Gabe continued his climb, moving with deceptive ease, the muscular rhythm of his walk devouring distance. Janeth knew he had slowed his pace to accommodate her, yet she was still exhausted. Finally Gabe stopped and turned to her. Without a word he pointed to a ridge before them. It was laden with broken trees, dead tree trunks, and old wood lying flat, piled and strewn upon the surface of the ridge as though some giant hand had flung them there like discarded toothpicks.

"Avalanche path!" Gabe Martin explained, pointing to the sharp smooth peak above the ridge. They picked their way through the broken timbers, past the ridge, and then Janeth became aware of the sound of trickling waters. They plodded on and soon found themselves on a large, high plateau. Janeth gasped. The entire area looked like a punch bowl in the heart of the mountains. At the head of the meadow a stone wall was festooned with a series of three waterfalls, as white as bridal veils against the dark, wet stone. Everywhere in the bowl of the meadow, small streams and rivulets trickled downward. The grass was thick and high and wild blossoms bloomed in profusion.

Surrounding the meadow were stands of timbers as strong and straight as any Janeth had ever seen. But the meadow itself was treeless, and she felt she had been ushered into some glorious secret. Gabe, watching her exultant expression, smiled.

"Perhaps you will find something here," he said.

They worked together collecting plants throughout the rest of the day. By evening Janeth was too tired to return to the sheep camp.

"Will it be safe for me to camp in this meadow?" she asked Gabe. "I will need to work here at least one more day."

"Of course it is safe," he replied. "I will keep watch."

That night Gabe built a fire and they ate the food Janeth had brought. Wearily Janeth prepared her bedroll, while Gabe banked the small fire and indicated a distant ledge in the upper meadow that would give him a view of the entire area.

"I will camp up there," he said, and moved off into the night.

Janeth rolled herself into her blanket and lay down on the soft grass. As tired as she was, she found it hard to fall asleep. She knew it was foolish to trust herself to a man about whom she knew nothing, and yet, as she and Gabe had worked together through the day and she had listened to him talk about herbs and medicines, she had felt like a student at the feet of a great teacher, and her mind yearned to know everything he knew.

"Who are you, Gabe Martin?" she wondered as she fell asleep.

For the next few weeks Janeth established a pattern. On the days when she went into the mountains she would return to the last place where she and Gabe had met. Sometime during the course of the morning he would appear, always having some new place to take her. Occasionally he would bring plant preparations and would spend the morning showing her how to distill or dry and powder a particular substance. They discussed dosages, symptoms, limitations, and diagnoses. Janeth always recorded Gabe's information carefully in her notebooks. Finally Janeth felt they had covered all the available indigenous sources of medication, except for the mushrooms Gabe had mentioned on the first night.

One afternoon she closed her notebook as she prepared to leave. "Gabe," she said, "why haven't you ever taken me to find the mushrooms?"

He answered her in his slow, careful voice. "Because the weather has been wrong. We need a spell of rain."

170

There was a moment of silence. Then Gabe continued. "I'm leaving, Janeth. I've taught you all I know. Time to move on."

Janeth felt a clutch at her heart. She had never thought of him leaving. She had imagined him to be as much a part of the mountains as the wildflowers.

"But . . . not until you have shown me the mushrooms! You promised!" She knew she sounded petulant, like a disappointed child.

Gabe laughed. "Well, if the rain comes soon. Otherwise I must leave."

Heartsick, Janeth packed her bag and prepared to return home. Gabe turned to go as well, and she put her hand on his arm. "Please," she said, "promise me you won't leave without at least saying good-bye." She gave him a tender, crooked little smile, but her eyes were full of uncertainty. "I will see you again—tomorrow? I'll come back, right here, to this very spot. We'll go see the mushrooms—rain or not!" His face remained impassive and he didn't answer.

"Promise?" she challenged him.

Gabe shook his head slowly, his face impassive. "Promises are for children," he said, and moved off smoothly and silently past the stream.

The next day it began to rain. It was a midsummer downpour, and it lasted two days and nights, turning the roads into rivers of mud and beating the ripening cornstalks into the dirt. The barnyards became a mire of manure and black loam, and restless children pressed their noses against the rain-streaked windows, or ran, screaming and laughing, through the deep puddles on the front lawns. Janeth sat in the Garden House unable to work or think clearly. Would Gabe leave the mountains, driven away by the hurling rain, which must be bitterly cold in the mountains? Or would he hole up in some cave, waiting out the storm? Would he wait, now that it had rained, to show her the mushrooms?

On the third day the rain stopped, but the wind blew like a tyrant, and travel was out of the question. Finally, on the fourth day, the sun burst forth as hot and clear as a lover's eye, and Janeth was up at the crack of dawn with her old straw hat clamped on her head, striding up the lower foothills toward the shining, fresh-washed mountains. The wind of the day before had dried the trails and the hot sun continued to bake the water out of the earth. At times she would step into a puddle, or cross a spongy area of saturated grass, but for the most part her way was unhampered, and it was still morning when she arrived at the rendezvous spot. Restlessly she paced beside the stream, her eyes searching the surrounding rocks and approaches. By noon she was discouraged. The hot sun seemed to mock her and her fruitless wait.

Janeth turned from the stream and prepared to return to Pleasantview. She could not throw off a terrible feeling of loss and betrayal, yet her mind derided her for her feelings. "If he were really just a source of knowledge to you, then why are you so sorrowful? You have already gleaned most of the information he has to offer," she chided herself. "What does this man mean to you? You don't know who he is or where he comes from. You have never said a personal word to him nor he to you."

She was almost to the sheep meadow when she heard rocks slip behind her and turned to see small pieces of gravel rolling down the trail. In all the time she had known Gabe he had never dislodged a single stone. She looked behind her, alarmed, and there was Gabe, standing above her on the mountain, tossing stones from his hand and rolling them down toward her.

She laughed with joy and relief. "Have you come to show me the mushrooms?" she asked gaily. He nodded and came leaping down the mountainside to join her.

"We will need to hurry," he said, and set off at a wicked pace. Janeth, who by now was conditioned to the strenuous requirements of their explorations, matched his stride. They followed a defile at the base of Mount Ouray, and, as they penetrated more deeply into the wilderness, they came to two mountains, side by side.

"This is Taimago and Abajo," Gabriel said. They crossed a stream and worked their way up a steep canyon between the mountains. It was very rough climbing and Janeth found herself growing tired. The sun was cooler in the shadowed canyon, and, as they moved deeper into the heart of the mountains, she shivered. The stream was wider and deeper than most mountain streams, and its banks were treacherous and slippery with moss.

Suddenly the canyon walls narrowed and the stream seemed to have grown smaller where it spurted through the opening. Janeth thought they would have to end their journey and return the way they had come. She wondered if, for the first time, Gabriel had lost his way. Reaching the spot where the two mountain walls almost came together, Gabe carefully began to climb the stone canyon. He found handholds and small ledges. Frightened but determined, Janeth

172

followed him, and, a few feet above the gushing stream, they squeezed between the stone walls and edged their way into an upper canyon.

This new canyon was almost dark. The walls were so high that the sunlight scarcely reached the floor. The banks of the stream were wider here with plateaus of stone and steps of moss and trickling water making a giant stone mosaic filling the wide canyon floor. Tall, rustling aspens and maples reached toward the distant sunlight, and centuries of decayed leaves and rotting wood lay at their feet. With a delighted gasp, Janeth noted that one face of the canyon wall was like weeping stone, with water oozing and dripping from a myriad of tiny cracks and crevices. The entire stone face was black with moss and lush water-loving plants that clung to the water-washed cliff, like a giant hanging garden, with thousands of tiny fountains continually flowing.

In the strangely shaded gloom, with the musical sound of water playing a constant melody, Gabriel beckoned to Janeth and began to show her the countless mushrooms.

"The trick is to know the poisonous ones from the healthy," Gabe said. "Here, I will show you." He placed two mushrooms in front of her. "This is not always sure, but one way is to look for a ring or a cup on the stem." He showed her a small mushroom that she had picked. Around the base was a small cup formation. Another mushroom had a ring of tissue around the stem about halfway up. "These are amanitas," Gabriel said. "Deadly!" He picked one up, a beautiful pure-white mushroom with both a ring and a cup and small speckled growths on the cap. " 'The Destroying Angel,' " he said. "A killer!"

Then he began to sort the mushrooms. "Honey, Field, Helmet, Granular, Horse, Parasol, Oyster, Morel." He named each one as he put it aside.

When he was finished, he had three piles. He pointed to one pile: "Delicious!" he said. To another pile: "Poison!" And to the third: "Unknown."

Quickly, Janeth began sketching. "What about the unknown ones?" she asked. "Could some of those be useful?"

"Yes," Gabe answered. "I test them. It is the only way."

Unhesitatingly, he cut a small sliver off one of the mushrooms. "Never test one which has a cup or a ring. Also if they are extremely white, or extremely colorful, be careful." He put the small piece of mushroom in his mouth and chewed and swallowed it. "Now we shall wait," he said. "Also, do not eat a decayed mushroom, or one that has a milky juice."

Janeth continued to sketch, and Gabe closed his eyes and lay on his back in a spot of filtered sunlight.

After an hour Gabe sat up and carefully lifted the mushroom he had tested and put it in the "Safe" pile. Janeth gave a sigh of relief. "Don't test any more today!" she exclaimed. "It makes me uncomfortable."

Gabe nodded. "The varieties which are safe for eating have no medicinal value, but one or two of the poisonous varieties have limited use." He began to show her how to prepare and use the powerful poisons. She found the plants and the canyon somehow foreboding and oppressive. Finally she could stand it no longer.

"I think I must be going, Gabe," she said, and he, sensing her unease, picked up the specimens, wrapped them in a flannel cloth, and moved toward the narrow entrance to the canyon. The return was as harrowing and slow as the ascent, and by the time they had emerged from the canyon at the base of Abajo, it was midafternoon. The sun, which had deserted them in the deep canyon, shone down more fiercely than ever. Their clothes were spotted with mud and slime, and, as they walked, the heat, perspiration, and dust from the dried trail became almost unbearable.

The stream continued to widen. As they came to the base of Mount Taimago, it became a creek that wound its way between clusters of cottonwood and blackberry bushes. Mosquitoes began to swarm around them and Gabe cursed and swatted the back of his neck.

Janeth felt wretched and tired. "Gabe, couldn't we stop and rest for a bit?" she asked. He turned and shrugged, and she threw her shawl on a flat rock by the bank of the creek and sat down on it. Gabe walked down by the swift-flowing water and pulled out his fish line. The sun-baked stone felt good beneath her, and Janeth lay back and closed her eyes. In a moment she was asleep, the sound of the water soothing and steady.

She woke up minutes later, screaming. A huge cloud of gnats, black and vicious, hovered around her, biting, humming, filling her ears and eyes. They flew in her mouth as she screamed, and she spat violently and covered her lips with her hands.

Gabe was waist deep in the stream shouting at her. "Run to the water! They'll eat you alive!"

She leaped to her feet, ran to the creek, and threw herself in the water. As she felt the powerful current sweep over her, the biting cold was a blessed relief. Half swimming, half wading, she moved toward Gabe. He was submerged in the center of the stream, only his head above the water. He ducked under every few minutes. The gnats had followed them to the stream, although not in such thick formation.

"They smelled fresh meat," Gabriel said, chuckling. The gnats were swarming around Janeth's head and she ducked under the water for a moment. When she came up for air there seemed to be fewer of the insects. Gabe took her hand. Her footing was uncertain on the rough, mossy rocks. The water was swift and so cold that she could hardly speak.

"We'll move upstream," Gabe said. "Get as clean as you can in the water so they won't smell us, and then we'll rub jewelweed on our bites. Maybe we can find some citronella or laurel to burn and smoke them out."

Janeth nodded. The cold water seemed to be pressing against her chest, shortening her breath, and numbing her legs. They moved upstream, and she undid her hair and rinsed it in the icy water. She scrubbed her face and neck with the rough grass that grew at the side of the stream, and then, unable to bear the cold any longer, she pulled herself up on the bank, panting with exertion and shivering from the bitter chill.

Her clothing streamed water and clung to her heavily. Gabriel was still in the water. He had taken off his deerskin shirt and was slapping it up and down in the cold stream. She watched the play of the muscles in his arms and torso, startled by the whiteness of his skin in contrast to the deeply suntanned face and hands. She had not realized he was so fair, and the sight of his skin made him seem like a stranger to her. For the first time since their meeting, Janeth was acutely aware of the fact that Gabe was a man and she was a woman.

For so many years, denied the comfort of a true marriage relationship with Angus, she had schooled herself not to think of her sex. She had trained herself to be useful, to be intellectually challenging to Angus, and to pass her days in active, genderless pursuits. Perhaps this attitude was one reason she had been such an emotionally distant mother to Christina. Perhaps she did not dare even allow the feminine role of motherhood to intrude itself on the sterile, controlled life she had created. She made no effort to dress attractively, seldom looked in a mirror or busied herself with creams or combs.

Her feminine identification was cut to the bone, and she had grown to regard all people with the strict objectivity of a medical practitioner wherein sex was little more than a factor in diagnosis and treatment, and had no personal application. She had poured all her love for beauty and passion into her weaving. The colors, the patterns, the texture of the yarn, and the rhythm of the loom had become her only solace for all that was human and hungry within her. Why, then, after all these years should she be so moved by the sight of this man's body and the vigorous, physical ballet of his arms pounding and sweeping against the mountain stream?

Ashamed and dismayed, Janeth pulled her eyes away from the sight of her friend, and, dragging her heavy, soaked skirts, she moved slowly over to a copse of trees to gather kindling for a fire, fearful that the gnats would catch her scent and be upon her again.

Gabe waded out of the stream and came to help her. When the fire was started she knelt beside it shivering in her wet clothes. Gabe had pounded his shirt on the rocks until he had pressed and beaten most of the water out of the leather. He spread it on one of the sun-heated rocks. "That'll be dry in no time," he said with satisfaction.

Janeth looked at him with envy since her heavy, homespun cotton dress had absorbed water like a sponge. She had tried, ineffectually, to wring it out while she was wearing it, but she was still soaking wet.

Gabe went over to his pack and pulled an Indian blanket free. "Here!" he said. "You'd best go in those bushes and put this on. I'll get your dress dry for you."

Shocked, Janeth opened her mouth to object, but Gabe shrugged casually. "You can't hike in those wet clothes, and if we don't get started soon, you won't make it home tonight."

Realizing Gabe was right, Janeth did as he had told her, wrapping the blanket tightly around her after she had taken off her dress. She handed it out to Gabe, who wrung it with his strong hands and then rigged it up by the fire to dry. Shyly, Janeth walked to the far side of the fire and sat down in the cocoon of the blanket. The smoke from the fragrant wood seemed to keep the insects at bay, and she sighed with relief.

A strange silence fell between them. It was as though Janeth could sense a thread of tension and awareness strung between the two of them; it seemed to grow tighter and more painful with each quiet moment. She could not bring herself to look across at Gabe. Her mind held vividly the imprint of his naked torso. She had often seen

176

men stripped to the waist as they labored in the fields, chopped wood, or swam—why was this suddenly so different, so disturbing?

The heat of the sun and the fire began to warm her, and she loosened the blanket around her neck so that the cooling breeze could enter. Suddenly, impatiently, Gabe jumped to his feet and walked over to the rock where his leather shirt was drying. He picked it up and shook it, water flying from the fringed sleeves, then he threw it over his head and jerked it down. As he strode back toward the fire Janeth stared at his long, muscled legs, watching where the leather outlined them like a second skin, and she felt her cheeks flaming with emotion.

Gabe came within five feet of her, and then he stopped abruptly and dropped into a squatting position, the same one he had assumed when she had opened her eyes and looked upon him the first time many weeks ago. He remained still and alert as he had been then, and his eyes devoured her with their intensity.

Janeth moved in discomfiture under his curious gaze, and the blanket fell down around her shoulders. The black mane of her hair, loose and drying in the sun, blew like a dark cloud around her face.

"Who are you, Gabe?" she asked, her voice strained and tense. "How have you come to this place?"

It was a long moment before Gabe answered, and for a while Janeth thought he would not say anything. She had broken their unspoken code of no personal questions.

"New England," he finally said. "I was a young medical student. Gambling, debts, disgrace—my family sent me west and hoped to forget I ever existed."

"But how?" Janeth did not know what questions to ask.

"How did I come to the mountains?" Gabe shook his head slowly. "I'm a squaw man, Janeth. It's that simple. I lived in Fort Laramie for a time when I first came west. Did a little doctoring, and then I met a raven-haired beauty, and I went to live with her and her people.

"You know the irony of it?" he continued. "Her people were kinder, more generous, more intelligent, than the people I had left behind. They taught me new kinds of medicine—some more effective than anything I'd learned in the ivy-covered halls. I could have stayed with them—maybe should have. But I found I couldn't live their rules any more than I could live those of my own people.

"So . . . the mountains became my people."

"But what about your—wife?" Janeth asked, sorry the minute she had said the words.

"I'm with her in the winter," Gabe said. "I sometimes go to the summer camping grounds too. But less and less. . . ." His voice trailed off, and Janeth saw a bleak look come into his eyes.

"Is that where you are going now?" she asked.

He shook his head. "I don't know," he answered. "I only know it's time for me to move on."

She felt as though she could not breathe. Air simply would not fill her lungs, and she gasped softly and quickly. He watched her distress and his eyes clouded.

"You are not an Indian, Janeth, but you are all that I thought the Indian people would be. I imagined they were the last true primitives, filled with pure emotions and at one with nature. Perhaps at some time in the distant past they were whole, but the white man has brought them to corruption and decay.

"But you, Janeth, you are like the first woman. The only woman. When I saw you in the meadow of Tokewamna, sleeping among the wildflowers, I felt as though I had discovered the first woman sprung from the womb of the earth."

Janeth was hypnotized by the sound of Gabe's voice. It was as though each word he spoke pierced into her unshielded heart. A tear formed in the corner of her eye. She felt it coursing down her cheek but did not move to brush it away. "Your hands," he said. "They hold the miracle of healing. I knew it the first time I saw you handling the plants without so much as a filament disturbed. Your eyes, as dark as night, and yet so straight and honest, and your face! Oh, Janeth, can you imagine what it is to look into such a face—as calm and guileless as the surface of a lake and yet filled with hidden mystery!

"I must leave now, Janeth, because the woman in you cries to me too strongly and I cannot turn away any longer. Before I hurt you—before I destroy what we have built together—I must leave this place."

"But, Gabe!" she cried. "I—I don't want you to leave. Can't we stay just as we are? Friends? Companions? Healers?"

Gabe gave a soft, short laugh. "You are the most desirable woman I have ever seen," he whispered. "You have made me wish that with one stroke of my hand I could wipe away my past—all the things I have done and not done. I want you, Janeth, and in all my life, I have never before hesitated to take what I want. But for you, for the first time, I have not—and I must leave you now, before I return to my old habits."

His voice was heavy with self-disgust and pain, and Janeth instinctively raised up on her knees, stretching her hands toward him, and the blanket fell to the rock. She did not know what she wanted to say or do, she only knew that she wanted him to stay. For the first time since she had arrived in Pleasantview she felt her heart, open, passionate, yearning, intense, and she felt alive and beautiful.

Still looking at her as though he wanted to burn the memory of the sight of her upon his mind forever, Gabe remained where he was, unmoving. He took a deep, ragged breath that sounded like a sigh from the depths of the earth.

"Oh, Janeth. If you could only see yourself now!" he whispered hoarsely. "You must remember what I say always. You must not hide that burning heart of yours, that fierce mad passion, that glorious body. No man could resist the woman in you, and you have kept her in prison—for whatever your reason. How wasteful! How foolish!"

Suddenly he stood up and hurried over to the sapling that held her dress. He snatched it up and threw it at her. "Put it on!" he said roughly. "We need to start back! Now!"

With her mind in turmoil, Janeth dressed. They moved down the trail swiftly and silently. Gabe had not touched her, and yet she had felt his love and passion as surely as though he had overcome her. It was early twilight when they arrived at the mouth of the canyon. The high meadows stretched before them. Wordlessly, Gabe turned away and began to reenter the shadowed trails of Ouray.

"Gabe!" she called after him desperately. But he was gone.

And now, a decade older, she leaned against the sill of her lonely bedroom, unloved, with her heart and mind fastened on Angus, the one great passion of her life. Somehow the gifts that Gabe had given her—his profound skill with medicine, his knowledge of the mountain's secrets, and, most of all, his deep reassurances of her own womanhood—had become a powerful talisman against the slights, the pain, and the enduring isolation of her life.

She looked at the mountains and let herself remember Gabe's passion. Something firmed within her, a solid conviction, a quiet resolve, a flame of hope. If Gabe had seen her desirability, then it must be there still. Somehow, some way, in the next few days when she was alone with Angus, she would use that womanhood to ignite a flame once again in her husband. Her body, aching with unfulfilled longing, glowed with the fierceness of her needs, and she rose from the floor and walked slowly to the narrow bed that had been her prison and her refuge. "Tomorrow," she whispered as she fell asleep, and her face glowed with the joyful anticipation of a young bride.

The next morning at the crack of dawn the two traveling parties prepared to depart. Jeremy, Sam, and Christina and their pack horse were the first to be ready. Angus had dismantled Janeth's loom and was strapping it to a pack animal. The loom would be rebuilt in Nephi, so Janeth could continue weaving during her days of exile.

Christina had said restrained farewells to her parents, still feeling confused and miserable from the conversation she had overheard the day before. As she prepared to mount her horse, Jeremy grabbed her leg to give her a boost and she kicked out at him angrily. "Keep your hands off me, Jem!" she shouted, her face bright red with fury.

Jeremy, offended and equally angry, stamped over to his own horse. "That's the last time I'll try to help you, missy!" he growled.

"That's fine with me!" Christina retorted. "I don't need help from any boys anyway!" With that she dug her heels into her horse, and the surprised animal sprang ahead and began to canter down the road. Sam, Jeremy, and the pack animals followed after her quickly.

Angus watched the ragged departure of the group with a look of dismay. "That girl!" he exclaimed. "No one ever knows what she will do next. I hope Matty and Zina have more luck with her than we have."

Sitting on her horse, Janeth said nothing. Her heart ached at the thought of her separation from Christina and at the impending farewell she must say to Angus, but another part of her heart was singing as she thought of the coming days and nights alone with this man whom she had loved since she was a young girl. She watched his strong hands at work, tying the thongs. She stared at his broad shoulders and strong back. His voice, firm and authoritative as he spoke to the restive animals, filled her with joy, and she longed for him to turn and look at her, to acknowledge the wonderful secret memories they shared. In her heart the strange conviction stirred once more, and she knew, as surely as she knew the stars would appear, that somehow, somewhere in the next days, they would come together once more and nothing could restrain their love. Nothing would dam the pent-up feelings of all these years. They would spill out like a mighty flood that would carry them both beyond the threshold of anything they had imagined or experienced in the past. Perhaps they were on the verge of being old, but still, in their bodies the flame of youth would burn for this one last brief and glorious time.

In the pale dawn light, their horses walking slowly, with the pack animals plodding behind, Janeth and Angus rode side by side down the wide, empty streets of Pleasantview. Suddenly Angus reached out and took Janeth's hand and held it tightly as they left the town he and his brothers had built. They turned their horses toward the upper trails. Earlier in the morning Angus had been told by his scouts that a party of men sent from the federal marshal had ridden up the pass road. The federal men had examined the roadblock and then had ridden back to the west, but Angus knew that within days a large party would return to find a way into the valley. The time of testing was at hand. He had gotten his families out just in time.

That night as Angus made camp on the western hills overlooking the Virgin Valley, Janeth stood gazing over the town, with its patchwork of fields and farms around it. The turbulent river seemed nothing more than a shining silver thread in the distance.

Angus had stowed the gear and hobbled the horses. He could not take the chance of building a fire and so his work was finished quickly. He walked over to Janeth and stood beside her silently.

"Can you bear to leave it?" she whispered. "It is so much a part of you."

"Aye," he said quietly. "But it has taken on a life of its own. It will survive, with or without me." He sighed. As she looked up at his face in the gathering twilight, she saw a somber smile lighting his eyes. "I had forgotten how beautiful the valley looks from this spot," he said, and she heard the pain in his voice.

"This is almost the exact place from which we saw the valley for the first time." He looked around wonderingly. "Matty and Johnny and I—we climbed up that ridge, right over there. Couldn't believe our eyes. It was so beautiful."

He turned back to the view of the valley, now so dark that the mountains were indigo and the line of the river the only bright spot in the twilight-shadowed bowl beneath them. A backdrop of stars pinpointed the eastern sky. "In the evening light it seems unchanged!" he exclaimed. "Right now, you could believe the McElins had never come—that it was still untouched—undiscovered!"

Janeth laughed with sudden understanding. "You wish you could do it all over again, don't you?" she baited him. "The exploring—the finding—the adventure!"

Angus turned to her with a smile that was almost boyish. "Aye!" he admitted. "It was a bonnie time."

Janeth felt the brush of his rough sleeve against her arm and could smell the scent of his soap and the saddle leather and crisp mountain air in the wool of his riding jacket. She trembled with desire. What was Angus feeling? She knew that he must be filled with sadness as he left this beloved valley, and perhaps there was no room in his heart for anything else.

All these years she had waited for him to come to her, sure that he wanted her as much as she wanted him, that only his iron sense of honor and responsibility had kept away. Now, however, he was free to express his love, and she was filled with doubt, wondering if perhaps the years of quiet friendship had destroyed the fires of their past.

The evening wind rushed up from the valley, and Janeth, poised on the brow of the hill, reached up and undid the pins that held her long, heavy hair. Her hair uncoiled and fell in a dark tumbling mass across her shoulders and down her back, and the wind caught the soft tendrils and blew them in a shifting cloud around her face.

Angus, a few steps behind her, watched this enigmatic woman who had been a part of his life for so many years, lover yet unloved, wife, friend, advisor, and the mother of his child. Her body was still graceful and strong as it had been when he first met her, and each movement she made, as he watched her silhouetted against the night sky, was mysterious and sensual.

"Janeth!" he whispered and moved toward her. She turned, surprised, thinking he had gone back to camp. In two massive strides, and before she could say a word, he reached her, grasped her in his powerful arms, and kissed her soft, astonished mouth with a hard, yearning desire that filled her heart with joy and madness.

"Oh, Angus." She gasped. "You do love me!"

For an answer he kissed her again, and she felt as though the mountains rocked under her feet and the earth gave way. She sank to the ground, and he held her and knelt with her above the valley.

The wind took her long, dark tresses and wound them around his arms. He felt himself captured by the silken cords. The cloud of her hair brushed his face and cheeks in countless caresses, hiding and revealing her face in the moonlight, like a dancer's veil.

He kissed her again and again, his lips drinking in the sweet, soft ripeness of her mouth, the smooth column of her throat, her eyes, lidded with satin. Her hands, strong and knowing, held and touched him, until he felt loved, desired, and desirous as he had never felt before.

Under the stars they heaped their clothes and made a nest of wool and homespun, and then, together, they lay beneath Janeth's down-soft shawl. He felt the flowing lines of her body, warm and fragrant next to his, and his hands discovered the curves and hollows, the firm limbs and womanly tenderness, and the supple yearning flesh of this woman who had given herself to him completely, as no one else had ever done.

In a burst of glorious joy he threw back her shawl and looked at her body radiant in the silver light. Her hair was like a shadowed halo around her and her sweet face was smiling at him. He reached out and took her to him with a love he could not have believed possible, and when it was over he lay beside her, spent but filled with a happiness so complete that he almost feared it.

Lying beside him, Janeth felt the tears of joy washing her face. All her years of longing and humiliation were washed away, and she felt herself newborn, as though Angus's love had baptized her. She was filled with a sense of beginning and could not wait for tomorrow, —for all of the tomorrows beckoning to her over the rise of the mountain where she and Angus would journey the next day.

Later, as Angus slept, Janeth walked once again to look down upon the dark valley. Some deep, sad voice of warning whispered to her: "Don't be in a hurry to return to the places where there are people." She knew that in the towns and homes where she and Angus would stay, and even if they returned to Pleasantview together someday, Angus would find it difficult to recapture the sense of rapture and abandon they had known tonight on that wild, forgotten hillside. The whispers and eyes of people would follow them. Their love was too intense! The world would want to domesticate it—to place it in bounds.

"I hope it takes forever to reach Manti," she thought with a smile. She shivered with delight as she remembered his hands and their compelling touch upon her body. She hurried back to the campsite needing to be near him, to feel the solid warmth of his body and to be assured it was not a dream.

Chapter Nine

In the spring of 1887 the Edmunds-Tucker Bill was passed into law even though many congressmen claimed it was little more than legalized persecution. The bill disincorporated the Church of Jesus Christ of Latter-Day Saints because of its advocacy of polygamy. By early summer United States Marshal Dyer had taken possession of all real estate and personal property belonging to the Utah Church. The Church, in order to retain use of its own business and tithing offices, was forced to pay an onerous rent. The Church Immigration Fund, accumulated over the years through the dedication and sacrifice of thousands of Saints, was confiscated by the federal government. The only buildings left to the Church were those used exclusively for religious services or burial grounds.

Under these terrible strictures, the pressure on the structure of the Church became enormous. Church leaders, such as Angus McElin, had become exiles in their own territory, forced to conduct Church business from hiding places, trying to avoid arrest while their lawyer struggled desperately to find a reasonable, legal solution to the legislative confusion and persecution.

In spite of the struggles and concerns around her, Christina was safely situated in Matty and Zina's cozy St. George home where she was having one of the happiest summers of her life. Picnics with other young people, square dancing, quilting bees, and morning walks in the wide fields of southern Utah filled her days. For the first time in her life she had friends. They accepted her as Matty's pretty niece and treated her with uncomplicated goodwill. Away from Mary and the Big House, Christina began to feel admired and attractive. Aunt Zina and Uncle Matty's children were grown and gone and they were delighted to have Christina living with them.

Once, out for a stroll in the morning, she and her friends walked past the lovely home that had been President Brigham Young's summer home, and Christina told the other girls how her papa had been called by Brigham Young himself tō settle the Virgin Valley. The girls' voices were hushed with awe, and they asked Christina a dozen questions. Christina experienced a thrill of delight at the unusual experience of being the center of attention.

Matty was often in meetings with solemn-faced men of authority who rode down from the north. Often the men would arrive by stage from Salt Lake and would be closeted with Matty for hours. Christina and Zina carried refreshments to them—plates of sliced turkey, golden slices of homemade bread, garden-fresh fruits, cold lemonade, and peach tarts that melted in the mouth like butter. "Food is meant for enjoyment as well as for sustenance!" Zina always said. Christina had noticed, however, that no matter how much food Zina made—no matter how much Matty ate—her uncle never seemed to gain an ounce. It was as though his tall, lean frame refused to bother itself with any extra burden.

Christina helped Zina by setting the living-room table with the trays of food, and, while she passed each dish around to the men, she learned through snatches of conversations about the serious hardships being imposed on her people. Yet the information scarcely seemed to make an impression on her. It seemed to her that none of the dreadful things these men discussed could possibly change the sweet, summery-pleasant pace of life in St. George. Christina did have an occasional pang for her father's safety, but Matty reassured her that he had received word her father was well and in no immediate danger.

The summer moved on, almost like a dream to young Christina. Zina had bought her some lovely fabrics—calico, ginghams, poplins, and voiles. Together they stitched and fitted, until Christina had a wardrobe as pretty as any of the other young girls in St. George.

One evening, in her small upper bedroom, Christina pulled one of her new dresses from the closet. It was dusky pink with a tight fitted bodice and long sleeves. The skirt had a small draped bustle in the back and soft pleats in the front and was trimmed with a dainty froth of white lace, which Zina had tatted. Around Christina's slender neck the lace looked like a web of snowflakes, cool, fragile, and exquisite. She stared at herself in the mirror with a feeling of wonder. She found it hard to believe the fashionable creature in the mirror was actually herself! Her eyes looked enormously green and mysterious, her auburn hair crackled with vitality and blazed around her face, and the smooth line of her bodice showed the womanly curves of her breasts, which made her a little embarrassed and yet abashedly pleased.

Christina knew she wasn't really pretty—not like her new friends with their pink, rosy cheeks, their soft dimpled faces framed by golden-brown curls. "Everything in me is too angular," she thought, "too defined, too colorful." But still, in the dim evening light, looking at herself sideways in the mirror, she felt a small half smile of satisfaction tug at her lips. Maybe she wasn't so bad! If only she didn't have that square jaw. Perhaps if her eyebrows were not so dark, her eyes not so large and alert. There was no softness in her face, Christina decided, trying to be objective. It was a face of cheekbones and color, and only her full, chiseled lips showed any sign of softness.

She turned from the mirror, ashamed that she had been so entranced with her own image. "What would Mama think of such mooning?" she wondered. It was the first time she had thought of her mother in days. "I must write a letter to her!" she thought guiltily. Glancing out the window, she caught sight of several young men and women walking down the path. Her girl friends were dressed in pastel colors and the young men were wearing white shirts and light flannels. The group made a pretty picture in the play of light and shadow on the walk, and Christina snatched up her button shoes and quickly put them on, not wanting to keep them waiting. Evenings could become chilly, and Christina reached into the wardrobe shelf to snatch a shawl. The first one that came to her hand was a light woolen wrap her mother had given to her when they had parted in Pleasantview. The shawl was woven of mohair and was as light as a feather. It was dyed with a rare pink dye that varied in intensity, giving the fabric a rippled pattern, as though the color was seen through moving water. Threaded through the weave was a fine satin strip that caught the light like a slip of pink silver through a cloud. It was a creation uniquely Janeth's—color, weave, wool, satin—all extraordinary and different. Christina stared at the shawl thinking of her mother and resenting her mother's oddity. She yearned now to be just like everyone else. These new friends knew nothing of her mother—nothing of her childhood. No power on earth could have induced Christina to wear the conspicuous work of her mother's hands. She put the dramatic garment back onto its shelf and pulled out a simple lace stole, and then hurried down to greet her friends. The young people were on their way to attend an evening lecture at the church hall.

186

"The month of July is almost over," Christina thought to herself as she sat in church listening to the insects buzzing around the gaslights and absently watching the full moon as it hung in the night sky outside the open windows. Several women were fanning themselves slowly, but the evening was growing cooler and Christina was feeling pleasantly relaxed and a little sleepy, as she listened to the earnest voice of the returned missionary who was discussing the growth of the Church in Germany.

Suddenly the repose of the meeting was shattered by a noisy rattle of harnesses and horses being ridden at full speed. All heads turned as a messenger alighted with a thump on the church steps and ran up the center aisle of the chapel. Without pausing, the man hurried to the podium and whispered a few words to the astonished missionary, who nodded and stepped aside.

"Brothers and sisters," the new speaker called. The whispering and curious buzz of conversation that had attended his arrival ceased abruptly and the room became as silent as the stars.

"Brothers and sisters," the man repeated. "I bring you sorry news. We have just learned of the death of our beloved president, John Taylor, who has died as he has lived, in the service of his Father in Heaven. He was a victim of persecution, forced to live his final years in cruel hiding, a man who never did anything but good in his life and has now gone to the great reward which he so justly earned. Let us continue to be of courage in these times of grave trial. Our Saviour is with us, and our Heavenly Father watches over us."

As the Church officer spoke, women bowed their heads to cry, and several men, overcome with grief, pulled out handkerchiefs or covered their faces with their hands and wept. Christina, for whom President Taylor had only been a name, nonetheless comprehended the vulnerability of the Church at this moment. What a terrible time to lose a leader! Suddenly she felt the loss of the president as though she had lost an anchor in the midst of a storm. Her father hiding in the mountains. The whole structure of her world at risk! She bowed her head in panic, wanting to pray, but all that would come were the words "Oh! Please . . ." and then she could not think what to ask for. So instead of praying, she began to cry, and she watched the teardrops splash on the pink cotton of her dress, staining where they fell. They looked so dark on the cloth it almost seemed like drops of blood had fallen.

When the meeting had ended one of the young men escorted Christina home. She was somber and quiet all the way, but as soon

187

as she entered the house she hurried to find her uncle to tell him the news. She discovered him in his small office across the hallway from the dining room, and as soon as she saw him she knew by the slump of his shoulders and the strained look on his usually merry face that he had already heard.

"Oh! Uncle Matty!" she cried, the tears starting afresh. "Whatever shall we do? What is to become of the Church without President Taylor? What will become of Father and Mother—and all of us?"

Matty came over and embraced her tenderly and then led her to a chair. "There, there, my girl. No need to be afraid."

His voice was calm, and she felt herself growing more peaceful as he spoke. "This Church cannot be destroyed by persecution, or biased laws, or even federal marshals. The Council of Twelve will direct us now until a new president is chosen. It is not lack of leadership we need to fear, Christina. The only harm that can come to our Church is if we, who are its members, are found wanting in faith or courage or goodness. It can only be destroyed from within."

Christina looked at Matty with shining eyes. Something in his voice gave her strength, and she found herself wishing with all her heart that she could be as fine as he was. "Oh, Uncle Matty!" she exclaimed. "I do so much want to be good! I mean, really good, like Peter and Paul and all the great Christians—and you."

Matty looked at her as though slightly astonished at her fervor and then he chuckled. "I'm glad to be thought of in the company of biblical heroes, Christina, but I assure you, I am just a man—and not much of a one at times—as Aunt Zina will surely attest. It's the 'trying' that counts, my girl. It is what we all must do. And now, off to bed with you. Sufficient to the day is the evil thereof, and I think this day has had its fill! Don't be concerned about your father. He will be sad to lose an old friend in President Taylor, but he remains safe and in hiding. If it's any comfort to you, Christina, I have the feeling that this situation will not long endure."

Christina heard his reassurance with a relieved smile and hurried off to her bedroom. She did not hear the comment her uncle added softly as she climbed the stairs. His eyes clouded with thought, and he repeated quietly to himself, "Aye, something will change—for the better or the worse. It cannot go on as it is."

When Christina had told her uncle about trying to be more righteous, she had been speaking from a well of guilt and shame that had grown inside her during the summer. It seemed so glorious to be living away from Janeth's odd, brooding presence, at last outside the

188

shadow of the Big House, which stood through her childhood like a constant bitter reminder of the fact that her mother was a second wife.

Frequently she would find herself wishing Zina was her mother. When Zina smiled, hummed, and flitted about the bright, sun-filled rooms of her St. George home, with its bouquets of fresh-cut roses on the tables, plump, plush pillows on the velvet chairs, and the rich, red carpets adorned with woven flowers, Christina felt she must truly be in heaven. She could not help wondering how different her life might have been with a mother such as this.

She fastened her desires on becoming as much like Zina as possible, and she followed her aunt around, observing her little mannerisms, her daily schedule, her clothes, and her speech.

One day, as the two of them were walking through the garden, Christina caught sight of an unfamiliar plant and pointed to the bloom eagerly. "What is the name of that orange-colored blossom, Aunt Zina?"

"Oh, that's some type of lily, Christina," Zina answered absently.

"What type?" Christina persisted.

"My lands, Christina!" Zina exclaimed, laughing lightly. "You are just like your mother. She would have known every name and the product of every plant in my garden. I'm sorry, dear, I am just not as smart as your mama. I just plant 'em and enjoy 'em."

If Zina could have read faces, she would have known what a blow it was to Christina to be told she was just like her mother. Everything in Christina cried out that she did not want to be like Janeth. She did not want to be thought strange. Couldn't Zina see? Christina's life was going to be free and full of joy like her aunt's—not like her mother's quiet, shadowed existence.

Christina felt guilty when she found herself rejecting her mother in this way. She was convinced that she must truly be evil to think such wicked thoughts.

Burned across the feeling of rejection toward her mother was the awful half-hidden memory of the passionate conversation she had overheard between her father and mother. She hated her memory of that encounter and all that it implied. Again she found herself making an unflattering comparison between her parents and her Uncle Matty and Aunt Zina, who, although their relationship was gentle, loving, and sweet, nonetheless never gave any indication of subliminal undercurrents of passion or darker emotions. Since there was no one with whom Christina could discuss such things, she held her peace and prayed that the thoughts would simply go away.

In keeping with her resolution to be a better person, Christina made a secret vow to write a loving letter to her mother. She spent days planning what to say. "I will make it warm and loving," she thought, in penance for all the unkind things she had been thinking. "I will tell her about St. George, and make it amusing and bright— but reassure her that I miss her and Pleasantview." This last sentence gave her pause for a moment of reflection, because she did not want to compound her sins by telling her mother a lie. "Well," she equivocated, "I really do miss Pleasantview, and Mama, and Papa— even if I don't miss the Garden House!"

She wrote and rewrote the letter in her mind during the next weeks, but life was busy, and she never managed to get her thoughts down on paper.

The same 1887 Congress session that had passed the Edmunds-Tucker Bill also authorized the Indian General Allotment Act. This act too had far-reaching effects in the Utah Territory, and allowed the federal government to appropriate over 85 million acres of reservation land from the Indian people. Much of the land that remained was to be divided up among the Indians living on the reservations and would become their personal property. The tragedy of the act was that it did not recognize the fact that most Indians had no concept of land ownership. It would eventually prove to be the coup de grâce to a once proud and free race.

Matty, who acted for Church authorities in matters that concerned the Indians, foresaw the tragic effects of this congressional action. During the weeks of July and August, Christina and Zina were kept running to provide refreshment and care for the hundreds of Indians and concerned officials who streamed through Matty's little office and spilled out into all the rooms of his home.

Over and over again, Matty warned the Indian leaders not to sell their land for any amount of money since he knew the greed of land speculators who would try to buy the choice property for beads, rifles, pots, and finery. "You must keep the land for your children."

"How he loves these people!" Christina would think wonderingly as she walked among the quiet men, some of them seated on blankets on the floors and others sitting uncomfortably on Zina's Victorian settee, serving them cornbread, milk, cool water, and wheat cakes.

The Government Indian Agent in St. George hated the new law as much as Matty did, and the two of them often talked late into the night, thwarted and frustrated by the blindness of the men who controlled their destinies from over three thousand miles away in the cool halls of Washington.

Late in August on a hot, sticky night when the air in Christina's room seemed as thick and heavy as clotted cream, she lay on top of her bedcovers in a light cotton shirt, tossing and turning, unable to sleep. She was filled with a strange sense of unease, and even though she was weary, she could not seem to quiet her restless mind, or shrug off a sense of foreboding.

All day heavy clouds had been massing over the red rocks of the cliffs that surrounded St. George, and the sky had lowered until it seemed to be resting on the very rooftops of the village in a gray sullen mass. Zina had predicted rain, but not a drop had fallen, and the air was black and still.

Christina thought it must be almost midnight, and she felt like a prisoner in the darkness. Somewhere in the house beneath her she heard the abrupt sound of knocking and then the murmur of voices and tired, heavy footsteps. Doors were opened and closed, and she could hear voices, louder, more anxious, and more footsteps.

Alarmed, she sat up in bed and threw a wrap over her light nightgown. She was preparing to go downstairs when Zina appeared at her doorway carrying a small, lighted lantern.

"Christina!" Zina whispered. "I was afraid you might have been wakened, dear."

"I wasn't asleep, Aunt Zina. Is anything wrong?"

"No, no, dear!" Zina whispered quickly. "Please go right back to bed. I will explain in the morning. Don't be troubled, my poor, sweet girl!" Zina came to Christina and led her back to bed. She placed the lantern on the table and sat beside her niece, patting her hand.

"Have I told you, Christina, how much Uncle Matty and I love you? And how happy we are to have you in our home? This has been one of the happiest summers of my life." Zina turned her face away, but not before Christina saw the tears in her eyes. "I just wanted you to know that, dear," Zina whispered, picking up the lamp and holding it so that her face was in shadow. "Try to sleep now."

Zina slipped out the door, and, as the glow of the lantern faded, the darkness seemed to flood back a hundred times more heavy and oppressive. Puzzled but deeply touched, Christina mulled over what her aunt had said to her. At last, her tired young body took control and she slept heavily and wearily.

Toward morning the storm broke. The first loud thunderclap jolted Christina from her sleep, and she heard the wild rush of heavy rain and saw the gigantic scar of lightning gash across the night sky, illuminating wet cliffs, trees, and houses so that they looked painted in phosphorous for one mad, wild moment. Then everything disappeared into blackness once more. She had left her window open and the onslaught of the rain drenched the curtains. Leaping out of bed, Christina ran to the window and tugged down the swollen sash. She crawled back into bed, and the blessed coolness which was driven before the storm bathed her body. She turned face down on the coverlet and was almost instantly asleep.

When Christina awakened, bright sunlight was streaming into her room. Knowing that she had overslept shamefully, she dressed hurriedly and crept down the back stairs to the kitchen. Zina was not there, and the kitchen looked unused. She moved to the hallway where she could hear women's voices coming from the parlor. Not wanting to interrupt, she walked softly toward the main room, hearing bits and pieces of conversation.

". . . some relief at last . . ."

"Grover Cleveland . . ."

"So sorry for Matty's brother . . . to be mourning two wives!"

"Will Matty be gone long?"

"Dreadful about Mrs. McElin! Such a sad thing, to lose both baby and mother . . ."

"Well, at her age! It's always a danger. Maybe she should have known better than to . . ."

"Rather shocking, so soon after the first wife's death . . . hardly a decent interval!"

Zina's voice interrupted sharply. "Do not say such things, Neila. It is not for us to judge! Janeth loved Angus very much and Lucy was always very possessive. Janeth deserved happiness—not this."

There was an awkward pause then another voice asked, "Have you told Christina yet?"

Christina stepped into the parlor, her face white, and the women turned to stare at her with concern and consternation. Zina was sitting on the sofa with three other women in a small circle around her. All of them seemed at a loss for words, but Christina looked squarely at her aunt. "Have you told me what, Aunt Zina?" she asked in a proud, determined voice. She was not going to let those nosy women see that she was frightened and upset.

Without hesitation, Zina stood up and walked to her niece. "Come with me, dear," she said softly. Turning to the other women, she nodded her head in a gesture of dismissal. "Please, will you excuse us? I'm sure you can let yourselves out." Gently Zina led Christina to Matty's office. It was empty, and Matty's saddlebags, which usually hung on a rack on the far side of the desk, were gone. The floor was stained with muddy bootprints, and the room had a look of disarray.

"Please sit down, dear," Zina urged. Christina, suddenly aware that her knees did not seem able to support her, sat down abruptly. Zina pulled Matty's desk chair in front of Christina, sat down, and took the young woman's hand.

"I hardly know where to begin, Christina. I think perhaps I should give this to you first and then you may ask me any questions you want."

Zina handed her an envelope. Christina opened it to find a short letter in her father's writing. The date at the top was one day ago. She looked up at her aunt with a perplexed frown, but Zina motioned her to go on, and so Christina concentrated on the sheet of paper: "My Dear Daughter Christina, It is with sorrow and regret that I must tell you of the death of your mother. She passed away two weeks ago lovingly cared for by the Saints with whom she was staying. They have assured me all that was possible was done for her but her life could not be saved. She died as she lived, nobly and quietly. I know that our Heavenly Father has welcomed her home with open arms."

The paper fell from Christina's nerveless hand. Too shocked to cry, or even comprehend what she had read, she felt the blood draining from her head, and Zina watched in horror as the young girl fell from her chair in a dead faint.

It wasn't until much later that Christina became conscious of where she was. She was lying in her little bedroom, and Zina was carefully sponging her face with a cool cloth. As Christina opened her eyes, her aunt gave a sigh of relief. "You gave me quite a scare, dear girl!" she said, smiling tenderly. "I know you have had a great shock, and I am truly sorry you had to learn this tragic news with so little preparation."

"Please, Aunt Zina, tell me everything!" Christina begged. "How did she die? Where is Papa? What is going on?"

"Oh, dear!" Zina seemed flustered and upset. "There is so much to tell. You see, your father brought the news last night. Poor man! He could not even attend the funeral. The federal marshal was waiting in Nephi to arrest him if he came. Your mother died—"

Zina hesitated and averted her eyes, and suddenly Christina felt, irrationally, that there must be something shameful even in her mother's manner of dying.

Zina took a deep breath and turned back to look Christina straight in the eye. "I think you are old enough to understand this," she said. "Your mother died from miscarrying. She was going to have a baby, Christina, and the child came much too soon. They couldn't stop the bleeding. It—it—sometimes happens when an older woman . . . that is . . . it is not uncommon when a woman is over forty. . . . I think perhaps if your mother had been able to administer to herself she might have lived. She was an amazing healer, Christina. I hope you remember that, dear. She has saved many, many lives. I feel so sad that there was no one who could have saved hers." Zina burst into tears, and through her sobs, she tried to smile. "She was one of the finest women I have ever known."

Christina watched her aunt crying, but she could not feel any tears. Somewhere, where the tears should have been, she felt a great hollow void, cold and dark, ballooning inside her. She almost felt as though the real Christina wasn't even in her body. The real Christina was standing over in a corner of the room watching sweet, tearful Aunt Zina tell a stranger on the bed what had happened to her mother.

"Why didn't Father come in to see me last night?" Christina asked, her voice dull and lifeless.

"He didn't dare talk to you, Christina! He wasn't sure whether he had been followed by the marshals and he thought it best, if they should question you, that you could say, honestly, that you had not seen him. He wanted to see you very much. Uncle Matty is traveling back to the Virgin Valley with him."

Christina nodded, but her eyes held no emotion.

"Anyway, dear," Zina went on, "with all of this terrible news, I have some good news. It looks very possible that President Grover Cleveland is planning to give amnesty to the men who have been jailed on charges of plural marriage. There is every indication that this terrible persecution is coming to an end. We have abided by the law in every way, and people have begun to see that we are, after all, loyal and responsible citizens who are trying to serve our God and our nation at the same time. Your father feels it may be only a matter of weeks before you will be able to return to Pleasantview."

For the first time Christina showed emotion. She sat up suddenly, her eyes blazing with distress and fear. "Not the Garden House! I can't go back! I will never go back there!"

Zina reached out soothing arms and laid Christina gently back upon the pillows. "No, no, dear!" she said soothingly. "Of course not back to the Garden House. I understand. You could never want to live there again—not with all the sweet memories of your mother. Besides, now that it is just you, Mary, and your father, you will all live together at the Big House, of course. You will need to take care of him now. He loved your mother very much. . . ."

Christina lay back on the pillows and let her mind slip away again. She felt herself swirling out of the room, while Zina's voice seemed to come from some distant place. "Loved her very much," the voice said, and then her own voice repeated the phrase, mockingly, laughingly. The sound of a creaking bed, her mother and father riding off together, their horses almost touching. "That's how babies are born . . . even to old women. . . ." *You have it all wrong—she was the one who loved him! She coaxed him, wooed him, seduced him. And now the whole world knows! Everyone knows about her passion and they're laughing at the strange wild woman who was your mother!*

"Why couldn't she do anything like other people?" Christina wanted to scream. "Even her dying! It couldn't be private—circumspect—hidden!" Aunt Lucy scarcely cold in the grave and her mother filled up with the seed of her father's love because she had begged for it, wanted it. Had she no shame? Her mother had flaunted her love—old and plain though she was. Her mother had died because of her hunger, her passion, her needs.

In black confusion and misery Christina wanted to cry out—she wanted to rage at her mother and father, at the sorrow and the humiliation and the pain she was feeling. Somewhere in the whole massive weight of her terrible emotions she recognized a fierce, crazy pride for her shameful mother, and oddly enough, on the underside of the black sense of bitter betrayal, she felt the odd sharp sliver of an emotion she refused to accept because she recognized what it was. It was jealousy. She did not want to know how such an emotion came to be in the dark black crush of her pain.

* * *

In October, just before the snows came, Christina received word through her uncle Matty that her father had returned to Pleasantview. With the death of his two wives and the civil annulment of his marriage to Sarah, he was no longer sought by the federal authorities. Throughout the Territory of Utah there was a softening in the official stance, and many leaders who had been on warrant lists now returned to their homes and families and began to set their long-neglected affairs in order.

"Your father needs you at home, Christina," Matty told her. "He has sent for Mary too. He wants you to come help him get the Big House into running order and to prepare the Garden House for rental."

With a heavy heart Christina prepared for her return to Pleasantview. The dream she had cherished since her earliest memories to live in the Big House had now become a reality, and yet the thought held no pleasure for her. With all her soul Christina wanted to remain in St. George with her aunt and uncle.

On the day she was scheduled to board the stagecoach to Manti, Christina's heart felt like lead. Zina had cried all through breakfast and morning prayers, and now, as she fussed over Christina's luggage, her tears started afresh.

"You won't forget to write to me, Christina dear!" Zina exclaimed, as she retied the ribbons on Christina's bonnet. "You look so pretty. My, how you have grown and matured this summer! You are such a beautiful young woman!" Zina's voice was choked by another sob. "I am going to miss you so much!"

Tears sprang to Christina's eyes and she threw her strong young arms around her plump little aunt. "Oh, Aunt Zina! I don't want to go! You have been so good to me and I love you and Uncle Matty so much!" Zina struggled to control herself and patted Christina on the back gently. "There, there, dear. We will see each other again, soon. If I didn't know how lonely your poor papa is I don't think I could stand to see you go!"

Matty came over and took one of the crying women under each arm. "Now, you two! Enough of this bawling! You'll have the whole Ute tribe down on us, thinking we are sending out a war cry!" His firm, no-nonsense voice gave Christina strength, and she hugged him quickly and stepped up onto the high step of the stagecoach doorway.

"Thank you, Uncle Matty and Aunt Zina," she said. "I shall write, I promise! Come to Pleasantview soon!" The horses started moving with a great rattle of harnesses, and Christina leaned out of the window and waved until the sight of St. George was swallowed up in the dust.

Zina turned to Matty with a sigh. "Poor little motherless lamb!" she murmured sadly.

"Aye," Matty replied. "But she has my mother's spunk. I think she will not have an easy life, but she will be equal to it—no matter what comes. She's a fighter!"

Zina frowned thoughtfully. "She's had to fight for everything she wanted, but inside, she is frightened and unsure. If we could only have kept her another year or so. . . ."

Christina's homecoming was not at all what she expected. Her father, rather than looking the part of a weary, sorrowful, aging man, was fit, tanned, and filled with energy. He had spent his summer hiding in the mountains surrounding the valley, and, using the charts and maps in Janeth's old notebooks, he had visited many of the areas his second wife had explored years before.

Often during Janeth's long-ago summer of wandering she had begged Angus to come with her and view the large stands of mature timber on the backs of mounts Pisgah, Taimago, and Abajo, but for one reason and another he had always been too busy. During his own summer in the mountains he had been amazed at the breadth and daring of her wanderings, and when he located the timbering areas she had recorded for him years ago, he was astonished at the wealth of the harvest waiting for his axe.

These hidden forests were Janeth's last legacy to him. What an astonishing woman she had been! He returned to Pleasantview enthusiastically to start a new industry, lumbering, in the mountains above his beloved valley. His fervor filled him, renewed his youth, but it also made him less sensitive to his daughters and their needs.

He had greeted Christina warmly, but from long habit their relationship was too formal and tentative to allow either one of them to speak freely about Janeth. Their unspoken loss stood like a palpable barrier between them, making both father and daughter more awkward and stiff even though they yearned to feel close and more natural with one another.

And Christina could not overcome the uncomfortable feeling that she was an unwanted guest in the Big House. When Mary arrived from Salt Lake, the feeling was intensified by her immediate assumption of leadership and superiority. Christina found herself feeling more like a hired girl than a daughter of the house.

Christina's first season in the Big House turned out to be one of the coldest winters ever recorded in the Virgin Valley. Angus bought muffs and hats for Mary and Christina and fur-lined capes and boots. The girls made a lovely picture on Sunday mornings as they hurried to church, their hats at a rakish angle and their chilly hands snug in their soft muffs. Mary's cape was a deep-blue velvet with black braid trim and black seal lining. Christina's was the color of claret, with beaver lining. They made a charming contrast, Mary, cool, smooth, and dark, and Christina, colorful, vibrant, and exuberant.

Gradually, as the winter progressed, Christina and Mary developed a pattern that made their days together workable. They stayed out of one another's way as much as possible. Angus was extremely busy organizing his new lumbering venture. He and Johnny spent hours together in the business office on the first floor and hired a clerk to handle their voluminous correspondence.

Shortly after Christmas Angus left for Salt Lake City to file incorporation papers and arrange for delivery of equipment in the summer, and to subcontract the lumbering crew. It would be a long and hazardous journey, and the girls did not know how soon he would return.

A few days after Angus's departure, Christina was walking up the stairs carrying some freshly ironed bed linens. As she walked down the hall she heard the sound of crying coming from Mary's room and so she tapped on the door.

"Mary!" she called softly. "Are you all right?"

There was no reply, only the continued sound of sobs. Christina turned the handle and pushed the door open slowly. She could see Mary lying face down on the brass bed, her shoulders shaking.

Impulsively, Christina put down the linens and hurried over to the bed. She sat beside her crying sister and patted her awkwardly on the back. "Mary, what is it? Can I do anything?"

Mary sat up abruptly and lifted her tear-stained face to her sister. "Oh, Christina! I think if I have to stay in this awful place another day I shall die! Pleasantview is so provincial and I'm so bored!" She was weeping with rage and frustration. "Why couldn't Papa take me with him to Salt Lake! I begged him, but he said the trip would be too difficult. I don't care how difficult it is! I'd do anything to get away from here! There's nothing to do—no one to talk to—no one worth knowing here!"

Relieved to know that nothing serious was the matter, and stung by Mary's thoughtless words, Christina blurted out the first thought that came into her head. "You mean that Peter Saunderson isn't here! If he were here you'd think Pleasantview was better than Salt Lake!"

Christina had only meant to tease, but she had struck a tender spot. Mary sprang from the bed, her eyes flashing and her fists clenched. She was taller than Christina, and when she drew herself up to her full height she was imposing. In a voice as cold as the icicles hanging from the eaves of the house, she challenged, "Don't you dare make fun of me!"

Without responding, Christina walked calmly over to the door, picked up the bed linens, and prepared to leave the room, but, just as she reached the door, she turned with a saucy smile and said, "Don't worry, Mary, no one could make fun of you—because you don't have any fun in you!"

With a cry of anger, Mary picked up her pillow and threw it with all her force at Christina, but her sister was too fast for her, and the pillow bounced off the door as it closed.

Late that night Christina got up and put on her woolen robe. The air was icy in the house, and the wooden floors were so cold they almost froze her bare feet. She ran swiftly down the runner rug in the upstairs hall and knocked on Mary's door.

"Mary!" she whispered, shivering. "Let me in!"

"What do you want?" Mary called, her voice alarmed but sleepy.

"To talk!" Christina answered. "Let me in before I die of the cold."

Very reluctantly, Mary called, "Come in, if you must!"

Christina walked into the freezing room. Mary was buried up to her nose in comforters and quilts. Standing in a chill ray of moonlight by the window, Christina shivered, and through chattering teeth she apologized.

"I know I shouldn't have teased you today, Mary. Please forgive me. I didn't mean to hurt you. I was just trying to be funny." Christina gave a nervous giggle. "You're right, it is pretty boring around here."

From deep under the bedclothes came a muttered, "I forgive you!"

"What did you say?" Christina yelled. "You mean it? No more bad feelings?"

"Oh, for heaven's sake!" Mary said impatiently. "Will you stop hopping around on your bare feet like a two-year-old! You'd better get in here and warm up, before you go back to your own room."

Christina didn't need a second offer. In a twinkling she had hopped into the wide bed next to Mary, sliding blissfully under the cloud of covers and curling up into a shivering ball.

"Mind you don't put your cold feet on me!" Mary warned. "You'd think you didn't have the sense you were born with, walking around after the fires are out on a night like this!"

Christina didn't care how much Mary scolded. She lay in the dark room listening to Mary's voice and feeling the blessed warmth of the quilts beginning to relax her shivering muscles, and she smiled to herself in the darkness.

Chapter Ten

As soon as the spring thaws came, men for the lumbering crew began to filter into the valley. For the most part they were a rough-and-ready group, men who had roamed the west, shearing sheep, cutting timber, turning their hands to any task that took strong arms and no questions asked. When they wearied of a place, or their work was done, they packed their few belongings and set off again. They drank whiskey, smoked or chewed tobacco, and fueled their meals with thick black coffee. To the Mormons they seemed as exotic and frightening as creatures from the inner ring of Dante's Inferno.

The mothers of Pleasantview cautioned their daughters to beware of the "lumbermen," and so the young girls of the valley cast their eyes downward when the men passed them on the streets, but more than one pretty young thing found herself staring out the corner of her eye to catch a glimpse of excitingly wicked masculinity.

One day Mary and Christina had a group of girl friends in the front parlor working on a quilt. The conversation turned to the topic of the lumbermen.

"I think those loggers are so handsome!" one dark-haired beauty exclaimed, giggling. "When you pass them on the street, I declare they are bold as brass!"

"You'd better watch how they treat you!" cautioned another friend. She was plump, with a round, firm chin. "Mama says those kind of men know all sorts of ways to lure young girls to"—her voice dropped to a whisper—"be with them!" She rolled her eyes meaningfully.

"Oh, tish!" Christina said impatiently. "I think they're a very ordinary-looking lot, and kind of scruffy too. Besides, most of them are so old!"

"Fiddle-dee-dee!" said the dark-haired girl. "You just don't know a real man when you see one, Christina! I suppose it comes from all those years of tending sheep when you should have been tending to important things—like boys!"

The girls laughed, and Christina felt the blood rising to her face, but then she saw the girls' merry eyes and realized she was being teased. With a shrug of her shoulders, Christina joined in the laughter.

Not all of the work crew that was being assembled for the summer logging camp came from outside the valley. Many local men saw this as an opportunity to earn hard cash, and even Jeremy had signed up. The upper mountain trails were still blocked with snow, and so the gathering men grew restless waiting in the valley with little to do until the roads opened. A number of loggers worked during the day to widen the lower roads and trails that led to the upper slopes. Teams of oxen and heavy horses were being collected in the valley, and large lumbering wagons were being constructed to carry the cut timbers down from the mountains. The air grew thick with a sense of change and excitement.

Late one afternoon Jeremy's younger brother knocked on the front door of the Big House. Christina answered the door. "Hello, Russell," she said, surprised to see her young cousin. "What can I do for you?"

The red-haired boy was out of breath from running. "Please, Christina, could you go fetch the cows home for me this afternoon? I've got a ballgame at school. Jem usually goes for me when I have to play ball, but he's still up at the roadwork today and somebody's got to fetch the cows! Would you do it for me?"

Christina laughed. "Yes, Russell, I will."

The relief on the boy's face was almost comical. "Jem said you would! He said, 'If you ever need help, just ask Christina. She's a good egg!' "

"I appreciate the compliment, Russell. Good luck with your game."

The McElin milk cows were pastured in the community field outside the town limits. In the evening it was hardly a matter of driving the animals home, since they were docile creatures, and, with their udders heavy and uncomfortable, they were happy to head back to their own barns and the relief of milking.

Christina snatched up an old calico bonnet, bunched her skirts up at the waist, and set off at a sprightly pace for the town pasture.

Gathering the animals together proved to be a more difficult chore than she had remembered. By the time she had them bunched together and moving down the muddy road toward town, she was hot and dirty. She cut a long willow switch, and with the light end of it she flicked the cows' rumps to keep them in line.

For some reason that night the animals seemed restless and jumpy. They probably missed young Russell. Nonetheless, Christina kept the little herd together and they began moving along quite nicely.

Suddenly behind her on the road she heard the clamor of a galloping horse. Startled, she whirled to stare in alarm as a single rider bore down on her and her herd. The rider was a young man, and his head was turned looking back over his shoulder as he ragged his horse onward with his hat. It was not until the horse was almost upon Christina and the cows that the rider turned and saw where he was headed. In the resulting confusion Christina had three distinct impressions: She saw a horrified look of concern in a pair of flashing blue eyes; she saw the feet of the horse as it reared from the abruptly pulled reins; and she saw her cows bawling in fear and scattering, running awkwardly, their heavy milk sacks swaying and tugging as they trotted and leaped away from the road and the rearing horse.

Furious and unafraid of the plunging horse, Christina ran toward the man. "You fool! Look what you've done to my cows!" she shouted.

"Look what you've done to my horse!" the man replied a little unevenly as he struggled to master the frightened mount.

Christina gave a wordless scream of rage and frustration. "I haven't done anything! You—careless! wild! thoughtless person!" she shouted the last word as the worst epithet she could think of at the moment. "Why don't you look where you're going?"

"Why don't you herd your cattle on the road frontages where they belong?" he retorted. His face was tense from concentration on his horse, but his eyes and voice were touched with humor. Christina regarded his amusement as the last straw.

"This isn't funny!" she shouted. "Look at those poor animals! Do you know how much damage they could do to themselves running like that with full udders? I'll never get them herded together. Oh-h-h!" She let out a wail of fury and stamped off toward the nearest cow, wielding her gentle switch.

Without a word the rider, his horse calm now, cantered over the field. As Christina watched in astonishment, he rode his horse deftly among the cows, calling to them and encouraging them. The horse, equally gentle, nudged the cows back toward the road. If one of the animals strayed, the horse gracefully and instinctively moved from side to side until the cow, shown its path, moved toward the gathering herd. Within minutes all the cows were back together again and heading smoothly toward town. Christina had seen dogs work the sheep in much the same way, but she had never seen a horse and rider collaborate so deftly.

At last the horse came up beside her, and its rider, with an ironic grin, raised his hat to her.

"I expect you think I should thank you," Christina said tartly. "But since you caused the problem in the first place, I'm not sure that gratitude is in order." She knew she sounded ungracious, but there was something about the assurance and calmness of this man that she found incredibly irritating. He didn't seem to feel sorry at all. He even seemed to find her, or the situation, slightly amusing.

He rested his hands on the pommel of his saddle and continued to regard her with his quiet blue gaze. He was handsome, she had to give him that, but she found his looks as irritating as his manner. Did he think because he was handsome she would smile and forgive him?

"You might say something!" she exclaimed angrily, uncomfortable under his silent scrutiny.

"I'm afraid to," he replied, the quiet note of humor still present in his deep pleasant voice. "I don't know what to say that won't set you off again. I believe what I've been told—hell hath no fury like a scornful woman!"

Her face flamed with fury and shame. Controlling herself with difficulty, she turned her eyes and concentrated on the cows that, sensing the closeness of their barns, had picked up their pace. "The correct quote is 'a woman scorned'!" she stated haughtily.

He grinned and nodded, and she realized belatedly that he had been baiting her. She refused to smile back at him.

"Besides," she said, turning to give him one last look, her small square chin raised in defiance and her eyes flashing, "the quote should really say that 'hell hath no fury like a McElin woman'!" With that she marched briskly toward the cows, and the young man, pulling his horse to a stop, watched her go with a look of speculative amusement on his lean, suntanned face.

Tired, cross, and dirty, Christina entered the back door and slammed it after her. Sister Hammond was in the kitchen taking a chocolate cake out of the oven.

"Best wash up quick, Christina," Sister Hammond said. "Your papa has guests for dinner and your Uncle Johnny and Aunt Hes and Aunt Min are here too. They're in the parlor getting set to go to the table right now."

Sister Hammond worked at the Big House as housekeeper and cook. She was a cheerful, hard-working woman who tried to mother the two sisters, but the girls remained rather aloof and cool toward her. The McElins were too private to allow anyone easy access to their personal lives.

Christina hurried up the narrow kitchen stairs. She didn't want to be late and face her father's displeasure, or try to explain what had kept her.

In her bedroom, Christina stripped off her soiled workclothes and boots and put on a white shirtwaist with a high neck and a simple dark skirt. She smoothed her hair with a brush and pulled it back in a big white bow at the neck. Quickly she rinsed her face and hands and dotted some fresh-smelling cologne on her wrists.

A glance in the mirror told her that she looked presentable, and so she hurried down the hall to the front stairs. She could hear Mary laughing happily, and the voices of men and women mingled. As she entered the parlor, Papa saw her and came to her with a smile of relief.

"We were getting worried about you, Christina! Where have you been?" he asked kindly.

"I brought the cows home for Russell, and it took longer than I expected," she explained.

"Good for you," her father said proudly. "You do have a way with animals. Now come over here and meet Mary's friend. Then we shall all go into dinner together."

Johnny, his wives, and Mary were standing talking to a man

whose back was facing Christina, but even before he turned around she knew who the man was, and her cheeks flamed.

"Peter," Angus said, touching the guest on the shoulder, "I've someone else I'd like you to meet."

Christina was prepared for the blue eyes and the calm half smile that met her gaze.

"My daughter Christina," Angus continued, putting his hand lightly on her shoulder. "Peter Saunderson." He nodded at the tall, muscular young man—the same person Christina had seen less than an hour before on the road into town.

"So this is Peter Saunderson!" Christina thought. "He is every bit as good-looking as Mary said he was. I bet he knows it too. Well! You are not going to charm me, Mr. Saunderson!" she thought defiantly.

"It is a pleasure," Peter said, taking her hand. "I have heard so much about the McElin women!" His voice was deep and confident and there was a glint of irony in it.

Angus looked slightly puzzled.

Christina gave Peter an exaggerated smile and said in her sweetest voice, "And I have heard a great deal about you too, Mr. Saunderson!" She pulled her hand away brusquely and turned to greet the other guests.

As the group moved toward the dining room, Peter came over beside her and murmured in a voice too low for the others to hear, "That was a quick change. You don't look anything like the furious cowgirl anymore—you look quite like a lady in those clothes." His eyes regarded her appreciatively.

Christina fixed him with a frosty glance. "It would take more than clothes to make a gentleman out of you!" she retorted.

"Don't stay angry with me." He laughed. "The cows are safely in their barns and I am sorry for what happened. Please accept my apology and let's start from scratch."

Everything in Christina was irritated by this impossible young man. Just when she felt she was justified in treating him badly, he apologized with such sincerity that she knew it would be stupid and ungracious for her not to accept.

Very stiffly, she nodded her head. "Very well," she said grudgingly. "Now let us go in, or we will keep the others waiting." Out of the corner of her eye Christina could see Mary watching them with a tight frown on her narrow face.

For everyone but Christina the dinner was a success. She had

205

never seen Mary so animated or cordial. Peter was not a talker, but when he spoke he was amusing and his observations were intelligent. He was obviously well read and became an animated speaker when the conversation turned to a discussion of books. Angus and Peter had a heated interchange concerning the character of Macbeth.

At one point Peter said he felt Macbeth's greatest mistake was his willingness to allow his wife to influence him. Incensed, Angus countered by declaring that a man's mistakes were his own responsibility. To that Peter replied, "True. But what is a man to do if his wife is a creature of irresistible emotions or unbendable will?" As Peter asked the question he deliberately looked across the table at Christina and held her eyes with his for a moment. Then he smiled in a slow, provocative way and continued the conversation by asking Mary what she thought.

"Mary, her cheeks tinged with pink, looks very pretty tonight," Christina thought, "and a little flustered—which is unlike her."
"Oh—I'm not sure, Peter," Mary stammered. "Perhaps his biggest mistake was marrying that particular woman in the first place!"

Everyone at the table laughed, and the conversation flowed on to the establishment of the lumber camp, which would be moving up into the mountains the following week. As the talk continued, Christina ascertained that Peter had come to work with the logging crew. She thought of the dark, worldly men who made up the bulk of the work force. It satisfied her to regard Peter Saunderson as a man lost to the church social circles and the parlors of decent folks—a wild, wandering man whom she was justified in snubbing. Still, her practical mind reminded her that he hardly fit in that neat category of "lumberman" since he was there in her very own home dining with her father and sister, who were the very souls of probity.

After dinner, Christina excused herself early and went up to bed. She could hear the sounds of laughter downstairs for a long time, and it seemed to her that it was hours before she finally fell asleep.

When the logging crews left to establish the first camp on the plateaus at the back of Mount Pisgah, the town became quiet and dull. Mary sulked around the house, and Christina found she missed Jeremy more than she would have thought possible.

The work crew's schedule kept them on the mountain from Monday morning until late Saturday afternoon, when the men were dismissed, and they came streaming down the three-hour trail from their camp into Pleasantview. The town had grown dramatically in the past months, with houses and sheds thrown up on the outskirts, and a new cafe on the incoming road that provided a piano player and sold spirits. The church-going population was horrified at this new addition to their community, but they were realistic enough to recognize that they could not hold back the world forever.

The professional lumbermen found their Saturday night fun in the rowdy cafe, but the young loggers who came from Pleasantview and the surrounding towns were welcomed at church socials and in the homes of the leading citizens.

The weekdays were slow and dull, but Saturday nights became a round of merriment, with parties, dinners, and dances. The air was full of excitement, vitality, and a feeling of prosperity just around the corner as the magnificent trees came rumbling down the mountains, shorn of limbs and bark with the terrible cut across their bases showing in hundreds of rings the trees' years upon the earth.

During the early part of the summer Christina had become aware of a subtle change in her father. Angus, uncharacteristically, sent to Salt Lake and ordered himself a set of new clothes. Always neat and conservative in his dress, he became even more meticulous in his grooming. He bought a pair of matched grays for his carriage. The horses were blooded and sprightly, and he harnessed them with a special-order harness of supple black leather trimmed with polished silver.

About the middle of June, Angus told the girls rather sheepishly that he was hiring a new accountant and secretary to handle the increasingly heavy load of paperwork for the thriving lumber company. Something about the way he made the announcement made it seem mysterious. On a bright, sunny morning their father left the house early, dressed in his new morning coat with white piping at the vest and a freshly starched shirt, with a silk cravat, to "fetch" the new clerk.

Although Angus's hair and beard were sprinkled with white, his face and carriage were still that of a younger man. His clear, piercing eyes and well-muscled vitality commanded admiration and respect. His girls thought of him as "old," but he was, in reality, at the very height of his manhood and power.

Christina felt a prescient spark of apprehension as she saw her father drive off with his magnificent team. The morning passed slowly, and it was close to lunchtime when Christina heard the sound of Angus's carriage returning. Her father entered the front door with a pretty woman in a dress of creamy daytime silk. It was elaborately draped and stitched, with an embroidered inset in the front, and she wore a matching hat tied with a fetching bow and decorated with silk blossoms and a dotted veil.

The blond woman was laughing at something Angus had said. Her head and eyes were turned toward him with a look of proprietary affection. Christina felt a chill in the pit of her stomach.

"Girls!" Papa said, calling them down from their places on the stairs. "I'd like you to meet Sister Louella Minton." The pride in his voice was unmistakable.

With watchful eyes and blank expressions, Mary and Christina came down and shook the woman's hand. "How do you do, Sister Minton," they said in formal, expressionless voices.

With a mannered laugh Louella Minton looked at Angus archly. "Why didn't you tell me they were beautiful, Angus? It is hard to believe you are the father of two such grown-up girls. Why, I expected them to be mere children the way you speak of them, and here they are—young women. Almost ready for homes of their own."

She fixed the girls with her bright, penetrating eyes. "I'm so glad to meet you at last!" she exclaimed. "Your papa talks of nothing else but his two wonderful daughters—and of course his lumber company! Always in that order!"

Louella swept into the parlor and the others followed her. With a quick appraisal of the room, Louella again turned her eyes on the girls, her smile still radiant and warm. "You must not call me Sister Minton. After all, I'm not all that much older than either one of you. Please just call me Louella."

Dutifully, the sisters nodded, and Christina was sickened to see how her father was beaming upon the scene, as though he thought it was the most wonderful thing he could imagine to have them all together in one room.

"I'm so glad to see the three of you getting along!" he declared expansively. "I knew you would like one another. It's important because Louel—I mean, Sister Minton—will be working in my office here at the Big House. You'll be seeing a lot of one another."

"Where will you be living?" Mary asked primly. "Do you have a home in Pleasantview?"

"Oh, dear me, no, Mary! I'm from Manti. After my husband passed away, I continued to run the telegraph and post office there. That's how I met your papa. He was doing so much business by telegram and mail trying to get his lumber company going, I almost felt like his full-time employee. So he decided to make it official, and asked me to come work for him."

Again she smiled into Angus's eyes. Christina could have sworn she actually batted her lashes at her poor defenseless father, who smiled back with delight.

"It is such a privilege to have the opportunity to work for a man with the vision and capability of your father," Louella added.

Christina thought she was going to be sick. Surely her father could see through such obvious flattery and manipulation. Angus, however, simply smiled back at Louella, his face showing nothing but pleasure and satisfaction. The whole situation was a nightmare.

If Christina and Mary had been close, loving sisters, they might have developed a means to fight the invasion of Louella Minton. She did not sleep at the Big House, since Johnny and Hes had given her an extra bedroom in their home. But that was the only time she was absent. Louella came early in the morning to have breakfast with Angus and his daughters, during which time she and Angus began talking about the day's business. She spent hours in his office working on accounts and correspondence. Louella also ate supper with the family and often stayed into the evening talking to Angus, or finishing up his books, or sometimes even bringing a bit of sewing. She would make herself at home on the settee next to Angus, who seemed content to have her there.

In a very short time Louella had involved herself in every decision and activity of the house. When Angus went out for a meeting, she fussed over the way he looked, and more than once Christina had seen her straightening her father's tie or refolding his handkerchief. The Minton woman insinuated her own tastes into the dinner menus and ordered Sister Hammond around until the good woman threatened, obliquely, to quit.

For Christina, the final straw came one morning when she ran upstairs to change into her walking shoes and found Louella standing in her bedroom.

"What are you doing in my room?" Christina asked, her voice cold and furious.

"Now, Christina, dear!" Louella said in a mollifying tone. "I wanted to get to know you better, and I thought maybe if I could see your room it would give me some clues. You are such a mysterious young woman!"

"You know me as well as you need to!" Christina answered shortly.

"But we should get to be great friends!" Louella persisted. "I know we could! Mary is starting to like me better all the time."

Truthfully, Mary had not taken quite such a resolute and instant dislike to Louella as Christina had. Also, Mary was more pragmatic, and, since she could see the writing on the wall, she had decided to try to make some kind of adjustment to the older woman's presence. Christina suspected that such a lot of Mary's thinking was focused on the excitement of having Peter Saunderson nearby, that her sister was simply able to ignore Louella and the threat she represented. Christina had no such buffer.

She glared fiercely at Louella, her eyes hard and her jaw stiff with resistance. In the harsh light of the whitewashed bedroom Christina could see that behind the enforced gaiety and the subtle use of cosmetics, Louella's face was older than Christina had imagined. "Why, she must be forty if she's a day!" Christina thought. Still, Louella was younger than Angus, and everything she did emphasized that youthful impression—her clothes, her walk, and her determined sprightliness. Angus was obviously entranced by her.

Behind Louella's facade of feminine sweetness Christina suspected there was a shrewd and aggressive mind. Listening to business discussions between her father and this woman, Christina was sure that Louella had a firm grasp on the lumber company and was not adverse to influencing Angus in his decisions. Her father seemed to respect the Minton woman's opinion, even on matters in which she had no responsibility.

"You know, Christina!" Louella broke the cold silence in her most friendly voice, but Christina could detect the iron will underneath it. "This could be made into a lovely room, with that western exposure! If we just brought in some wallpaper with soft pink roses, we could add some fleece rugs and get Sister Hammond to make a Dresden quilt in cream and pink. We could make this a beautiful room for you—and it would make a nice guest room too."

"No!" Christina almost shouted. "This is my room. I will keep it the way I want. There is no such thing as 'we' for you here. You work for my father's lumber company. You are an employee. You have nothing to do with me, or my sister, or our home! You don't even have a right to be in here! This is my room! My house!"

The smile left Louella's face, but she did not seem taken aback by Christina's outburst. Instead she looked at the eighteen-year-old girl in front of her, with her auburn hair bursting from its pins, her dress stained with flour from the morning's baking, and her brilliant blue eyes blazing. She saw a formidable foe, but Louella was too sure of her own ground to feel any fear.

"Well," she said calmly, "I do want to be your friend, Christina, but it doesn't matter a lot if we are or we aren't. You see, this really isn't your home, it's your father's, and we shall see whose home it is by the end of the summer, won't we." Louella turned with a swish of her moiré taffeta skirt and walked gracefully down the center hall to the front stairs. Her wide rustling skirt seemed to fill the entire corridor. Christina went into her room and slammed the door.

That weekend Angus announced he was taking Louella for a brief visit back to Manti. Since he also had some business to conduct, he said they might not return for several days.

"May we have an Independence Day party at the Big House next Saturday?" Mary begged. "I will get Uncle Johnny and Aunt Hes to chaperone!"

"If Sister Hammond agrees, it's fine with me," Angus replied.

The week was spent in mad preparation. Bunting was hung on the porches, and the kitchen was filled with the smell of baking. There was to be a huge buffet on the porch followed by games on the back lawn, and then dancing in the parlor. The evening was to end with a fireworks display. Jeremy was going to bring the young men from the lumber camp, and Mary and Christina's girl friends were bringing cakes and flowers. Homemade root beer cooled in the cellar, and Johnny had contributed a huge ham from his own smokehouse.

Christina had to admit that Mary had never looked prettier or seemed happier than during that busy week. Christina knew it was because her half-sister was looking forward to seeing Peter. On the few occasions when Christina had seen Peter Saunderson during June, she had felt the same unreasoning antipathy toward him. He irked her because he was always in control of himself and she felt at a disadvantage. He seemed to hold himself aloof from others, as though he were an observer or perhaps a philosopher who used people as his laboratory. It puzzled Christina that Mary, so cool and proper, thought she was Peter's "girl." Although he was always cordial and attentive to her, Christina could detect no hint of courtship in his manner. Christina was the first to admit, however, that she knew nothing of such things. And, anyway, it was certainly Mary's problem, and Mary had not chosen to confide in her for months.

The Independence Day party was a great success. Young people poured into the Big House. The men from the lumber camp ate like ravenous wolves, but the buffet was copious. Root beer fizzed in crockery barrels and laughter and good spirits filled the evening air.

The relays on the back lawn became highly competitive. Christina and Jeremy ran in the three-legged race. Jeremy put his arm across Christina's back with their left and right ankles tied together. She was so short that he could almost pick her up with one arm. They practiced their pace until their rhythm was perfectly synchronized. Peter and Mary were going to run together as well, although Christina could tell by Mary's face that she was terrified of the athletic contest. A starter shouted "Go!" and the field was off. Before the teams had run ten yards several couples stumbled and fell on the soft grass, laughing and rolling. Mary and Peter were still struggling at the starting line, Mary awkward and embarrassed and Peter patient. Only one couple gave Jeremy and Christina a run for their money, but the cousins did not let the pressure fluster them. They kept their steady, rhythmic pace and, just before the finish line, the other couple, desperate to win, tried to sprint, broke pace, and fell. Christina and Jeremy won!

Everyone cheered, and Christina laughed until she cried. The games continued, and Christina collected five first-place ribbons, which she pinned on her dress. Finally, exhilarated and rumpled, she went into the house in search of a glass of root beer. A number of the more sedate young people had already begun to dance. Christina took a glass, smoothed her hair, and walked over to the settee to watch. A moment later Mary came in, with Peter in tow, and clapped her hands. "All right, everybody! One more dance, and then we shall go outside for the fireworks!"

A young man Christina had met at church came over to ask her to dance. As they began spinning around the parlor floor, the front door opened and her father and Louella walked in. As their host entered, the music stopped and the guests became respectfully quiet.

"Father!" Mary exclaimed. "I'm so glad you got back for the end of the party anyway! You are just in time for the fireworks."

"Yes," Angus said. "We tried very hard to make it back in time for the celebration. Especially since we have something of our own to celebrate. Mary! Christina!" He looked at each of his girls and then at the attentive guests. "I would like to introduce you to my wife, Mrs. Louella McElin. We were married in the Manti Temple yesterday. We wanted to surprise you."

The dancers gasped with delight, and someone started clapping while people called out congratulations.

Angus stood beaming in the wave of goodwill from the guests, and Louella smiled, blushed, and looked admiringly at her husband—the perfect picture of an adoring, adorable bride.

Mary, showing the breeding and character of her dignified mother, controlled her shock and dismay with rigid determination. With a forced smile, which was nonetheless beautiful, she went to her father and kissed his cheek. "I hope you will be truly happy," she whispered.

Then she leaned forward rather stiffly and gave Louella a formal kiss on the cheek. "Congratulations," she said, trying to make her voice sound natural.

Louella laughed nervously, her voice a little too high and shrill. "Thank you, Mary, dear. But you got it mixed up. You say 'Congratulations' to the groom—and 'happiness' to the bride." Everyone laughed appreciatively.

Angus looked searchingly across the room to Christina. Their eyes, so much alike, met in a direct gaze, and Christina felt impelled to move by the wish in her father's eyes. It took all of her self-control to walk to the hall. She could not force herself to speak, but she did embrace her father, and then, with arms as heavy as lead, she embraced Louella. Again the guests at the party applauded. Laughter and music began again as friends lined up to congratulate the newlyweds. In the confusion, Christina slipped through the crowd and out the kitchen door. She ran across the darkened lawn where the fireworks were to be held, and, for the first time since her return to Pleasantview, she found herself in the yard surrounding the Garden House. She ran on past her old home until she came to the animal shed, long empty and unused. She pulled the rusty door latch. The hinges screeched, but the door opened enough to let her slip inside. The air was dusty and it was so dark that she could not see anything, but instinct led her toward the pony stall where her foot struck a pile of hay. With a groan she sat down and put her hands tightly around her legs. She pulled herself into a fetal position and bowed her head so that she was like a small, tight, closed ball. Silence, darkness, and the smell of past summers surrounded her and filled her senses.

"Mama!" she cried to herself. "Mama!"

After a while she heard the sound of fireworks. The first rocket burst in the air, and its flash of light caused tiny silver streaks to show through the cracks in the boards of the shed. For a brief instant everything was etched in silver and then it was dark again. She listened for a second boom, but instead, in the silence, she heard the sound of someone opening the shed door. The explosion of a starburst cracked in the air, and in its light she saw, for an instant, the outline of a man standing in the partially opened door. Then silence and darkness again. She was quiet in her corner, thinking whoever it was would go away, but then she heard the door close and the creak of shoes walking toward her. She instinctively moved backward, and the hay rustled underneath her.

She gasped as a voice whispered, "Christina?"

"Who is it?" she called angrily.

"Peter," the voice replied, much closer to her now. She heard someone sitting down in the hay on the other side of the stall, just a foot or two away from her.

"What are you doing here?" she demanded angrily. "How did you know where to find me?"

"I followed you," he said quietly, his voice patient and calm in the darkness.

"Why?" she challenged him.

"I thought you might need someone to talk to," he responded in the same even tone.

"I don't!" Christina retorted defiantly. "I came here to be alone! And even if I wanted to talk to someone it certainly wouldn't be you. I hardly know you."

"That's true," Peter's voice replied. Another rocket was shot off, and in the brief light she could see his outline. He was sitting so close she could have reached out her hand and touched him.

"Christina," he said gravely, "I came to take you back. If you return to the party now, with all the confusion of the fireworks, no one will have missed you. If you wait, everyone will notice that you've gone—and they'll guess why. You can prevent that embarrassment and hurt to your father if you come back with me now."

"My father!" she shouted, her voice breaking with bitterness. "My father! Why should I care about causing him hurt and embarrassment? What about me—he causes me nothing but hurt—what does he care about me, about my pain and shame?" she cried again. "I hate my father! I hate him!" And somewhere from the past she heard the echo of her child's voice screaming at her mother: "I hate him! I hate him! He is never fair!" The memory hit at her, striking like a hammer from which random bolts of pain flashed like sparks and pierced the last remnant of her self-control. She began to weep wildly, like a child abandoning herself to grief.

She felt Peter's arms go around her. She didn't know how he had reached her so quickly, but he had raised her from her crouched position and was kneeling in front of her holding her in his arms, and she, torn by the force of her sobs, gave herself up to his strength. In the darkness it was not Peter who held her, it was simply someone's arms—there in the secret blackness—arms tight around her, and a warm solid body leaning against her, shoring her up, cushioning the fury of her emotions and making her secure from herself. Slowly her crying began to quiet and the wonderful warmth of those strong unknown arms seemed to wrap themselves around not only her body, but her mind, her heart, and her soul as well. In the total darkness she felt as though she had fallen into a magic place of comfort and peace. The arms pulled her closer and closer, and she became aware of the hard-muscled chest pressing against her own breast, and she felt the smooth, solid stroking of a firm hand against her trembling back. Suddenly she was consumed with the need to cling to this presence, to hold on, as though she were drowning on some dark and bitter wave, and she must reach up to fasten her own arms to this place of safety. She clasped her arms fiercely around Peter's waist and felt the heat of his body through the fabric of his suitcoat. Her tears were gone now, and so was the fury and hurt, but in their place was a frantic restlessness, an urgent desperate hunger that was nameless to her, and yet it compelled her, in the darkness, to press herself against the man who held her. She moved her arms upward around his neck and pulled him toward her, not even knowing what she was doing.

It was as though, in the blackness of the empty stable, neither of them were really people, only collections of needs and wants. All that was in the dark stable was the hunger for love crying in Christina's heart and those warm strong hands, and two beating hearts and the mystery of some great and dreadful unknown that had hung over Christina since before she could remember.

She felt Peter's head press against her cheek and then his mouth, soft as silk, brush against her once, and then again, more fiercely, and then he bent and kissed her neck, her ears, her chin, her throat—sweet, rich kisses, like nothing she had ever imagined. His hands were in her hair pulling her face toward him, smoothing her tangled mass of curls with long, tender strokes, as she lifted her face, her mouth half open, soft and hungry. Her breath was as light and quick as the beating of a startled sparrow's wings, and in the thick velvet darkness his unknown lips reached down to her and filled her hunger with his own. She had never dreamed of such feelings—had never known such desperate sweetness. Again and again she kissed his silent lips and felt herself falling into a vortex of forgetfulness and joy that released her from every moment of her past.

Another rocket burst in the air. It startled them apart, and in the faint afterlight she looked up to see Peter's grave eyes looking at her. In his eyes she thought she saw the remnant of the pain that had left her. Seeing his face brought her back to herself, and to reality. This was no disembodied being who knelt next to her in the Garden House barn. It was a flesh-and-blood man! She felt a hot blush rise to her face. The blessed covering darkness returned, but Christina had grown stiff in Peter's arms.

"You must go back to the party, Christina," he whispered urgently. "You are almost out of time. You must return for yourself and your father." She pulled away from him, her anger directed now at herself, as well as at him and her father.

"And you will have such an amusing story to tell!" she exclaimed bitterly.

Silence greeted her thrust, and she was ashamed to have accused him because she knew that Peter would never tell a living soul about what had happened. The thought gave her little comfort though, because Peter himself would know, and she felt her acquiescence had given him an advantage over her. Still, in spite of herself, she felt a warm glow and relief from her anger at her father. She wasn't sure what had happened to her there, but in her confusion and turmoil she felt shy about facing Peter in the light.

Christina stood up abruptly. "I *will* go back!" she said decisively. "I think perhaps there is less to fear out there than in here." Her voice cut through the darkness. In response she heard a chuckle.

"For both of us, I think," said Peter's soft voice.

Christina rushed to the door and pulled it open. The night air was redolent with the smell of gunpowder. The western sky was filled with stars that were brighter than fireworks. Christina could hear the murmur from the party on the back lawn, and saw the guests in silhouette sitting in a semicircle, their faces looking upward, waiting for the last rockets. She brushed her skirts and smoothed her wayward hair. An old patch of mint grew nearby, and she plucked some fragrant leaves and crushed them in her hands to dispel the scent of the dusty stable. "In the darkness, I'll do!" she decided and walked

216

swiftly across the lawn to join the straggling edge of the party just as the final rockets lit up the sky.

Behind her she saw the tall figure of Peter Saunderson striding across the lawn toward Mary. Mary looked up at him and smiled. He sat down beside her, nodding to Angus and Louella on the other side. The sight of Louella and Angus together brought back Christina's anger and sorrow in a rush. A sense of hopelessness settled over her like a cloud across the moon.

Christina could not live in the same house with Louella and her father. She could not bear the sight of them together, or the terrible lurking thoughts that bombarded her when she thought of them together in her father's small dark bedroom. She lay awake trying to think of some way out of her terrible dilemma. She considered writing to her Uncle Matty and Aunt Zina, but Aunt Zina was not feeling well and she didn't want to burden them. Where could she go?

In the end it was Jeremy's mother, sweet, silent Min, the solid enduring second wife of Johnny's happy double marriage, who gave her the answer.

Min had come over to bring a bowl of sweet cream for Sister Hammond, who was making a batch of sugar loves. Christina was sitting glumly in the kitchen, trying to stay out of Louella's path. Something in the girl's dejected appearance struck Min. She recalled that Jeremy had said Christina had taken her father's new marriage very hard, and Min, for one, could see why. Min was the kindliest soul in the world and would never say a harsh word about anyone, but in her heart of hearts she thought that Angus's new wife was the most grasping woman she'd ever met.

"Well, Christina," Min said, sitting down at the table with an exaggerated sigh, "seems you're not quite yourself today. I think you need something to do. I always find that work is the best medicine for anything that ails me."

Christina smiled at her plump, cheerful aunt. She really liked this hearty woman, even though sometimes Min's well-meaning advice was wide of the mark.

"I'm tired of hoeing the garden, Aunt Min." Christina laughed. "That's no help for boredom anyway. And Papa won't let me herd the sheep anymore. He says I'm too old, and it's unladylike. So do you have any other suggestions?"

"I certainly do!" Min exclaimed. "Did Sister Hammond tell you

217

that she and I are going to finish the summer running the cooking crew for the lumber camp?''

"No!" Christina exclaimed, looking over at Sister Hammond with a surprised expression. "I didn't know!"

"If you'd listen to what's going on around you, you'd know, Christina. You've been in a fog all week," Sister Hammond said impatiently.

"The men have been taking turns doing the cooking, and there's been a lot of complaints," Min explained. "So your father has set up a second smaller camp, with cook tents and enough sleeping spaces for eight or ten women. We're going to go up during the week with the men and take care of the cooking."

"You mean, you'll be living all week right up in the mountains?" Christina's eyes sparkled at the thought. "Oh, Aunt Min! Take me with you! I promise you I'll work like two women. Aunt Min, I've just got to go."

"That's sort of what I was thinking too, Christina," Min said with her gentle smile. "I'll talk to your papa."

Christina would never know what a fight Min had in getting Angus to agree to let Christina go with the cooking crew to the mountains. Angus felt it unseemly to have the daughter of one of the owners working at the camp, but Min pointed out in her gentle, practical way that she was the wife of one of the part owners and she was going to be working with them.

Even Johnny joined in the discussion, reminding Angus how much Christina had always loved the mountains. Angus countered with his fears of sending a young woman to work among the rough element that existed at the camp, but Johnny pointed out that three other young women from good homes were planning to accompany the cooks, and Min and Sister Hammond were excellent chaperones.

It was finally Christina herself, though, who won the argument without even knowing it. After two days of saying no, Angus came to supper one evening and observed his young daughter. She was sitting in her place at the end of the table, as far from the others as possible. In the past weeks she appeared to have lost weight, and her face seemed pale and listless. Even her hair seemed to have lost its luster. She looked for all the world like an injured, caged bird, and his heart twisted for this child of his love. This daughter, so like his own mother in appearance and yet so like Janeth in her heart. How precious she was to him! He felt he could almost see the light in her dying before his very eyes.

He cleared his throat. "Christina!" he said. "Would you like to go with Aunt Min to the mountains?"

A flash of brilliant sunlight seemed to illuminate Christina's face. "How mercurial she is," her father thought. "Her emotions are so fierce and extreme, so close to the surface!"

Her face was radiant with joy. "Oh, yes, Papa!"

"Very well," he said sedately. "You have my permission."

Mary frowned as Christina leaped up from her chair and embraced her father exuberantly. "Thank you, Papa!"

"Ugh!" Mary said. "How can you want to spend a summer doing slave work and living with flies and dirt!"

Christina laughed. "Sounds wonderful to me, Mary!" she exclaimed and ran upstairs two at a time.

The work in the cook camp was hard. From sunup until sundown Christina and the other women toiled. The men had ferocious appetites in the thin, clear air of the mountains, and their grueling physical labor required huge quantities of food. Christina carried water, washed and peeled bushels of vegetables, scrubbed pans, kneaded dough, cut kindling, waited on tables, and ladled food from great pots that steamed on the serving lines.

Her dreams of spending days in the freedom and glory of the high mountains were quickly dispelled, since she scarcely had enough energy left at the end of the day to peel back the covers of her cot, say her prayers, and fall into bed.

The men worked to exhaustion. Occasionally a logger would make a flirtatious remark, or tease the women in the cook camp, but for the most part the timber men ate their meals with heavy concentration, enjoying the improved quality and quantity of the provisions, and returned directly to their labors. After the evening meal, the lumbermen did not linger near the cook tents. Those who used tobacco would indulge in an evening smoke. Others might return to the logging camp for a brief game of cards, or a round of jokes and banter by the campfire, but most of the crew headed for their beds, conscious of the early dawn and the requirements of the coming day.

It was inevitable that Christina should see Peter, but she did not speak to him and, when at all possible, avoided meeting his eyes. He did not press her for any acknowledgment, but when she could not avoid looking at him she caught him regarding her with a calm look of amusement, as though he could read her mind.

In mid-July an afternoon thundershower stopped the timber work early. The cookstoves had been extinguished by the downpour and the women prepared a cold supper of cornbread, rice pudding, ham slices, fresh tomatoes, buttermilk, and applesauce. The meal was served and eaten quickly. For the first time, the work of the camp was finished before darkness.

The rain had stopped and the men built a roaring fire in the center of their camp, hanging up their soaked shirts to dry. One of them pulled out a banjo, another a harmonica. Soon their music lured the women from the cooking camp to the edges of the men's area. The tunes were sprightly and the men's voices took up the refrain of a well-known folktune. Min, standing beside Christina, began to sing in her deep, hearty voice, and a lumberjack standing nearby turned to grin at her.

"You are one fine cook, ma'am!" he said to Min. "I don't think I have ever et better in my life. I don't suppose you dance as well as you cook?"

With a girlish grin, Min's plump cheeks dimpled in a pleased smile. "Don't mind if I do!" she said in her forthright way.

The lumberjack stepped over to her, bowed with awkward courtesy, and led Min over near the fire.

"Grab your partners, gents," the man called. "Let's form a square!"

Before long nearly everyone in the camp was dancing. The men formed squares with other men, and they were clowning and laughing their way through the Virginia Reel. Christina, shy and wary of being asked, stepped back into the shadows of the trees. The sweet quiet of the mountains began to seep into her consciousness. For the first time since coming up to Mount Pisgah she was alone—and there was still an hour of daylight! The rain had washed the air clean, and the beds of pine needles at her feet glistened and sparkled in the evening sunlight.

She loved this time of summer when the twilight lingered like a shimmering mantle upon the earth, and the ferns and sweet wildflowers decked the mountain's breast while the full-leaved trees rustled above. Without thinking, Christina began following a faint track that led upward through the dense growth of pines. She wanted to move through the mountain grove and up, past the treeline, where she could see open sky and the Virgin River cascading below. She had no idea how high she would need to climb to find an open place, but instinct led her upward, as the sounds of music and merriment faded below. Her mother had walked these paths, she knew, many years before, and Christina, caught in the silent mystery of the pines, was overwhelmed at the thought of Janeth's strange courage.

How long she climbed, Christina did not know, but the sky was still glowing with afternoon light when she came to a rocky ridge. Carefully planning her footholds, she pulled herself up over the rough face, and, as she breached the top, she was rewarded with the sight of a slope stretching upward in front of her. The slope was broken with levels of rock, but no trees. Above her she could see the summit of Mount Pisgah, and she was certain, if she could get a little higher and move east, she would be able to see the turbulent Virgin River far below. With that goal in mind she began to edge her way along a rough stone canyon defile. She had only gone a few hundred yards when her foot struck a rock and her ankle twisted. With a sharp groan she sank down onto the canyon floor. Shooting pains radiated up from her ankle, and she grimaced. "How stupid of me!" she said impatiently, reaching down to extricate her foot from the rocks. As soon as she touched her ankle she felt a sickening wrench in the pit of her stomach. "It can't be broken," she muttered, feeling the injured area gingerly.

Already her ankle was swelling like a balloon, and she sat waiting for the pain to subside to manageable proportions. A chill wind blew down the canyon. She shivered and looked up at the sky, which was beginning to turn silver gray. For the first time she felt a pang of fear. What would happen if she couldn't walk? Nobody knew where she was. Carefully she pushed herself to a standing position and searched around for a stick, or something to lean on, but she was above the treeline and the canyon floor yielded nothing but rough, barren rocks.

She tried to hobble for a few steps, but her foot could not bear any weight. "I shall crawl," she decided, and got down on her hands and knees and began, painfully, to pick her way across the rough stones. Concentrating on her slow progress, she did not know what alerted her to danger. She felt a prickle of apprehension along her spine and a terrible alertness warning her of hazard. With pounding heart she turned her head and saw, perched above her on the canyon rim, an enormous golden cougar. The predator was crouched on a projection of rock, its amber eyes watching Christina and its tail moving slowly. Christina's mouth went dry, and her whole body turned cold with fear.

She froze, staring hypnotically at the hunter. The cougar bared its teeth and made a menacing sound more like a scream than a growl. Christina, terrorized, screamed with the animal as she saw it bunch its powerful legs and spring into the air directly above her. It seemed to Christina that the whole world exploded around her. The animal's wild scream, her own mad voice, the explosion of the cougar's magnificent muscles, and another sound, like a furious thunderclap. Then everything went black.

When Christina came to her senses, she could feel her body jolting, bumping, swaying. There was a blaze of pain from her foot and she moaned. The motion stopped and she felt herself being settled gently on something soft and fragrant of pine.

"Christina!" It was Peter's voice. "Are you all right?" She opened her eyes and saw that she was in the forest. The luminous evening sky shone above the tops of the trees. Peter was leaning over her. There was no amusement on his face now, only anxiety and concern.

"Yes," she whispered. "You shot the cougar, didn't you! You followed me—and saved me again."

He laughed with relief. "You foolish little girl!" he exclaimed. "I think you need to keep me around. You seem to need a lot of saving!"

She bridled, and a hot retort came to her lips, but she looked at Peter's eyes and knew he was not laughing at her. In his eyes she saw the same thing she had felt in his arms in the barn—safety and strength and comfort.

"I'm more trouble than I'm worth," she murmured.

"Not to me, you aren't," he whispered. "Never to me!" With that he reached down and picked her up in his arms. She felt as light as thistledown as he carried her down through the trees, with his long, swinging strides.

Her ankle was not broken, but it was severely sprained. Min, scolding and angry with relief at Christina's safe return, bandaged the injured limb and confined Christina to her cot for the remainder of the week. Christina remained in camp with a few retainers over the weekend, and during the next week she began hobbling around on a makeshift crutch Peter had fashioned for her.

After the accident, Peter spent all of his free time with her. He visited her as she lay on her cot, and then, as she was recuperating, he led her on small forays into the surrounding area. He showed her glens and hidden places of beauty he had discovered in his summer's explorations. They did not talk a great deal, but between them there was a comfortable and natural communion, as though, looking at the same thing, they understood one another's feelings without having to verbalize them.

Min was a very cautious chaperone. The young people could not be alone for long or wander far, and she kept a careful eye on all of Christina's comings and goings. But secretly Min thought the tall, silent young man was the best thing that had ever happened to her niece.

Peter had lived most of his life as a wanderer. He prized his freedom and privacy. "What is it about this red-headed waif of a girl," he wondered, "that makes me feel tied to her?"

Since the day he had almost trampled her on his horse, he had sensed the tender, vulnerable child beneath her independent, proud exterior. He was not sure what had ensnared him—her womanly beauty—or that child within her—he only knew she needed him and she had somehow come to fill his heart and his mind until now he needed her more than he had ever needed anything.

He wanted to take her away from anything that made her frightened or unhappy. He wanted to care for her, to soothe her, to make her smile, to lighten the secret burden she seemed to carry. He knew it wouldn't be easy, but he was confident he could find a way to reach her. It would take time, but he was patient.

Christina, in turn, could not understand her feelings toward Peter. She guessed that he pitied her, and she resented his pity. Not believing herself lovable, she could not imagine that she was loved. Her own tender, warm feelings of first love frightened her, and she did not want Peter to guess how much she wanted him or how eagerly she waited for the sound of his step and his voice. She only knew that when she was with him, in spite of her confusion, she was happier than she could ever remember being.

"Will you be going down to Pleasantview?" Christina asked Peter wistfully as the weekend approached. "Aunt Min says I must wait another week to make the trip." She couldn't bear the thought of Peter leaving.

The two of them were sitting beside a small brook that ran through the ferns below the lumber camp.

Peter was tossing small stones into the water and she watched him bemusedly. His hair was light brown and wavy, but the sun had bleached it to the color of ripe wheat. His blue eyes were shaded by his deep brow, and his features were bold and regular. When he smiled, his white teeth gleamed in his darkly tanned face. His plaid shirt sleeves were rolled back, and she noticed that the muscles of his forearm were burnished by golden hairs. She stared in fascination, unable to take her eyes from the play of his muscles as he fingered the stones and flung them into the water.

"I think I must go to Pleasantview," he said after a long silence. "I must speak to your father."

"My father?" Christina exclaimed, puzzled.

"Yes," Peter replied. "I intend to ask him for your hand in marriage. And then I shall ask you!"

Christina began to tremble. "What are you saying, Peter?" she asked, as though she could hear his words but could not comprehend their meaning.

He did not move or touch her; he continued to throw the stones into the bubbling stream. "I want you to be my wife, Christina," he said, and she saw the slow smile. "Although, as you warned me when we first met, I am taking my chances marrying a McElin woman. I believe it will be either heaven or hell."

Never in her life had Christina felt such a rush of emotions, but over and above all others she recognized pure, magnificent joy, and she threw her head back and laughed aloud.

"Perhaps a little of both, Peter!" she said.

Neither Peter nor Christina was prepared for Angus's vigorous denial of their request to marry. Angus told Peter that he felt his itinerant work pattern made him a poor candidate for the hand of his younger daughter. Peter's lack of activity in the Church was also brought up, as well as Christina's youth and inexperience.

Christina raged at her father's objections. Rather than seeing his caution for what it was—an attempt to make up for years of neglect by seeing his daughter comfortably settled with a suitable husband—she interpreted his reluctance to allow her marriage as another sign of his careless lack of concern for her.

After weeks of argument, Angus agreed that the two young people could marry if they would wait for a year. Christina returned to the Big House, but after one week of living under Louella's scrutiny and with the cold, silent fury of Mary, who felt that she had been tricked by her younger sister and spurned by Peter, Christina knew she could not exist another day in that environment.

Christina assaulted Peter with her passionate tears and entreated him to take her away and make her his wife. On a wild, rainy night at the end of August, Christina slipped out of her whitewashed bedroom by the back stairs for the last time, and she and Peter eloped to Manti, where they were married outdoors in the rain by a reluctantly awakened justice of the peace. No Church official would marry them without Angus's consent.

Their wedding night was a disaster. In a wretched boardinghouse on the outskirts of Manti, Peter climbed into a hard, narrow bed with his young bride. She was exhausted, upset, and filled with anger at her father for making this hasty, clandestine marriage a necessity.

"Papa is happy to enjoy the fruits of wedded bliss with whomever he pleases," she muttered, "but he will not allow anyone else the same privilege."

"No! No!" Peter soothed her damp hair back from her face. "Hush now, Christina. We will speak no more of him."

The bed creaked ominously under their combined weight, and he felt Christina shudder at the sound and grow rigid under his arm. "Don't move!" she hissed. "They'll hear you!"

Peter, inflamed by the nearness of this beautiful woman whom he had desired since the moment he had seen her standing with her cows on the muddy road outside Pleasantview, did not understand her fear. Oblivious to the timidity of his tender bride, he took her with her nightgown still on, his passion roaring in his mind with such heady delight that he was scarcely aware of the dismay of the young girl beneath him. Her mind cried in humiliation at the dreadful noise of the bedsprings, and when Peter had finished she pushed away from him, moving as far to her side of the bed as possible. Her back was turned rigidly toward him. Peter embraced her tenderly. "It will be better tomorrow when you are not so tired," he whispered, but she would not turn to him and, after he slept, her hot tears wet the pillow.

The next day the newlyweds returned to Pleasantview. Peter, without apology, his head held high, walked up to Angus and told him straightaway that he and Christina were married.

The directness of Peter's manner and his solid confidence softened Angus's wrath. Realizing that he could not change what had happened, Christina's father accepted the situation and did what he could to make the marriage as successful as possible.

Angus informed Peter he had signed the Garden House and all of its attendant property, as well as one of his small sheep farms, over to them. "I will not take your charity, Mr. McElin," Peter answered proudly. "Christina and I will make our own way."

"But, man!" Angus exclaimed. "This is Christina's rightful

property! You would not deny her what's hers. You can sell the lot of it if you wish, but if you do, where will you go? What will you do? Don't you think your days as a lumberman, cowboy, and sheepshearer are over? You have Christina to think of now.''

Peter was silent, but his eyes took on a thoughtful cast. Later, when he told Christina what her father had done, she smiled excitedly. ''Oh, Peter! He must love me after all, to have given us so much! How shall I thank him?''

Her delight was a stone barrier to Peter. He wanted to explain to his new wife that the property was a two-sided gift. It provided security for the newlyweds, true, but it also tied them down to Pleasantview. Peter had had dreams of spiriting his lovely bride away from this place where she had so many sorrowful and troubling memories. Seeing her face light up at the thought of her father's generosity, Peter did not have the heart to spoil the gift for her, and so he lost the opportunity to make her truly his own.

The newlyweds decided to move into the Garden House, and Christina began a period of feverish activity. She was determined to make it a real home, as it had never been in her childhood. The square rooms and the unornamented plainness of the walls and windows were daunting. Her mother's room, where they slept, held old ghosts, and one night she woke gasping. Peter raised up and put his arms around her. ''What is it?'' he exclaimed.

Frightened, she jumped out of bed and ran to the closed door that led to her mother's old weaving room. She threw open the door to the room and saw the moonlight shining on the dust motes in the air of the empty room.

Shivering, she ran back to bed and hid her face in Peter's shoulder. ''I thought I could hear the loom going! I know I heard it—I was sure she would be there!'' Still half asleep, she whimpered, and he rocked her gently in his arms.

''Sh-h-h-h,'' he murmured and slowly she fell back to sleep.

Peter used the money he had earned at the logging camp to buy domestic stock and a prime flock of sheep for the farm. On the surface things seemed to be going well, but at night, nothing had changed from the first day of their marriage. As soon as they were in bed together, Christina grew tense and resistant. She avoided Peter's embraces and lay under his lovemaking as tightly as an overstrung bow. Her lifelong training in modesty and her confused and frightened perceptions of marriage filled her with shame. She would not allow him to see her dress or undress, and his efforts to remove her nightgown were rewarded with such a recoil of fear that he stopped. He could only guess at the dark struggle she was waging against the deep scars of her childhood insecurities and her battered perceptions of love and passion and morality.

When the Garden House was settled, Christina made a visit to the Big House to retrieve her belongings. She entered by the kitchen door and walked up to her old room. The bedroom walls had been papered with roses, and the entire room had been redone to Louella's specifications. Nothing could have expressed to Christina more dramatically the fact that she no longer belonged to the Big House, if, indeed, she ever had. Her belongings were packaged in neatly marked boxes and piled in the corner of the room.

She hurried out into the hall carrying the boxes and almost ran into Mary. Her half-sister gave her a look of cold fury and turned away.

"Oh, Mary!" Christina exclaimed impulsively. "Please let bygones be bygones. Let us be friends at last."

Mary opened her mouth once or twice, as though anger and indignation had robbed her of words, but then she began speaking in a voice of such quiet and determined loathing that Christina flinched at the sound.

"You ask me to be friends. Friends with someone who is as evil and treacherous as a serpent. All my life you have mocked me and stolen the things which are rightfully mine! Your mother was a thorn in my mother's breast all of her life. You were born of an unholy passion which robbed my mother and me of our husband and father. And now you have robbed me of the only man I will ever love. Oh, I knew that Peter didn't love me—not like I loved him. But if you had left him alone he would have grown to love me. You always wanted everything that was mine! Well, now you have stolen him too. Much good it will do you. You don't understand him, and you never will. You are too full of yourself, Christina, so you can't see anybody else's needs. You will destroy Peter. But I don't care about either of you now. From this moment on, you are not my sister. We no longer bear the same name—and I no longer know you! I shall never speak to you again as long as I live!"

Tears were running down Christina's cheeks. She was frightened and devastated by Mary's bitter fury. "Oh, please, Mary. Don't say such things!" Mary turned from her sharply and ran down the hall. Shuddering with emotion, Christina picked up her boxes and returned to the Garden House. She never told Peter of her confrontation with Mary, and the next week Mary left to return to Salt Lake City.

Louella, married to the most prominent man in the valley and rid of his daughters, now had what she wanted. She was mistress of the Big House, and she thoroughly enjoyed her role. As Mrs. Angus McElin she entertained and joined the best women's clubs. During the winter she had a large addition built onto the house, and as early spring came she began to invite parties of houseguests from all over the state. Christina and Peter were seldom included in the elaborate events—dinners, assemblies, political events, luncheons, and evenings of music and drama.

The winter had gone hard for the young newlyweds. Although Peter was a good sheepman, he had little patience with the day-to-day running of a farm. The work of husbandry seemed dull and undemanding, and he retreated more and more into the books that were his solace. His mind, while he fed the stock and mucked the stalls, was struggling with the paradoxes of Plato's *Republic*, or musing over the prose of Dickens. Christina, never reflective, with her restless, active body, found his quiet, measured pace and meditative silences a source of endless frustration.

Their sheep were not doing well, and she feared for the coming year when their small hoard of money would be gone if there were poor proceeds from the farm. Her tongue grew sharper as the winter passed.

In early April, Angus came over to tell Christina he had received word that Mary was going to be married to a wealthy merchant in Salt Lake City named Samuel Ostler. Brother Ostler was ten years older than Mary, but he loved her very much, and Angus was sure the marriage would be a happy one. He and Louella were going to Salt Lake for the wedding, and Angus wondered if Christina would like to accompany them.

"No," Christina said sadly. "I think not." She did not tell Angus the reason for her refusal, but she was well aware that her presence would have spoiled Mary's happiness.

After Angus and Louella left for Salt Lake, Christina felt a lightening of her spirits. "Does Louella's presence brood over my existence even though we live under different roofs?" Christina wondered.

One afternoon that spring Peter came into the kitchen. "I'm riding out to the farm this afternoon," he said. "The new crop of lambs is in the pasture. Would you like to ride with me and see them?"

"Oh, yes!" Christina exclaimed, delighted with the prospect.

They rode out to their property together. The fresh mountain wind buffed Christina's pale cheeks and her hair crackled in the sun. They walked across the rough field to the lambing pen and climbed up the log fence. In the pen the new lambs, still wobbly on their spindly legs, staggered toward their mothers. Christina watched the eager little mouths reach for the ewes' full teats and laughed delightedly at the little tails wagging as fast as hummingbird wings as the lambs drank. Deep within her, Christina felt a yearning. Standing close to her, Peter reached for her hand, and they stood watching the animals with their fingers entwined.

Together they tramped their fields and assayed the work that needed to be done that spring. Early in the evening they rode up to the little cabin that was the farm homestead.

Christina had never spent a night in the cabin. She had been too busy getting the Garden House ready for winter, and when the winter came, the rough cabin was not warm enough to be lived in. The April air was still chilly, so, while Christina prepared a simple supper, Peter built a roaring fire in the stone fireplace that dominated the one-room cabin. Wind blew through cracks in the log walls, but the area in front of the fire grew warm and cozy. There were some carded sheep fleeces piled in a corner that Peter threw on the floor, and they sat down and ate their supper like a picnic, with the roaring fire as their only light.

Christina started to clear the food away, but Peter restrained her. He pushed the utensils out of the way.

"We are staying the night," he said gently.

"But I didn't bring night things!" Christina protested.

"Hush!" he said softly and put his finger on her lips. Then slowly and tenderly, he moved his finger back and forth across the soft fullness of her mouth until she thought she could not bear it any longer. With deliberate care, his eyes holding hers, he moved forward and kissed her, his lips scarcely touching her. Still wary and afraid, she held back, but her face involuntarily lifted to his and, without touching her with his hands, he began to kiss her again. A warm flush began to spread through her body, and she felt herself yearn toward him.

"No!" she exclaimed weakly, shaking her head. "No!"

But he silenced her fear with his lips and she felt herself drawn irresistibly toward him.

She melted in the gentle whisper of his lips and the heat of the fire like a moving tongue darting in and out with the rhythm of their breathing. He pulled her toward him and his arms encompassed her as his hands lightly and smoothly undid the buttons of her dress. She was scarcely aware of what was happening until he reached up to pull her dress from her shoulders. Startled and on guard again, she threw up a restraining hand. Instead of resisting her, he took her hand, still holding her around the waist, and kissed her palm. His bent head moved her and she placed her other hand on his hair. Lifting his head, he kissed her throat, and slowly she felt her dress sliding from her shoulders.

Suddenly Peter stopped kissing her. He removed his arms from around her and leaned back. Christina's eyes flew open. Peter was staring at her. His hands held hers lightly, but his eyes were devouring her. He was breathing in a deep measured rhythm that made Christina's heart beat quickly, and he was staring at her bare shoulders and her breasts like a man seeing a vision. She felt the firelight playing on her glowing skin and she could feel the heat of the flames through the thin cotton of her camisole.

"Christina!" Peter whispered. "I love you." He reached forward and untied the satin ribbons that laced her camisole. The garment fell open and dropped from her shoulders, and Peter's face flamed with joy as he crushed her to him. Before Christina could think or react, he laid her gently back upon the soft fleeces and they were lost in a storm of passion—heedless, unthinking. They were no longer themselves, but timeless lovers caught in the first wild mystery of the body and its hidden joys.

Peter woke first in the gray dawn. The cabin was shabby and filthy in the morning light, and the dead fire could not hold back the chill wind from the mountain. With intent and serious eyes Peter looked at Christina, who was lying hunched in a ball against the cold. Her glorious red hair obscured her face, but her bare shoulders, white and thin in the pale light, twisted his heart with desire and tenderness. He reached out to place his jacket across her as she slept, but his motion wakened her. She sat up bewildered and shaken and glanced in horror at her state of undress. Grabbing her clothes from the floor, she turned her flaming face from Peter and began to dress herself hastily. She refused to look at him.

"Christina!" Peter said tenderly, reaching out to touch her. "It's all right. We are man and wife." But she pulled away from his grasp and sprang to her feet, still averting her face. With her back to him, she stood in the far corner doing up the buttons and laces of her clothing. The silence in the cabin was heavy, and Peter stood up and began to pull on his clothes as well.

Suddenly Christina staggered out into the yard and began to retch. Peter ran to her side and held her while she trembled and heaved until nothing but dry, choking sounds came from her throat. He picked her up in his arms and carried her back into the cabin. Placing her in a chair, Peter groped for a kerchief in his back pocket and gently wiped her face. Then he grabbed a pan and swiftly ran out to the water pump. When he returned to Christina's side, he gave her a sip of the icy water. She shuddered and closed her eyes, and as he looked at her he thought how small and young she was.

"I am better now, Peter. But I want to ride back to Pleasantview." Her voice was filled with shaky determination.

They returned to the Garden House, but Christina's health did not improve. In the next two weeks she was sick every day, and she became tired, irritable, and depressed. In her secret heart she thought that during her shameless night of love on the cabin floor when she had forgotten herself so completely, she had somehow injured her body or her immortal spirit. Sometimes, in the morning, she felt so sick she wondered if she might be dying in penance for unbridled passion. Christina's anger and resentment toward Peter grew silent and deadly, and she brooded on the thought of his hands upon the private places of her body, his mastery of her emotions. As she remembered that night of dark passion, though, a part of her shuddered with joy, and a secret longing that she could not erase filled her heart.

At the end of her second week of illness, Christina had to talk to someone, and so, in an agony of humiliation, she sought out her Aunt Min. Min was in the midst of baking pies, and her rotund face glowed from the warmth of the ovens. Her hands were covered with dough and streaks of flour dusted her apron. She welcomed her niece's visit and discerned that Christina wanted to talk about private matters, but it took Christina most of the afternoon before she could bring herself to explain her health problem. Scarlet with embarrassment, Christina asked if she might have "damaged" something by having "intimate" knowledge of her husband. The question was asked so delicately that it took Min a moment to understand what Christina meant. It had never occurred to Min that anyone could have reached Christina's age—severals months a married woman—and still be as ignorant of the process of child-bearing as her red-haired niece appeared to be.

With a hoot of surprised laughter, Min figured out what Christina was asking. "Child!" she exclaimed heartily. "You are not 'damaged.' You are simply doing what the good Lord intended for you to do. You are going to have a baby!"

"A baby?" Christina asked, flushing scarlet, recognizing immediately that what Min said was true. "I didn't know. . . . I thought it would show more. . . . Is it right to be so sick? Do you think there's something wrong with the baby?" Her voice rose with anxiety.

"Oh, dear!" Min said, her voice filled with warm-hearted sympathy. "I should have thought . . . Your mama never had a chance to tell you about these things before you were married. Now, hush, Christina. Don't worry. There's nothing wrong with your baby. You'll always feel a little sick at first. How far along do you think you are?"

Christina looked at her blankly.

Min sighed impatiently. "When did you have your last monthly issue of blood?" she asked. "That's how you can tell."

Christina thought carefully. "I think about two months ago," she answered, a trace of alarm in her voice.

"Fine!" Min said matter-of-factly. "That means you are about six weeks along. That's a nice start. Only seven and a half months to go!" Min chuckled. "You and Peter certainly didn't waste any time!"

Embarrassment crimsoned Christina's cheeks. In a choked voice she asked, "When will other people be able to tell?"

"Oh, it depends, but I would say in another three months—four at the most—everyone will know you are going to be a mother. It's not so bad, Christina. Get some loose shirtwaists and let out the bands of your skirts. Of course, you won't want to be seen in public, but you can certainly do everything at home that you normally do. It isn't bad at all! And, when it's over, you'll have a little girl or boy of your very own to love and care for!" With an expansive smile, Min came over and planted a kiss on Christina's cheek. Christina thanked her aunt quietly and walked home toward the Garden House. Her feet felt like lead, and her heart was heavy.

"You and Peter didn't waste any time!" Min had said laughingly, not meaning to tease, but Christina, sensitive and ashamed of her mother's reputation, was sure that everyone would be secretly thinking the same thing. Would they be laughing at her behind her back? Would they guess how her willful body yearned for wanton pleasures? No hiding the fact from the world now. Everyone would know— including her father.

The next morning Christina got up to fry the bacon for Peter's breakfast. He came in from tending the chickens with the cold fresh scent of spring in the folds of his woolen shirt and his face scrubbed red by the mountain wind.

In his usual self-contained and quiet way he sat down at the table, waiting for Christina to join him. She came and stood by her chair but did not sit. He gazed at her calmly and his eyebrows raised slightly in silent query.

"Aunt Min says I am going to have a child." She threw the words at him in her quick, passionate voice. "It will be about seven months in the coming."

Her mouth snapped shut, but her eyes blazed at him with a confusion of emotions. Peter's smile lit up his face—open, unhindered, and completely joyous. It was a smile of such intensity that it would have blinded a spirit of less will and seething ferment than Christina.

In two strides he covered the distance between them and reached to take her in his arms—but she pulled away from him sharply.

"Don't touch me!" she cried. "I have done my duty to you as a wife! Now I must bear the mark of it while you roam far and free. Men are always free while women wait and pay for the men's joy! Now they will say I am just like Mama!"

"Christina!" Peter replied in a steady, restrained voice. "You are yourself. There is no one just like you. Why won't you accept yourself and be happy?"

She turned upon him in fury. "You're a man," she accused him. "You cannot understand."

Peter continued to regard her with his intent and compassionate gaze, but he said nothing. He refused to be drawn into any argument where reason and thought were not the final measures, and Christina, torn by her fears and passions, could not bear his silence. She wanted to wrench from him his forbearance and calm rationality. More than anything else she wanted to see him join her suffering and rise to her anguished fury—to fight her, struggle with her, and destroy or conquer her wild, half-known demons.

To Peter the raging, tempestuous woman who was his wife was an enigma, but he could not let himself be drawn into the vortex of her fury. His eyes watched her with deep concern, but he remained composed. She felt anger at his silence rising like a tide. Scarcely knowing what she said, she began to heap upon him her pent-up frustrations. Her bitterness at their poverty, his ineptitude with the sheep and farm, his cruel silences, all these she threw at him, pacing the floor, wringing her hands. Her fear of having the baby channeled into every crack of her dissatisfied existence.

"What is to become of us? Shall we live forever like paupers at my father's back doorstep? Can you expect me to bring a child to this? You must work harder, Peter!"

She began running her mind through the rooms of the Garden House. "We must paint, and get new furniture, and new clothes and live like McElins, not like itinerant sheepshearers! What if Mary came to visit? What if she saw how we live? I cannot bear it! Peter! You must be ambitious! You must work, and I will work beside you! Oh! The disgrace!"

The storm would not abate, and Peter stood unflinching in the flood of disjointed and irrational anger, waiting for Christina's fury to blow itself out. Finally, spent with rage, she slumped in her chair and, placing her face in her hands, wept distractedly.

Peter walked over to her but did not venture to touch her shaking shoulders. In his steady, deep voice he said, "Having a baby is no disgrace, Christina."

She raised her tear-streaked face to him and said bitterly, "When a woman is past forty, and a second wife who has not lived with her husband for almost twenty years, having a baby is a disgrace! People talk about such a woman and they will talk about her daughter too."

"What are you saying, Christina?" Peter asked softly.

She refused to answer him. Standing up abruptly, she hurried over to the stove and brought his breakfast, which she dished up with sharp, angry motions.

"You'd best hurry and eat and get out to the sheep farm. Those animals can't manage on their own, you know!" she said. The joy had gone from his eyes, but he made no reply. Without hurrying, he finished the breakfast she had prepared, and listened, without comment, as she worried aloud about the flocks and the spring hay crop. She had always been inclined to be critical and demanding about his work habits. She had been raised with men who worked from dawn until dusk, and, when they could not work, they worried. Peter never seemed to worry, and, although he worked long hours, he worked with an unhurried pace and an inward eye fixed on thoughts that had nothing to do with fields and animals. He was a lover of the wilderness and would stop midstride to test the wind or feel the soil. Some days he left his hoe in the midst of a row and tramped across the fields to roam the high cascades, returning long past dark.

In the evenings he read by lamplight, and Christina, anxious to hear what he had accomplished that day, watched impatiently as he turned the pages, a quiet withdrawn smile on his lips. This was the way he escaped her, and she felt the only way she could bring him back to her world was with her tongue, which grew increasingly sharp from fear she would lose him altogether.

She knew when he went to the farm that his saddlebags were crammed with his books, newspapers, and journals, and she fretted through the day for fear he was not really working but sitting in the fields, or in the little cabin, reading.

In her desperation to change him, she forced him to become more and more the man she would not have him be. He refused to match her head on or to be drawn into her shrillness or the flare of her quarrels, so Christina lived with the unconsummated fury of one who quarrels alone, and her quarrel, unpartnered, could never be ended.

Late in October, Christina's body, misshapen and heavy, seemed to grow bloated. Her feet no longer fit her shoes and her hands were stiff and puffy. The day was cold with the first hint of snow in the air and the last tomatoes on the vines of the kitchen garden were ripening in the cool autumn days, protected from frost by newspaper tents Peter had fashioned.

As Christina had predicted all summer, the sheep farm had not done well. Their hay crop had been poor, and their sheep had suffered several accidents that had depleted their numbers. Also, the lambs had been disappointing, and the yearlings were a scrawny lot.

"We have to improve our stock!" Christina had exclaimed as she had tallied their books. "You must borrow money from Father, Peter, and buy better stock. You can't raise fine sheep from mongrel strains."

For the first time her ranting had drawn blood, and Peter had lifted his eyes from the book he was reading—*Bleak House* by Dickens. His face was not angry but his voice was rigid. "I will not borrow money from your father, Christina," he said. "I will not be in debt to any man." His eyes returned to his book and Christina had felt him slipping away from her again.

"Peter!" Christina called. The October morning had chilled the milking porch where she was skimming the cream from the night's leavings. "The milk has ice crystals! You must get out there and harvest the last of the tomatoes or we'll lose them!"

Everything she said to him had a tone of challenge and accusation in it. He came out onto the porch wearing a heavy gray sweater, his hair gleaming in the pale October light. His face, tanned from the summer, was lean and strong, and his shoulders seemed to have broadened through the labors of the year. He smiled gently at Christina as she stood by the straining table. She was wearing a blue gingham Mother Hubbard over a white high-necked shirtwaist, and her unruly hair was pulled back into a smooth knot that was tied with a bow at the nape of her neck.

He smiled with his deep, mysterious quiet eyes. "You're a pretty thing, Christina Saunderson," he said softly.

Her face flamed with astonished self-consciousness at the unexpected warmth of his compliment, but before she could bite the words back, her tongue, schooled in quick and acid responses, said, "You won't get out of work with flattery, Peter!"

Peter's face did not change, but the smile left his eyes and he walked outside.

Angry with herself and feeling her emotions in a jumbled state, as though she had been picked up and shaken like one of those Christmas tree ornaments that are turned upside-down while little white flakes whirl wildly around, Christina tried to forget the look in Peter's eyes and carefully addressed herself to the task of separating the milk and churning the butter.

Still feeling restless and curiously uncomfortable later in the morning, she sat in the kitchen scalding and peeling the tomatoes from the root cellar that Peter had brought in the night before. She was planning to use a recipe for chili sauce that had been her mother's, but somehow the smells of the cloves, vinegar, and other spices made her stomach churn. She wondered if she should leave the tomatoes for a while and go lie down, but the thought of Peter seeing her resting during the daytime goaded her, and she determined that she would continue her task until the last tomato was done.

"And where is that Peter?" she asked herself irritably. "He's been out in the garden for over an hour. Plenty of time to have picked those last few tomatoes!" She walked stiffly over to the door, stepped through the milking porch, and looked out onto the backyard. In the garden she saw Peter. He was standing beside a half-filled bushel basket of tomatoes, leaning on his hoe. In his hand was a newspaper from the frost tent. Something in the paper had apparently caught his eye, and he was reading with complete absorption. Behind him the milk cow, who had escaped the barnyard— she had a trick of lifting the gate-latch with her nose—was plodding solemnly through the garden, tramping down the remaining vines and smashing the plump, red fruit with her heavy hooves. The sight of this destruction and Peter's oblivion was too much for Christina.

"Peter!" she screamed and started running toward him, trembling with anger. "Can't you see the cow's in the garden? She's ruining my tomatoes!" Christina was half crying, half shouting, and she was beside herself with fury. "How could you do such a thing?" she yelled at him. She ran toward the cow. "Shoo, you old thing!" she screamed. "Get out of my garden! Get out of my beautiful garden!" Scarcely knowing what she was doing, she struck the stolid animal on her flank. The old cow turned her head and gave Christina a surprised, uncomprehending stare.

Peter walked over and caught his wife's hand as she prepared to strike the animal again. "That's enough," he said firmly. With that he grasped the cow's halter and led her back to the cowyard, securing the gate with an extra piece of wire.

He came back to where Christina was pacing up and down among the mangled rows of tomatoes. Tears were staining her cheeks and she was ranting at the ruined garden. "Look at these tomatoes! Smashed! Useless! What a waste!"

"Christina!" Peter said curtly. "Stop it! Now!" She looked up at him sharply, her eyes flashing in defiance, but something in the firm set of his jaw stopped her.

"You will make yourself sick for a handful of tomatoes," he said, taking her arm and guiding her toward the house. She was beyond his reason, however. The incident seemed to have set off some streak of fury in her.

She choked on a deep, angry sob. Suddenly she bent double and screamed. "Peter!" she screamed again. "Peter! Peter!" She looked at him with shocked and terrified eyes, her mouth forming another scream. This time the scream was all the more horrifying to him because it was silent. Without a pause he picked her up in his strong arms and hurried into the house, taking the kitchen stairs two at a time and placing her upon their bed in the bare room that had been Janeth's. The door to the weaving room stood open and he could see the tiny cradle, which he had built for the new baby during the long summer evenings. Christina had quilted a tiny patchwork blanket, which lay over the waiting cradle. "It's too soon," Christina whimpered.

"Will you be all right for a minute if I leave to get Aunt Min?" he whispered urgently.

"Mama!" Christina called hoarsely, her eyes unfocused with fear and pain. "Not Aunt Min. I want Mama!" Christina's voice was coming in strange spurts, more like a groan rather than a voice, and Peter felt his blood run cold. He knew this was not the onset of normal labor and he was frightened.

"Christina!" he whispered, kneeling beside the bed and gathering her in his arms. "It's all right. Aunt Min will come and we'll fetch the doctor. Do you understand me?"

"Not Papa!" Christina cried in fear. "Don't tell Papa! Just Mama. I want Mama!" She was mumbling incoherently, and her face had a strange gray cast and was shining with heavy, unhealthy perspiration.

"Christina!" Peter called more loudly and shook her shoulders gently. "Listen to me. I must get help! Hold on! Please!"

For a minute her eyes cleared and she looked at him directly. He saw fear and pain in their depths, but he also saw her comprehension and courage. "Yes!" she whispered clearly. "Get Aunt Min."

After going through hell for nearly thirty hours, Christina was finally delivered of a fine healthy baby boy. The child was blond like his father, and, even though he was a few weeks early, he was a good size, robust, and well featured. After the delivery, Christina went into convulsions. Her life was saved by the quick-thinking doctor, who wrapped her in wet, icy sheets and then, as her muscles relaxed, covered her with warmed quilts. He and Min watched with relief as the bright pink color flowed back into her young face.

A tear coursed down Min's plain, soft cheek. "She's past the danger now, Min," the doctor reassured the tired woman. "See that she is kept warm and gets lots of rest."

It was nearly a week before Christina's mind cleared enough for her to recognize the little bundle that was placed at her breast as her own baby son. Feeling, for the first time since her delivery, fully conscious and bright, she held out her arms and Min placed the squalling infant in them. Christina undid his swaddled clothes with trembling hands and looked at the baby's fine-textured skin, his lusty chest, and soft round cheeks, the gleaming silky baby hair like a fine dusting of gold on his little shoulders and at the nape of his neck. Her son's cry was powerful and self-confident, and his little fists beat the air like tiny hammers.

As much as Christina had hated her pregnancy, that was how much she instantly loved her child. Hers was a fierce, intense, protective love that was almost as hard as hate because it was so complete and irrevocable.

Chapter Eleven

Christina had grown thinner in the years since Cameron had been born, but she had lost none of her intensity. If anything, the trials of poverty, hard work, and motherhood had increased her proud fierceness, her determination, and her sharp tongue until they had crowded out of her personality all the softer emotions of peace, tenderness, and quiet. Her mind never rested from worry, and with the birth of her second child, Russell, she had folded him into her heart also and with him the full load of care and burning commitment to his future, his safety, his protection. There were no soft corners in Christina's mother-love. It flamed like a brand across her soul.

The summer had been a disastrous one for the Saundersons, despite the fact that Peter had labored long and hard. He had planted oats and flax, two of the newest money-making commodities. After years of barely surviving, Peter had become determined to produce a crop that he could sell for good money to give him some working capital. He had risked everything but he had never labored so carefully, preparing his soil, buying the finest seeds, even hiring a young man to work the fields with him. By early July it looked as though it would be a bumper year. His oats were heading up full and plump, and his flax lay like a sea of blue, merging with the mountain sky.

Christina and the boys loved to drive out to the fields in the wagon at sunset. The boys didn't understand the significance of the ripening grain, but they knew that their mother's face had a sweet, golden cast as she smiled out over it and they liked her this way—quiet and happy.

Early in July, after a long, sultry day, Christina and Peter lay in their upstairs bedroom unable to sleep because of the heavy air. Suddenly, above the mountains, they saw the jagged crack of lightning, and then on the roof they heard the sound that strikes terror into the heart of all who work the land. On a gust of wind so strong that it shook the windows came the staccato noise of hailstones. The wild tattoo grew louder until the din of the pounding ice filled the rooms of the Garden House. The two little boys, awakened, came running into their parents' room and screamed and huddled in the bed against their mother and father.

The hail lasted less than fifteen minutes. The next morning, by the light of dawn, Peter galloped out to the farm and stared in bitter defeat at his ruined fields. Where only yesterday had stood the rich, ripening stands of gold and blue, now lay flat, muddy stretches of empty ground. The grain had been pounded into the earth as if by a great mallet, sheared with an icy scythe and buried under the beaten earth. Without a backward glance, Peter mounted his horse and rode home to the Garden House, packed his work clothes, and left for the timber camps to hire on as a day laborer.

Later that day Angus McElin came to visit his daughter and her husband to express his regret at their loss. The whole Virgin Valley was reeling under the hail's damage, but the farmers who were raising wheat had time to replant a winter crop, and the alfalfa fields would reconstitute themselves. It was only the early cash crops such as oats and flax that were a complete loss.

When Angus heard that Peter had already left for the lumber camp, he frowned with genuine concern. Over the years he had grown to like Christina's husband. He knew Peter was a strong, wise, and compassionate man, ill-suited to be a farmer and yet caught by circumstance to labor in that profession. Even though Peter was not a man with a natural feel for the land or for animals, he did have a natural feel for business. On many occasions Angus had sought Peter's advice on investment and capital matters and was always amazed at the younger man's grasp of the subject. Angus had offered both to pay for Peter's advice and to hire him to work in the McElins' increasingly diversified business operations, but Peter adamantly refused to accept the offer, seeing it as charity or another obligation of gratitude that would tie him even more closely to his wife's family.

"I would gladly advance Peter the money for winter wheat to seed. It still wouldn't be too late for him to recoup some of the loss," Angus told Christina, feeling inadequate and awkward in expressing sympathy to his difficult, proud daughter.

Christina tossed her head, her back stiff with pride. "Nay!" she said, unconsciously using her father's word. "Peter will not take your charity. He will work to earn money this summer, and we shall have better luck next year."

"But if he works at the lumber camp, who will mind the sheep?" Angus inquired. "Could we lend you some assistance there? Perhaps run them with our flock for the summer?"

"No!" Christina exclaimed. "We shall manage ourselves. *I* will run the sheep this summer!" Her voice was sharp, but her father could hear the edge of tears in it, and his heart wrenched.

"Very well, my girl," he said, rising with a sigh. "You always were a good hand with the animals."

Even though she was a grown woman and a mother of two sons, Christina felt her heart give a lurch of joy at this unexpected praise from her father. Did it still matter to her so much, then? Did she still want so earnestly to win his approval?

Peter worked the summer at the logging camp and enjoyed his renewed association with the quiet, hard-working men. The weeks in the mountains were a respite from the constant weary struggle of his relationship with Christina. He wondered at the fact that he found himself still wanting her. He still desired her body, which had grown slender and supple as a willow whip. Her gleaming, untamed hair, her flashing eyes, her quick fierce glance, all drew him like a hypnotic flame. Perhaps misery with Christina was sweeter than peace with someone else! Nonetheless, during the summer he had thought of leaving her. He knew, as he stretched his body in the satisfying labor of the timber cutting and, in the evenings, as he sat in the silence of the whispering pine groves, that he could not live the rest of his life without some moments of peace. He sensed that Christina was happier, easier in her mind, when he was gone. Without him as an adversary, her complex passions seemed to become soothed and less importuning. For a time he examined the thought that they should separate.

When Peter returned from the final camp he entered the back porch hungry for the sight and smell of Christina, his mind filled with the need for her. From the kitchen she called sharply, "Peter! Mind you take off that flannel jacket before you come in! I don't want you in here smelling like a horse!"

With a sigh Peter hung up the heavy mackinaw. He stood for a moment in silence in the darkened porch, and then he sighed and moved to the kitchen door. When he opened the door and entered it he understood how deep was his commitment. Whatever they were, enemies or lovers, they would never be free of one another.

When Christina's third son was born Johnny came to see the new baby and gave a bark of amusement. "Hah! It's our Angus reborn!" he exclaimed. "Bless my soul it is! A 'wee Angus'!" Christina had laughed in response, because there was no mistaking the child's strong resemblance to her father. Despite their Highlander names, her two oldest boys, Cameron and Russell, were pure Swedes like Peter. They were sturdily built, tall for their age, well muscled, with golden skin that drank in the sun, dark-blond hair, and deep-blue eyes. They were good-natured, quiet boys, wise and caring beyond their years. Her new baby was smaller boned than her first two. He was beautifully formed, with fine clear features and jet-black hair. He had an alert, pleasant expression on his little face that seemed to greet the world with a curiosity and joy almost miraculous in one so tiny.

Angus felt a special tug of attraction to this appealing baby grandson. As a father Angus had been stiff and unbending, but with the birth of this little boy, he seemed to open up the tenderest corners of his heart. He would hold the baby for hours, seeming content to have the infant on his lap. He rejoiced in wee Angus's first steps and first words, boasting of the child's quickness and brilliance. Perhaps the grandfather's partiality would have been harder to take if Angus had not been a genuinely endearing little boy. His older brothers responded to Angus's lively, pleasant nature with unaffected love and found it impossible to feel jealous of one who wore his adulations so lightly.

Christina knew in her heart of hearts that she was partial to her youngest child. Nothing could diminish her devotion to her older sons, but in young Angus she saw the mirror of all that she had ever yearned for herself, and she spoiled the child wholeheartedly, watching him with hungry, vivid eyes as though she could never have enough of his sweet presence.

As Angus grew older his grandfather would take him for rides in his buggy, or ask if the child could come spend the afternoon at the Big House. Louella McElin spent less and less time in Pleasantview. Angus had bought a large home for her in Salt Lake City, and Louella, caught up in a steady round of entertainments, spent most of her time in the capital now. Angus traveled between Salt Lake City and Pleasantview, but as he grew weary of the constant social events, he spent more and more time alone at the Big House trying to escape the "season" when the balls, dinners, and evening salons became too much for him.

"Cameron!" Christina called from the back stoop. "Come in this minute and bring your brothers!"

Five-year-old Cameron, the oldest of the three Saunderson sons, climbed down from the barnyard fence with alacrity and grabbed the hand of three-year-old Russell. The two boys ran in their heavy, cobbled boots across the muddy yard, awkwardly carrying the old egg basket.

"Mind you don't break any eggs!" Christina shouted.

"No, Mama," Cameron puffed, and turned to call over his shoulder to his youngest brother, Angus, who was building mud pies in the cold, damp earth of the harvested garden.

"Hey, Angus! Come on! Mama wants us!"

Angus raised his dark little head and smiled at his oldest brother. He threw down the ball of clay he was molding in his muddy hands and ran toward the two older boys on his swift two-year-old legs. His small feet made mud splatters in the water-soaked ground.

The boys had reached the porch where Christina was waiting for them.

"How many eggs did you gather?" Christina asked Cameron. "And don't you dare walk on the kitchen floor in those muddy boots! I have just scrubbed it," she added sharply.

Cameron held up the egg basket. She took it from him as he entered the mud porch, removed his shoes, and began scraping the mud off with a sharp stick.

"Eight," she counted, frowning. "That old biddy hen trying to nest again!" she exclaimed.

Russell answered, "She pecked at my fingers when I reached under her, and I think she must be hiding her eggs somewhere 'cause she didn't have any in the box." Christina clicked her tongue in annoyance.

"I was hoping to make an angel food cake for Grandpa's dinner tonight, but it takes thirteen egg whites and I don't see as how I'll have enough!"

She bent to kiss Angus's dark curls absently. "You let Russell take off those muddy shoes, wee Angus," she said. "I'll get a warm cloth to wash off your dirty hands. Did you make some nice mud pies?"

The little boy smiled up at his mother, and his deep-blue eyes filled with love and happiness. "I made a dish for you, Mama! This big!" He held his hands in a wide circle. "But I left it in the garden."

Christina laughed out loud with pleasure. "That's all right, Angus!" she soothed him. "We'll get it tomorrow."

She took his tiny hand and led him into the house. "Come on, boys!" she called to her two other sons. "Let's get these eggs in, and then I'll give you some lunch."

Later in the afternoon the three boys, hands scrubbed clean and hair slicked back, were kneeling on chairs around the kitchen table in their stocking feet waiting for their boots to dry out in front of the stove. Their mother was whipping up the angel food cake, and Cameron watched in fascination as his mother's slender, deft fingers cracked each precious egg and then carefully juggled the golden yolk back and forth letting the silver whites slide out between the two halves of the shell into the mixing bowl. As his mother had said, thirteen eggs—all of the ones they had gathered today, and five from yesterday's precious store. His mother sold eggs, and Cameron knew the egg money was important. He wondered what could be so special about Grandfather's dinner that night that his mother would squander two days' lay of eggs. Fascinated, he watched as the pile of empty shells grew and the copper bowl filled with the clear whites and the brown bowl with the golden yolks. Once, during the separating, his mother made a mistake and a thin sliver of yellow yolk fell in with the egg whites. Christina almost cried with vexation, and ran to get a small piece of brown paper with which she painstakingly fished out the offending yellow streak.

When all thirteen whites were in the shining copper bowl, his mother pulled out a wire whip and, with her strong thin arm, she began to beat the whites. Before his eyes Cameron could see them begin to foam and grow in volume, multiplying under the vigorous stroke of her arm. Whiter and whiter the mixture became until it looked like a mound of snow. The little boys' eyes grew wide with wonder.

"Gee!" Russell breathed.

"Russell!" Christina said sharply, almost by reflex. "Watch your language! And don't breathe on the egg whites!"

But the boys could tell by their mother's secret smile that she was pleased with their wonder.

The cake was going well, and her success with the project made Christina more expansive than usual. "This is going to be a special dinner tonight," she confided to her boys. "Aunt Louella is coming home from Salt Lake for a visit." The boys made a face. They didn't like Louella very much. The Big House was lots more fun when Angus was there by himself. When Louella was home she scolded them if they ran in the halls, ate anywhere but in the kitchen, or spoke too loudly.

"Aunt Louella is bringing home Aunt Mary and her husband," Christina went on. She saw the puzzled look on the boys' faces. "Aunt Mary is my sister," she explained. "Well, my half-sister," she added. The boys were looking at her with their bright, curious eyes. They said nothing because they wanted their mother to go on talking. They loved it when she talked to them about something besides the chores, and they waited, wide-eyed, to hear her explain more about this mysterious Aunt Mary.

Christina, seeing the insatiable curiosity behind their looks, suddenly gave a sigh and shook her head. "I don't know how to explain it to you," she ended abruptly. She paused, and then went on rather curtly.

"I want Aunt Mary and her husband—whose name is Samuel Oster—Uncle Samuel—I want them to have a nice time tonight, and to know how glad I am to welcome them home. That's why I'm making the cake." Christina tried to make her voice sound light and gay, but her boys, attuned to the finest nuance of her moods, sensed the apprehension and nervousness behind her cheerful facade.

"It's going to be a beautiful cake, Mama," Cameron assured her.

Christina tried to smile, but her heart was as heavy as lead. She had not seen or spoken to Mary in all the years since their last bitter parting. Louella often described to Christina the elegance of Mary's Salt Lake home and the courtesy and sophistication of her sister's wealthy husband. Mary apparently saw enough of her father in Salt Lake City that she had felt no need to return to visit her childhood home. Christina secretly believed Mary was trying to avoid ever seeing her and Peter again.

All week Christina's thoughts and emotions were in a whirl. She was eager to see Mary and yet she was afraid and shy of meeting her after so many years and with so many harsh memories. Christina was shamefully embarrassed by her own poverty and the marks of hard work and worry that she knew made her look older than she was. For the first time in years she worried about her appearance, her red, work-roughened hands, her thin body, which she called scrawny, and her wild, fly-away hair.

"What shall I wear?" she fretted at Peter. "Everything I own is threadbare and old!"

Peter remained silent, but early that morning he rose from their bed and left the house without explanation. She was furious with him, leaving her to manage the whole day alone, even though he knew she must be ready for the family banquet that Louella was planning that evening. Matty and Zina were in town and coming to the party. Johnny, Hes, Min, and Jeremy and his new bride would all be there as well.

As Christina fed the boys their supper of bread and milk, and instructed the teenage girl who was going to care for them, Peter rode into the backyard. Christina walked to the kitchen door with her quick, impatient steps, ready to scold him for his tardiness. He was sitting in the yard on his saddle horse, and the late October sun sent a shaft of light across his head and his hair blazed in the light. His tanned, noble face, and easy grace in the saddle gave him an appearance of command. For a moment, while he did not see her, she stared at him as though at a stranger, and she saw how unfitted he was for the life to which she had brought him. For love of her he had left a life of freedom, action, and challenge. He was a Viking king, and she had put him in a peasant's yard. With a sigh she returned unseen to the kitchen.

Moments later he came in with a box in his hands. His face was raw with the cold, and she could smell winter in the folds of his sheepskin coat.

"Snow tonight," he said, handing the box to her.

"What is this?" she demanded, awkward in her surprise. "What foolish thing have you done now, and we with scarcely enough to see our way through the coming winter?"

"Sh-h-h!" he said sharply, shaking his head and glancing meaningfully at the children.

"It's a present for your mama!" he whispered to the boys conspiratorially. They grinned and leaned toward her like sunflowers turning their faces to the light.

Flushed with the unaccustomed attention, and still fussing at Peter's misuse of money, Christina pulled the string from the box. Inside lay a dress. It was made of heavy silk poplin, a rich russet brown, with a black velvet trim and jet buttons. The skirt was full and trimmed with velvet piping and the waist was as narrow as a handspan. The dress was dark and heavy, and a little old-fashioned, but Christina knew instinctively it would look excellent on her. However, before Peter could delight in her happiness, Christina turned from him and closed the box.

"Of course we can't keep it! It is much too expensive! We can't afford it! I will wear my black skirt and shirtwaist and you can return this wherever you bought it tomorrow."

"No," Peter said, and his voice was cold and final. "I will not return it tomorrow or any other time. I bought this dress for you. You are my wife and you will wear it tonight."

She was furious that he would order her in such a fashion, and she turned to him with blazing eyes. "I can't make you return it! But you cannot make me wear it!" She seemed to turn every emotion into anger. She was like a cornered field animal that turns in spitting defiance, unable to discern a friendly hand from a threatening one.

"Do as you will," he said. "It was you who complained of having nothing to wear." He picked up wee Angus and, with Cameron and Russell following, left the room.

From that moment nothing in the evening seemed to go right for Christina. Her cake, which had been cooling on the table, was ready to remove from the pan. In doing so, the soft, fluffy height of the masterpiece began to settle, and, by the time the cake was glazed and on the cut-glass plate, it had shrunk, and she knew its texture was ruined.

The matter of wearing the new dress was solved for her when she realized the flounce on her old black skirt had come unsewn. With no time for mending, she was forced to take out the new dress and put it on. It fitted her small figure to perfection, but she knew as she looked in the glass that the style and fabric were too heavily tailored for an evening dinner party. She felt overdressed and awkward in the high-necked, stiffly boned bodice.

The night was cold, and Christina put on the old fur-lined cape her father had given her years before. The trim had faded and the fur was worn, but the wrap was still comfortable and warm. As Peter and Christina walked toward the Big House, which was ablaze with lights, a beautiful open carriage with gleaming coach lamps and fine black horses pulled up to the front gate. Out of the carriage stepped Mary, her posture more regal than Christina had remembered, her jet hair gleaming and smooth. Mary was bundled in a wrap of extravagant luxuriousness. The fur was pale gray, and beneath it shone a full red satin skirt. Christina saw the flash of diamonds at Mary's ears. Instinctively she stepped back into the shadows, but Peter's hand on her elbow was firm and he propelled her out into the light.

The two sisters faced one another across the steps of the Big House. The cold, brisk wind swept down from the mountains, a harbinger of snow and frost, and Christina shivered as her half-sister swept her with a glance as cold as the wind itself.

"Well, Christina," Mary said coolly.

Fury swept over her at the sound of her sister's unforgiving voice. Christina quickly mounted the steps until she stood even with Mary's eyes. She knew Mary had taken in with a glance Christina's old cape, the dark heavy dress, and her thin body and overworked hands, but Christina did not care. Pride stiffened her, and she thrust out her chin, her eyes crackling with their old challenge.

"Well, Mary," she replied, tone for tone, and the two sisters walked into the front hall side by side, as erect as queens.

The evening was a disaster for Christina. Louella and Mary chatted at the head of the table like old friends, talking of people and events unrelated to anyone else there. The men were all dressed in formal evening attire, even Peter, who had kept his old dinner suit from his unmarried days. The suit still fit him perfectly, and Christina, stealing a glance at him, had to admit he was by far the best-looking man at the table. He was seated near Samuel Ostler, Mary's husband, and the two of them were engaged in an intent conversation. Samuel was a man in his forties, with dark hair salted with gray, and a neatly trimmed beard and moustache. He was not handsome and was slightly shorter than his wife, but he had shrewd and kind eyes and a smile, though rare, that was warm and appealing. In spite of herself Christina thought she could grow to like her sister's husband. Apparently Peter did, because he and Samuel were laughing jovially together, and, when they rose from the dinner table and the ladies prepared to retire to the parlor, Samuel came over and clapped Peter on the shoulders as though they were old friends.

Christina saw Mary frown at the friendly gesture. Watching Mary and her husband, Christina decided that Samuel treated Mary much as a spoiled and adorable daughter—and that he would brook no interference or suggestions from his young wife as to his own behavior. Samuel Ostler was obviously used to being his own man— and a successful and powerful one.

"How are your boys, Christina?" Zina asked, sensing that her niece was feeling awkward and unhappy. "I hope to get over to see them before we leave for St. George!"

"Fine, Aunt Zina. We would love to see you."

Even Zina's concern for her made Christina uncomfortable because she sensed behind it a feeling of condescension and pity—the kind of attitude one takes toward "poor relatives."

Louella had overheard Zina's mention of the boys and she exclaimed to Mary with overdone enthusiasm, "Can you imagine Christina the mother of three boys! And such healthy, robust boys! Oh my, the size of them! All except wee Angus, of course, who takes after the McElin side and is much finer of frame. I declare, Christina. I don't know how you are doing it—bringing up three such vigorous boys in that little house! I should think you would be stepping all over one another. I know when they are here at the Big House they seem to fill it up."

Christina glared at her stepmother. "Well, if they are too much for you, Louella, I can certainly see they do not come over while you are here," she said in a voice like cracked ice.

"Oh, no!" Louella protested sweetly, looking around the room at the other women with a helpless expression that said, What are you going to do with someone that sensitive! "Of course not, Christina! Their grandfather and I love to have them! Especially wee Angus—he is such a little gentleman."

Christina was about to make an angry retort, but Zina patted her on the hand and gently shook her head. Christina fought down her fury with her stepmother and got to her feet.

"We must be going," she said abruptly. "Peter has a difficult day tomorrow and we must not leave the children any longer."

Mary stood up as well. "Must you go so soon?" she asked in the same emotionless voice with which she had greeted Christina. To Christina the whole scene seemed to be such a travesty of human affection that she wanted to scream. Feeling the insults and slights, imagined or real, of a lifetime, she faced her old adversary.

"Yes!" Christina answered hotly. "The sooner I leave the better, I think." She turned to Louella, and her voice, barely courteous, rapped out the words. "Thank you for the lovely dinner." Turning to her aunts, she gave each one a stiff kiss and then marched out of the room with her head held high. Walking on the plunge of her anger, she burst into the library where the men were talking. The men looked up in startled surprise as she entered. "Peter," she announced without preamble, "I think we must be leaving."

Peter was sitting in one of the central chairs, and, from the way the other men were grouped, it was obvious they had been listening to him. Sam Ostler was looking at his newly met brother-in-law with frank appreciation, and her father was standing with one hand on Peter's shoulder.

"Surely you can stay a little longer, Christina," her father said mildly. "Sam and Peter were just having a most enlightening discussion about the federal monetary system and the banking needs of the west. Most enlightening!"

Without thinking, Christina said scornfully, "What does Peter know about banking!"

Her father's eyes grew stern and angry, and she felt rebuked knowing she had insulted Peter appallingly. "I—I'm sorry," she stammered. "I mean, I'm sure that Mr. Ostler has had so much more experience . . ."

Samuel Ostler turned and looked at her with perceptive eyes. "Your husband has studied the issues thoroughly, and I find his knowledge surpasses my own."

"All that reading!" Christina thought bitterly. "When he should have been out tending the crops!" But she didn't say any more, only looked at Peter with silent urgency and he slowly rose from his chair.

"Thank you for the dinner, Angus," he said, shaking her father's hand. "Samuel, I am glad to have met you at last." The two men shook hands, and Johnny and Matty in turn said their good-byes. In the front hall, without a further word, Peter retrieved Christina's old cape, and the two of them walked silently home across the rough, frozen ground as the first flakes of winter dusted their faces.

The next day Mary came unexpectedly to visit the Garden House. Christina was kneading bread, and the laundry kettle was boiling on the stove. The children's toys were scattered on the floor.

"Is Peter gone?" Mary asked.

"Yes," Christina replied, trying hastily to straighten up a place for Mary to sit down. "Would you like to come into the parlor?" she asked stiffly.

"No," Mary said calmly. "Go on with your bread making." The two young women talked in a careful, desultory fashion about their lives. Mary did not take off her wraps and sat perched on the edge of her chair as though she disdained contact with the rest of it. Christina called her children and introduced them to their aunt. Mary acknowledged the children in the same distant, fastidious voice she had used in every interchange with Christina since their meeting the night before. However, when wee Angus came up to her with his wide, bright eyes and sweet smile, and hugged her skirts, Mary gave a small gasp of pain or recognition. "There is certainly no mark of Peter on that boy," she said emphatically. "He looks like my father." Christina was stung by Mary's use of the word "my" when referring to their father, and she glared at her sister, but before she could say anything, Mary turned her face to look at Angus again, and she said very softly, "He could even be mine, he looks so much like me."

A moment of awkward silence followed while Christina punched the bread dough and Mary surveyed the room with her cool eyes. Unable to stand Mary's penetrating appraisal, and convinced that she had come to gloat over the evidences of her sister's poverty, Christina blurted out belligerently, "Why have you come here, Mary?"

With a slightly raised eyebrow and a sardonic smile, Mary regarded her volatile half-sister. "To see for myself," she answered calmly.

"You will never forgive me, will you, Mary?" Christina exclaimed with horrified intuition. "You talk about love and family, and Christian living, but when it comes right down to it you have no heart! How could you go on hating after all this time? Surely we do not need to be enemies anymore!"

Mary's face was whiter and colder than ever. "You were born my enemy, Christina," she replied bitterly. "Oh, don't flatter yourself to think that I still want Peter. My Samuel could buy and sell you and Peter a thousand times over. All your conniving ways have gotten for you just what you deserve—your mother's ugly hovel of a house and an unhappy failure of a husband."

"That's enough, Mary!" Christina lashed out, her face as white as Mary's. "You will not speak like that in my house! Get out of here, before I forget myself in front of the children and throw you out!"

"Oh, yes, the children!" Mary said, moving leisurely to the door. "Is that how you trapped your husband, Christina?"

Christina walked toward her sister menacingly. "How dare you speak to me like this! You are only jealous because your cold, lifeless body is as barren as your heart!" Tears of fury, hurt, and humiliation stung Christina's eyes, but Mary stared at her as though she were something less than human.

Without another word Mary turned in a swirl of her black broadtail cape and left. From the window Christina watched her sister as she walked across the frozen path to the Big House with her head held high.

Tears streaming down her face, Christina moved back to the table and began beating the dough on the flour board. Cameron ran over to her. "Are you all right, Mama?" he asked anxiously.

Christina did not answer. She went on pounding the bread dough, and her tears fell down and were kneaded into the mass.

In the following days Angus frequently came over to the Garden House to fetch wee Angus. He was spending the week showing Samuel and Mary his properties and the changes that had occurred in the Virgin Valley since Mary had left. He took the Ostlers touring in a handsome new closed cabriolet, which was warm and snug. Since wee Angus loved these outings with his grandfather, Christina felt she could not refuse her father's requests, although she missed the child desperately when he was gone.

Little Angus talked sometimes about "Aunt Mary" and told Christina that he had sat on her lap, and she smelled "nice." He also talked of Aunt Mary's pretty "shine things," which Christina took to mean Mary's jewels. One night as she tucked her youngest son in bed, he reached up and ran his little fingers through her hair. "It's soft, like Aunt Mary's coat!" he murmured sleepily. Jealousy twisted on Christina's heart like a knife, but she consoled herself with the thought that Mary and Samuel would be leaving in a few more days.

Early in the evening before the day of the Ostlers' departure, Christina and Peter were sitting in the kitchen by the table. The kerosene lamp spilled yellow light in a circle around them while Peter read and Christina mended stockings. There was a knock on the door, and Peter, answering it, discovered Samuel and Mary on the doorstep. "Come to say good-bye, have you?" Peter asked with a smile. "Come in then."

Christina stiffened at his cordial welcome, but she stood to greet the guests. She urged that they go into the parlor, but the front room was cold, so Peter suggested they remain in the warm kitchen, and he placed chairs for the visitors.

The four of them sat in uncomfortable silence while Mary and Christina stared at one another like wary contenders. Mary was first to speak. "Christina, this is between you and me, and I want you to hear me out without anger. Your temper always prevents you from understanding what people say to you."

Christina was offended by her sister's reference to her temper, but Peter gave her a warning glance. "Very well," she said coolly, "I will listen."

"In the past few days," Mary began, "I have spent a great deal of time with wee Angus. I have never seen a child so bright and gifted. He is a McElin through and through, and I honestly believe there is nothing he could not attain if he were given the education and opportunities which would make it possible."

Mary hurried on, earnestly, almost beseechingly. "Surely you have seen this!" she exclaimed. "You must realize what an extraordinary boy he is. It is only for that reason that Samuel and I . . ." She turned and looked appealingly at her husband, but he said nothing, merely shook his head and regarded his well-manicured hands, as though removing himself from the situation. "We have discussed the matter thoroughly," Mary continued determinedly, "and we have come to the decision that Angus should be raised in a situation where every opportunity which money can buy is available to him."

Christina's eyes grew dark with suspicion and horror. Was Mary suggesting that she and Samuel pay for Angus's upbringing—or that they send him away to school? Whatever Mary was saying, it was horrible and insulting, but Christina had an almost morbid need to hear the rest.

Mary took a deep breath and then blurted out, "Samuel and I are proposing that we adopt Angus." The words were so appalling that Christina heard herself gasp, and even Peter took a deep breath that sounded almost like a moan.

"Stop right now, Mary!" Christina warned in a voice so low that even Mary should have realized she had gone too far. However, Mary was so convinced of the rightness of her argument that she could not stop.

"No!" Mary cried. "You promised to hear me out! How can you raise a delicate, refined boy like Angus in this poverty? What can you give him? Hard work, a brawny back, a broken spirit? Surely if you really love him, you will be unselfish enough to give him this glorious opportunity! We would love him like our own. You would know that he was cared for in luxury and that his every wish would be granted. How can parents who say they love a child deny him these things?" Mary was almost weeping with her arguments, and, floating in a haze of disbelief and pain, Christina could imagine the fantasy that poor childless Mary had built in her mind, of the beautiful dark-haired child who looked so much like her running through the halls of her mansion, laughing in his playroom, which would be filled with the finest toys money could buy, accompanying Mary on shopping trips and afternoon expeditions. A showpiece of a child in the center of her glamorous hollow life.

Christina shuddered, as though she had witnessed something so ugly and despicable that it did not deserve to see the daylight. "Mary!" she said, and her voice was cold with loathing. "As long as I can remember you have resented everything I have had. You wanted to destroy my talents, you diminished my accomplishments, you demean my husband, and now you have tried to steal the one thing I have left which you envy, my youngest child! You are the smallest person I have ever known. Go back to your mansion, and your furs, and your fine friends! I will tell you this—you have nothing of value to give to a child! Nothing! Do you hear me?"

Peter stood up and faced Samuel. His jaw was hard, and his eyes were unfathomable. "I think perhaps you had better go," he said quietly. With a nod, Samuel put his arm around Mary's shoulder and led her to the door. Mary was weeping, her narrow shoulders shaking under her furs, but Samuel's expression was pitiless and his hand that guided his wife was as firm as a rod.

Long into the night Christina agonized in guilt and pain. "Is it true?" she asked in a storm of tears, alternating between anger and fear. "Are we selfish to deny him this opportunity?

"All of our relatives see how we struggle!" she ranted. "Do they all feel like Mary does? Are we undeserving of our children? Are our children going to grow up in scorn and ridicule? Oh, Peter! I am so afraid! What have we done!

"How can she hate me so? What was Papa thinking? Did he know she was coming? How could he let her ask me such a thing? Maybe Papa thought it would be best for Angus too!"

Peter watched her as she paced and agonized. When she would let him, he held her, but after a moment she would tear herself from his embrace and walk the floor again. Mary had struck at the very root of her sister's insecurities, and there was no comfort for Christina, only fear, doubt, and pain.

Toward morning, as exhaustion stilled her agony, Peter brought her to bed and lay quietly beside her. Just before she fell asleep he spoke into the silence.

"You never need think of this matter again. It was not your decision one way or another. I would never have let him go." Peter's voice was as firm and deep as the bed of the sea. With a sigh, only half comprehending all the implications of what her husband had said, Christina fell asleep.

In the morning, Peter was in the barnyard milking the cow when he heard a rap on the barn door. Looking up, he saw Samuel standing there in his traveling coat.

Peter stood up, his face impassive and dignified. "Well, Samuel?" he asked.

Samuel, almost a head shorter than his brother-in-law, walked to him and put out his hand. After a moment of hesitation Peter shook Samuel's hand, and they looked straight into one another's eyes.

"It wasn't my idea," Samuel said. "You know that."

Peter nodded.

"I knew it was a foolish and cruel thing," Samuel went on, "but I have fallen into the habit, since my marriage, of allowing Mary her own way, and she would not be denied. I knew she would come alone, and I thought it better if I were there."

Peter nodded again.

Samuel smiled ruefully. "It is not easy being married to these McElin women," he said. "They are willful, proud, immoderate, and independent. They are also easily wounded, fragile, and"—he smiled—"very lovely. What is a poor husband to do?"

Peter smiled and raised his eyebrows.

"One last thing, Peter," Samuel continued, and this time his face was totally serious. "I had wanted to offer you a job as manager of my new bank. I see in you a wisdom that is rare. We both realize such an offer would be impossible now. I am afraid the breach between our wives will never be healed. Mary will never forgive Christina for having the things which she wants. If you moved to Salt Lake I know my wife would find every way possible to make your lives a misery. However, Peter, I want you to know that I think you should seek an opportunity in business. You should leave Pleasantview behind you forever. I know you could be successful in business, and I know your marriage will be better if you can leave this valley with its memories and ghosts. I have seen what devastating things this place has done to my wife in the few short weeks we have been here. How can you expect your wife to free herself as long as she remains in these shadows?''

Peter gave the weary smile of someone who is being told things he already knows. "You have said it yourself, Sam, my wife is a McElin. If we leave because I demand it, she will never forget or forgive. We must leave when she is ready—and not before."

The two men sighed, and then Samuel walked forward and gave Peter a comradely embrace. "If there is ever anything I can do for you," Samuel said, giving Peter a look that was as intense and true as a written contract, "no matter what it is—ask and it will be yours. I owe you that much for having allowed you to be subjected to last night."

"I will remember," Peter answered.

Afterward, as Samuel was riding in the coach with the heavy fur robe tucked around his feet, Mary, her eyes puffy from angry weeping, sleeping beside him, he found himself wondering exactly what Peter had meant by his last statement. "What would Peter remember?" Samuel mused. Thinking of Peter, he shook his head. "What a waste of a great man," Samuel murmured to himself. "What a waste!"

After Mary's astonishing proposal to adopt Angus, Christina became almost frantic in her effort to care for her children. Her floors were scrubbed until they were white. The children's clothes were boiled, starched, and ironed. She cooked rich, huge meals and urged the boys to eat. From dawn till dusk she plied her sons with homemade toys, stories, games, lessons, and admonishments. Each child was given a slate and chalk and she began to teach them to cipher and learn their letters. She was not a good teacher because she was impatient and her expectations were too high, but the children reveled in her attentions and tried with earnest dedication to perform well. Her praise, to them, was the rarest and sweetest of life's gifts. Her love, especially toward little Angus, became increasingly possessive.

In February, the child fell ill. At first she thought it was nothing more than a cold, but in a few days the boy became feverish and listless. Christina's father came to visit, and, upon seeing how sick the tiny boy was, immediately sent for the doctor. After a short examination, the doctor broke the bitter news to the family. Wee Angus and diphtheria. The older two boys were immediately dispatched to Johnny's home and the long vigil of the desperately sick began. From the beginning of the illness the doctor did not doubt the tragic outcome. Angus was simply too little and too frail to fight the onslaught of the cruel disease. After four days of anguished pain the child was gone.

Peter wore his mourning deep within him, like a silent, secret wound. Only Christina's father suspected how sore and bitter was his grief, but Angus McElin was sorrowing so greatly himself that he could spare little comfort for the young father. Christina was destroyed by her child's death. She was like Medea of old, driven mad with grief, anger, guilt, and sorrow. Alternately she raged, wept, paced, and thrashed, then she would become silent, dark, cold, and withdrawn. Peter, Cameron, and Russell had ceased to exist for her. Even when she again took up her household responsibilities, cooking their meals and doing the laundry once more, she was like a hollow puppet of a woman in their midst. The real Christina had gone somewhere where they could not reach her.

In early April Christina asked Peter in a disheartened voice, "Why aren't you buying seed for the summer crops?" Peter had just come in from the barn and was pouring foaming milk from the pail into the separation tubs. He turned to look at his wife. Christina's hair was dull and lifeless. Her clothes hung on her tiny frame, and her face was gray and sunken. Her blue eyes were opaque and she seemed to him to be fading like an old daguerrotype.

"The rest of us never mattered to you, did we?" he asked. There was no blame in his voice, just a deep resignation. "Now that Angus is gone, you don't care—whether we are here or not makes no difference."

She lifted her eyes to look at him with an effort, but she said nothing.

"That's why I'm leaving, Christina. I have only stayed here for you, but I can't find you anymore! Much as I hated your anger and your quarrelsome tongue, I infinitely preferred it to the cipher you have become. Our son is gone, nothing can change that, and I will spend my life mourning him. But we have two other sons, and I cannot stand what you are doing to them. I used to think we also had each other, but now I know I never had you. That's why I'm leaving."

Even the repeated announcement did not seem to have the power to rouse any emotion in Christina. She continued to stare at her husband, but it was as though she could not comprehend what he was saying. The effort was too great.

257

"I am leaving at the end of this week," he said again, in a weary and defeated voice. "I am going on the sheepshearing circuit, starting in Arizona and moving northward to Montana."

Still she said nothing.

"It is to earn enough money to leave Pleasantview," he went on, wanting to shake her, wanting to rouse some response. "When I return in August I will take the boys and we will go somewhere to start again."

Her head dropped, but she was still quiet.

Anguish filled Peter's voice. "Do you understand what I'm saying?" he shouted. "I cannot live this way any longer! The boys cannot live this way—a mother who is no mother, and the weight of a thousand memories that aren't even their own pressing in on them!" Peter moved over to Christina and put his arms around her unresponsive shoulders. Tenderly he pleaded.

"I want you to come with us—more than anything in the world. If you want to stay here, the house and farm will be yours. You could run the farm and probably become quite wealthy." He gave a short bitter laugh. "You always were a better farmer than I. If you come with me, though, I promise you I will do everything I can to love you and care for you and make up for all the things you have lost. Let me do this for you Christina, please."

She turned away from him, her motions stiff and mechanical. Wordlessly, she began placing the straining cloths over the tubs of milk. Her silence was like a wall of rock between them.

Spring and summer passed slowly. Pleasantview had become a bustling, thriving community with a large feed and grain center, mercantile stores, and wide, busy streets. Christina, after consultation with her father, had rented the sheep farm to a neighboring rancher who was raising wheat in the fields and running his sheep in the pastures. She had accepted a percentage of the season's profits for rent. When she rode out to inspect the farm she knew her profits were going to be significant. The thought of the money gave her no satisfaction, however. Since little Angus's death, Christina had felt as though all of her emotions had been drawn out of her. She remembered how, as a little girl, she would pull on the tall corn stalks after they had been harvested. She would tug and wrench and tear away, until at last the whole root system, weakened and loosened from its moorings by her onslaught, would lift out of the rich black soil, and she would see the hundreds of tiny capillaries and the complexity of the root system lying exposed and dying in the sun. The black earth where the plant had grown lay empty and lifeless, sifting back to fill the emptied passages where the living roots had lain. So it was with her spirit. It felt as though her whole system of emotions, good and bad, had been wrenched whole from her heart, and she lay as empty and lifeless as the winter garden.

Peter wrote short notes during the summer that she read to the boys. He recounted his adventures and told them where he was in case they needed to contact him. The first emotion Christina was conscious of feeling since the death of Angus was a wave of resentment at the cheerfulness of Peter's letters. The thought that he seemed to have forgotten Angus's death made her feel bitter toward him. She hugged her own suffering closer, as though she must try doubly hard to keep the flame of sorrow burning.

As the heat of summer waxed full, and the days took on an endless, languid quality, she found herself responding unexpectedly to small things around her. Her two sons, who had borne her ingrown mourning with a stoicism beyond their years, began to touch her heart with their patience and thoughtfulness. One evening, as she sat by an open window, struggling for a breath of cool air, Cameron came to her with a glass of cold water. Afraid to speak for fear she would be annoyed at him for interrupting her private thoughts, he handed the glass to her with a hesitant smile, and she, seeing his fear, was smitten with remorse and horror at what she had become. For the first time in months she felt her heart fill with warm emotion.

She accepted the water from his young hand, and then, to his dismay, she burst into tears. He could not know, however, that these were not more tears of sorrow for little Angus's death. These were tears of healing and pity for her two living sons.

Gradually, Christina began to bestir herself. She cleaned her neglected house, made new clothes for her children, washed and cleaned her own clothing, and asked Min to trim and set her hair.

The family heaved a sigh of relief as they saw signs of order and vigor returning to Christina's life. She began to ride out to the farm daily, overseeing the work of the farmer who was sharecropping. She took her two sons with her and taught them all she knew about the animals and fields. The boys proved to be eager and apt students. As her healing process continued, Christina seemed to be infused with a white-hot burning energy that would not let her rest. As though to make up for her lost months, she threw herself into a

259

frenzy of effort, whitewashing the Garden House and outbuildings, hoeing and cultivating the garden until her produce became so abundant that she let the boys open a small roadside stand from which they sold the surplus vegetables and fruit. Each penny was hoarded and added to the small cache of savings even Peter did not know existed. Christina's fear of humiliation and dependence was great, and through the years of her marriage she had scraped together every possible penny and had secretly saved it against the possibilities of future penury or failure until she had a substantial, secret savings account.

As the time for Peter's return grew nearer, Christina yearned, in spite of herself, for his homecoming. At night, alone in bed, she railed at his invisible presence. "How dare you go and leave me alone to struggle with the farm and the boys and my sorrow?" she demanded of his unseen face. "How can you say you love me and then go on your merry way?" But she longed for his solid body and his silence. "You never let me in! Never let me have you—and when I needed you more than you could know, you left me!" She wanted him desperately, and for the first time she understood that Pleasantview was not her home—Peter was.

In the past, how many times had she shouted "Leave me alone!" at him, and when he had done just that she hated him for it—and yet she could not bear her life with him gone.

The week before Peter was to come home, Christina's cousin Jeremy walked up to her as she was hanging clothes in the backyard.

"Peter due home next week?" he asked laconically.

"M-m-m," she answered, her mouth full of clothespins. "Next week or whenever he decides to come back," she added bitterly.

She reached to get another wet sheet out of the clothesbasket, but Jeremy put his hand over hers and stopped her. "Let's talk for a minute, Christina," he said. "You know that I love you like a sister."

She nodded and smiled. "I know, Jeremy."

"I don't understand—I never have—your relationship with Peter," Jeremy stated. "For two people in love you are the most quarrelsome, difficult, stubborn, obtuse pair that I have ever seen." Jeremy gave her an affectionate smile. "Anyone watching you two would think you were hell-bent to destroy one another. The funny thing, though, neither one of you seems complete without the other. I don't know why, Christina! Heaven knows, you've done everything you could to push Peter away, but I'm telling you, Peter loves you more than life itself.''

She squinted at her cousin in the sunlight. "It's a strange way to show love."

"You left him long before he left you, Christina," Jeremy replied soberly.

She looked at him with a wary eye.

"You need him, Christina. Maybe you don't know it. Maybe you feel you stand alone, but I know you better than anyone alive. You need him. When he comes home, swallow your pride and stubbornness and go with him. Give yourselves a chance. You've got to go somewhere where you can be Christina Saunderson—not Christina McElin.''

"I know, Jem," she said. "I've known for a long time. I . . ."

Jeremy grasped her arms tenderly and looked deeply into her eyes. "Leave us behind, all of us, Christina. You don't need your father or the memories of your mother—or any of it! Forget you ever were a McElin. Go with him! Wherever he wants to take you—go!''

Three days later Christina heard Cameron running up the back walk shouting, "It's Papa, Mama! Russell saw him down the road. He's coming home!''

Christina took off her apron and hurried down the path to the road. Cameron ran ahead of her, his legs pumping with excited speed. She watched as her two sons flung themselves down the road toward the approaching figure of a man.

Peter stopped and held out his arms to the boys, and they hurled themselves into his embrace. Then he looked up toward the house and he saw Christina standing there waiting.

He stood up slowly staring at her across the distance. She did not move, but something in her posture told him all he needed to know, and with a whoop of joy he picked up a son under each arm and ran toward her. When he got to where she stood he put the laughing boys down and, for a brief moment, searched her eyes and her face.

Suddenly she smiled, a smile both sad and sweet, and he gathered her to him and whirled her around with happiness. Then he kissed her firmly and she put her arms about his shoulders and clung to him. He knew she had accepted him as her only refuge at last.

Part Three

THE FRUITFUL BOUGH

1898–1925

. . . let the mountains shout for joy and the hills rejoice, let them all burst forth into song . . .

Chapter Twelve

It was early September of 1898 when Peter and Christina left Pleasantview. Peter had assessed his prospects and he knew exactly what he wanted to do. He had sheared sheep in Rock Falls in northeastern Idaho and had met a man who owned the general store there. The man was a crotchety old Slav named Buckovic who had made his way down from Canada and had started the mercantile business in Rock Falls, but owning a business establishment had proved too confining for the old wanderer and he had become tired of the heavy snows and isolation of winters in the Idaho mountains. Buckovic and Peter had talked many evenings. The wrinkled, be-whiskered man had assured Peter that he'd gladly take the first reasonable offer he received for his store and all of its stock and then head south.

Peter wrote Buckovic from Pleasantview and made him a fair but low offer. Peter was thrilled when he received a letter by return mail from Buckovic. "Come and get it!" was all the old man had written.

As Peter made ready for the family's departure, he went to his father-in-law to arrange for the sale of the sheep farm and the Garden House. During the summer the Saundersons had acquired more cash money than they had ever had at one time in their lives. The sharecropper's harvest and sheep sales had been excellent, and Christina's portion of the profits was significant. Peter's earnings from the shearing tour were substantial, and even the little boys, Cameron and Russell, had managed to put aside a tidy sum of money from their roadside stand.

Angus McElin was saddened to hear that Peter and his family were leaving Pleasantview, but he was a wise enough father to realize it was the best possible decision.

"Where do you plan to go?" Angus asked Peter.

"I sheared up in northeastern Idaho this summer," Peter answered. "Now that Idaho is a state, the government is eager to see it settled, and there's land up there for the asking!"

"But I thought you didn't want to be a farmer!" Angus protested.

Peter smiled. "I don't intend to farm," he said. "I figure where there are people settling, there will be a need for stores, banks, hotels, lumber companies—business!" Angus nodded. He understood Peter's plan. This could be a beginning for Peter in business where his bit of capital could go a long way, with very little competition.

"Well, I wish you the Lord's blessings." Angus nodded soberly.

"About our property here . . ." Peter began.

"I'll buy it from you," Angus interrupted. "If you'll let me."

Peter frowned. "That isn't necessary. I'm sure we can sell it on the open market. I am not asking you for—"

"I know," Angus replied hastily. "I am not buying it to give you charity. For heaven's sake, Peter. Don't be so touchy! I'm buying it because it is part of my original family property, and I don't want it to fall into other hands."

"Very well," Peter said. "I'll ask your lawyer to set a fair market value. Whatever he suggests will be my asking price."

"Very good," Angus answered, and the two men shook hands warmly.

The value of the two properties was considerably greater than Peter had imagined, and, when the money had changed hands, Peter had more than enough capital assets to accomplish his business plans. For the first time in years he felt buoyant hope and the lighthearted eagerness for challenge that had been so much a part of him as a younger man.

Taking little else but their linens, bedding, and clothing, the Saunderson family traveled to Manti and boarded the train. Through the warm days of early autumn the train clacked rhythmically along the tracks, the boys watching open-mouthed as the beauty of the intermountain wilderness passed by the windows of their slow-moving train.

Christina had packed flour sacks with bread, sausage, fruit, and cookies. Occasionally the family got off the train during a long stopover, to walk around the station or buy fresh produce or a glass of milk or a phosphate before heeding the warning whistle and boarding the train once more. In this comfortable manner they moved northward, passing through Salt Lake City, where Christina refused even to leave the train. Peter took the boys out on the platform to view the spires of the newly completed temple, with its gleaming golden statue of the angel Moroni blowing his trumpet on the highest pinnacle. Cameron and Russell danced with excitement and never forgot the sight as long as they lived.

In Logan, Utah, the family switched to a narrow-gauge railroad called the "turkey trot." The second train was less spacious than the first and sometimes, going up a sharp mountain incline, Christina would glance in apprehension at Peter, certain that the train would be unable to make the grade. However, the plucky engine seemed to surmount every obstacle and soon the family crossed the border into Idaho. At the first stop in Malad, an old settler who'd been in the territory for years climbed on board and began regaling the two little boys with tales about Idaho and its history.

"Did you ever see a picture of what this new state looks like?" the old pioneer asked the boys. Cameron and Russell shook their heads, so the old man searched in his pockets for the stub of a pencil and a piece of paper and finally produced a rough drawing of the oddly shaped state. "You know why it looks like this—with this funny panhandle reaching all the way up to Canada?" the man asked them. The boys shook their heads.

" 'Cause they gathered up all the scraps that was left from the old Oregon Territory. Washington, Montana, Wyoming, Oregon—they had already set their borders. We were the last state around here to come into the Union, so the government just gave us everything that was left!"

The little boys laughed. The old man told them about the Bannock Indians, and the Nez Perce, and the last great fight of Chief Joseph. The hours passed swiftly.

The bumpy train bed turned to follow the Snake River, and now the family could see stretches of the river's canyon and occasional glimpses of the magnificent falls that marked the river's progress across the state as it ran from the northeastern corner, westward and southward.

"Where you folks headed?" the genial man asked Peter.

"On up to Idaho Falls," Peter answered. "From there we will get outfitted and head out, up the Lemhi River, to the Salmon, and follow that northward a piece to Rock Falls."

The man whistled. "Good luck to ye! I hope you've got a place to stay when you get there. Winter's comin', and the snows can be something fierce in these mountains.''

The following day the family arrived in the bustling new city of Idaho Falls. Gold and silver had been discovered on the Orifino River, and the little ''gold rush'' that resulted had spurred growth and immigration. Primarily the settlers were farmers, however, and the land surrounding Idaho Falls was cultivated and beautiful, with neatly harvested fields and prosperous-looking farms.

In Idaho Falls Peter purchased a heavy buckboard, a team of strong draft horses, a sleek milk cow, and sacks of flour, wheat, bacon, oatmeal, sugar, and dried beans. He strapped the family's luggage, bedding, and foodstuffs onto the wagon. As he was completing his purchases he saw a fine cookstove with enamel trim and heavy cast-iron decorations. On impulse he purchased the stove for Christina and lashed it on top of the load, with the long stovepipe tied to the side of the buckboard. Under the wagon he hung the copper milk buckets and washtubs.

The family had stayed in a boardinghouse in Idaho Falls while Peter was getting outfitted. The owner of the boarding establishment owned a fine collie, which had grown too large and active for the confines of the lodging house. When the dog came bounding into the living room, the boys, forgetting their manners, got down on their knees to tussle and roll with the joyful animal. Mrs. Welch, the boardinghouse owner, was appalled and sent the three of them, dog and boys, out into the backyard.

''I am going to get rid of that animal!'' Mrs. Welch assured her other guests. The morning the Saundersons left Idaho Falls, Peter went to Mrs. Welch and purchased the collie. With a joy that almost could not be contained, the two brothers lifted the big dog into the back of the wagon with them and Peter Saunderson began the last leg of his family's journey with the sound of his sons' laughter in his ears.

Christina sat beside Peter on the high box of the wagon as they wended their way along the Lemhi Valley. Almost one hundred fifty miles had to be covered, through areas of rugged beauty. Following narrow roads blazed between struggling little settlements, trails left by Indians, and flatlands carved by ancient rivers, the Saunderson family wended their way northward. The mountains became grander and the broad green flanks of their spreading skirts flowed out into prairies and rolling valleys. Even the rivers seemed newer and fresher than rivers Peter and Christina had seen before. It took the family two weeks of arduous traveling to reach Rock Falls, but the weather remained felicitous, and the boys loved camping at night, sleeping in the small canvas tent with their parents and cooking over a fire.

One evening on the trail Christina took the shotgun, and with Lad, the collie, following her, she tramped out across the fields behind their campsite. She was gone for a long enough time that Peter began to worry. At last he heard the crack of the rifle being fired three times. Soon, he saw Christina walking toward him through the waving prairie grass. In her hand she was carrying three partridges.

"Mama!" cried Russell, jumping up and down with excitement. "How did you shoot them?" He was thunderstruck with his mother's marksmanship.

Christina gave a rare smile. She was wearing a heavy calico apron over a blue shirtwaist and long poplin skirt. Her black boots were dusty and worn, and her hair was pulled back in a plain bun. She stood near the edge of the camp, the gun in one hand and the brace of birds in the other. The dog was jumping around her with pride and excitement. "Lad flushed them, and I shot them," she said. "My cousin Jeremy taught me how to shoot years ago!"

Peter came to her and took the birds. "You are a marvel to me, Christina!" he said with his generous smile. "Always another surprise!" All of her men were so pleased and proud of her that Christina felt embarrassed, and so she became brusque to hide her shyness.

"Well, don't stand there looking! Do you expect me to do all the work? Get out my heavy Bay kettle. Peter, you clean the birds while I make up the dough. Cameron, get out the Dutch oven."

The partridges were covered with cold water and simmered over the campfire with a little salt until they were tender. Flour was added to the gravy to thicken it while the meat was pulled from the birds' bones and sliced. Christina in the meantime had cooked several hardboiled eggs. Now she pulled out her heavy Dutch oven, laid the meat in it, poured the thickened gravy over it, added salt and pepper, covered the mixture with sliced hardcooked eggs, and then covered the pan with a thick heavy pastry. She brushed the top of the pastry with butter and cut a few lines to let the steam out. The top of the Dutch oven was added, and the whole was pushed into the coals of the fire.

That night, the temperature plummeted and the stars above the campers twinkled like flakes of ice in the night sky. The fire blazed and kept them warm as the children licked the last crumbs of

269

partridge pie from their tin plates and gathered under heavy quilts to lie by the fire. Giving a deep sigh of contentment, Peter leaned back on the deep grass of the lush valley.

"Christina," he said, "with a wife who can cook like that, a man could die happy!" The boys huddled closer to their mother, feeling the warmth of her strong, young body and, even though she was quiet, they felt she too was, for this evening at least, pleased and contented.

It was a cold day near the end of September when Peter and Christina and their two boys plodded behind their wagon through a low pass in the mountains, following a winding tributary of the Salmon River. To their west and north lay the Idaho panhandle, to the east rose the Grand Tetons. The valley around Rock Falls was lost in a crescent of land that was rimmed with mountain range upon mountain range, and in between each range lay another hidden valley with lakes and streams that jumped with fish. The elevation of Rock Falls was high, and the Saundersons knew the winter season would be long and brutal, but the bounties of nature seemed profligate around them as they rode toward their new town.

"Perfect cattle country!" Peter pointed out. "Look at the natural pastures—the fresh water! Mountains for built-in fences! Perfect!" Christina and the boys watched carefully as the wagon journeyed down the narrow rutted road toward Rock Falls. They saw the few scattered farms and ranches with fat cattle grazing, and a few sheep, like white blossoms in the green fields.

Peter had driven them down by the river and showed them their first view of the glorious rush of Rock Falls and the deep pool frothing at its basin. "This is where I shall build my lumber mill," Peter said quietly.

Christina looked at him with a frown. "Don't you think we should find out if we have a place to live first?" she asked with some asperity.

Peter laughed and said, "Some day all of this will be yours, Christina! You can live anywhere you want—any way you want!"

They drove from the falls into the little settlement and for the first time Christina saw the place that was to be her new home. The main street was one block long and boasted several commercial buildings. All the buildings were fronted by a boardwalk that was built higher than the road so that it would be out of the dust and mud. The storefronts had no decoration—square flat facades hammered in front of plain two-story gable-roofed wooden houses. Two large windows on either side of the doors were for displays and tall narrow windows on the second story above marked the rooms where the owners lived.

In front of the largest building Christina saw a hitching post and a watering trough where two ragged ponies and a heavy, saddled gelding were standing together. The sign over the largest building, in fading paint, read "Buckovic General Store."

The year the Saundersons arrived in Rock Falls a dying century was trying to give birth to a new age. America, just over a hundred years old, had burst its bonds from its old mother and had spilled, rolled, reached, and struggled until it finally had begun to fill each lost and forgotten corner of its own manifest destiny. Frontiers had been found and tamed—brought, kicking and screaming, into a new, more civilized and man-made world.

Peter Saunderson was a man on the threshold of his own wilderness, his own destiny, and his mind was itching to encompass it, to discover its possibilities, to subdue it and make it fruitful. As for Christina, she had no visions. She came to Rock Falls as a refugee, escaping from her own past.

Mr. Buckovic welcomed the little family with open arms. He was eager to conclude the sale of his store and agreed to meet Peter in the land office the next day to sign the final deed. That night, in a high-backed wooden bed with a crown of flowers carved at its peak and a heavy footboard decorated with a matching garland, Peter moved in the darkness and put his arms around Christina's shoulders.

"This is our real wedding night, Christina," he whispered. He kissed her gently on the brow and soothed her hair. In the darkness he lightly traced her features, the high brow, the firm, straight nose, the silken eyelids, the satin cheeks, and the full, rich mouth. His fingertips skirted the curve of her chin and the slender column of her throat. With delicate patience he touched the soft roundness of her shoulders and the hollow at the base of her neck. Slowly and lightly he untied the lacings of her gown, and his hand reached the velvet softness of her breast. She stiffened almost instinctively, but he held her closely and felt her body warm and open tentatively to him. The fires that lay in her, masked by her myriad of fears, angers, and misconceptions, flamed briefly toward his need, and, in the deep comfort of the unfamiliar feather bed, Peter knew his wife as Jacob had known Rachel, and he knew himself to be the most blessed of all men.

Twin girls were born to Christina and Peter the following June after their first long, hard Idaho winter.

Chapter Thirteen

Peter made steady progress in his business goals. His first step in his new life was made when he signed the lease for old Buckovic's store. Peter took the pen in his hand and signed his name "Peter Saunders" rather than "Saunderson." "From now on," he told Christina, "our name is Saunders. Saunderson is too long, too difficult to remember."

Peter Saunders, his wife, and their young sons spent the next week inventorying and reorganizing the store. Peter built new shelves, and before the first snows fell he had put in a feed and grain section with storage bins in the back lot. He also applied and won the franchise for the town post office and was officially designated Postmaster of Rock Falls, Idaho.

Upon discovering the unused storage rooms and bedrooms on the second and third floors of the store, Christina prevailed upon Peter to finish them. She purchased beds and linens to equip four guestrooms and then put out a modest sign saying "Rooms for Rent—Day or Week." During the first winter Christina's "hotel" had two permanent guests—government surveyors who were mapping the region—and several families who came to stay while they waited for legal papers for their newly acquired farmlands.

The hotel paid well, and Christina discovered she could make even more money by serving good food and accepting extra guests for meals only.

Winters in Rock Falls were bitterly cold, with heavy snow. Traveling was difficult, but neighboring farmers and ranchers came into town by sleigh and snowshoe. The settlers yearned for a place where they could gather and visit, and the general store and the adjoining hotel dining room became the logical choice. Peter kept the Franklin stoves red-hot, and the atmosphere in his commercial establishment was as cozy and hospitable as in a gracious home.

272

Over the years Christina's cooking became a legend in Rock Falls. In the winter she learned to compensate for the lack of fresh foods by using her ingenuity. She made a wonderful lemon meringue pie using vinegar instead of lemon because lemons were not to be had. On snowy days she boiled up molasses and let the guests run out to pour it in the snowbanks where it cooled into a delicious "snow taffy." Her bread was light and fluffy; her porridge, made from whole wheat soaked overnight, cooked in a thick double boiler and topped with creamy butter, brown sugar, raisins, and heavy cream, was a dish fit for a king.

On cold nights Christina would serve a creamy potato soup flavored with chicken broth and onions. For quick breads she made johnny cake, rock current buns, and pancakes with homemade syrups. Baked hams were served with a special raisin sauce flavored with cloves and cinnamon and heaping side pans of scalloped potatoes.

She always had plenty of fresh-churned butter, milk, eggs, cheese, flour, and wheat for cooking. Her children and the boarders became pink and healthy.

The little twin girls—Leah and Ruth—grew to be as unalike as a rose and a field lily. Leah, the older of the two by fifteen minutes, was dark and small-boned. She was a McElin, like her grandfather Angus, with fine-chiseled features, jet-black hair, and deep violet eyes. Her skin was the color of summer roses, and she was as lighthearted and carefree as a mountain breeze. Ruth was taller than Leah and fair like her father, with thick hair the color of wheat shining in the sunlight and eyes as blue as flax. In the summer Ruth's skin was touched with bronze from the kiss of the sun, and its golden tones glowed. She was quiet and gentle with the sweet good humor of her father and older brothers. The twin girls loved one another with an affection deep and intertwined. Neither one of them could imagine the world to be complete without the other. They played private games, and, when they were very small, even spoke a language of their own that no one else could understand.

Leah and Ruth were good students, happy, healthy, and filled with zest, but Christina found them a handful and not nearly as useful around the house as she expected them to be. Their father spoiled them inordinately and Christina scolded him for his indulgence.

Cameron and Russell thrived as well, excelled in their schoolwork, and with their father's encouragement and instruction became accomplished workers.

After school the boys threw themselves into any chores their

273

parents asked of them. At a very young age they were clerking in the store, milking cows, doing minor carpentry repairs in the hotel, running errands, saddling their father's horses, and taking care of the carriages and buckboards.

Peter loved his sons with a full man's love. Their willingness and skills made him feel expanded, as though they stretched him wider than his own capabilities. "So this is what it is to raise sons!" Peter would think happily, as he would assign the boys a task and leave on his own errands, knowing full well the job would be done when he returned.

The store prospered, and Peter bought out the establishments on either side, enlarging the general store and post office. On one side he built a square, spacious building that housed his thriving feed and grain supply, and on the other side he built a new lobby and dining room for the hotel, adding six more bedrooms above to rent out. He also bought property by the falls and opened a lumber mill.

However, none of these businesses was the main source of Peter's expanding income. From the very first winter in Rock Falls he began lending money discreetly to the cattle ranchers and farmers. He started out by financing a small herd for one of the younger ranchers. Soon the word got around that Peter was a good man with money, and settlers came to him to deposit their own cash in his company safe. Gradually Peter found himself functioning more and more as a banker.

After two years in Rock Falls, having made excellent profits on his loaned capital, Peter wrote to Boise, the state capital, and applied for a bank charter. By his third year he was running a small-scale, fully operational bank that occupied a tiny office between the hotel lobby and the general store. When ten years passed and Peter's banking operation was still expanding, he began construction of a large granite bank at the head of Main Street.

The Rock Falls Bank, when it was finished, was tall and imposing, with wide stone steps, four Roman columns, and heavy walnut doors with brass fittings. Inside, the floor was polished marble, and two tellers stood behind black barred windows. At the back of the high-ceilinged room was the enormous vault with its thick door and massive combination plate. Peter, as bank president, sat at his desk in view of the banking floor but segregated from the public by a polished mahogany fence and gate. From his desk he could watch the townspeople and farmers as they came to transact business. Peter's bank became the heart of Rock Falls. There was not a ranch, farm, or commercial business that Peter had not helped financially in

274

some way, and there were few members of the community who did not owe their start to his generous but shrewd lending policies. No man in Rock Falls was more respected and loved than Peter Saunders.

Over the years the bank business had become more demanding, and on the eve of Cameron's eighteenth birthday Peter decided to turn the running of the general store and feed and grain operation over to his oldest son as a birthday present. Russell, almost sixteen, was working in the bank. The younger son seemed to have his father's natural feel for money, and Peter felt certain that both boys would do well with their heavy responsibilities.

Peter and Christina had planned to surprise both boys on Cameron's birthday. Peter had gone to his lawyer and had drawn up the papers to incorporate the businesses with Cameron and Russell as corporate officers. A huge gold-leafed sign reading "Peter Saunders and Sons" had been hung early in the morning for the two boys to discover when they came down for work.

Christina, in her kitchen, finished tying bows in the girls' braids. "Now run off to school, you two!" she snapped. "You dawdle so much that I'm going to have to start getting you up an hour earlier. If I hear the school bell ring before you are on your way, you'll have double duty tonight."

"Oh, Mama!" Leah laughed. "Don't be cross!"

"Leah couldn't find her buttonhook," Ruth answered softly. "We're sorry."

"Out with you, or the teacher will be after you with a switch!" Christina warned.

As the twins grabbed their lunch pails and dashed through the front door, Cameron came into the kitchen from the back lot. He had been up since dawn unloading the sacks of seed wheat that had been delivered the day before. His dark clothes were dusty from handling the sacks.

"Sorry I'm late for breakfast, Mama," he said in his fine baritone voice. "I'll run upstairs to wash and be with you in a jiff. Where are Father and Russell?"

"They're in the store office going over some accounts," Christina answered. "I'll tell them you're here and the three of you can eat together." She turned to her oldest child as though she had something more she wanted to say. Her eyes fixed him with her clear blue gaze, as if to embrace him with her deep maternal look, even though she found it hard to show him any outward sign of affection.

"Yes, Mama?" he asked. "Is there something else?"

"No—just happy birthday, Cameron," she said stiffly.

"Thank you, Mama," he replied equally formally, and turned and hurried up the stairs to get cleaned up for breakfast.

Peter and Russell came into the deserted dining room.

"Cameron's on his way down," Christina told them.

Peter smiled conspiratorially at his wife. She smiled back and took her place at the far end of the table. Cameron entered the room a moment later. His wet hair was slicked back and he was wearing a white shirt and tie. When he opened the store he would put on a heavy gray-striped apron. He was a fine-looking young man, taller than Russell, with heavy muscular shoulders and blond hair that had darkened as he had grown older. The past summer he had grown a moustache, which gave him a dashing air, and his eyes, filled with intelligence and gentle good humor, were a wonderfully startling blue.

Whenever Christina looked at her sons, she felt such a rush of pride that she had to immediately counter her delight with some quick negative comment so that she would not spoil the boys. And as a child, Christina herself had so seldom heard a loving word or unrestrained praise that she had simply never learned how to express thoughts of the same kind to her own children.

"Well, Cameron," Peter said in a mock-stern voice. "What kind of a time is this to appear for breakfast?"

Cameron laughed. "I'm keeping banker's hours, Father!" he replied, and sat down at his place, tucking the linen napkin over his tie.

"I could eat a horse, Mama," he continued. "Hoisting those grain sacks makes a man hungry!"

Peter was not to be put off. "Look here, Cameron, this is no laughing matter. It is almost eight o'clock, and it is our policy to open the store at eight on the dot! You mean to tell me you will sit here taking your ease, enjoying your mother's hot muffins while some hapless customer cools his heels on the boardwalk?"

Cameron looked at his father, a puzzled expression on his face. He could not tell whether or not his father was serious.

"Well, sir," he replied, "if you think I should open the store now, I certainly will."

"Good idea," Peter said jovially. "We'll all come to help you!"

More mystified than ever, Cameron walked out the hotel doors followed by his father, brother, and mother. He reached in his pocket for the heavy key ring to open the front door of the general store.

"Here!" his father exclaimed. "Just a moment. I'm not at all sure I like the way you have the window displays arranged. Let's step down onto the road and look at them from a distance."

Cameron looked at Russell with an expression that asked, "Do you know what's going on?" Russell shrugged his shoulders. The two boys followed their father down the steps from the boardwalk and turned to survey the storefront.

Russell saw the new sign first. He read it twice before its import sank in, and then he whooped with joy and threw his arms around his brother. "Did you read it, Cameron? Did you? Some birthday present! Wooeee!"

Cameron was staring at the sign, a huge smile lighting his face. He pounded his brother on the back, and then he turned to his father, and the two men embraced.

"Welcome aboard, son," Peter said.

Peter turned to Russell, and they shook hands and then embraced. "You too, Russell, even though it isn't your birthday. We decided to do it all at once."

Christina stood to one side watching the love that flowed between Peter and his sons. She yearned to join their easy circle, to ease her restrictions of shyness and ineptitude to show them her open and unfettered heart that was filled to the brim with the same love. But habit and the fear of appearing foolish held her back.

Cameron turned to her, where she stood so primly, her back straight as a rod and her proud head held high.

"Mama!" he said, smiling warmly. He walked to her and embraced her. She raised her arms stiffly and patted him on the back. He kissed her cheek. "Thank you, Mama! It is a wonderful present!"

Tears stung Christina's eyes, and she turned away quickly, before he could see them. "Well, no sense standing out here acting the fools. Breakfast's getting cold!" she scolded. "Peter, bring your boys and come to eat so that we can get on with the day!"

Peter grinned at the two stalwart sons who stood beside him in the fresh morning air. "The voice of duty calls!" he said lightly. "If we are wise we will obey." Laughing, the three men walked behind Christina into the dining room.

That night Christina and Peter lay in the darkness and comfort of their bed, discussing the day's events.

"I think the boys were surprised and pleased," Peter said happily.

"They have earned their share in the family business. I think the future holds great things for all the Saunders family!"

"Yes," Christina answered softly. "It was a nice birthday for Cameron." "For all of us!" she thought to herself, thinking of the twins, Leah and Ruth, as they had fluttered around the supper table, hugging their brother and bringing in the birthday cake they had made with her help.

"There's one more thing I plan to do, Christina," Peter continued. "Don't start arguing before you hear me out. I know we've talked about this before, and I still say there is no logical reason why you will not let me build a house for you. I don't want you working at the hotel anymore, slaving for our boarders. I want the girls to grow up in a home, not in a commercial establishment."

"It was good enough for the boys!" Christina answered hotly. "Why do you always want to mollycoddle the girls? They need to learn how to work—they need to learn the value of a dollar!"

"Christina!" Peter interrupted firmly. "They are still children— and they are girls. I don't want them to grow up making sacrifices they don't need to make. What's the use of my working so hard and earning all this money if my family can't enjoy some of the benefits?"

"I don't see how you could replace me at the hotel!" Christina protested. "I've always made good money here—even the first winter. Where could you find someone who could manage it half so well? I—I—" Each time Peter raised the question of building a private home for the family and having her quit her work at the hotel, she was filled with an undefinable sense of panic and frustration. "I—I feel like the hotel is mine," Christina faltered. "I don't know what it is, exactly, Peter, but I feel proud of it. I like it—I even like the work of it."

Peter was silent for a moment. "I know," he said finally. "You've done a fine job here, Christina. But can't you see, it looks ridiculous for me, as president of the bank, to have my wife working as manager and cook in the town hotel and for my family to live, like itinerants, above the public rooms. Besides, Christina, you've worked hard through all these years and done without so much—won't you please let me give you something beautiful?"

Christina sighed and would not answer.

"You say you feel the hotel is yours. Very well, I will make it yours! I will deed it to you—in your name alone—and you can run it any way you wish, just so long as you agree not to do the work yourself!" Peter told her.

"I don't want to talk about this anymore tonight," Christina said miserably.

Peter sat up in bed. His voice was soft but adamant. "You can't put it off forever, Christina. I have bought property on Elm Street close to the school. You will love it! It's a shady lot with old, beautiful trees and a small brook in the back. I'm having an architect come from Idaho Falls next week. Please be reasonable about this, Christina!"

Christina sighed and turned away from him. "I don't see that you are giving me much choice!" she said bitterly. "You can build your house—but you can't make me live in it."

"Christina!" Peter exploded in exasperation. "Most women would give their eye teeth for the kind of home I want to build for you, and you manage to make me feel as though I am punishing you! I swear I will never understand you if we are married to one another till Kingdom Come!"

Christina said nothing, and Peter lay back against his pillows. In a subdued voice he continued, "I wanted to tell you about another decision I have made. I talked about it with Cameron today. Next September I am going to send Cameron to the university in Salt Lake City."

Christina gasped. "Why?" she said. "You have just given him management of the store and feed company. He can make a fine living. . . ."

"For now," Peter answered. "But our business interests are going to grow with this territory. Competition will come in, and we have to be prepared for it. Cameron is going to need a lot more than I can teach him in order to be ready for the future. Besides, I want to give him a few more years of youth than I had. Russell will join him in a year."

Reeling from the thought of being parted from her sons, Christina was suddenly assaulted with another idea. "Why Salt Lake City?" she demanded. "There are other universities!"

Peter was quiet for a moment debating whether he should inform her that it was because Samuel Ostler was on the Board of Trustees of the university and had arranged for Cameron's admission. Peter and Samuel had stayed in touch through the years. Both men regretted the animosity between their wives and yet felt unable to change the situation.

"Won't Mary's adopted son be attending the university too?"

Christina demanded. "Mary could cause all kinds of trouble for our boys."

Peter laughed. "Christina, there are several thousand students attending the university. I hope the boys do meet their adopted cousin—but I hardly think that Mary, or her son, Greg, or anyone else has much power to do harm to our sons, socially or emotionally, in a city as large as Salt Lake."

Christina sprang out of bed and began to pace the floor in the darkness. "Peter!" she exclaimed in an agitated voice. "You never consult me. You make decisions without any regard for my feelings. I will not accept this! We are just fine as we are! If you must shake up the world, go out and do it to somebody else's home and family, not mine!"

"My dear wife," Peter's voice was deep and soft. "I *am* your family."

Too upset to sleep, Christina left the room and went down to the kitchen. She lighted a small lamp and sat at her smooth, scrubbed baking table, where the wood was as white as flour from the hundreds of loaves she had kneaded on it. Slowly she sipped a glass of cool milk, and, in the pool of light, she looked at her hands, thin and strong, as they lay folded on the familiar wood.

The next day Russell came home for lunch from the bank. He was still taking some high school courses, by correspondence, and often worked at home for a few hours in the afternoon.

"Father asked me to take you for a walk," Russell told his mother. Reluctantly she took off her apron, and Russell led her down Main Street, until they turned off onto a tree-shaded side street. Several large homes had been built on either side of Elm Street, most of them clapboard with wide porches, high gabled roofs, and generous dormers. Far to the end of the street past the playgrounds and neat brick square of the new school building, they saw a piece of property that was backed by a grove of aspen trees. The lot was covered with underbrush and deep ferns bordering a lively brook that ran through its rear.

"This is it!" Russell said proudly. "Home!"

"So your papa has roped you in on his side, has he?" she demanded.

"Oh, Mama!" Russell exclaimed, coloring in confusion. "I—I guess he didn't have to rope me in. I think the house is a cricket idea!"

"A 'cricket' idea?" Christina mimicked. "Are you telling me that you don't think our present home is good enough for you?"

Russell was not put off by his mother's accusation. "Not at all, Mama! I just think we've outgrown it, that's all. Come on, Mama! Wouldn't you like to have the most beautiful home in Rock Falls and live like a lady for once in your life?"

Christina's eyes were as cold and dark as winter. "I am a lady, Russell. I don't need a house to prove it!"

Instantly contrite, Russell took his mother's hand. "Oh, Mama, I know that! It's just that—why do you make it so hard for people to do nice things for you? Why won't you let us try to show you how much we love you? Papa just wants to make your life happier."

"Then he should just let me be!" Christina retorted. With that she turned on her heel and headed for home. She passed the schoolyard, walking with her swift, proud stride.

"Mama! Mama!" voices called. It was Leah and Ruth playing hopscotch during recess. They waved their hands vigorously and came pounding across the grass toward her, their pigtails bouncing on their backs and their pinafores billowing around their legs. Coming up to her breathlessly, they threw their arms around her.

"What are you doing? Hi, Russell! Where are you going?" The twins were thrilled at the unexpected sight of their mother away from the hotel during the day.

"Run along, girls," Christina said, gently pulling their hands from her skirts and setting them on their way. "You must get back to your school, and I must get back to my work." With that, Christina continued on her brisk way while Russell and the girls stood staring at her fast-disappearing back.

"Just out for a walk," Russell explained with an ironic shrug. The three of them laughed and he hurried off after their mother.

The following summer passed quickly. Peter's architect came up from Idaho Falls and Christina refused to meet with him. She knew that Peter had had the final plans for the house drawn up, and she suspected construction had begun, although she never made mention of it and neither did Peter. She discovered, from overhearing conversations of customers in the store, that the foundations had been laid. The issue of the house became a silent contest of wills between Peter and his wife.

One night at the dinner table Cameron sat down with a wide smile across his handsome face. "I heard the darndest story today, Father," he said to Peter, who was ladling out a clear chicken broth.

"What is it?" Peter asked.

"Hyrum Mitchell was in today to pick up a batch of lumber and nails. Seems he's going to have to build his wife a house this summer after all."

"What?" said Peter, interested. "I thought they were going to live in their sod house for the first year, until they got on their feet financially."

Cameron laughed. "Hyrum did too, but seems his wife has other ideas. Yesterday she was rocking the baby in the sod house, and looked up at the ceiling because she thought she saw something move. Darned if there wasn't a tiny garter snake hanging right down from one of the sod bricks. In a few minutes she could see a whole tangle of the little things, hanging down and squirming together. Well, Hyrum says she let out a scream he could hear all the way in the back forty, and she grabbed up the baby, and the two other children, and ran like the wind!"

Ruth and Leah squealed in delighted disgust, and Christina shuddered. "Oh, that poor woman!" But the men laughed.

"That must have been some sight!" Peter exclaimed. "I bet a hunk of that sod was filled with snake eggs, and the warmth from her cooking fire just hatched them."

"Anyway," Cameron went on, "Hyrum says she refuses ever to set foot in the sod house again. She and the little ones are living in the tent until he can get a wood cabin built."

"Some women appreciate the importance of a good home," Peter said, with a teasing glance at Christina.

"And some men appreciate the accomplishments of their wives!" Christina retorted hotly.

Peter refused to argue, and so an uncomfortable silence settled on the table. The family ate their meal quickly and went their separate ways.

The Saunders marriage became more and more like an armed truce. No open shots were fired, but Peter continued determinedly to build the new home, and Christina adamantly refused to discuss it or go see it. She, equally determinedly, cleaned, refurbished, and redecorated the hotel until the rooms were fresh, bright, and inviting. Everything she did seemed to be her way of saying to the family, "See, isn't this a pleasant place to live?" The hotel showed a solid profit, and Christina took great pleasure in balancing her books every Friday evening and writing the final total in black ink.

At the end of August, Cameron packed to attend the university. Russell would act as store manager in his absence. Christina had become reconciled to the need for Cameron to go, although she still struggled against the thought of her son living in the same city as Mary.

The sisters had never written or spoken to one another in the long years since the death of little Angus. The child's death was like rock salt that had been rubbed into all the countless wounds of their childhood conflicts, and it had become a wound that could not heal. Christina had heard from her father that Mary and Samuel Ostler had adopted a young boy years ago and had named him Greg. Apparently the boy was a sickly child, and they had given him tutors because he was not well enough to attend a regular school. Angus wrote that Greg had grown into a bright enough young man and was attending the university with plans to enter his father's business when he graduated.

Christina did not cry when Cameron boarded the train for Salt Lake with his heavy club bags filled with a fine new college wardrobe his father had bought for him in Idaho Falls. She felt as though a part of her heart was being cut out of her, but she numbed herself to the pain. When the train left she turned from the platform to walk back to the hotel, but something in her bowed shoulders proclaimed that with Cameron's leaving she had lost a part of her youth forever. For the first time Peter, walking behind her, saw the shadow of aging in his wife's slender frame.

The next day Peter came into the dining room where Christina was supervising the setting of the table. The twins were off to school, and Christina heaved a sigh of relief. "At least in school," she remarked to Peter with her customary asperity when speaking of the twins, "they are required to use their time wisely."

"I want you to come with me," Peter said. "We won't be long."

She looked up at him with an impatient frown. "I'm busy, Peter," she answered. "What is it?"

He smiled with a warm, mischievous look in his eyes. "Come on!" he insisted. "I can't tell you!"

"Not the house . . ." she said warningly.

"No"—he sighed—"not the house. It's something else."

Intrigued but still slightly reluctant, Christina pulled off her apron and put on a broad-brimmed dark hat. She buttoned up her fall coat, which fitted her small waist and slender hips to perfection, and pulled on her fine leather gloves. "What is it?" she repeated impatiently.

He tucked her arm through his and they strolled together down the boardwalk, nodding pleasantly to the townspeople who were hurrying past them on their business errands. The early fall sunshine was bright, but the air had a nip in it that promised cool weather, crisp apples, and golden leaves.

At the end of their walk Christina found herself on the platform of the railroad station once again. She looked puzzled, but she waited quietly, and soon they heard the rumble of the approaching train.

The hurtling machine gave a loud hiss of steam and pulled up to the platform. Conductors and porters came down the steps while an unloading crew appeared and heaved open the heavy doors of the freight cars. Wooden crates, trunks, and shipping packages were unloaded, and then a large ramp was pulled up to the door. Christina watched in amazement as a large black automobile was rolled out.

There were only two automobiles in Rock Falls—loud, coughing machines that hurtled up and down the roads raising dust and frightening the horses. This car was bigger and more substantial than any she had ever seen.

"Ours," Peter said, nodding at the awkward-looking machine as the men rolled it down the ramp onto the road in front of the station. He was grinning from ear to ear.

Christina could not believe her eyes. "Peter Saunders!" She gasped. "When did you get it in your head to do a fool thing like this? It's a good thing you didn't ask me about it. I'd have talked you out of it for sure!"

"No, you wouldn't, Christina! What you see there is the future. In no time at all everyone will be driving an automobile. Now come along, I want to take you for the maiden drive!"

Still protesting, Christina allowed Peter to lead her down the ramp and place her in the car. He obviously had prepared for the arrival by learning how to operate the contraption, because in no time at all he had cranked the car, started it, and they were bumping down the rough road that led out of town into the surrounding countryside.

Cows fled at their approach, dogs barked, and farmers, wives, and children stood with open-mouthed stares as the noisy machine clattered by raising a shoulder-high trail of brown dust along the road.

Peter drove until they reached the Salmon River and the Rock

Falls. He stopped the car on the far side of his lumber mill. The mill was silent and the afternoon light filtered greenly through the trees lining the riverbanks.

For a few moments Christina and Peter sat in companionable silence drinking in the beauty of the scene.

"Do you remember when we first came here?" Peter asked. "We came to this very spot and I told you that someday all of this would be yours."

"Yes," Christina murmured. "I remember."

"Well, it is yours," Peter affirmed. "I have earned it for you. I have kept my promise and given it to you—for a gift. Why won't you accept it?"

"It's the house again, isn't it?" Christina said impatiently. "Everything always leads back to the house."

"Yes," Peter said quietly. "Don't you see? The house is the symbol of everything I've tried to accomplish since we came here."

"And can't you see that the hotel is what I have accomplished? It makes me feel secure—and independent—like I'm somebody—not just Peter Saunders's wife, or the children's mother. Why do I have to give that up just so that you can impress people with your success?"

"And it doesn't matter to you that we—the children and I—can't stand living in the hotel? We're tired of the lack of privacy, tired of living on the main street of the town, tired of having no trees, no garden, no lawn, tired of seeing you work for strangers and have so little time for us!" Peter exclaimed in a low, quiet voice.

"I don't see that any of you have suffered overmuch!" Christina flared.

Peter climbed out of the driver's seat to crank the engine with a groan of exasperation. "The house will be finished next spring, Christina," he said, and his voice held a note of finality.

Chapter Fourteen

The next week Peter packed for a short business trip. His plan was to drive the car as far as the Peterson ranch over near the Bannock range. There he would hire a saddle horse and meet a guide who would take him into the northern mountains where a new company, the Double Bar, was attempting to begin mining the lead and antimony ores that had been discovered there. The area was remote and the costs of developing the strike would be significant. Peter's bank had been asked to lend the company a part of the needed capital, and he had decided he needed to see the operation for himself before he decided.

"Why would you want to get mixed up in mining?" Christina asked.

"Because it looks like things are heating up in Europe," Peter answered. "If there should be war of any kind, these minerals will become even more valuable."

Christina shook her head. Peter thought so much farther into the future than she either cared or dared to do.

"I'll be back on Saturday," he called as he clattered off down Main Street in the black car that was already dusty from use. Leah and Ruth clapped their hands and laughed every time their father started the motor. They thought riding in their father's car was the closest to heaven they ever expected to get.

The days passed slowly. Only two guests were staying at the hotel, and both of them left on Friday. Russell went to the church to see a play on Saturday night and Leah and Ruth had gone to bed early. Christina was turning down the lights and preparing to retire when she heard the roar of a motor car. Looking out the window through the lace curtains, she saw Peter's car in front of the hotel. Peter was helping someone out of the front seat.

Christina flew out the front door and down the stairs. In Peter's arms she saw a dark figure, but in the obscurity of the night she could not make out any details, except that the man seemed taller than Peter and very weak. He was leaning on her husband's arm, and his feet dragged across the boards of the sidewalk.

"Let me help!" Christina cried and rushed toward them.

"No!" Peter panted. "We're all right. Run and open up the bed in the lean-to."

The lean-to was a small bedroom off the kitchen that Christina used for overflow guests or live-in help. It was a small room with a wooden sleigh bed and a washstand. The floor was covered with a rag rug that Christina had braided, and there was a small cupboard for clothes and linens. The door to the room was connected to the kitchen by a short hall. Christina ran through the front rooms of the hotel, back to the kitchen, and flew to open the door of the bedroom. By the time Peter and his heavy burden had reached the room, Christina had pulled back the quilts and the snowy linens were waiting to receive the man. As Peter lay down his human cargo, Christina lifted the lamp from the table beside the bed and in its glow she saw the man's face for the first time.

It was a face that, even in its pain, was so powerful it made her gasp . . . the beak of a nose, the high prominent cheeks, the full-lipped mouth, and noble brow crowned with hair the color of a raven's wings with threads of pure white running through it.

"He's an Indian!" Christina whispered—horrified, fascinated, and moved, all at the same time.

"No," Peter said simply. "He's a man who needs our help very badly."

Christina had inherited Janeth's assurance in the sickroom. Like her mother, she did not fear illness or injury—she confronted it. Without questions or hesitation she helped Peter undress the strange man, gently washed his scarred torso, and covered him with the fresh linens.

Peter called the doctor, who was half asleep and obviously irritated to see that his patient was an Indian. However, the doctor was in debt to Peter and so at Peter's request he set about examining the injured man. Christina went into the dining room to wait, and finally Peter and the doctor emerged from the kitchen.

"Thank you, Dr. White," Peter said. "We'll be in touch."

The doctor tipped his hat to Peter, nodded, and left by the front door.

"Well," said Christina. "Now can you tell me what this is about?"

"He's a Shoshoni chief," Peter told her. "He apparently left the reservation in Montana and tried to return to his tribal lands—somewhere up there west of the Bannocks. I don't know if he was riding a horse and it threw him, or if he was on foot and had a bad fall. Either way, he must have been lying up there in the rocks, helpless, for several days. We wouldn't have found him at all except for the early snow. The snow covered our higher trail and so we had to take a steep shortcut down the side of the mountain. We found him lying there in a ravine."

"Surely it must have been dangerous to bring him all the way back here. Why didn't you leave him at the Petersons' ranch?" Christina asked.

"Mrs. Peterson doesn't like Indians," Peter answered shortly.

Christina nodded. "What does Dr. White say?"

"Bad knock on the head, but no skull fracture that he can find. Several broken ribs, dehydration, malnutrition, and exposure. In other words, nothing fatal, but a lot of things that are going to require time and care if our patient is going to get well," Peter answered.

"Well, I imagine some hot broth would be the best place to begin." Christina rose with decision.

The next few days saw little improvement in the Indian's condition. Christina kept him clean, bathed his wounds, wrapped his injured chest, and fed him herb teas, broth, and fruit juices. He seemed to be resting more easily, as though his pain and discomfort were eased. But he still slept most of the time, and, when he was awake, did not speak to her, only watched her with his coal-black eyes as she moved about tending to his needs.

At first she had thought him to be very old, but, as his face began to ease from its harsh lines of pain, she realized that he was not much older than Peter. He was a man in his prime, but it was clear life had dealt with him harshly.

If it had been anyone but Peter Saunders who had brought the Indian into his home, the criticism in the town would have been ferocious. As it was, many of the townsfolk raised their eyes at Peter's "foolishness" and whispered dire predictions that the family would wake one morning to find themselves scalped in their own beds. Peter ignored the whispers, and soon the talk died away since

288

nothing spectacular happened. The Indian remained quiet and very sick in the small lean-to bedroom.

Christina kept the door of the chief's room open to the kitchen so that she could hear him if he was having any difficulties. The hotel staff was reluctant, at first, to do anything for him, but, as they watched Christina administer to him in her brusque, no-nonsense way, they began to feel at ease with the task themselves, and often the maid would run in if she heard the chief groaning, to give him a sip of medicine or to straighten his bed.

Russell, Leah, and Ruth frequently visited the Indian's room where they talked to him briefly—even though they got no answer. The chief would look at them with his solemn eyes, and Leah whispered to Ruth, "Maybe he doesn't understand our language." Ruth nodded with wide eyes.

Peter spent the evening hours with the man, helping him with his nightly preparations for sleep and turning him carefully in the bed so that he could rest more easily. Apparently the Indian spoke to Peter occasionally because he had gathered more information about their strange guest.

"He is a Shoshoni chief," Peter told the family at supper one night. "His name used to be Gray Owl, which means he must have been swift, wise, and fierce," he explained to the girls. "He has changed his name to Broken Arrow. That is the name he gave himself when he left the reservation." Peter turned to Christina. "You know the deep scar across his chest? He cut that himself when he changed his name to signify that he was cutting all ties to his past."

Christina clucked her tongue. "What nonsense!" she cried. "Why would anyone deliberately punish themselves? There's enough hurt in this world without creating more!"

"I've tried to hire a nurse to relieve you of the extra work, Christina, but I can't find anyone who is willing to take care of an Indian." Peter frowned. "Imagine! This man was once king of all the lands we enjoy. He was a man of power and wealth, and today no one will give him the due they would give a beggar."

Christina stood up to clear the table. "It's all right, Peter," she said. "I don't mind. He isn't that much extra work, seeing's he's right by the kitchen."

The family was eating in the kitchen, alone. The hotel guests had already been served.

Peter looked at Christina with warm eyes. "Sometimes you surprise me so pleasantly, my dear," he said, smiling, and Leah and Ruth smiled at one another. It felt good to hear their mother and father talking pleasantly to one another.

Christina observed that Broken Arrow reacted to his illness and injuries much as a wounded animal. He remained silent and still, but she had the feeling it was because he was conserving all of his strength and energy to focus it upon the healing process. It seemed his natural instinct was to pull all his conscious and unconscious energies into a deep central source, and then turn them upon the area to be healed. She felt as though the Indian's true self was hidden deep within the unmoving frame that lay on the bed, and, although he was utterly quiet, she sensed that within him an intense and powerful struggle was taking place as he fought the destruction and weakness in his body.

It came as no great surprise to her, therefore, that on the first day on which he spoke to her, he also sat up in bed and began to feed himself. She knew that it was his way of telling her that he had won his battle and would soon be independent again.

His first words startled her. She had come into the room to change the dressing on his head wound and to encourage him to eat some hot milk and biscuits. As she entered the room he opened his eyes and looked at her directly.

"Thank you, Mrs. Saunders," he said in a voice as deep as distant thunder. "I am grateful for the care you have given me." He pulled himself into a sitting position. She moved as though to help him, but he waved her away. When he had propped himself against the headboard, she saw perspiration standing on his brow and knew the price he had paid to raise himself.

She nodded her approval but said nothing. He liked her silence, and her appreciation of his effort seemed more profound because she had not put it into words.

"Chief Broken Arrow has returned from a long journey," he continued, his voice weakened from his exertion. "I had seen the light shining in the outer darkness and for a time I had wished to continue my journey toward that far light, but it is better that I have come back. I will see once more the land of my fathers and then it will be time for me to finish my journey."

Christina brought him the biscuits and milk. "If you want to go journeying again you must begin to eat more," she said crisply. She handed him the bowl. "Finish this, and then sleep. You have done quite enough for one day."

Chief Broken Arrow's lips stretched in a faint smile. "Mrs. Saunders is 'Chief' in her own right. I will call you Chief Little Fox." His voice had a tone of amusement that made her smile in spite of herself.

"Why on earth would you call me 'Little Fox'?" she asked.

"Because your hair is the color of the fox's coat and you are quick and wise and fierce."

Christina shook her head and laughed. "Well, I never!" she exclaimed, flushing, and stepped briskly across the threshold. "Enough of this nonsense. I must get back to work, and you must get well."

Chief Broken Arrow watched her go, and then he ate several bites of the mash she had given him. Wearying quickly, he laid the bowl on the table beside him, slid carefully down into the bed, and fell sound asleep once again.

By the time of the heavy snowfall in late October, Chief Broken Arrow was up on his feet. He was about the same size as Cameron, although still thin and emaciated, so Christina gave him some of Cameron's work clothes to wear. He began to spend short periods out of the sickroom, and Christina put him in a chair by the fire in the kitchen. One day he took one of the knives from the kitchen holder and began carving a piece of wood. He fashioned a small elk, a moose, and an Indian pony, which he gave to the twins.

Ruth and Leah were delighted with the gifts, which appeared like magic from his whittling knife. As Broken Arrow grew stronger he whittled less and began to assume many of the kitchen chores. He chopped the kindling and mended broken chairs with thongs of strong leather. He plucked and skinned fowl, and, as the winter progressed, he helped with the butchering of the Christmas pig.

It was a quiet holiday that year. The only guests in the hotel were a family consisting of a mother and father and two small children. Cameron had exams right after Christmas and did not feel he could make the long, cold journey by train to Rock Falls, as the hazard of being snowed in was too great. He spent Christmas with Christina's father, Angus, in his Salt Lake home.

The Saunderses and their hotel guests gathered around a small tree decorated with paper garlands, popcorn, and dried berries to sing carols. Chief Broken Arrow, who had grown stronger every week, had asked Russell's permission to borrow his snowshoes and had gone out for a walk. Every day the recuperating man had walked a little, at first going only as far as the back gate or the barnyard. Christina could see strength returning to Broken Arrow's powerful frame.

The chief had developed an enormous appetite. He ate by himself on the back porch, apparently indifferent to the cold. The family had invited him to share their table, but he declined the offer, seeming uncomfortable with the thought of a meal as a time for social gathering.

The night began to grow dark and cold. A freezing wind had begun, and snow was blowing against the windows. Every few minutes Christina glanced at the panes apprehensively. Finally, when the last carol was sung, she turned to Peter and whispered, "Will the chief be all right?"

"I'm sure of it!" Peter answered. "He has lived in this region all of his life. He will know how to handle a storm. Besides, he can't have gone far. He'll be home any moment." He patted her hand in reassurance.

They sat in the parlor listening to the murmur of Leah and Ruth as they showed their new paper dolls to the visiting children. There was a peaceful atmosphere in the room, all hushed except for the sound of the fire crackling.

Suddenly Christina jumped up. "We must go look for Broken Arrow. I have no intention of all those weeks of nursing being wasted for his foolish desire to go walking."

She stalked off toward the kitchen to pick up her heavy cape and bonnet. No sooner had she entered the darkened kitchen than she sensed the Indian's presence. He was sitting in the chilly room by the cooling stove. In the gloom she could barely see the outline of his proud head and the massive shoulders held as straight as an arrow.

Not believing how relieved and happy she was to see him there, she gave a little gasp, and he turned to her in the darkness. "Little Fox," he said, "are you well?"

She wanted to laugh with relief, but she was also furious that he should have worried her needlessly, and so she did not acknowledge his question but asked instead, in her sharp, defensive voice, "Why do you not call yourself Straight Arrow now that you are healthy and strong?"

The abrupt question caught him off guard, and he was silent. At last he replied, in a soft voice, "I shall never be well or whole. A chief without his people is a broken man. His heart is broken away from him."

She could not think of anything to say, and suddenly, in the darkened kitchen, she felt a great urge to cry—to cry for all her children broken away from her—to cry for the father and mother who had never been hers—to cry for the people she loved whom she held away with her fierce, self-wounding pride.

"I know," she whispered. "Chief Little Fox is a chief without a people too."

With that she turned on her heel and rejoined the family in the parlor. Peter was holding his heavy sheepskin coat. "You needn't go looking," Christina said. "He is in the kitchen."

After Christmas Chief Broken Arrow seemed completely recovered, although he and Peter decided that it would be best for him to spend the rest of the winter in Rock Falls. Russell, Peter, and the chief spent a weekend clearing out a small storage room in the feed and grain store. They put a stove, a bed, and other furniture in the room, and the chief moved his few belongings there.

"Thank you, Peter," Chief Broken Arrow said solemnly. "You have been a brother to me, and I will repay you. You have given me my life, and I hope someday to give you something more precious to me than the life you have saved."

Peter shook his head and clasped the chief's shoulders. "You owe me nothing," he said earnestly. "We are brothers."

It was one of the coldest winters the Saunderses could remember since moving to Rock Falls. Leah and Ruth wore heavy plaid, woolen dresses to school with several woolen petticoats and long dark leggings underneath. They each had warm, fur-trimmed coats and bonnets, heavy wool mittens, sturdy boots, and long mufflers that Christina wrapped around their faces so their cheeks and noses would not be frostbitten.

The girls were beginning to change rapidly as they approached their teens. Leah was maturing, with small womanly breasts and a dainty waist. She, like her mother, would never be tall, but already she looked like a young woman. Ruth, on the other hand, seemed to grow taller by the day. Christina let out Ruth's hems three times during the long winter days. Ruth was slender and graceful, with a much more childlike figure than her twin. She regarded Leah's curves with unconcealed envy and often, at night, would glance surreptitiously in the mirror and pull her white chemise tight against her chest to see if any pleasant roundness was developing.

The boys at school were already teasing Leah and vying for a

293

place beside her at lunchtime. Ruth felt forgotten. When Leah was surrounded by boys, she laughed and giggled and flashed her violet eyes at them, until Ruth thought she would be sick. She didn't even seem like her sister anymore! The worst of it was she didn't feel Leah even noticed her, and, since the twins had always been one another's best friend, she found she was without other friends to fill the gap.

Ruth hated that winter. To her it seemed that all of the things and people she had counted on had changed somehow. No one seemed to notice her. Her mother and father were so preoccupied with Chief Broken Arrow, the hotel, the bank, the stores, and their quiet battle over the new house that they didn't even seem to see her. Leah was always flitting around talking about boys, clothes, and parties, and Russell talked of nothing but joining Cameron at the university next fall. Cameron might as well have been dead and gone for all he counted in her life anymore—he didn't even answer her letters. It was as if he had jumped on the train and gone to a different planet!

As the winter progressed from storm to storm and the little town of Rock Falls bound itself up in its winter isolation, Ruth and Leah grew further apart, and Ruth became more and more quiet. The Saunders family was living like a cluster of separate islands in a sea of silent ice.

The battle over the new house, although silent, was nonetheless intense. Christina knew from hints dropped by Peter and the children that the house had been framed in before the cold weather began and that interior work was continuing on schedule. But whenever the house was discussed by family or friends, she left the room or changed the subject.

One evening, as the winter drew to a close, Peter and Christina were sitting together at the kitchen table. The children were in bed, and they were drinking a cup of hot cocoa together before retiring.

"You're going to have to face it sooner or later," Peter said quietly. As he made the remark the back door opened, and Chief Broken Arrow came through the door. Besides helping in the feed and grain business, the chief had taken upon himself the responsibility of keeping the wood boxes filled for Christina. He was carrying a huge load of freshly split logs, and the wood, where it had been cut, gleamed like gold in his arms.

He did not speak or look at the Saunderses but walked to the stove and began carefully stacking the logs in the large wood container.

Christina and Peter were so used to his comfortable, quiet presence that they continued the conversation as though he were not there.

"I've said all I am going to say on the subject, Peter. You have built this house on your own, and I think you may have to live in it on your own."

"Christina!" Peter said warningly. "Don't say foolish things that you may regret!"

"You could sell the house tomorrow and make a handsome profit," Christina stated. "Dr. White would love to own it. Let someone live in it who needs that kind of fanciness."

"For heaven's sake, Christina!" Peter exploded. "I can't sell it! It's our house—it's what I've dreamed of giving you all these years. I'd blow it up before I'd let someone else live in it. I don't understand you at all. Why won't you leave this dreary hotel? You don't need to work like this anymore! You can have all the maids and help you want! You can invite people in, and entertain, and have a place for our grandchildren to come—when we have them. The girls will have a decent place to bring their friends. We can take our proper place in this town! What is it that you are afraid of? Why are you fighting me on this?"

Peter shook his head in exasperation and Christina took a sip of her cocoa with a trembling hand. "It may be your house," she said. "It is not mine."

Neither one of them heard Chief Broken Arrow as he let himself softly out of the back door.

In April the new house was ready to be furnished. Peter begged Christina to come see it, but she refused, so he sent for a decorator from Idaho Falls to make the final arrangements for the furnishings.

"It will be ready the end of May," the decorator told Peter. When Christina heard the news she felt as though she could not breathe. A trap seemed to be closing in on her. The inexorable days rolled by, but Christina worked at the hotel with frenzy, ignoring the silent pressure of the rest of the family, who had made up their minds, and would not give an inch. Leah and Ruth whispered in excited voices about the wonders of the new house. They visited Elm Street every day after school, and Christina could overhear their breathless exclamations about the satin curtains, the carpets and plush couches. Christina turned a deaf ear to their delight. Russell too visited the almost-completed project with his father. Christina could always tell when they came home from an inspection of the other house. Their faces would be glowing. They would look at her with slightly guilty smiles and an eager entreaty in their eyes that unnerved and frustrated her.

Nothing would hold back the month of May. In Peter's quiet and contented smile Christina sensed he felt he had already won the victory. He was waiting for some word or gesture of conciliation and he would sweep her off her feet and carry her into the mainstream of his dreams, represented by this absurdly extravagant house. But for Christina it had become a matter of pride, and she would not back down.

During the second week of May, Christina made an announcement at the dinner table that made the family realize that Peter had not yet won the battle, as they had supposed. As Christina served them pieces of her feathery light strawberry shortcake, she announced, "Peter, I plan to leave next week on the train and take Ruth and Leah with me. I am going to Pleasantview for my father's eighty-fifth birthday. On the way back we will pick up Cameron in Salt Lake and come home with him. I believe his school is over on June the eighth."

Peter raised his eyebrows and tilted his head with a sardonic smile. "My compliments, my dear," he said. "I am playing chess with a master, I see."

Sharp words sprang to Christina's lips. "This is not a game, Peter! I want to see my father again before he passes away. And he has not seen the twins since they were born. I think it is time I went home. I'm sure this isn't too much to ask!"

"Not at all," Peter said equably. "I think you should visit your father. But why would you choose to go now, when it means taking the girls out of school?"

Ruth and Leah were sitting in an agony of indecision and suspense. They were dying to go on the trip, to see their mother's hometown, to meet their grandfather . . . to miss the last month of school. Nonetheless they also understood that the house would become ready for occupancy while they were gone, and the whole question of where they were going to live, and when, would remain unsettled for several weeks more. They loved the new brick home on Elm Street. Already they could imagine themselves living in the high-ceilinged rooms, running up and down the wide curved staircase, and bringing their friends into the sunny, grand bedrooms, side by side with a connecting door, that their father had designed for them.

296

They were sure they would die if they didn't get to move in the minute the beautiful house was ready.

Peter looked at his wife. Her eyes were flashing and her jaw was set. She was ready to sail into battle if he uttered a word. It wasn't the first time she reminded him of a frightened, cornered wild thing, and he wondered again what it was that made her fear his outstretched hand so terribly.

Calmly, Peter replied, "Very well, Christina, if you think this is the best plan, go, with my blessing."

Everyone at the table heaved a sigh of relief. There was to be no horrible war, but neither had any decision been made, and everyone recognized that fact. All Christina had done with her bold maneuver was to postpone the inevitable confrontation.

As Christina cleared the table, Ruth and Leah began chattering about the trip. "What shall we wear? When are we leaving? What will the principal say?" Christina, half-listening, answered their questions, but her eyes and her thoughts were on Peter, who was still sitting at the dining-room table going over some papers that he had brought home.

Sensing his wife's eyes on him, Peter looked up at her soberly. "You know we will move in while you are gone," he said softly and firmly.

"Not my things!" Christina warned. "You are not to touch those! They are to be left here!"

Peter sighed but said no more.

The night before she and her daughters were to leave for Pleasantview, Christina went in search of Chief Broken Arrow to bid him good-bye. The chief had worked hard through the winter at the feed and grain company and had helped Christina as well.

Christina's good food, the warmth and comfort of his room, and the vigorous exercise of his work had worked a miracle. He had grown strong, and Christina could hardly believe the tall, dignified, handsome dark man was the same broken, emaciated creature her husband had carried into their home on that dark night in early winter.

In the past weeks, as spring spread its soft green mantle on the earth, Christina had noted marks of restlessness in the chief's behavior. Many nights Broken Arrow slept outside under the stars even though there was still frost in the air. In the early mornings he went for long runs in the countryside beyond the village of Rock Falls. She had spied him occasionally standing in the lot of the grain yard oblivious of his surroundings, his piercing black eyes staring intently at the blue rim of the distant mountains.

Peter had noted the changes in the chief as well. "We won't keep him much longer," he had remarked to Christina. "I'm sure he would not have stayed this long, except he feels indebted to us. I wish I knew a way to relieve him of that burden. He is an honorable man, and I know he does not feel he can leave us until he has repaid us fully. He won't accept our help as charity."

Christina nodded. "He had enough of the white man's charity on the reservation!"

"I can't convince him that between friends there are no debts," Peter added.

When Christina found the chief he was sitting on a stack of full grain sacks. He was turned to the west where the sun was setting in a bath of red light. The Indian's powerful face was filled with such inestimable sorrow that Christina could not bear to disturb him. She turned to leave, but in leaving her foot broke a twig, and he gazed at her with his wise eyes.

"I have come to say good-bye, Chief Broken Arrow," Christina murmured.

He smiled his rare smile and stood up in a smooth, uncoiling motion.

"When you return, I will be gone," the chief told her quietly. She nodded as though she already knew.

"Your husband is a fine man," Chief Broken Arrow said. "I count him as my brother. No other man is left alive who I call brother."

"You are welcome to stay, you know," Christina whispered.

"I know," the chief replied, and his eyes again sought the sunset and the distant hills.

"My people love the mountains too," Christina said softly.

The chief nodded solemnly. "I have seen that in you. The far look—it is the mark of mountain people."

Christina was silent, and the chief, after a pause, began to speak.

"Chief Little Fox," he said, "I owe my life to your woman's hands. Among my people, this is not unusual. Our women are fine medicine workers. The medicine man calls upon the spirits, but it is the women who care for the flesh. You are a thing of beauty—like our women. It is a beauty not only outside, but something that shines in your eyes. Trees, rocks, water, the sky—all these things have great and noble spirits. Women have wondrous spirits too. Our women were among the great and noble ones, and you have their Sister Spirit within you.

"In my tribe it is custom that when a woman is to marry, her suitor travels many days in forest. He does not eat or drink until he finds the tallest, straightest tree. Alone, he brings it to the ground with his axe and strips the tree of its limbs and bark. Alone, he carries it back to the camp. The tree is the lodge pole of his bridal tent. As he struggles to bring it out of the forest, he is dreaming of the spirit of the woman to whom he will bring it and the labor does not seem hard.

"When he gives the lodge pole to the woman of his heart, it becomes hers alone. He adds other poles, the hides for the lodge, the robes for the beds and sleeping places. Each trophy he brings to the lodge becomes the property of the woman alone. She owns the place of their lodging. It is his gift to her."

Christina stood listening, confounded and fascinated by the things the chief was telling her. He had never spoken at such length. Broken Arrow continued, fixing Christina with an intent gaze. "The brave shows his regard for his woman by giving her the gift. It is hers alone. He must trust her to let him live there. The woman shows her regard by accepting the gift. In accepting the gift she is giving herself as the gift to the brave."

The chief paused and his dark eyes looked deeply into Christina's. Evening was falling, and she was transfixed by the nobility of the man before her.

"Do you understand, Chief Little Fox? The proud Shoshoni woman is not too proud to humble herself and accept the lodge pole. Receiving is the hardest part of giving."

"Why have you told me this?" Christina breathed.

"It is my gift to you for giving me my life. I have another gift for your husband, which I will give to him, and then I will be gone."

"Where will you go?" she asked anxiously.

His eyes clouded over and he withdrew from her into his solitary and inscrutable mystery. "I am a chief without a people," he said at last. "I am a wanderer with the stars."

Chapter Fifteen

Pleasantville had scarcely changed. Christina sat on the porch of the Big House and watched Ruth and Leah, acting much younger than their years, splashing bare feet in the cool irrigation water that sparkled in the narrow troughs at the sides of the street. Jeremy had inherited his father's house when Johnny had died two years earlier. One of his boys was close to the twins' age and was squiring them around, teaching them how to shoot and taking them on riding expeditions to the old sheep meadows. The girls had never been happier, and Christina found herself wishing that she could have remembered more of the joys of Pleasantview and fewer of the sorrows. The houses in the center of town seemed to her exactly the same as when she had run between them as a child. The lawns were brilliant green, and daisies, nasturtiums, and roses bedecked the yards with flashes of vibrant color.

Although Pleasantview had not changed, Christina's father had. With the passing years he had become sparer and more lean. His hair was white as snow and his blue eyes had faded until they were pale as water. In his eighties, he had developed a slight stoop that made him seem smaller and more fragile than he really was. Only his keen mind remained the same. He and his daughter sat in rockers next to one another, staring at the panorama of the Virgin Mountains stretching beyond the town's limits.

Louella was in the house making last-minute arrangements for Angus's huge birthday party. She had grown stout with a firm double chin and fading hair, but the years had been kind to her, and she still had a fresh complexion and pretty features that gave her an illusion of continued youth even though she was in her sixties.

"Louella doesn't seem to slow down at all!" There was both admiration and bewilderment in Angus's tone. "I think it's the parties that keep her going. If she had to stop planning socials I think she'd pine away.''

Christina gave a short laugh.

They rocked in silence for a few moments. "Pity that Peter couldn't come with you—and the boys.''

Christina said nothing.

"Everything's all right between you two, isn't it?'' Angus asked. "Prying is the privilege of old men,'' he added.

Without taking her eyes off the mountains, Christina began rocking faster. "Oh, Papa, I don't know. Peter has built a new house. It's *his* house, big, and fancy and showy—and all of the things I'm not. And I've worked so hard on the hotel, made it a place of comfort and beauty and—and—it always brings a profit—we'll never be in need if we stay there! How can Peter be so callous—so cavalier—to think I will leave the home that I have made, the business that I have created, and merrily go hopping after him? All to satisfy some grandiose whim of his!''

Angus gave a rusty laugh. "Christina, you are the only woman I know who could turn a present into an offense!''

"I don't see the house as a present!'' Christina retorted. "I see it as Peter trying to control my life against my wishes. I followed him to Rock Falls, Idaho! Isn't that enough obedience for one lifetime?''

"That's enough obedience for a lifetime, Christina,'' her father replied. "But I don't think this house is about 'obedience.' I think perhaps it's about 'love,' and there can never be enough love for a lifetime.''

"Poppycock!'' Christina exploded.

Her father glanced at her sternly, and his gray, unruly eyebrows knitted in a frown. "It is not poppycock, daughter. Love is essential to the human spirit. I have been fortunate to have been loved by three remarkable women, one of whom was your mother.'' His voice was still powerful, even in old age. "I know you have not liked Louella, or approved of my marriage to her. She may not be the most warm-hearted or sensible woman, and you have had reason to resent her, perhaps. But even with her faults, I have never for a moment regretted marrying her. You see, she has had to put up with a lot too. It is not pleasant to marry someone a good deal older than you are. Something is gone forever from our ability to love when we are no longer young—some fire or freshness—I do not know quite what it is, but I know that Louella has missed it. So she and I have made our peace with the things we could give one another.

"I will tell you this, Christina, we have had a happy marriage. She has been good to me—as best she knew how—but the one thing she has been able to do—which has given me the most pleasure—has been to allow me to give her things. She has let me lavish her with gifts to my heart's content. I have enjoyed the giving."

The sounds of splashing water and the laughter of the twins wafted up to the porch and Christina sat in pensive stillness.

"Chief Broken Arrow told me the same thing," she said. "To accept his gift, and with it the obligation of returning my love to him. I don't know. . . ." She rocked some more, and her voice became very soft.

"Would I own the house, or would the house own me—or would Peter?"

She heard a soft purring sound and looked over to see that her father had fallen asleep, his white head resting on his chest and a soft snore bubbling from his lips.

Angus's eighty-fifth birthday party was a roaring success. Everyone in the Virgin Valley and many old friends from Manti and Nephi came. Mary and Sam Ostler, however, were spending the summer in Europe and had not been able to attend. The Big House was decorated with Japanese lanterns and baskets of flowers, and tables were heaped with food.

Louella had insisted that Christina have a new party dress made for the occasion, and she was wearing it that night. It was made of soft chiffon in a robin's-egg blue, and had a wide collar, a narrow skirt, and a satin sash tied around her tiny waist. Even with silver streaks in her hair she looked young and pretty. Ruth and Leah squealed with amazement when they saw her.

"Mama!" Leah exclaimed. "You look like a new bride!"

Christina laughed. "You look very nice yourself, Leah." She turned to Ruth. "So do you. Very nice indeed!"

The twins were standing in Christina's old room at the head of the kitchen stairs. They were dressed for the party—Leah in pink and Ruth in yellow. Their new dresses were made of organdy, with taffeta bows and puffed sleeves. With her face flushed in excitement, Leah's porcelain-pink skin and her rich black hair made a warm contrast with the color of her dress. Her violet eyes were sparkling and her well-shaped breast was fluttering with agitated breathing. She was as beautiful as a freshly opened flower.

Ruth, more composed in her excitement, was also rich with color.

Her shining golden hair fell on her shoulders, and her skin was the color of sun-warmed apricots. Ruth's startling blue eyes and serene face gave her a look of maturity and beauty. The dramatic contrast in the twins' appearance struck Christina, and she thought to herself it was no wonder people acted surprised when they were told the girls were twins.

The young men of the valley kept Leah and Ruth dancing on the lawn through the evening, although it was Leah for whom the boys lined up. Christina suspected she had encouraged many of the boys to ask Ruth to dance after their turn with her. Ruth graciously accepted each invitation and entertained the boys with her quiet charm and sweet humor.

"She is like her father," Christina thought. "She does not fight against what is—she accepts it and makes the most of it."

As the evening wore on, Christina glanced over at her aging father, who had been standing in an informal receiving line, greeting the many guests. There was a lull in the party, and Christina was struck by how tired and old he looked.

She picked up a plate and a cup of punch and went over to him. "Won't you come sit with me on the sofa, and eat a bite?" she asked.

"Yes, Christina," he replied. "I would like that very much. Excuse me, my dear, will you?" He nodded to Louella. "I think I will go with Christina and rest my legs for a moment."

"Of course, Angus!" Louella replied. "I think most of the guests have already arrived. It is a lovely party, don't you think?"

"Yes, my dear." Angus patted Louella's hand, and then put his arm through Christina's and followed her to the sofa. She handed the punch cup to him, and he drank from it gratefully.

"I believe you mentioned someone named Chief Broken Arrow when we were talking yesterday," he said with the directness of the very old.

Briefly Christina told him about Chief Broken Arrow and the amazing way in which he had come into their lives.

Angus smiled. "Your mother knew a mountain man once," Angus said. "He was a good friend to her. Taught her many important and wise things." He nodded his head for so long that Christina was not sure if he was reminiscing or falling asleep again. Finally he lifted his head and looked her squarely in the eye.

"You should go look through your mother's things in the Garden House. She kept notebooks on what the mountain man told her—

herbs, medicines, weeds, and things like that. You might find it interesting." He was nodding again, and Christina lifted the cup from his hands.

"Are you all right, Father?" she asked.

"M-m-m-m," he murmured. "Yes. Just thinking. You know, Christina, I told you when you left Pleasantville that the Garden House would always be there for you, but I know you are never coming back to it. When I die Louella will have it taken down, I know it. She has always hated having it in the backyard. Before you leave you must make the time to go through the things in the house and save everything that was your mother's. Otherwise it will all be gone—and with it, her memory. I don't think your children should lose Janeth!

"She was the best of the lot, you know!" he whispered. "Janeth. The best."

Louella was bearing down on them, and Angus gave a sigh. "It's hard work turning eighty-five," he said with a smile, rising to greet his wife.

"Now, Louella! What do you have planned next?" he asked, with a touch of mischief in his voice.

"The Caldwells just arrived, Angus, and they want to wish you happy returns. You will excuse us, won't you, Christina?"

Christina nodded. Jeremy came from across the room and asked her to dance. "I haven't danced in years!" she demurred, but her cousin persuaded her and they whirled out across the lawn.

"You look as young as you did the summer you came home from St. George," Jeremy told her. "How do you do it, Christina? It must be because you don't carry an extra ounce of meat on you."

She laughed. "Only a farmer would evaluate a woman like a piece of livestock!"

They spoke easily about their families and the events that had taken place since Christina had left Pleasantview.

"Jem," Christina said abruptly, "could I ask a favor of you?"

"Of course, what is it?"

"Papa says I must go through Mama's things. They are stored at the Garden House. He wants me to take whatever I decide to keep."

"Yes?"

"I don't want to go back to the Garden House alone. Won't you come with me and help me?"

"I'd consider it a privilege." Jeremy nodded. "Just let me know when you want to do it."

The days passed. Pleasantview swarmed with memories for Christina and they were not as unpleasant as she had thought they would be. Images of her childhood came to her that made her think it had been happier than she had let herself remember. For such a long time she had clasped to her heart the memory of a lonely childhood, of love withheld, of cold, empty rooms, but here in the heart of her childhood places—by the empty swing in the old apple tree on Uncle Johnny's lawn—she was assailed with memories of sunshine and laughter.

One day she came out to the porch to see her father walking down the path alone inspecting his roses. He was walking with a cane because his knees were giving him trouble. With his slightly bowed back and the sun shining on his soft white hair, he looked as small and fragile as a child. A poignant feeling pierced Christina's heart. Her papa was mortal—and nothing more nor less than a fallible man—a fine man, a good man, but still, a man! She had wanted his love so badly through the years and had felt it was her only possible security. She could understand now, for the first time, that it was not his love that could give her a life. His love was only meant for the foundation of her childhood. A father's love could not be an end—it was only a beginning!

He turned on the walk and began to make his painful way back to the house. She waved to him, and he raised his head and waved back at her. His eyes were shining and he smiled as he looked at her.

"Good morning, Christina dear!" he called happily. He stood there in the morning sunlight, with the profusion of roses at his back and his face suffused with such pleasure at the sight of her that she wanted to cry. "He does love me!" she thought, amazed. "He has always loved me! Perhaps it was just that he was like me—he found it difficult to show love. He didn't know the way any more than I do!"

She hurried down from the porch and took his arm, and together they walked toward the Big House.

It was not until the day before their departure that Christina could face the expedition to the Garden House. She had arranged to meet Jeremy there early in the morning. Just after dawn she went to waken the twins.

305

"Come on, you two sleepyheads!" she called. "Up and at it! Time you got out of this vacation schedule!"

Leah groaned and turned over in bed, but Ruth pushed back her covers and slipped her feet over the side. The day was already hot.

"It's going to be a scorcher," Ruth said.

"Yes," replied her mother. "Pity us up in the attic of the Garden House. It can get to be an oven up there, as I remember."

Ruth leaned over and punched Leah. "Come on, Leah. Let's get going. I'm dying to see the place where Mama grew up."

Ever since arriving in Pleasantview the girls had been asking to go inside the Garden House. Christina had found a dozen excuses to avoid going, and the girls had become steadily more curious, until now they were certain that the house must be something either as wonderful as the Taj Mahal, or else as sinister as Bluebeard's castle. They didn't much care which one—either would be exciting!

"It's just an ordinary house, you know," Christina warned them as they hurried across the dew-wet lawn. "You're going to be disappointed."

The girls skipped ahead of her, laughing and talking to one another.

"I wonder if Grandmother Janeth's loom will still be there," Ruth whispered.

"I wonder if there'll be a treasure!" Leah squealed with anticipation.

"Stop that nonsense, you two!" Christina said sharply. "It is a plain old farmhouse, with a minimum of furniture. There certainly won't be any treasures."

Jeremy met them at the Garden House door, and Christina put the key in the lock and stepped into the milking porch. Even after all these years the smell of milk clung to the boards. The separation table and butter bowls were stacked neatly. She opened the door into the kitchen, and a streak of light illuminated the bare, dusty floor and the wooden table and chairs pushed into a corner. The old black stove stood cold and unused. The rest of the room was empty. Someone had taken the rugs, curtains, and kitchen utensils. Angus had probably given them to one of the younger cousins when they had set up their home.

The twins, unable to move at the slow pace of the adults, began racing through the rooms—the parlor, the front hall—and soon Jeremy and Christina could hear their young feet pounding around in the bedrooms upstairs.

Christina was assailed with memories as though someone had cut open a feather tick and showered her with a load of feathers, so thick they seemed like a wall—soft, claustrophobic, and frightening. Jeremy, sensing her dismay, put his hand on her elbow and guided her toward the stairs.

"Let's head for the attic and get those boxes sorted out before the day gets any warmer," he suggested.

They mounted the kitchen stairs together and came into the large bedroom, which had been Janeth's and then Peter and Christina's. The sight of the room, so full of so many memories, saddened her. Jeremy put his arm around her shoulder.

"It's all right to cry a little, Christina. Only be sure you cry for the happy memories as well as for the sad."

She turned to him, and tears welled in her eyes. "It's so hard to remember, Jem," she murmured. "I hate it! Memories are so—so—arbitrary!"

He laughed. "The arbitrary ones can't hurt us. It's the ones we choose to remember that leave the most cruel marks."

They climbed up the stairs to the attic. Ruth and Leah were there before them, standing by a little window at the side of the chimney stack that poked through the attic and out of the roof.

"I can see the high sheep meadow from here!" Leah cried.

"See how much closer the mountains seem!" Ruth echoed. "Pleasantview looks smaller from up here!"

They began opening the stored boxes. Much of what had been saved was simply the detritus of several generations of life in the same house. Old magazines, rolls of unused wallpaper, damaged toys, and musty clothing.

The little group looked over the items and marked most of them for disposal. Jeremy began to make a pile in one corner of the attic. "I'll have one of my boys come and cart all of this stuff away," he said.

Christina separated out some old dresses that would make good keepsakes. She also found a few toys that had belonged to her dead son, Angus. At first she thought she might take them home with her, but then she decided she did not want to live with a tangible reminder of that still-painful loss. "Give these to your little Andrew to play with," she said to Jeremy.

"Thank you," Jeremy replied. He and his wife had been blessed with another son who was turning one year old this summer. Jeremy doted on the little child and extolled the praises of "mature" fatherhood.

At last Christina came to the heavy leather boxes marked "Janeth" in fine, old script. These boxes were made of superb leather and were beautifully crafted. When Janeth left Denmark she had brought her belongings in these expensive trunks, which were discards from the luggage rooms of the royal house. The trunks were still in excellent condition. The leather remained a rich, deep, lustrous brown and the metal caps that rounded the corners gleamed softly in the attic light.

The girls drew close to their grandmother's old possessions and touched the surface of the decades-old leather with reverent hands. "Lovely!" Ruth exclaimed.

"Open it, Mama!" Leah clapped her hands and giggled. "If there's going to be any treasure, it's bound to be in there!"

Jeremy laughed. "Your grandmother was a treasure herself!" he said. "Perhaps you'll discover something of her in there."

Christina found herself hesitating. She was experiencing an almost pathological reluctance to open her mother's boxes. Did she fear another wave of memories, which like the creatures from Pandora's box would fly out at her as soon as she lifted the lid? Slowly her hand found the clasp, and, as luck would have it, she could not open the box after all. The clasps were intricate and difficult to unlatch, so it was Jeremy, ultimately, who broke open the long disused trunks. Christina and her daughters peered down at the legacy that Janeth had neatly packed before leaving on her final journey with Angus, fully believing that she would return someday to live out the rest of her life with her husband in the Big House.

Two boxes. One contained Janeth's finest woven shawls and swatches of woven fabric, packaged with camphor, bay leaves, and cedar chips. The fine woolens were as fresh and beautiful as the day they had left Janeth's loom nearly a quarter of a century earlier. Through experimentation and accumulated knowledge Janeth had created dyes that had not faded. Their subtle colors glowed in the depths of the trunks.

In the other box they found Janeth's notes. Many of her scientific and botanical observations and experiments were written on loose sheets of paper that had been compiled in sheafs and tied with strings. In the bottom of the box were her notebooks. There were ten of them in all, each one filled with carefully detailed drawings and meticulous notes written in her careful, sloping hand.

Ruth was enchanted. Slowly she turned the pages of the notebooks, her eyes growing round with wonder. "They're beautiful! Mama," she whispered. "Did Grandma really draw all of these plants? She knew so much!"

"Yes!" Christina said impatiently. The notebooks had brought back her feelings of resentment toward her mother. Her mother had cared more about those silly books than she had about her only child. What did they amount to after all? A few dusty volumes tucked in the bottom of an old trunk that no one would ever see!

Suddenly Christina wanted to get out of the Garden House. She wanted to be free of the dust, and the stifling air, and the rush of memory.

"Jem, I'm too tired to sort all of this. If you don't mind, I think I'll have you ship Mama's trunks to Rock Falls for me, and I'll sort them out there when I have the time."

Jeremy nodded.

"Oh, Mama!" Ruth begged. She was sitting on an old rocking horse, lost in the pages of her grandmother's notebook. "Couldn't I keep one of these out to read on the train?"

"I suppose so," Christina answered impatiently. "Let's move along now, girls. We have our packing to do."

Leah, disappointed by the ordinariness of everything they had seen, was as impatient as her mother to be gone. It had been fun seeing Mama's old home, meeting the McElin cousins, and playing on the farms, but Leah could not wait to get back to Papa and the new house. She was homesick for Russell and Cameron as well, and for the familiar town with its narrow streets and well-known shops.

Ruth walked out of the attic last of all. She gave the low-ceilinged room a final reluctant glance, as though she wanted to fix the image in her mind. As she left the house, she walked through each of the rooms once more and then she slowly came out of the back door where the others were waiting for her.

"Close the door tightly," Christina said impatiently. "It will latch by itself. My goodness, Ruth, you have certainly taken your time!"

Christina turned to walk away, but Ruth's voice followed her. "I think it must have been a splendid place to have grown up, Mama! There is something so . . . so honest about that house. I liked it!"

As the train sped toward Rock Falls, Christina became aware of the ticking of the time bomb set in her life over a year ago that she had squirmed and twisted to avoid. The hours clicked by with the rhythmic rattle of the train wheels as she watched the countryside through the windows of the moving train. How vividly she remembered journeying through the wilderness of Utah and Idaho to Rock Falls with Peter so long ago! She saw scores of new settlements where before there had been nothing but open tracts of land, lush fields of untouched grass, wild mountains and hills, untapped, rushing streams and waterfalls.

The memory of Peter came to her like a dream, as she leaned her head against the ash-stained window and stared at her own dim image reflected against the scrim of nature. Peter had not been a part of her memories of Pleasantview, but now thoughts of him came thick and fast as she sped toward their reunion. She remembered him comforting her in the stable when her father had announced his engagement. She remembered him saving her from the cougar. In her mind she saw his strong hands and his young face with a soft golden stubble as it had been at the lumber camp—their hurried marriage—his gentleness and patience. With shame she thought of the hundreds of ways she had sought to hurt him because she was so wary of his love. Had she deliberately and cruelly tested him, pushed him, fought him, to prove to herself that he would not fail her? She didn't know, but the thought made her remember the time when he had left her, that terrible summer after Angus's death when she had found that any life with Peter was better than the easiest of lives without him. But what was it that made her treat his gifts as though they were sentences of oppression or the imposition of his will upon her? Why did she put herself against his kindness and love, as furiously as she did against his efforts to understand and help her?

She saw now that her father had loved her—in his own way—and yet throughout her childhood she had refused to believe in his love. Did she mistrust love so completely that she would not allow herself to be loved? Or was it her pride? Was there something so unbending in her spirit that she refused to accept love for fear she would be bound to it, would be caught in its web and would have to yield the gift of herself to another? Wasn't that what Chief Broken Arrow had been trying to explain to her?

Behind her she could hear Ruth and Leah quarreling over Janeth's book. Leah had picked the notebook up and was reading it, and Ruth had snatched it away from her. "You mustn't flip the pages like that, Leah!" Ruth exclaimed. "You will rip the binding! It's very fragile!"

"Oh, pooh!" Leah responded. "All you've been doing this whole trip is mooning over that dumb book! Why don't you go up and sit by Mama and let Cameron come and sit by me if you're going to be so boring!"

Cameron had joined the family in Salt Lake. He looked even handsomer than Christina had remembered, and he was eager to get home and reinvolve himself in the family business.

He told Christina he had had a fine year at the university and that Russell would be crazy about it too. During one conversation Cameron laughed and said, "Gosh, Mama! I don't know what it is that you and Aunt Mary have going between you, but it must be potent! It carries down to the next generation!"

"What do you mean?" Christina asked anxiously, instantly on guard. "Did you meet Aunt Mary?"

"Not on your life! She didn't want to have anything to do with me! I met Uncle Sam though. He came to my rooms one day to introduce himself. Told me if there was ever anything he could do for me, just to let him know. Nice fellow."

"Yes," Christina said crisply. "I don't see how Mary deserves him."

"I met Greg too," Cameron went on. "At a fraternity social. I was thinking of pledging that fraternity. Went to an invitational. As soon as Greg figured out who I was—he was on the membership committee—he avoided me for the rest of the evening. When I was getting my hat and coat he came out on the porch and growled, 'I'll save you a lot of time and effort, Saunders. Don't try to pledge Kappa Tau because you won't make it!' That's all he said, but I got the message!" Cameron chuckled.

Christina was furious. "That Mary! How could she teach such spite to her son! And an adopted son at that! What is he like anyway? He sounds absolutely dreadful!"

"Oh! He's sort of a scrawny fellow. Dark, slick hair, sharp dresser, oozes self-confidence," Cameron replied. "He runs with a mighty fast crowd! Lots of money, and it shows! He seems bright enough—sort of shrewd and savvy."

Clucking her tongue, Christina responded, "Sounds like the sort you'd be best off without! Did it bother you not to get into the fraternity? If it did, I'm going to write Mary and give her a piece of my mind!"

"No, Mother! I didn't want to join that crowd anyway. As a matter of fact, Uncle Sam proposed me for his old fraternity—the Beta Phis—and I made it in without a hitch. I'll see that Russell gets in as well. I'm not much for the fraternity thing anyway, it's just that it's nice to be able to stay in the frat house." Cameron shrugged.

"Speaking of houses, Mother, what are you going to do? Papa has moved everything into the new house. He wrote me about it."

"That is between your father and me," Christina said, snapping her lips shut in a way that told Cameron he would not get another word out of her on the subject.

Peter was waiting at the station with the car. The family embraced one another and the twins squealed in delight at the familiar sights of Rock Falls. Christina was fussing over her luggage and waiting for her mother's trunks to be unloaded. Peter came up to her and said quietly, "I will have the boys drive the girls home. You and I will walk."

Cameron drove off in the car, sitting very tall in the front seat, proud to have been trusted by his father to take the family home.

Once the luggage was collected and neatly piled, Peter paid the carter to haul it to the house and he gave Christina his arm.

"By 'home' I suppose you mean the new house," Christina said.

"Yes," Peter answered firmly. "That is our home now—your home."

"And the hotel?" Christina challenged defensively.

"It is fine. I have a new couple running it. If you are unhappy with them you are welcome to replace them. I have had the whole thing deeded to you."

"Chief Broken Arrow?" Christina asked.

"Gone," Peter answered. "I'll tell you all about it this evening. But for now, we are going home."

They walked across Main Street onto the quiet residential vista of Elm Street. Tall leafy elms spread like an arch across the street and at the far end, framed by the majestic trees, Christina saw the wide brick facade and the tall, shuttered windows of the home Peter had built for her. As they drew closer she noted the graceful wrought-iron fence, the fanciful eaves, the deep cornices and chaste white trim. The wide front steps, rather than seeming imposing, appeared to spread in a glorious welcome. Even the landscaping was complete, with beds of marigolds and hardy petunias lining the wide brick walk. The windows sparkled in the afternoon sunlight, and every aspect of the house was one of spacious and pleasant appeal.

Christina said nothing, although she could sense Peter waiting for her slightest response. They entered the wide double doors, and she stood in the large entrance hall with its sweeping staircase and sliding doors on either side, one leading to the front parlor and the other to a combination office and library. She could hear the children upstairs in the hallway, the girls' voices warbling with delight and the older brothers laughing at their enthusiasm.

Solemnly and silently Peter led Christina through each of the rooms: the living room with its plush patterned carpet in rose and cream; the ivory walls, and the velvet rose furniture, with splashes of gold and turquoise as accents.

The dining room had a walnut chair rail under a pale green and gold Chinese tapestry paper. The room was centered with a crystal chandelier hanging from a plaster rosette that decorated the ceiling. The table was shining mahogany surrounded by graceful chairs with petitpoint seats and a rich Oriental rug on the floor. Throughout the house the wood parquet and the plaster motifs showed the excellence of the craftsmen who had worked there and the attention to detail that characterized everything Peter undertook. The home reflected good taste and quiet restraint, and Christina knew that Peter had built it with her in mind.

When they reached the kitchen she gasped. One entire wall was filled with a bank of beautiful steel stoves: four ovens, eight burners, a broiler, and a large steamer unit. In the center of the enormous room was a long, heavy wooden table, with a surface of finely finished wood and a marble inset for candy-making at one end. The kitchen was lined with cupboards and shelves on three walls, and a large pantry door opened from the other end. "Your iceboxes and vegetable and flower sinks are in the pantry area," Peter told her, his eyes smiling.

She walked over to the stoves and looked at the gleaming metal. "What meals could be cooked in this room!" she thought. The kitchen was filled with freshly minted sunlight, and she realized that Peter had removed the trees from around the kitchen windows so that light would pour in to make the room even more cheerful.

In spite of the warm summer afternoon the house was surprisingly cool. Christina knew that was a sign that the walls were thick and the ceilings high. Could it be true that such a marvel of a house was hers? She shook herself.

"Come," Peter said, and led her up the staircase.

The children were quiet now. All of them had gone to their own rooms, to unpack or simply enjoy the new luxury of privacy. Peter led Christina down a carpeted upper hall to wide doors at the end of the corridor. He pushed open the doors and she stared at the master bedroom. The room was shell pink, with tones of lavender and pale blue. The walls were a pastel paisley, with delicate shell-pink woodwork. The carpet was a soft, carved Oriental, pale blue, with corners and center medallion decorated in deep-pile lotus blossoms of soft pink and green. The wide bed was covered with a spread of shot-taffeta in creamy pink, and canopied in the same material. Gold leaf decorated the trim of the doors and the tall regency mirror that hung above the taffeta-skirted dressing table.

Christina walked across the carpet, and Peter followed her, softly closing the door behind him. She moved to the elaborately draped window and looked down onto the green lawn that fell away from the back of the house to the dancing brook bubbling among the ferns.

Peter stood close behind her and raised his hand to touch her shoulder, but she pulled away from his touch. "No," she whispered urgently. "Don't touch me, Peter Saunders. I have something I must say and it is going to be very hard for me."

She gave a long shuddering breath and moved toward the center of the room, turning to face him. He remained where he was, his face calm, listening.

"I—I don't know why it is so difficult for me to accept things, Peter. Even from the children—when they bring me a cluster of wildflowers or a picture they have made at school—I am so pleased with the gift and yet, I cannot tell them. It makes me feel awkward and uncomfortable. I know sometimes I must seem hard and unfeeling—but I'm not! I'm truly not! I just find it so difficult to—"

Peter nodded. "I know, Christina," he said quietly.

There were tears in her eyes. "Peter, this is a beautiful house. Any woman would be proud to live here, but it frightens me! Can you understand that? It is such a commitment! It is a gift so full of expectations—and I will feel the need to live up to it. This house takes away all the familiarity and security of my life. It challenges me to live a new way—to be a different person—and I don't want that. I am forty years old and I have grown comfortable and used to my old patterns. Can you understand any of this, Peter? Because I'm not at all sure that I do—I only know that I have hated the idea of this house! I have blamed you for pushing me out of my cozy nest into a world which you have created."

"*We* have created," Peter corrected her. "This is your achievement as much as mine, Christina! I couldn't have done any of it without you.''

She shrugged and went on. ''I only want you to know—none of those feelings have changed but, in the past few weeks, while I have been gone, I have remembered something.''

''What is that?'' Peter asked.

''That I cannot live without you, Peter,'' Christina said softly, forcing the words. Her face flushed with the effort of speaking private thoughts, but she continued. ''I know I will always struggle against you. You are strong and, in your quiet way, you dominate and control. You never fight like I do, you simply go your own way, and no one—or nothing—deters you! I have one of two choices—either I follow, or I am left behind. What you see as love, I see as domination—and sometimes I have to fight to feel I am real.''

''I never . . .'' Peter began, but Christina shook her head and he stopped speaking.

''I know, you never mean to dominate me,'' she said, ''and the strange thing I have discovered is that, as strong as my desire is to struggle against you, I would be destroyed if I won! What I am testing, I suppose, is not your strength, but your love. No matter how often you tell me—no matter how many ways you show me—I still cannot believe you love me!'' She was trembling, and her troubled, tear-stained face looked like that of a lost and sorrowing child.

''I know I can't change—not entirely—but I know I want to try! I have come very close to the edge of a precipice, and I have looked over the edge and seen how bleak and dark my life would be if I destroyed your dreams and with them your love for me.'' She took a deep breath. ''I will live in this house, Peter. I will try very hard to be the woman you thought I was when you built it.'' Tears were streaming down Christina's face, and Peter moved toward her.

''Let me hold you,'' he whispered, happiness filling his voice. He put his arms around her and bent to kiss her wet cheek. She was sobbing, and he gently kissed her hair and then kissed her forehead, her eyes, and at last her trembling lips. Again and again he kissed her, and gradually her weeping changed to a sweet urgency and her tender lips opened to his and he kissed her with the fervor of passion. She responded to his demanding embrace and kissed him furiously.

He picked her up and placed her on the taffeta coverlet. Her glorious hair spread out across the shining fabric like freshly struck coins, and her slender, lovely body, so exquisitely formed, seemed like the incarnation of all women and all men's dreams of womanhood.

With loving, patient hands he undressed her, holding her and kissing her softly as he removed each garment until at last she lay before him with the late-afternoon sunlight filtering through the lace curtains, her body glowing like a pearl. Each magnificent detail of her filled him with joy and desire.

He picked her up and held her close against him. "Christina," he whispered. "You are more beautiful than anything I have ever seen in my life! This house—this world—are nothing compared to your loveliness."

He threw back the covers and laid her on the cool white linen sheets. Hurriedly he undressed, watching her as she lay before him. She had closed her eyes, and he could see the weariness and emotional exhaustion that had weakened her to the point where she could not resist him—but he also saw the subtle change in her, her tentatively opening heart. She was trying to give herself more freely, and, although he knew that the struggles of their marriage would always be as much a part of them as the shape of their hands, he also knew that sometimes they would break through to deeper levels of loving and understanding than they had known before. Tomorrow Christina might regret this moment, but he did not care. Today he would take her proffered gifts just as she had taken the house—and the price would be worth the cost of all his tomorrows.

With a groan of delight he lay beside his wife and passed his hand gently down the long curved line of her body, a column as rich, smooth, and voluptuous as a classical statue. He touched her breasts and she turned to him with a tiny moan. He could contain himself no longer, but clasped her in his arms and feasted upon the touch and sight and taste of her, and she responded with a sweetness that made his heart roar with happiness.

Later that evening Peter ate dinner in the dining room with his children. Mrs. Lennox, the housekeeper he had hired, served a festive meal of chicken, fresh vegetables, buttery biscuits, and lemon ice with raspberries.

"Where is Mama?" the children inquired anxiously as Peter sat down at the table without Christina.

"She is sleeping upstairs," Peter answered. "The trip has tired her out, and I did not want to waken her."

"Then she's going to stay here?" Ruth asked with careful joy.

Peter grinned from ear to ear. "Yes." He laughed. "She loves

316

the house. Of course she will stay! We are a family!'' Never had he said the word with more conviction.

Peter brought a tray of supper up to Christina and wakened her gently.

"I thought you might want a bite to eat," he suggested. She pulled herself up on the large, downy bolsters at the head of the bed and sat looking at him. She had put on a lacy wrapper that tied high on her neck, and she looked small and sleepy in the big bed.

"Thank you." She nodded as he placed the tray in front of her. She could not meet his eyes, and the color in her cheeks was very high. He understood she felt shy and awkward with the memories of their lovemaking and the elegance of the unfamiliar room. He pulled a chair beside the bed, not sitting too close—but close enough to give her a feeling of comfort and care.

"Tell me about Chief Broken Arrow," she said.

"He came to me about a week after you left and told me it was time for him to go," Peter said. "I urged him to stay. I told him I had never had a finer friend than he had been to me, and I would be honored if he would work with me for the rest of our days."

"What did he answer?" Christina asked.

"He didn't say anything in reply. Just smiled. We both knew he had to go. He is not a man for walls and a roof, or the paved streets and silly conventions of a town."

"No," Christina said softly, "he is a man for the sky and the wind."

"Anyway," Peter continued. "He asked if I would make a short journey with him before he left me. I said yea, so we traveled together up into the mountains, past the area where I had found him, and on to the next valley—through a high, difficult pass. The valley was magnificent. Rolling fields and mountains cropping around in a series of lovely plateaus and soft foothills, up to the highest, craggiest peaks you've ever seen! A dazzling waterfall that comes like a series of bridal veils, down a sheer rock face, and sends a small river rushing through the heart of the land. The chief stood at the opening of the pass looking out and his hand swept the whole of it. 'This is my place,' he told me. 'The place of my people. Now my people are no more, and I am a wanderer until the Great Spirit takes me with his mighty wings.' "

"Oh, no, Peter!" Christina exclaimed softly. "He is like a man without a family—without a country! So lost. . . ."

"I know," Peter replied. "I tried to reason with him. 'Broken

Arrow,' I said, 'join us. Join the white man. You are part of us too. Let me help you! I'll lend you money—you can run cattle on this valley and build a place for yourself.' But he replied, 'No, it is not my way. I do not want to live a life with two faces. I will leave as I have come, a man of my people, a man of honor.'

"He said to me, 'You are a man who gives money to other men, and they must repay you. A banker understands that a man must pay back his debts or else he becomes their prisoner. I am in your debt and I wish to be free!' I protested that he was not in my debt—I did what I did for him because all men are brothers. He answered, 'If you are truly my brother, you will let me repay you so that I may be free to care for you as a brother.' What could I do? I understood what he was saying, and I knew he felt it necessary to give us something in return for saving his life.

"We talked through the day. In the evening we caught a rabbit and roasted it over the campfire. Three days we spent together in the valley, and on the third day he had almost convinced me that I wanted to spend my life as a Shoshoni too!

"At last, when we knew our time together had ended, he told me what he wished to do. It seems that in the General Allotment Act in 1887 his father, who was then chief of the Shoshonis and living on a reservation, was given deed to the large section of the territory which Broken Arrow had brought me to. The deed was now in Broken Arrow's name, and it was his desire to repay us by giving us a portion of his land. I protested vigorously, but he had obtained my word that I would let him repay me in whatever way he saw fit. Of course, at the time I had given my word to that bargain I had no idea he had anything to give!

"He brought out a large piece of deerskin which was bleached and smooth as parchment, and on it he had written my deed and—amazingly—had even had his signature witnessed. Apparently he learned a great deal about white man's ways while he was on the reservation."

Peter walked over to a small table and pulled out the top drawer. "I knew you would want to see this," he said.

Christina took the soft leather from his hands and unrolled it. On the parchment surface in dark ink, written in a careful, large hand were the words "To Peter Saunders I deed the following portion of my lands. From the rim of the Coyote Pass a day's ride to Moon Mountain and from the eastern peak of Crowsnest Mountain to the Mountain of the Three Song Falls. Lines from these four points to be drawn to form a perfect square. All territory and earth, all waters and things under the earth, all plants and animals upon the earth within that square belong to Peter Saunders and to his children and their children forever. To this I have put my hand." The signature was clear and firm, and the witnesses were two businessmen from Rock Falls.

She looked at Peter with tears in her eyes and handed the deed back to him. "What did you do?" she asked him.

"I thanked him. His gift was given with friendship and dignity. I had to accept it in the same way. We embraced, and I promised him that I would care for his land with the same love and respect he and his people had given it.

"One thing more," Peter said. "I had the deed registered and officially surveyed, so it's legal. I intend to keep my promise. I will work the land and put a portion of its proceeds in trust for Broken Arrow, should he ever return."

They sat in silence a moment. "Do you think he ever will?" Christina asked.

"No," Peter said. "He has watched his people die one by one of disease, starvation, battle wounds, and broken hearts. When he changed his name he vowed he would become a wanderer to the end of his days, he would submit to no man, not in friendship, fealty, or duress. He will never return because he has grown to care for us, and he does not want his heart in bondage."

For a moment Christina thought of her friend, dark, lithe, noble, and fierce. "Perhaps he knows the way to the Great Spirit," Christina murmured, "or perhaps it is only in searching that he finds rest. I think we will never see him again."

Peter nodded. Then Christina looked at him out of the corners of her eyes. In her expression there was a look of humor that surprised Peter. Humor was rare with her! There was, however, a distinct note of amusement in her voice as she said, "He didn't need to repay you with his land, Peter. You owe him more of a debt than that!"

"What?" Peter asked.

"This!" Christina said, indicating herself and the bed. "My being here! It was Broken Arrow who made me understand that I must come. We both owe him more than we can imagine."

Chapter Sixteen

Once having acknowledged the fact that she would live in the new house, Christina became a termagant about setting it in order. Peter may have built it, but she was determined to place her imprint upon it, and so, in the first weeks of living there, she rearranged the furniture and brought several loved objects from the family rooms at the hotel and installed them in places of prominence. She replanted the flowerbeds with flowers more to her liking, and although she retained Mr. and Mrs. Lennox as caretakers, Christina did much of the work in the house herself, and the kitchen remained her domain. Even when she did not do the actual cooking she supervised every menu—choosing the recipes and insisting that preparations follow her detailed instructions. She also insisted that Ruth and Leah do their share of the chores, and she gave them regular lessons in the kitchen.

Late in August, as the harvest season was beginning, Christina sat on the front porch, peeling a basket of peaches. The fuzzy golden globes of fruit, with their soft, rosy blush, were firm and juicy. Carefully Christina handled them without bruising, and she filled her quart bottles with perfecty arranged slices ready for the heavy preserving syrup.

She looked up apprehensively as Sy Warner puffed up the walk on his old bicycle. With fruit-stained hands she gingerly accepted the yellow envelope he handed to her, and thanked him, but she was in no hurry to read the contents. Her heart was heavy with a prescient knowledge of the message. The telegram was brief:

ANGUS PASSED AWAY PEACEFULLY IN SLEEP MONDAY STOP FUNERAL
SERVICES WEDNESDAY STOP MARY IN EUROPE STOP LOVE LOUELLA

Christina felt hot tears sting her eyes and she sat down heavily, oblivious of Sy Warner, the telegram man's departure. It was Wednesday.

Had Louella deliberately delayed sending the telegram? No. She would not be that unkind. It was probably the telegraph company's fault.

Poor Papa—neither of his daughters at his funeral to mourn him. Christina thought about the way her whole world had been circumscribed by her father when she was a child. How she had yearned for his love and approval! How she had feared and resented his indifference and had struggled for his attention!

A flood of gratitude came over her as she thought of her visit with him earlier that summer, and then the tears came, warm and natural and free.

"I love you, Papa," she whispered, and somehow she was comforted as though she felt his strong hands on her shoulder and his voice whispering, "I know."

Peter and the children were saddened at Angus's passing as well, but the family's mourning was tender and restrained, and the pace of life at the end of the summer became brisk. Christina found little time to lose herself in sadness as the regular chores of canning, drying, preserving, and bottling the harvest began; the two girls, now teenagers, were pressed into daily service, peeling, paring, slicing, and scrubbing fruit.

Both Russell and Cameron were busily preparing for their departure to the university. Christina mourned inwardly but she kept herself busy and tried not to think about the passing days. So many changes in her life, crammed into so brief a span!

Leah was also a great concern to Christina. Leah had developed into a beautiful young woman, and the young men of Rock Falls were eager for her company. Every night in the front parlor a group of them would assemble. They brought their ukeleles and their friends and spent the evenings laughing, telling jokes, dancing, singing, and vying for the honor of sitting next to Leah. Ruth and some of the other girls of their social set were usually in attendance, but the circle was always drawn around Leah.

"Lee" was what the young people called her, and Leah asked her family to start calling her Lee as well. "My name is so old-fashioned!" she had complained. "Everyone calls me Lee. I refuse to answer to 'Leah' anymore!"

This vigorous announcement was made at the dinner table. Cameron turned to Ruth. "Well, I guess we'll have to start calling you 'Ru'!" he said with a grin.

Ruth did not smile. "I don't suppose it matters much what anyone calls me," she said quietly. Then she smiled ruefully. "Probably 'Lee's sister' would be the most accurate nickname."

Christina frowned at her. "What kind of a thing is that to say?" she asked sharply. "You are yourself—and don't forget it!"

But Leah's family could not get used to calling her "Lee" and so they continued to call her "Leah." Soon she had forgotten all about her request to be known as "Lee." It was simply another one of her enthusiasms, picked up, tried, and forgotten.

Cameron and Russell left for school, and winter set in very hard. The news from Europe became more and more disturbing, but life in Rock Falls remained much the same. The new house was cozy and bright, and the twins had a short walk to school, so even on the coldest days they did not feel much hardship. There were several cars in Rock Falls now, and the streets were plowed regularly. As the winter progressed the piles of snow on either side of the roads were as high as walls, and the sidewalks like white tunnels, with the snow head-high on either side.

Christmas that year was the happiest the family had ever known. The boys managed to get away from school for the holidays, although their train was snowbound in Lemhi Pass for nearly six hours. A plow got through and cleared the tracks and they chugged into the Rock Falls station at three in the morning on Christmas Eve day. Christina had planned an open house and invited their old friends from church, school, business, and community. Leah and Ruth were busy for a week hanging green boughs and garlands and decorating the house with bayberry and juniper. Red velvet bows garnished the greenery and bright platters of candied fruits, nuts, mounds of rosy apples and oranges pierced with cloves decorated the tables and mantels. The house was filled with the sight and smell of Christmas.

Russell and Cameron slept most of the day while Christina attended to the final food preparations. In the early evening guests began to arrive—families from all around the valley as well as from town. The driveway was jammed with automobiles, horse-drawn sleighs, cutters, and a few saddle horses tied to the hitching posts.

Many of the Saunderses' friends had walked from their homes, and the street, lighted with arc lamps, made a lovely picture as people streamed toward the brightly glowing house. A gentle snow was falling, and it gave the scene a mystical, festive look.

Christina and Peter greeted their guests at the door, and then the company went into the dining room where a table of holiday food was spread before them. There was dancing in the back parlor, visiting in the front parlor, and games in the library. The house hummed with merriment.

It was not until late in the evening that Christina saw Leah for the first time. Christina had been busy and had given the twins permission to buy their own party dresses. Ruth had bought a bright-blue velvet dress with a dropped waistline and a band around her hips. The skirt was narrow, with a small slit at the side, and the collar was a beautiful circle of pointed lace. When Peter saw Ruth he embraced her. "You look very grown up, my dear," he said. "And very lovely." Her golden hair was brushed and hung past her shoulders in a shining fall. It was held back with a single satin ribbon.

"She is just about the age you were when I first saw you," Peter remarked to Christina as they watched Ruth walk away.

"What a disconcerting thought!" Christina exclaimed. "Where have the years gone!"

She looked at her budding daughter more carefully and felt a wistful pride that Ruth was so close to the flowering of her womanhood.

Her reaction was quite different when she saw Leah. Leah had chosen a dress of scarlet taffeta. The neck was cut low and wide. The dress had a slight bustle effect that drew dramatic emphasis to Leah's tiny waist and her full young bosom. To emphasize the effect, Leah had put her hair up, and the column of her neck, bare but for a double strand of pearls, was tantalizingly displayed. Christina was scandalized. "Peter!" she hissed. "Have you seen what Leah is wearing? I insist that you tell her to go change at once!"

Peter glanced around and saw his young daughter sitting in the library in the midst of a cluster of young men. She looked like a glowing ruby on a sea of black velvet. The young men's faces were turned to her in adoration, and Peter thought they looked as though all they asked in life was to be able to stare at her. He could understand why. She was beautiful in the same piquant way her mother was, only Leah's coloring was more conventional—more appealing to most people, and her features were softer and more delicate.

"You shall have to get used to it, Christina. So shall I. It isn't what she is wearing. It's Leah herself. She attracts attention and we cannot stop it."

"Well!" Christina snapped. "We can certainly keep her from such a foolish display of her body!"

Peter put a restraining hand on Christina's arm and his voice was stern. "Christina, you are not to say a word to her until the party is over. The dress is perfectly all right, and I won't have you humiliating her in front of her friends."

Christina pulled away from Peter, her eyes flashing. "You have always treated those girls as though they could do no wrong! I hope you do not live to regret it!"

With that she whirled on her heel and walked furiously into the kitchen.

Despite Christina's anger the evening was a great success. At its close, friends and neighbors said their farewells with warmest thanks and stepped out into the night air, which was sparkling with delicate flakes of ice and crystals of snow. A departing guest struck up a carol, and the Saunders family, standing happily in the doorway waving their farewells, heard the sweet strains of "Silent Night" wafted up through wintery air.

When the last good-bye was said, Christina turned her glance to Leah. "You will take that dress off this minute, Leah! I never want to see you dressed in such shameless fashion again!"

"Oh, Mama!" Leah cried in defensive outrage. "There's nothing wrong with this dress! Everyone said I looked beautiful!"

"Mama," Cameron said softly, "don't spoil the evening. The dress is a little too modern for you, maybe. All the girls in college . . ."

Christina did not let him finish. She fixed him with an angry glare. "Stay out of this, Cameron! She is not in college yet! She is a fifteen-year-old girl, and anyone with a sense of decency would know this dress is not appropriate! Take it off immediately, Leah, and when you are dressed to retire you may bring the dress to me. I will dispose of it!"

Furious and hurt, Leah ran up the stairs, trembling with indignation. Ruth gave her mother a reproachful look and followed her sister up the staircase. When she arrived in the room Leah was tearing at the dress, almost ripping it from her body. "Oh!" she cried when Ruth entered her room. "How can Mama be so hateful! Sometimes she is so mean and unfair I could scream! I hate this dress now! I hate Mama for talking to me like that! Did you hear her, Ruth? She treated me like I was a child, in front of Cameron and Russell!" Furious tears were streaming down Leah's face. The dress was in a heap at her feet and she kicked it. "She makes me so angry!"

Ruth came over and picked the dress up and folded it neatly. "I'm sorry, Leah," Ruth said quietly. "But you knew the dress was awfully grown up! You even told me that's why you bought it. . . ."

Pulling the hairpins out of her hair, Leah walked across the room and threw herself across her bed. "I know!" She sobbed. "Because I feel grown-up inside! Everyone treats me like a grownup except Mama. She'd be happy if we never grew up, just stayed home and did our chores and behaved like good little girls!"

Leah sat up abruptly and rubbed the tears from her face. "Well, I won't stay home and be a good little girl! I'm going to have fun, and go to parties, and have lots of beaux, and . . ." Suddenly Leah's face changed, and, instead of anger, her eyes were suffused with anguish and she gave a wail. "Oh, Ruth, she hates me! She has always hated me, and I don't even know why! I can't do anything right!"

Ruth ran to sit beside her sister and patted her shoulder. "No, she doesn't, Leah. She loves you! She loves all of us! It's just . . . oh, I don't know. It's just Mama—the way she is. But I know she loves us." By now Ruth was in tears too, and the two sisters sat side by side on the bed and wept.

It was the last Christmas the family shared. The brothers stayed at the university for the summer semester. They were trying to speed up their graduation. On June 28 in the obscure town of Sarajevo, the capital city of the Austrian province of Bosnia, the Archduke Francis Ferdinand, heir to the throne of Austria-Hungary, was assassinated. Europe fell into war like a heap of unstable building blocks, and by the end of summer the countries of the continent had aligned themselves as the Central Powers—Austria-Hungary, Germany, and the Ottoman Empire—and the Allies—Belgium, France, Great Britain, Italy, and Russia. The events seemed very remote to the enclosed and isolated community of Rock Falls. In reality, however, in the new century, with machines, wireless, telephones, and radio, the world had entered an era in which nothing that happened on the face of the earth could be considered remote.

Peter understood this fact, and in the following year he worked harder than ever to help the ranchers and cattlemen upgrade their herds. His bank lent hundreds of thousands of dollars and the valley thrived.

"If there is to be a war it will soon involve all of us, and the need for food will be very real. We must be prepared," Peter predicted.

325

In May of the following year the *Lusitania* was struck by German torpedoes and America moved a step closer to war.

By the summer of 1916, even though America was still technically neutral, it was supplying food and arms to the Allies and President Wilson had established military camps across the country where young men could enlist to spend their summers in training. Among the nation's young men a great patriotic fervor took hold. Uniformed, with neatly wrapped puttees, close-fitting breeches, polished shoes, and sharp-brimmed hats, they found themselves surrounded by adoring women, and the fever was on.

Christina was adamantly opposed to the military, but in spite of her objections, Cameron and Russell enlisted in the summer army and were assigned to officer-training camp. If their mother had seriously thought there was any real threat of her sons being sent to war, she would have gone to Salt Lake City and thrown herself in front of the recruiting station. However, like most Americans, she was convinced the United States would never be embroiled in the ridiculous war on the other side of the Atlantic. She decided the army camp was a bit of boyishness that her sons had to go through, just as their father had found it necessary to spend his early years tramping with sheepshearing crews and living in lumber camps.

In autumn the boys returned to the university, and they could not come home for the holidays because of another army training session. In the spring, Christina and Peter went to spend the last week of school with their sons in Salt Lake City. Cameron was graduating with high honors, and Christina's heart swelled with pride as she watched her tall, handsome son receive his diploma. All she had to wait for now was one more summer of army camp and then Cameron would come home as a reserve captain, Russell as a reserve lieutenant.

Christina was very uncomfortable while she was in Salt Lake. Peter had urged her to see Mary, but, after the years of silence between them, it was impossible for Christina to make such a step. Peter had gone, unknown to Christina, to visit Samuel in his offices. Samuel had aged since they last met. His hair was white and the skin on his hands was almost transparent, but his smile remained vigorous and warm. The two brothers-in-law discussed the European war, their businesses, their sons, and, at last, their wives.

"I think their estrangement will never mend," Peter said with a sigh. "You have been a good friend to me nonetheless, Sam, and I am grateful. Thank you for seeing that my boys got into a fraternity and for keeping me informed along the way.''

"Nothing more than you would have done for me," Sam replied. "You have fine sons, Peter."

Peter nodded and smiled. "How is Greg?" he asked. "I had hoped to meet him sometime, but I gather he feels about our family much as his mother does."

"He's working for me now," Sam said thoughtfully. "He is a bright young man, and extremely ambitious. It seems odd that a young man who has never wanted for money should be so eager about acquiring more of it! I don't know—perhaps it stems from some basic insecurity because he is our adopted rather than our natural son. Who knows the vagaries of the human heart?" Sam shrugged and smiled.

Peter felt a concern that Christina did not share as they traveled back to Rock Falls from Salt Lake. He felt certain that sooner or later America would have to join the terrible battle that was tearing the Old World apart. He felt no one in the Western world could expect to emerge unscathed from the conflagration. Sooner or later America would be forced to act. She could not remain a bystander watching while Europe became a wasteland. He feared for his two sons because he was convinced they would be sent into the battle.

Both Christina and Peter were wrong. Not bullets, or an American declaration of war, or a German torpedo robbed them of their sons. The instrument of death was a small microscopic organism—a minute virus that made its presence known in the summer camp when a young soldier complained of a headache at reveille. By evening the private had a raging fever, and in three days he was dead. Spanish influenza tore through the army camp like a grassfire. Within ten days all work in the camp was virtually halted. The hospital beds were full and the barracks themselves were turned into clinics. Groaning men, aching in every joint, burning with fevers and torn by retching bowels, lay in their soiled linen, too ill to move, while their attendants became too ill to care for them.

Russell succumbed to the fever in the first week. Cameron nursed him carefully, and by the fifth day Russell was beginning to look a little better. He recognized his brother that morning for the first time since the illness struck, and he was able to hold down a sip of weak tea. The following day Cameron was hit. He woke in the morning wracked with pain and found he was too weak to move—unable to go to Russell. By afternoon Cameron was delirious, not knowing who or where he was. Russell, with no one to care for him in his weakened condition, slumped into a coma from which he never awakened. By the morning of the next day Cameron too had slipped away.

When the epidemic reached its peak and the authorities managed to bring in enough personnel to bring it under control, a count of personnel showed that out of every three young men who had entered the camp in the early summer, only one was still alive. When the two rough pine boxes bearing the bodies of the Saunderses' sons were deposited on the platform at the Rock Falls station, Christina and Peter stood dry-eyed as the station master decked the coffins with flags and loaded them on the flat bed of the wagon, drawn by two beautiful bays Peter had purchased for the final tribute to his sons.

The citizens of the town of Rock Falls gathered in front of the town hall. Cameron and Russell were eulogized by the mayor, the Mormon bishop, and an army colonel. Then a slow, sorrowing procession, with muffled drums, paraded down Main Street, past the brave, gold-leafed sign that proclaimed "Saunders and Sons," and continued out to the edge of the town where the Rock Falls graveyard lay under spreading maple trees.

A final prayer was said by the bishop, and the two coffins were lowered into the freshly dug graves as a lone bugle played. After the services the Saunders family returned to their home, and a procession of neighbors and friends came to pay their respects and offer sympathy. Throughout the day Christina stood like a statue, unweeping. She was white as alabaster, and her hands were cold as stone.

The death of Cameron and Russell was a blow so profound and deep it could never heal. Christina and Peter would live the rest of their days carrying their heart-deep pain like a terrible hidden injury.

"I should have given all of my sons to Mary," Christina said bitterly. "Perhaps she could have saved one at least. I seem to have no luck with sons."

Peter turned on her, infuriated. "You will not speak of our sons in that way!" he shouted. "They were fine boys—all three of them! If we had them for only one day each we would have been richer than not having had them at all!" He took a deep breath and calmed himself. "They have returned to their Father who is in Heaven, and someday we shall join them there," he said softly. "Until then we shall try to live with dignity, and with some joy for the sake of our daughters.''

Christina's face was closed and she said nothing.

The year of mourning passed like a dirge. Christina draped the house in black, and Leah and Ruth were forbidden to go to parties and dances. Peter threw himself into his work while Christina became more somber, brittle, and unapproachable as the months passed. It was as though the deaths of her sons had dried up all of her emotions. She worked like a demon, cleaning, cooking, caring for the sick and those in need, but it was her hands that worked. Her mind and heart were in some distant, hidden corner with her own sad thoughts.

In the spring Peter's prediction came true. President Wilson declared war on Germany and the United States of America mobilized. The price of beef soared. Peter was busier than ever making loans to the cattlemen of the valley.

Peter suggested the mourning crepe should be removed from the house, now that a year had passed, and Leah sprang to the task with vigor. The year of social inactivity had seemed endless to her. Every day the train brought troops through the town, and Main Street was crowded with young men who were being shipped to and from the camps. Rock Falls was close to a wilderness station where troops trained for maneuvers, and, in the evenings, the town was now filled with the sounds of laughter and dance music. Cafes stayed open late, and restaurants were doing capacity business. A new dance hall and nickelodeon had opened up, and churches held weekly socials for the young men in uniform. A patriotic enthusiasm pervaded the community and nothing was too good for the fine young men in their khaki suits.

Because so many men had enlisted in the army, it was hard to find adequate help for the Saunderses' businesses. Gradually Christina and her daughters found themselves working more and more at the hotel, general store, or feed offices. Ruth showed a natural aptitude for business, and before long she was keeping all the store's accounts. Her father opened a small office for her at the bank where she handled the financial side of the family's affairs while he taught her the fundamentals of the banking business.

Russell, as a young man, had shown talent for finance, but Peter was astounded at Ruth's astuteness and creativity. Peter began to look forward to discussing business problems with his daughter. She was incredibly fast with numbers and seemed to grasp the principles of accounting, capital, and investment almost as quickly as he could explain them to her. Ruth had never found anything so exciting as working at the bank. She began to be the first one to arrive and the last to leave at night.

Leah was a success at the store and the hotel, not because she was a good worker but because people enjoyed having the sprightly, beautiful girl wait on them. They didn't seem to mind when she made mistakes or gave them the wrong change. Leah didn't object to working in the store because she enjoyed seeing people, and anything was better than being cooped up in the house on Elm Street with her somber mother.

To Christina, Leah's easy, flirting manner was a source of constant distress. She saw each young man, and particularly those in uniform, as a potential threat. One evening, when she locked up the store, Christina discovered Leah talking to a handsome young captain on the boardwalk.

"Young man!" Christina snapped. "Don't you have anything better to do than speak to a young woman to whom you have not been properly introduced?"

The captain flushed and doffed his hat respectfully to Christina. "Pardon me, ma'am," he said in a courteous southern drawl. "I thank you for reminding me of my manners. Perhaps you would allow me to call one day with a proper letter of introduction?" He was obviously a man of breeding and character, but Christina was not to be mollified.

"My daughter is too young for callers and we are emerging from a period of mourning," Christina answered coldly. "Come, Leah!"

Leah pouted prettily at the young officer and ran after her mother. As soon as they were out of earshot she shouted at her mother, "That was mean and hateful! I am not too young for callers! And that young man was just asking what Papa's name was so he could arrange a formal introduction! What do you want, Mama! To bury me with Cameron and Russell?"

Christina gasped in horror, and even Leah was shocked by her own words. "Oh! Mama!" she cried contritely. "Please forgive me! I didn't mean . . ." But her mother rushed off down the street, her back as straight as a poker, while Leah stood weeping.

Once inside the front door Christina bent over like an old woman and, very slowly, began to mount the stairs, using the bannister for support as though she had no strength left in her legs. Something in her daughter's face had frightened and jarred her. Perhaps Leah wasn't as spoiled and selfish as Christina thought. When Leah had spoken those cruel words, her young face had looked not so much angry as frightened!

"Do I not know my daughters at all? Or am I just like my own mother? Am I so caught up in my own concerns that I do not see those of my daughters? Do I resent their womanhood because I know it will bring them nothing but heartache and refuse to forgive them for having been born women?"

She evaluated the terrible anger she had felt when she came out of the store to see the handsome soldier, captivated by Leah, and Leah confidently spinning her thread of magic around his heart. How easy it was for Leah to accept adulation and love! "Am I jealous of that?" Christina wondered. "Am I jealous of the ease of Leah's life? Jealous for myself? Jealous for Ruth? Jealous for all the women for whom life is hard and ungiving?"

Christina shook her head. It was too hard to figure Leah out. Her daughter was too extraordinary—too different from the restricted pattern of Christina's experience. How could a mother be expected to understand a daughter whose beauty was like a key to the treasures of the world?

That evening Peter came home with Ruth and the family ate a quiet dinner together. "Papa!" Leah said defiantly. "A Captain St. John may be calling you with letters of introduction. Will you see him?"

"Of course. I'll be glad to," Peter replied pleasantly. Leah gave her mother a sidelong glance, but Christina said nothing.

"Christina," Peter said, "I made a decision today. I'm going to run a herd of beef cattle on Broken Arrow's property. No reason we shouldn't help the war effort. That land could raise prime beef. I think I'll start looking for a manager to run it."

"Fine," Christina answered listlessly. Aside from the store and the hotel, she had taken little interest in the family's affairs since the death of her sons. What was the use of building an empire when their were no heirs to run it?

Chapter Seventeen

Ruth had never seen the valley that Broken Arrow had deeded to her father. When Peter said he was going to drive out to the property, Ruth begged to accompany him. She pulled on an old pair of riding pants and a fringed leather jacket, which had been Russell's, and hopped into the car beside her father. They drove out of town and down the long, dusty road that led to the mountains.

Two years earlier Peter had arranged for a narrow road to be cut through the pass into Broken Arrow's valley. He named the property the "Arrow Homestead" because he had fulfilled the homesteading laws to secure the lease. The house that he had built in the heart of the peaceful valley was situated on a small knoll above a bubbling stream. It was a log-frame cabin, nestled among a copse of aspen trees, scrub pines, and lacy mountain shrubs. There were three rooms in the house, a kitchen, a small parlor, and a large, unfinished bedroom. The house was unfurnished, had none of the amenities, and had never been inhabited.

Ruth was enjoying the drive. As they bounced along the rough road she asked Peter what he planned to do with the homestead.

"I figure if we can find the right man to work it, he could make himself a nice living up here!" Peter exclaimed. "Darned if I don't envy him the opportunity. If I were twenty years younger myself I'd be on fire to try it."

Laughing, Ruth rolled down the car window and let the wind tear through her hair. "If I were a man, I'd like to try it!" she exclaimed. "If it's half as beautiful as you say it is."

They were slowing to a snail's pace as they prepared to turn off the main highway onto the rutted road leading to the Arrow pass when they saw a man walking down the road in front of them. He was tall and broad-shouldered with a pronounced limp. He was wearing work jeans, a worn army jacket, and carrying an old army rucksack on his shoulder.

"What on earth do you suppose he's doing out here in this wilderness?" Ruth exclaimed.

"We'd best stop and ask him," Peter said. "He may need some help."

That was how Hal Morgan came into the Saunderses' lives. When he climbed into the back of the car, he gave Peter and Ruth a grateful smile, put his head back on the plush seat, and fell promptly asleep.

"I guess we'll go on up to the homestead and let him sleep in the back," Peter said. "When he wakes up we can ask him where he wants to go and take him there."

They drove slowly up the rough pass road. In places it was steep and so narrow and precarious that Ruth trembled for fear they would end up at the foot of the mountains, but the powerful car continued on its way, and they finally crested the pass and looked out over the magnificent valley.

"There it is," Peter said, waving expansively, and Ruth gasped at the lush richness of the land below.

They drove down to the cabin, the car bouncing and rolling on the rough ground. The young man in the back did not stir.

"Are you sure he's alive?" Peter asked, slightly alarmed.

Ruth stared at the stranger. She noted the rise and fall of his chest as he breathed and the drawn, exhausted look on his rugged face. "Yes," she said, "I think he is worn out—that's all!"

The air in the valley was crisp and cool. Peter got out of the car and beckoned to Ruth. "Let's gather wood and start a fire in the house, then we'll survey the area."

They were busy gathering wood and did not notice their young passenger as he stepped out of the car, stretched, and looked around curiously.

"Hey!" he called. "Anybody here?"

Ruth hurried out of the trees. Her golden hair was fluffed by the breeze and her cheeks were pink from exertion. "You can talk!" she called, laughing. "We were beginning to wonder!"

The tall man threw back his head and laughed, then he walked toward her with a grin and put out his hand. "Hal Morgan," he said.

"Ruth Saunders," she replied heartily, and took his hand in her firm handshake. "Nice to meet you!"

"Can I help?" he asked, nodding to her armload of wood.

"Yes, of course." Ruth was disconcerted. "Only—should you?—I mean, do you feel up to it?"

"Look," the young man said defensively, "just because I limp doesn't mean I'm a cripple!" He tramped off into the woods and returned shortly with a large pile of dead wood in his arms. Ruth had left the front door open, and he went into the house with his load and dumped it beside the fireplace.

She was fussing with matches and kindling. "Here, let me do that," Hal insisted. In minutes he had a fire blazing and had thrown a massive log on the flames.

"I see you've decided to join the land of the living!" Peter exclaimed, entering the room. "I hope you don't feel we kidnapped you. We didn't know what else to do. Give us a few minutes here to finish our look-around and then we'll drive you wherever you want to go."

Hal laughed. "No problem, sir. I'm not going anywhere. I was tramping around looking for a job on one of the local ranches. Seems no one wants a hired hand with a bum leg."

"Want to tell me about it?" Peter asked soberly.

"Not much to tell," Hal answered. "France. My second week of action. I was leading a squad out of the trenches and took one in the leg. They sent me back to a hospital in England. Thought I'd never walk again—but when the thing mended up a bit they decided to ship me home for treatment.

"Our first ship was torpedoed—a hospital ship! Can you beat that! Those Huns!"

He stopped talking for a few minutes, his face black with memory. It was not until years later that they would learn that Hal had spent hours in the water rescuing dying men and had been awarded the Medal of Valor for his actions.

"They took those of us who survived back to England and sent us out on the next ship. I was sent out west here for more hospital time, but I figured I'd seen enough of hospitals. When I arrived I asked for my discharge papers. Told them if I ever hoped to walk the only way I could do it was by walking. That's what I've been doing ever since. The leg gets stronger every day, but I guess I still look pretty gimpy."

"No!" Ruth exclaimed. "No, you don't!"

Peter stared at the young ex-soldier. Hal's shock of dark-brown hair curled on his forehead, and his face, with its strong, pleasant features, was marked with the shadow of the things he had seen. Although his eyes were dark with fatigue and pain, Hal's face had the rugged glow of a man who has lived outdoors. His shoulders, arms, and hands were strong-muscled and something in his body indicated a self-reliance and strength that struck a responsive chord in Peter.

"You're coming home with us, young man," Peter said with sudden decision. "At least until that leg is better."

"No, sir," Hal replied. "I won't impose on you."

"No, you won't," Peter responded. "I intend to put you to work!"

Ruth's eyes were glowing with happiness. "You must come, Hal!" she begged. "You will really like Rock Falls." Peter glanced at his daughter. She was looking at the tall young stranger with a look of sweetness and gladness in her eyes that touched her father's heart. "My stars!" Peter thought. "I believe our Ruth has finally met her match!"

Hal accompanied Peter and Ruth on their walk in the valley. He slowed them down a little, but he commented incisively on the layout for the proposed cattle operation. Peter listened with admiration as Hal suggested where the salt licks should be placed and recommended short lengths of fence between the mountain slopes to prevent cattle from wandering into the narrow canyons.

The grass of the valley was deep and rich, but Hal cited recent research showing great luck in breeding heavier, better meat-producing animals by supplementing grass with corn.

"You're a cattleman!" Peter nodded. "I should have guessed it."

"Not exactly," Hal answered. "I was raised on a ranch in Oregon. After my real folks passed away I was sort of adopted by a family who owned a ranch. That's where I grew up. I've seen a lot of cattle in my day!"

"You going back there?" Peter asked.

"No. I don't reckon so. The family sold the ranch and moved down to California somewhere. I guess I've sort of lost touch with them. . . ."

The ride home was a happy one. Ruth sat in the back and the two men in front. She leaned over the back of their seat to put her head between them, and they sang together. Hal's voice was a fine baritone and their voices blended nicely. Ruth, without thinking, started a church hymn, "Come, Come Ye Saints." Both she and Peter were astounded when Hal joined in.

335

"Are you a Mormon?" Ruth asked, astonished.

"Mm-m-m," Hal assented. "I guess that's what I am if I'm anything. You too?" he asked, looking at the Saunderses. They nodded their heads.

When Hal got out of the car, Ruth put her arm through his. "Oh, Hal!" she cried. "I can't wait to introduce you to the rest of the family!" Her brilliant eyes were like cornflowers, and her smile was dazzling. Peter had never seen her look so animated and lovely.

"Come along, Hal," Peter said. "Ruth will show you the guestroom."

As they walked up the flower-bordered path, Ruth could feel her heart dancing with happiness. From the moment she had seen Hal Morgan's face as he slept in the back of the car she had known she had found a man she could love. She had felt as though everything about him was familiar to her, as though she had seen him before, felt his limbs, heard his voice, listened to his heart beating. She could not explain it! She, who was usually so quiet, even, and logical—how could she explain this sudden dazzling joy? She felt her body burning at the touch of his arm in hers, and the rhythm of his awkward stride jolted her with delight. She wanted to ask him questions—foolish, inane questions—anything to keep him talking and herself hearing the deep, thrilling sound of his voice.

As Hal and Ruth entered the front hall, Leah came running down the staircase. She was wearing a white dotted-swiss frock, with a wide pink sash and a ruffled collar. Her magnificent dark hair was caught up in curls and loose tendrils framed her beautiful face. In her hand was a large-brimmed straw hat with a circlet of daisies around the crown.

"Ruthie!" Leah cried. "What have you here?"

She ran to the doorway, her eyes sparkling with laughter and curiosity, staring at Hal. "Is this what you are growing out on the homestead?" she asked, eyeing their guest with a mischievous grin. "If so, I'm going to go with you the next time!"

Hal Morgan looked at Leah and he grew as still as a hunter. Ruth could feel the muscles in his body tighten, and she glanced up at his face. His eyes were riveted upon Leah with such intensity that Ruth dropped her arm from his in a wave of despair and presentiment.

"Well!" Leah rattled on. "Have you two lost your tongues, or something? I'll introduce myself then! I am Lee Saunders, and who might you be?" She glanced up at Hal archly, and her dimpled smile flashed.

"Hal Morgan," he replied calmly. "A stray your father picked up."

"You are certainly a cut above his usual stray!" Leah laughed. "Are you staying for dinner, Mr. Morgan?"

Ruth found her voice. "Yes, he is, Lee," she said coldly. "He is also staying the night in the guestroom."

She turned to Hal, but all the animation had drained from her face. "If you like, Hal, I will show you your room so you can freshen up." Her voice sounded cold and formal, even to herself.

"Oh, for heaven's sake, Ruthie!" Leah demurred. "At least give him a moment to get his bearings! Come into the parlor, Mr. Morgan, and I'll get you a glass of cool lemonade. There'll be plenty of time to settle you in your room later."

Hal looked from one girl to the other, aware of the subtle contest. "I think perhaps I should go and wash up first. If you don't mind, Ruth, I'll take you up on the offer to see my room."

Leah laughed and shrugged. "I'm off to the garden to pick strawberries, then. I'll see you in a while." She was out the door before they could reply. Ruth watched Hal's eyes as they fastened on Leah's retreating figure.

"I'll show you your room now," she said abruptly, and marched in front of him up the stairs.

Dinner was a disaster for Ruth, but only her father noticed. Christina's maternal instincts were touched by the wounded young man, and she had been more hospitable and gentle toward him than Peter had expected her to be. She fussed over his room, making sure it was comfortable, and made a special effort with supper, urging Hal to eat seconds of the swiss steak, green-bean casserole, tender new potatoes, fresh rolls, and chocolate cake.

Leah kept up an effervescent conversation. She asked Hal about his war experiences, his childhood, his opinions on fashion, dancing, and cars. Her questions were often impertinent, and if anyone else had asked them they would have sounded rude, but Leah, with her lighthearted laugh and innocent smile, could ask anything she wished without giving offense.

Hal was not affronted by her interrogation. He answered the questions he chose to answer and parried the others. His quiet strength stimulated Leah. She regarded it as a challenge, and teased him when he eluded her probing inquiries.

"You are just trying to sound mysterious, Mr. Morgan!" she charged.

337

"Women are the mysterious ones!" Hal countered. "Isn't that so, Mr. Saunders?" he appealed to his host.

Peter laughed. "In my experience that's certainly the case!"

Ruth did not join in the conversation. She sat listlessly in front of her plate and picked at her food.

Hal turned to her. "I should think you would be hungry after all the walking we did today," he said.

She looked up at him with a little smile. "It didn't seem far," she said.

"No." He grinned at her. "It didn't!"

"I declare!" Leah chimed in. "Ruthie could walk to New York and back and not get tired! I have never known anyone with so much stamina!"

Peter saw the look of pain dart across Ruth's face. Hal Morgan was not a boy to be bowled over by Leah's practiced charm, but even Peter could see that Hal was absorbed by her beauty and gaiety. Tonight, in the dining room, Leah seemed to glow with a special vitality that gave a promise of renewal. Peter could only imagine what a glowing, free-spirited woman of such extraordinary beauty must seem like to a man who had looked death in the face. Peter could not blame Hal for searching Leah's face as though it were his salvation, but his fatherly sympathies were with Ruth, who watched and understood. "Is it possible for a heart to be broken in one day?" Peter wondered. "Surely she will get over this quickly. Life cannot turn on such small points of time!"

In the next weeks Peter and Hal worked together assembling a herd for the Arrow Homestead and hiring a small crew of men to live on the property. Peter had decided to give Hal the opportunity to manage the valley, and Hal had responded to the offer with a gratitude and dedication that were almost overwhelming.

Hal and his men drove a small string of cattle ponies up to the valley. They carted in furniture, food supplies, tools, and feed. Day after day wagons left Rock Falls carrying necessary supplies to the new spread while Hal and his men worked day and night to build a rough barn. The building crew was inspired by the heavy work the wounded veteran was able to do. Hal seemed to grow stronger daily. By the time the homestead was ready to receive its first herd, he came striding up the front walk of the Saunders home, and Ruth, catching sight of him from her bedroom window, was astonished to see that his limp was almost gone. She leaped from her bed to run downstairs to congratulate him, but before she could leave she saw a figure clothed in bright yellow dart out the front door and race down the path toward him. Hal smiled and doffed his hat as Leah ran up to him and threw her arms around him.

Ruth, watching, trembled and pulled the drapes over her window. With a sigh she picked up the heavy account books on which she had been working and walked down the back stairs.

"I'm leaving for the bank, Mama!" she called into the kitchen. Hal and Leah came through the front door, laughing and talking.

"Ruth!" Hal exclaimed. "I was hoping I'd see you."

"Hello, Hal," Ruth said.

"You've been quite a stranger lately," Hal remarked.

"Well, I've been busy setting up the account books for the new venture. You've been awfully busy spending money—you and Papa. I hope you prove to be as good at making it as you are at spending it!"

Ruth hadn't meant to sound snappish, but she knew the remark was mean-spirited, and she would have given anything to take it back.

"I hope so too, ma'am," Hal replied seriously.

Ruth let herself out the front door feeling like a fool. "Why did I say such a stupid thing?" She was furious with herself. "Because I am hurt, I didn't need to try to hurt him in return!" Feeling miserable, she hurried to the bank and when her father prepared to go home for supper she pleaded the need to finish up her work, and urged him to tell the family to eat without her.

Later that night she let herself into the darkened house and tiptoed up to her bed. For a long time she lay awake in the darkness thinking of Hal lying silently asleep in the room next to hers.

Christina was not blind to the attraction between Hal and Leah, and her attitude toward Hal had grown steadily cooler. It was with great relief to her that she saw him pack his things and prepare to move out to the homestead permanently. Hal had not stayed at the Saunders home except for those nights when he came in from the ranch, but he did keep a few clothes in the guestroom, and Peter had told him he was welcome to stay whenever he came to town. Christina had not been happy with the arrangement.

"Peter!" she accused her husband one night as they lay awake in their bed. "You cannot tell me you haven't noticed how Hal looks at Leah, or how she flirts with him. It is not suitable at all. She is only nineteen years old, and besides he is scarcely a suitable match for her—he's a penniless drifter.''

"Hardly a penniless drifter," Peter responded. "He is my ranch manager.''

"Hmph!" Christina sniffed. "Fancy title for glorified cowboy. And that's another ridiculous decision. What on earth makes you think the boy knows a thing about managing a ranch? You could lose every cent you've invested in this thing!''

"Possibly!" Peter conceded. "But even with the best manager in the world we could lose. If the winter is too harsh, or the cattle get sick, or prices drop—it's all a gamble, Christina dear. That's what makes it worthwhile!''

Christina clicked her tongue impatiently. "I don't believe in anything that isn't safe and sure!''

"Then you don't believe in anything," Peter said firmly. "Don't you know nothing of value can be made safe or sure—it wouldn't have any value if it were.''

"Well, I'm sure I'm happy that Hal Morgan is on his way out of our lives!" Christina stated emphatically, returning to her original thought.

"Not out of our lives, dear," Peter corrected. "Only out of our guestroom!''

Hal Morgan knew and understood Christina's reservations about his relationship with Leah. He even agreed with her point of view— but his need for Leah was too strong for him to give her up. Because he was a man of honor he would not deceive the Saunderses about seeing Leah, and so, with typical straightforwardness, he went to Peter.

"I want to talk to you because I believe what I'm going to say will upset Mrs. Saunders," he told Peter. "If you want to fire me after I have finished talking, I will understand.''

"What is it?" Peter asked.

"I want to court your daughter," Hal said.

"Which one?" Peter inquired calmly.

Hal looked puzzled for a moment. "Leah, of course," he answered.

"Oh," Peter said and nodded as though some inner thought had been confirmed.

"I am in love with Leah, Mr. Saunders! I think I have been in love with her from the first moment I saw her, and I want to court

340

her, to become engaged to her, and to marry her." Hal looked at Peter with his direct, honest gaze.

"You are right," Peter said after a moment's pause. "Mrs. Saunders will be upset. However, I believe I know my daughter Leah, and I think she has already made up her mind.

"I was just your age when I married Leah's mother, and her family did not approve of me either." Peter stopped speaking, his mind drifting toward the past.

"Then I have your permission?" Hal asked.

"Yes," Peter answered quietly.

Peter told Christina he had given Hal permission to call on Leah, and Christina was forced to accept the frustration of watching her beautiful daughter whisked off for dates in the wretched old car Peter had purchased for the homestead ranch. Hal was always prompt, courteous, and carefully proper in his conduct toward Leah, but nothing he could do or say seemed to win Christina's approval of the match.

Ruth buried herself in her work at the bank. She was performing all the functions of a bank officer, evaluating loans, investing the conservative portfolio, handling trust accounts, and tallying receipts.

The lead and antimony mines in which the bank had invested had done very well through the war years. Ruth had made a study of the mining industry and had followed the loan with particular interest. In the course of her involvement with the mining consortium she met several bank officers from the eastern banks who had also lent the mining company some of its early capital. Ruth was struck with how much more sophisticated and knowledgeable these easterners were, and she developed a burning desire to go out into the world and learn more about the finance industry. She began a subtle and persistent campaign to convince her father to allow her to go away to college.

"I've taught you everything you need to know, Ruth!" he protested. "It isn't as though you were a man and were going to have to make a career of it. This is something you can do until the right man comes along."

Her father's complaisant assumption about the "right man" and what she should and shouldn't do infuriated Ruth. She kept her peace, however, and continued to drop hints and explore possibilities.

Knowing that Hal and Leah were desperately in love had in no way eased Ruth's feelings for Hal Morgan. Ruth could not bear to be in a room with him. When he was near her every nerve of her body responded to him, and she could not release her mind and heart from their awareness of his hands, his face, the muscles of his strong, work-hardened body, and the lithe grace of his motion. She was sick with longing and despair, and to see him with Leah was more than she could bear! How could she stand to see the two people she loved more than anyone else in the world loving one another and having no place in their hearts for her? In her pain she knew she would have to leave Rock Falls. She could not stay and watch.

One day in late fall Peter asked Ruth to drive a truckload of grain up to the homestead. Ruth was one of the few women in Rock Falls who could drive. Several times Peter had taken her with him on supply trips to the ranch, and he had let her handle the truck. She had a fine sense of machinery and quick reflexes. "I can't drive up because of these visiting bankers, and there's a forecast of snow for tomorrow. The load has to go up this afternoon."

Reluctantly, Ruth agreed. She pulled on her work clothes and the fine leather driving gloves her father had bought for her. It was a new truck and handled well on the roads. The autumn air was cold, the ground frozen, and the road rutted, but not dusty. She wound her way up the pass and down into the Arrow Valley. The changes at the ranch surprised her. Hal had accomplished miracles. Smoke was curling up out of the cabin, and freshly painted barns and outbuildings spread behind the cattle yard. On the wide floor of the valley she saw a herd of sleek cattle grazing peacefully. Two cowboys were riding among the herd, deftly keeping it in order.

She drove into the barnyard, and one of the hired hands came over to unload the truck. The day was cold and her breath rose in a plume of vapor and the mountain wind stung her cheeks and brought tears to her eyes.

"You'd best run in the house to keep warm, ma'am," the man advised her. She was not dressed for the cold, and so she nodded gratefully at his suggestion and ran toward the cabin.

The kitchen was empty, but a fire was burning in the cookstove and one of the men had put a pot of stew on the burner. She glanced around the warm, cozy room and took a bowl from the cupboard and ladled a serving of broth from the simmering pan. Taking the bowl to the table, she began to eat the soup. It was hot and she ate slowly, blowing on the liquid to cool it.

"Good?" Hal asked, stepping into the room. He was dressed in a

342

heavy sheepskin jacket, with leather gloves and riding boots, and his wide-brimmed hat was jammed over his eyes. He brought the fresh cold air in with him, clinging to his clothes, and he seemed to exude the wide-open power of the Arrow Valley. The kitchen suddenly became constricting and small, and Ruth instinctively pushed her chair back and stepped away from him. "Yes," she said. "It's hot at least—and that is good."

He reached out and grabbed her hand in his. "You're freezing!" he exclaimed. "Get closer to the stove! Don't you have enough sense to dress for the weather?" He laughed. "It may still be autumn in Rock Falls, but it's winter up here!"

"So I see!" Ruth said. "I'll only be here a bit longer. Until the truck's unloaded."

Hal frowned. "I don't think you should drive back down alone. I'll come with you and ride a saddle horse back up tomorrow."

"Papa says snow is coming."

"I'm bringing up the chestnut gelding. We can make it, even if it snows."

"No!" Ruth exclaimed. "I am perfectly capable of getting home."

"Yes," Hal said quietly. "I know you are. But I need a ride to Rock Falls to fetch the horse." He grinned at her persuasively, and she knew she could not refuse without sounding impossible.

"Very well," she said grudgingly. An uncomfortable silence fell. Hal stood looking at her. "You're a mighty pretty woman," he said suddenly. She looked at him with fury, sure that he was teasing her, but then she saw the honest, blunt look in his eyes, and she realized he had no idea how she felt about him. He thought of her as his friend—and he was complimenting her with natural goodwill, one friend to another. He had no idea how much he hurt her! He assumed her feelings toward him were exactly the same as his toward her. "At least that's a small blessing!" Ruth thought ironically. "If he has no idea how I feel, I don't seem like such a fool!"

"You've performed miracles up here this summer, Hal," Ruth told him. "I think it's going to prove to be a very nice investment."

Hal laughed. "Coming from you that's high praise. I hope I can measure up to it! Are you feeling warmer?" he added.

"Yes, I'm fine now."

"Good!" He laughed. "Let me lend you some warm clothes and you can come with me and see the whole place."

"I'd like that," she acquiesced.

He found an old woolen jacket, scarf, and hat and she threw on

343

the clothes. They tramped through the fields as he showed her the feed lot where the cattle would receive their "finishing" with grain and troughs fed by clear spring water. He showed her the rotation schedule for the cowboys and the ranchhands and the newly completed bunkhouse. She saw the storerooms, the tack room, neatly organized and secure, and the fragrant barn with the domestic animals for produce and the calving stalls for difficult deliveries.

"Quite a place!" she remarked as they tramped across the last pasture. "I think you might find you could run a few sheep here too."

He nodded his head. "Next year we'll try."

The wind had grown colder and he put his strong arm around her shoulders. "You're shivering," he said. "Come on, let's get back to the house and warm you up."

He folded her against him and they began walking into the wind. She ducked her head into his side and smelled the scent of leather, barns, green grass, and the piney mountain air, mixed with the smell of his body, warm and masculine and solid. She shuddered with his nearness. He held her closer and they ran in step, her long, strong legs matching his stride. By the time they reached the house they were laughing with the cold, the physical exertion, and the freedom of the run.

"Ruth!" Hal exclaimed as they entered the kitchen. His eyes were brilliant and his face looked younger and more carefree than she had ever seen it. "You really are something! I don't know when I have enjoyed myself so much!"

"Me either!" Ruth replied, shining with happiness. "It's been a fine day, Hal."

Chapter Eighteen

That fall Hal made the trip down from the ranch as many weekends as possible to take Leah to dances or church socials, on automobile drives, or to visit with her in the front parlor of the Elm Street house. When the snows fell his visits grew further apart. Leah became restless and complained to her mother and father.

"It isn't fair. You should let him work down here at the bank, or at the store, so that we can be together. I know you sent him to work the ranch so we would be apart."

Christina sighed and pressed her lips together in disapproval, but Peter smiled. "Leah! A little absence is good for a relationship. If it is based on anything worthwhile it can outlast one winter!"

Christmas Eve had come again, and the girls were spending a quiet evening at home with their parents. Since the death of their two older sons, the Saunderses had stopped entertaining.

In the front parlor, the family was seated around the fireplace. Leah had been playing some carols on the piano, but since no one felt like singing she stopped and walked over to the tall front window. "It's snowing," she announced. The moon was bright as crystal, and the white snow sparkled in the deep blue of the night. "Do you remember the night of the open house?" she asked wistfully. "Wasn't it fun?" Leah's voice had been filled with reminiscent longing but suddenly she squealed, "Hal! It's Hal! Everybody! He's here! He's come for Christmas!"

She left the window and raced across the room to the front hall. Throwing open the door, she called out into the night. "Hal! How did you ever make it?"

They heard his deep laugh and his footsteps as he bounded up the stairs. "On Santa's sleigh!" he shouted. Peter hurried into the hallway where the young couple was embracing. Hal reached out his

345

hand. "Merry Christmas, sir!" he exclaimed heartily. "Thought I'd come and give you a report on the homestead!"

At this Peter chuckled. "I'm sure that's the only reason you're here," he rejoined.

"Mrs. Saunders, ma'am," Hal smiled, nodding formally to Christina. "Merry Christmas to you." He handed her a small package wrapped in gold foil.

"Thank you," Christina said stiffly, but she was pleased to see him in spite of herself.

"Hello, Ruth," Hal said, kissing her on the cheek. "Merry Christmas to you." He handed Ruth a brightly wrapped package.

Turning back to Peter, Hal handed him an envelope. "My present to you is in here," he said with another grin.

"Well!" Peter said jovially. "Let's not stand here in the front hall! Let's get back to the fire. Maybe now we'll have enough voices to sing a carol or two."

"What about me!" Leah pouted, hanging back. "Don't I get a Christmas present?"

Hal looked at her with a secret smile. "Later," he promised, whispering.

Hal had rented a room at the Rock Falls Hotel, but Peter insisted he stay in the guestroom. Christina's eyes snapped her disapproval of the arrangement, but she would not spoil the spirit of Christmas by being inhospitable.

After a late supper the family went to bed. When they bid one another good night, Hal slipped a note into Leah's hand. She could not wait until she got to her bedroom to unroll the scrap of paper. It read "Meet me in the parlor at midnight—Love, Hal."

"How deliciously exciting!" Leah thought. Fully clothed, she lay in bed until the house was absolutely still. She watched the small French clock beside her bed, and, when the hands pointed to twelve, she slipped out of the covers and opened her bedroom door softly. The hall was dark and empty. She closed her door with a tiny click and hurried down the steps. Her feet were as light as thistledown and she made no sound on the thickly carpeted stairs. Not even Hal heard her coming.

"I'm here!" she whispered.

He took two enormous strides toward her and swept her into his arms. "Leah!" he murmured. "I love you!"

She lifted her soft, beautiful face to him, and it glowed in the dark room like a gentle flame. "Hal!" she breathed. "I love you too!"

He carried her to the couch and placed her gently on the velvet seat, and then sat beside her. "Today I brought your father the first receipts from the homestead. We sold a carload of cattle to the army. The livestock's weight gain was excellent, and we made enough money to repay almost our entire original investment. By spring the ranch will be operating in the black!"

"Oh, Hal!" Leah exclaimed. "That's wonderful! Even Mama will have to be impressed with that. Another great businessman in the family!" she stumbled, realizing what she had said. "Well-l-l, sort of in the family!" She hung her head in embarrassment and giggled.

"That's what I wanted to talk to you about," Hal said. "I want you to be in my family. No!—I want you to *be* my family!

"Leah, I love you in ways I can't even understand. Without you I seem to be less than a whole person. It is as though someone has imprinted your image on my mind and there is no erasing it. I see you in everything I do. Please say you will marry me. I don't care when—we'll need to work on that with your parents—but I must know that you're promised to me and that our lives will be lived together."

Leah was laughing and crying at once. "Oh, yes, Hal! Yes! Yes! Yes!" she whispered, accenting each "yes" with a kiss. "I would rather be your wife than anything else in the whole world! I dream about it every night! I cannot wait until we are in our own room together—and not separated by silly walls!"

She moved closer to him. Her voice was soft as gossamer. "I lie in my bed and I think 'What if I went into Hal's room?' I could lift up the covers and climb into bed next to you! I could feel you lying there beside me, with your chest moving up and down as you breathe, and I could put my arm across you and press against you."

Leah moved across the couch until her soft, rounded body leaned against Hal and he could feel each curve and hollow. "I'd never have to feel cold or alone anymore," Leah whispered. "You would put your arms around me and hold me in the night."

Hal reached his arm around her waist and pulled her closer to him. He bent and kissed her full lips and they tasted of roses and honey. In a madness of desire he stood up, holding her in his arms, and moved toward the stairway. She had pulled his head to her breast, and he kissed the pulsing hollow at the base of her throat, as he strode across the dark hall, forgetting where he was, and who he was, devoured by his need for the bewitching woman in his arms.

"Who is there?" a tentative voice called from the darkness at the head of the staircase. "Is anyone down there?" It was Ruth's voice, sleepy and frightened. "Mama! Papa! Is that you?"

Leah gasped and stiffened, and Hal, brought to his senses in a flash of relief and pain, placed her gently on the floor.

"It's all right!" Leah whispered and laid her finger on Hal's lips. "I'll go up and tell her our news, then we'll all go back to bed and wait for Santa Claus!" She laughed softly.

"Before you go," Hal whispered back, "here's your present!" He groped for her hand in the dark and she felt him place a ring on it.

"You can look at it in the morning," he said.

Leah kissed him again and ran up the stairs quickly. "Sh-h-h!" he heard her say to Ruth. "Come in my room. I have something to tell you." The two sisters disappeared through Leah's door, and a moment later Hal walked slowly up the stairs.

In the morning Leah announced her engagement to Hal, and Peter congratulated the young couple warmly. Ruth and Christina were quiet, although they each expressed formal words of good wishes. The wedding date was set for April, and Hal left the day after Christmas to return to the ranch.

On New Year's Day Ruth came into her father's study. "May I talk to you, Papa?" she asked.

"I thought you might be coming," Peter said.

"I want to go back East to school," Ruth told him. "I am going, either with your blessing or without it! I have made enough money with my own investments that I could pay for my schooling if necessary."

She was stiff with fear and hurt and his heart reached out to her.

"Don't be impetuous, Ruth!" he answered. "If you want to go to school I'll support you, of course, but I want you to be sure you are not just reacting."

"I'm sure," Ruth said, simply.

In April, Leah and Hal were married.

The ranch was doing well, but Hal could not leave during the planting and calving season, so the young couple planned to have their honeymoon at the ranch.

The wedding was a lavish affair. The young couple stood under

348

an arbor of lilacs to greet their guests and a stringed orchestra played. The weather cooperated with a bright blue sky and a warm sun.

Leah was an exquisite bride. Her dress was Alençon lace, with a high collar and leg-of-mutton sleeves, and a waistline so trim that it seemed one of Hal's hands could span it. Her long train was spread behind her, and her skirt draped smoothly over her slender hips. Leah's color had never seemed so vivid and her veil, framed by lilies of the valley, touched her dark hair like a halo. To Hal the wedding day seemed like the longest of his existence.

At last the young couple had greeted everyone, Leah had thrown her bouquet of lilacs, tulips, and bridal wreath, and had changed into her traveling suit. She and Hal ran through a shower of rice to the truck, and through a chorus of "Best wishes" they rattled off down the road.

Leah chattered happily all the way to the homestead as Hal concentrated on the winding road. It was dusk when they arrived at the cabin. The hired hands had set a fire in the stove, and Leah exclaimed over the attractiveness of the rooms that Hal had fixed up and furnished for her. With desperate impatience, Hal threw their luggage on the floor and picked her up in his arms.

"You can see everything tomorrow!" he said, his eyes smiling. He carried her to the bedroom, over the threshold, and kicked the door shut behind him.

"But Hal!" Leah protested. "My beautiful nightgown and peignoir!" Her eyes were dancing with mischief. "Shouldn't I change?"

"We have no use for them," Hal whispered hoarsely, and began unbuttoning the buttons at the waist of her suit.

"None at all!" she assented and reached up to undo his tie.

Their passion lasted through the night. Leah's body was like a torch—it seemed to flare at his touch. She was made for the delights of love, and in their first encounter she was open, uninhibited, eager to experience and to rejoice in all the wonders of their union. He could not have imagined such a glorious, natural sensuality, as though she had no thought but the moment, no desire but the flesh, no delight but the response of her body! He drowned in her exuberance and seemingly insatiable need.

Toward morning Leah gave an expansive yawn and threw her arms around him one last time. "Oh, Hal!" she whispered. "It's more wonderful than I dreamed!" With that she turned away from him, rolled herself up into a ball like a young child, and in a moment was contentedly sleeping, her slumber as natural and uncomplicated as her passion.

Hal lay beside her, unable to sleep. He pulled up the covers and straightened the wrinkled bed, then put his arms under his head and lay in the room staring at the ceiling as the dawn began to lighten the sky. "Why," he pondered, "after a night of physical satisfaction more wonderful than most men could dream about, do I still feel a sense of emptiness?" Had it been too easy—as though Leah had thrown open all of her treasure boxes, dumped them in a heap at his feet without any needed effort on his part, and simply had nothing more left to give? Or was he beginning to realize that this was why he had married Leah—for this bed and her beautiful body lying in it—and suspect that this alone could not fill his long, weary days?

"Perhaps all men must choose one or the other," he thought philosophically. "Besides, Leah is her father's daughter. There's bound to be more challenge in her than I know now." Still, vaguely restless, like a man who has eaten too much and yet still is not replete, Hal fell asleep.

Leah did not like to cook. Hal discovered that fact in the first week of their marriage. He would come in from the fields, freezing from the cold, to find Leah propped in front of the fireplace with a magazine or a piece of sewing. The moment he entered the door she threw herself upon him and began kissing him. "Oh, Hal!" she would exclaim. "It has been such a long day! Come here and talk to me!" She would lead him to the couch, and he would find himself entangled in her beauty and the sweet humor of her blandishments.

He also found no supper waiting. After they had made love, he would go to the kitchen and scramble eggs, or heat up some leftovers. The men in the bunkhouse had their own kitchen, and soon Hal made a habit of stopping in the bunkhouse to eat a bite of supper before going home. Occasionally Leah would prepare a meal, but she was a casual and indifferent cook. Except for this one unexpected characteristic, Leah was a wonderful bride—cheerful, devoted, loving, a neat housekeeper, and always eager for lovemaking.

Hal tried to interest Leah in the workings of the ranch, but she was a reluctant horsewoman, and the cattle and barns did not interest her. With a great deal of help from the hired men, however, Leah learned to drive the old car, and once she could get to and from town on her own she was even happier, spending many days shopping and bringing things to make the house more beautiful. Hal worried about their budget, but he could not deny his lovely bride anything.

On a hot day in July, Leah returned from a daylong visit in Rock Falls. She had been to see her mother, and Christina, who had grown fond of Hal because of his goodness to Leah, had sent him a ham, some fresh-baked bread, a fruit salad, and scalloped potatoes for supper. Leah set the table prettily and the young couple ate by candlelight. Hal devoured the delicious food and stared at his lovely wife across the table. "You should go into town more often!" he suggested laughingly. "Your mother is a wonderful cook, and you look radiant with happiness! Is that what town does for you? I'm going to begin to think you have a secret lover down there, or something!"

Leah laughed her light silvery laugh. "I do have a secret something!" she glowed.

"What is it?" Hal asked, helping himself to another slice of ham.

"A wonderful secret which I bring to you from town."

"What?" Hal asked, his curiosity piqued.

"Dr. White is the one who told me," Leah whispered.

Hal stopped eating and stared at her. "Dr. White? Leah?" He looked at her with a joyful question in his eyes and she nodded her head.

"Yes," she said. "We're going to have a baby!"

Hal thought he would explode with happiness. He had been orphaned as a young boy and had been raised with kindness but with little affection. All of his life he had dreamed of having a child on whom he could lavish the love and tenderness he had never experienced. A child of his own! He thought his heart would break with joy.

"Leah!" he said almost reverently, and got up from his chair. He went to her, knelt in front of her, and buried his head in her lap. "You have made me the happiest man on earth."

It seemed that Leah was born to be a mother. She did not experience morning sickness or discomfort. At night, in bed, when Hal wanted to abate his passion, Leah, hungry as ever, demanded the fullness of his love, and her body seemed to thrive on it. The baby grew strong and robust within her, and, even though her frame was tiny, Leah carried the child with grace and beauty. She was the picture of health as winter approached, proud of her expanding form and filled with a sense of self-importance. The baby was due in January, and Hal encouraged Leah to go to live with her parents until the baby came, but she refused to leave him, so they greeted the first heavy blizzards together in their snug log home.

The first month of winter was not bad. Leah was sewing clothes for the new baby and Hal did not have to work such long hours in the cold months. They were able to spend more time together talking, playing games, and reading.

By the end of November, however, Leah's nerves were beginning to fray. She was growing heavier and her back ached. The house was cleaned to a fare-thee-well and it was hard for her to find enough activity to fill her days. She felt trapped in the ranchhouse, and as Christmas approached Leah sank into an unassailable gloom. Hal could not reason with her and she grew morose and silent, or angry and tearful by turns.

"How did you come see me last year at Christmas?" Leah demanded.

"By sleigh," Hal replied. "But it was a terrible trip."

"Is the snow worse this year?" she asked.

"No, about the same," he answered truthfully.

"Then I want to go home for Christmas," Leah said petulantly. "Once we get through the pass the roads will be cleared and it will be an easy trip. Please, Hal, say you'll take me or I shall die!"

"It wouldn't be good for you or the baby," Hal said flatly. "I can't take you. Wait a month or two—after the baby's born.

"Your mother will be here right after Christmas to stay with you until the baby comes. You can wait that long!"

"No! I can't!" Leah cried. "I want to go right now and be at home in Rock Falls when my baby comes. You can't expect me to have my baby up here—I need to be home with a doctor and all the right kinds of care."

"But it was your idea!" Hal protested. "I wanted you to go home! But not now when the roads are bad! The trip is too danger-ous now."

"You must take me!" Leah shouted. "Or I will go alone!" She was getting worked up and her face was blotched with red.

As the days passed Leah became more sullen and unreasonable. She was tense and withdrawn, and Hal watched her staring out the windows, her brows knitted in a furious frown. He had known when they married that Leah had been a pampered and spoiled child. Seldom in her life had anything been denied her. In their marriage this was the first time he had been unable to give her the thing she chose, and she could not accept it. She was enraged that he would not accede to her wishes.

On Thursday one of the steers was sick. Hal went to the barn to lance a boil on the animal's flank. It was a miserable job. When it was finished Hal washed up in the bunkroom and headed for his house. As he crossed the barnyard he saw a sight that chilled him to the bone. The sleigh was outside the gates, with the bays hitched up to it, and inside the sleigh, sitting with a heavy fur lap robe piled around her, was Leah. She looked like the snow queen in her large fur hat and cape, with her driving gloves and her neat little carriage whip in her hand.

"Leah!" he shouted, racing toward the sleigh. She turned and saw him and gave a triumphant smile, waved her hand, and flicked the horses lightly with the switch. The horses, feisty from their long winter stay in their stalls, plunged off into the snow, moving erratically. "Someone—one of the hands—must have hitched the sleigh for her," Hal thought desperately. "She must have told the men that I had agreed to it!"

Frantically Hal changed direction and ran diagonally across the yard to intercept the sleigh. He vaulted the fence just as the vehicle slid past, and he landed on the backseat.

"I'm going!" Leah shouted, looking back at him with alarm. "Don't try to stop me!" She lashed the horses with her whip. He reached forward to grab the reins, and she reached back and hit at him with the butt of her carriage switch.

Not wanting to frighten her, he sat down quietly in the back. "Leah!" he said in a controlled voice, "the horses are too fresh. Let me drive them if you insist upon going!"

She laughed gaily, thinking she had won. "Nonsense, Hal! The faster we go, the sooner we'll be there!"

"I mean it, Leah," he said, desperately frightened by the wild pace the horses were setting as they plunged through the snow. "I'll take you down to Rock Falls—only let me drive!"

"No!" she shouted. "I don't trust you!"

"Pull back on the reins!" he cried. "You've got to get the horses under control before we hit the pass!"

Too late, Leah realized Hal was right. She yanked back on the reins, and the bays, startled, swerved abruptly. The runner hit a snow-covered rock and the sleigh lifted up into the air. For a moment it seemed to Hal that time and motion were suspended. He could see Leah hanging in the air in front of him and the sleigh drifting above them in the sky, but then everything came crashing down. He hit the ground and felt the stab of pain as the sleigh dug into his foot. It slid across the snow and scraped the skin from his

353

leg, but he was free. Frantically, he rose and searched desperately for his wife. "Leah!" he screamed, but there was no answer. The horses were dragging the upturned sleigh, loping in terror back to the barn. Hal saw the pile of furs and the presents Leah had been taking to town scattered on the snow, and then he saw the dark mantle of her fur cape and her red scarf. But she hadn't been wearing a red scarf! Still, there was a red scarf streaming across the snow by her head—no, it was blood!

He dragged himself over to where she was lying. "Leah! Leah!" he cried, but he knew the minute he saw her it was hopeless. Her skull had been crushed by one of the sleigh runners, her life and her beautiful face were gone. At first Hal was immobilized by sorrow and horror, and then he looked at her skirt, spread across her body, and he saw the motion of the baby within her. Leah was dead, but the baby was still alive! Scarcely knowing what he was doing, he pulled out the knife with which he had lanced the steer. The knife had been sterilized and he had been returning it when he had seen Leah leaving. With trembling hand he cut a single thin line across Leah's abdomen. The skin split open and he could see the thin wall of her uterus and the baby moving feebly inside. Leah's veins were not pulsing—there was no life in her—and he knew he had less than a second to make his decision. Terrified, he took the knife and delicately traced a line across the stretched membranes with his sharp blade. The womb opened like a torn balloon, and he reached his hands into his dead wife's body and lifted out the warm, squirming child who lay within. Quickly he grabbed the fur robe next to him, wrapped the baby tightly in it, and, with tears streaming down his face, raced through the snow toward the warmth of the house that lay peacefully quiet in the circle of the pines, smoke curling placidly from its chimney like the timeless, unchanging symbol of haven.

Chapter Nineteen

By some miracle the baby lived. Hal named her Faith. One of the ranch's hired hands made it down to Rock Falls, and Peter and Christina came up to the ranch immediately, bringing medical help. They were too late for Leah, but the doctor was able to confirm the baby girl would be fine. She was small because she was a few weeks early, but she had a strong, lusty cry, and a formula was found that seemed to suit her admirably.

Christina begged to take Leah's baby home with her, but Hal was adamant. "I need the baby, Christina," he told her quietly. "If I don't have her, I think I will go mad!"

Peter and Christina understood. Their own grief was devastating, but Hal looked like a man who had lost his reason. The grieving parents reluctantly left him with the new infant and returned to their empty home to mourn.

Ruth had left for the East to attend Wellesley College in early September. She wrote enthusiastic letters about the things she was learning—majoring in economics, minoring in mathematics, and taking a smattering of liberal arts courses as well. She was spending Christmas at her roommate's home in New York City and, since she could not return home in time for Leah's funeral, her parents decided she should remain in the East to finish out her school year.

The empty house became a prison to Christina. She began spending her days at the hotel, supervising the kitchens and the accounts. Her manner with her staff was brusque and sharp, as though she had no patience for either incompetence or human relationships. Hard work was the anodyne for her sorrow.

She had suffered so much pain and loss that she stored her feelings away where they could not hurt her. More and more she buried herself in the work, and squeezed the human, feeling components in her life into a small compartment.

355

Peter and Christina were living like strangers. The only rooms in the house that were used were the kitchen and their bedroom. They walked to Main Street together in the morning—Peter to the bank and Christina to her office in the hotel. At night, in the winter's darkness, they walked home together, talking about business, if they talked at all, and ate a simple meal in the kitchen before retiring.

Occasionally they could break through to one another. Christina sometimes turned to Peter with tears of pain. "Oh, my poor daughter! My poor sons!" she would groan, and he would hold her. Often, in his sleep, Peter would cry out, and Christina would rub his shoulders and murmur to him in the darkness until he fell asleep again. Ruth and little Faith became their only two links to the world of feelings and emotion. The days when Ruth's letters arrived were like a holiday. Side by side they would read the letter silently, and then Peter would reread it aloud as Christina prepared supper. Long into the night they would discuss their absent daughter and speculate about her life in the East.

Faith was their one other source of joy. Through the winter the Saunderses visited the ranch as often as the roads allowed. Hal had grown somber and quiet, but he was raising Faith with loving care, and the little baby was thriving. She was dainty and pretty like her mother had been, but with blond hair and blue eyes, so that she resembled her Aunt Ruth in coloring. When Christina looked at the baby she felt she saw both of her girls rolled into one person—the best of each of them captured in the precious infant.

That spring Hal asked if he could leave Faith with Christina and Peter during the demanding planting season. Nothing could have given them more joy. Peter took the month off, and so did Christina. They filled Leah's old room with toys and baby furniture, and fussed over little Faith like young parents, bathing her, dressing her in mounds of pretty clothes, walking her in a fine new perambulator, and rocking her gently when she cried. Love flooded into the house like sunshine, and some of the pain in the grandparents' hearts was erased by the sweetness of the darling child.

Hal came for the baby in June, three days before Ruth was due to arrive from college, and Peter and Christina begged him to leave Faith with them a few more days so that Ruth could see her. Hal acquiesced and agreed to come back in a week's time. The Saunderses could see the effort on his face as he placed the baby back in Christina's arms. His eyes devoured his infant daughter, and the love and tenderness in them brought tears to Christina's own eyes. She reached out a tentative hand and touched Hal's sleeve lightly.

"Hal," Christina said softly, "I know I wasn't as approving of your marriage to Leah as I should have been."

Hal shook his head and turned away. He still could not bear to hear Leah's name.

"I just wanted you to know, Hal," Christina went on awkwardly, "I think you are one of the finest men I have ever known. We couldn't have wished for a better son!"

She had struck a chord in the grieving man's heart and he turned to her with a crooked smile, half sad, half joyous. "Thank you, Christina," he whispered hoarsely. "That means a lot to me. You see—" His voice choked and he cleared his throat. "I didn't know if you and Peter were blaming me. I wouldn't fault you if you were. I blame myself—horribly! If I had only done something different!" He turned his face away and struggled for control. "I keep reliving the accident and wondering what I could have done to save her. I would have done anything! Anything!" He was white with the intensity of his emotions, and Christina, with the baby in her arms, looked desperately at Peter. He stepped forward and put his arms around Hal and embraced him.

"You did, Hal!" he said firmly. "You did everything that could have been done—and more! You did the most courageous and best thing imaginable! You saved Faith! Nothing could have saved Leah."

Hal nodded and straightened up. Then he took a deep shuddering breath and walked down the path to his truck.

When Ruth arrived home the reality of Leah's death struck her for the first time. If it had not been for Faith, Ruth would have slipped into a trough of despair and mourning, but the little girl seemed like a miracle of renewal, and, although Ruth wept at each painful reminder of the loss of her twin, still, tending the baby helped her put Leah's death into a meaningful perspective.

"I know I will always miss Leah, Mama. But maybe the missing will get to be like breathing—I won't have to think about it all the time like I do now!" She had been crying in her room late at night, and her mother, up checking on the baby, had heard Ruth's sobs and had come in to talk to her.

Christina nodded. She could not talk about Leah's death yet, it was too close to her and too painful. She could only listen and give what sympathy she had to Ruth.

357

When Hal came for Faith, Ruth was shocked at the change in his appearance. "Oh, Hal!" she cried. "I should have come sooner!" He looked at her with dull eyes, and she walked to him and embraced him, the tears coursing down her cheeks. "You miss her most of all!" Her gesture of friendship was spontaneous and natural, and he remembered her goodness and it touched him. He held her while she wept.

"We're going to be all right!" he assured her. "Faith and I—we're going to make it!" She looked up at him with a tearstained smile.

"I know you will, Hal!" she said. "I know it."

The family ate in the dining room that night. Faith was asleep in her little crib upstairs, and Christina put on one of her wonderful feasts.

"I'd forgotten how delicious food can be!" Hal complimented her.

Christina had baked thick, juicy pork chops with an apple dressing. With it she had candied small carrots fresh from the garden and had tossed a salad with crisp new lettuce leaves and a light mustard and honey dressing. She had baked feather-light orange rolls and blackberry pies with a creamy frosting glaze.

Later, in the parlor, she served ice-cold root beer with homemade vanilla ice cream floating in the sparkling brew.

Ruth talked about Wellesley and the nearby city of Boston, which she had visited frequently while she was at school. She had seen the Boston Symphony Orchestra, operas, plays, and museums. She had boated down the Charles River and sailed on the Atlantic with friends who lived in Marblehead. With blithe familiarity she discussed national events, the Armistice, and the government's economic policies.

She had cut her hair, and, although at first the new style had been a shock to the family, as she talked animatedly in the mellow light of the room they could see she had never been so lovely. The short, shining, wavy hair seemed to suit the strong, lively features of her face. It somehow made the blue of her eyes more pronounced and showed off her long, slender neck and lovely, straight shoulders.

Christina and Peter decided to go upstairs early. Christina was tired from her kitchen exertions, and Peter seemed to have lost his old vitality. Ruth pulled Christina aside as she walked into the kitchen.

"Is Papa feeling all right, Mama?" she asked. "He doesn't look too well!"

"Oh, pooh!" she said her old sharp way. "We're just getting old, that's all! You can't expect your father to stay a young man forever. He's over fifty, you know!"

"That's not old!" Ruth exclaimed.

"Old enough!" Christina snapped, and walked into the kitchen.

Hal excused himself too. "I need to get an early start back to the homestead in the morning," he said. "Good night, Ruth."

Ruth was not tired. The excitement of the dinner, the memories of Leah, and seeing Hal had left her with a restless unease. She decided to go for a walk. Letting herself out the front door, she strode up Elm Street. The streetlights were not on because of the post-wartime economy, but a full moon dusted the landscape with silver and she could see the outline of trees and buildings distinctly. When she arrived at her old grade school, she stared at the dusky, moonlit playing field. Far across the way she could make out the outlines of the old swings. On impulse she hurried over to the swing and sat down, staring at the dark trees as she swung slowly back and forth. Her mind drifted as the night wind played through her hair.

In the stillness she heard the snap of a twig, and, instantly, she was alert. "Who is it?" she whispered.

"Hal," came the answer. "I saw you leave the house and I was worried about you being out alone. There are a lot of strangers in town these days. I don't think this is very safe." His voice was harsh with worry and anger.

"I'm sorry!" she exclaimed contritely. "I only wanted to get some fresh air."

"I think you should get it in your own yard, then!" Hal growled, his voice still rough.

"You're right," Ruth conceded. "I wasn't thinking."

Hal came over closer to her, and she sensed his anger had spent itself. "Want a push?" he asked with a short laugh.

She laughed at the unexpected request and held tightly to the chains on the swing. "Yes, I'd love it!" she said.

Firmly and smoothly he began to push the swing. She rose higher and higher, and the sensation in the darkness was one of flying to the stars. Back and forth she swung, above the trees and into the night. Neither one of them made a sound and she felt alone, lullabied by the darkness and the sweet earth and the gentle, star-struck sky. Soothed and comforted in ways she could never have explained, Ruth felt the swing beginning to slow, and gradually it stood still once more. Her heart was so full of love for the man behind her that

359

she could not trust her voice. She stepped away from the swing and turned to Hal, dark and silent behind her. "Does he feel anything for me?" she wondered.

"Thank you," she whispered.

He took her arm and they walked back to the house and went in the kitchen for some milk. Hal scarcely seemed aware of Ruth's presence.

"Hal," Ruth ventured shyly. "May I ask a favor of you?"

He was silent, but he nodded.

"Let me take care of Faith for you this summer. You're going to have to hire someone and I—" Her voice was filled with urgent entreaty, but before she could continue, Hal shook his head emphatically.

"No," he said. "I know you love her, but no."

"Why?" Ruth demanded. "No one would be better. . . ."

"Because you mustn't get too close to her. You can love her as an aunt, Ruth, but I don't want her to become the center of your life. That wouldn't be fair to you—or her! You've got to be free to go out, meet boys, make a life of your own. Thanks anyway," he finished. "Faith is lucky to have you—to have all of your family— and so am I." The subject was closed. Ruth put down her half-finished milk without further protest and left the room.

Hal took Faith back to the ranch the next morning. During the summer he brought the baby to visit the Saunderses frequently, and they made biweekly trips up to the homestead. The ranch was thriving, and it gave Peter great joy to see Broken Arrow's legacy put to such worthwhile use. Sometimes Ruth would accompany her parents to the ranch, but more often she found excuses to stay home. There were too many confusing and ambiguous emotions in her relationship with Hal.

Her father was aware of Ruth's unhappiness. He surmised that her love for Hal was as great as ever. Absence and sorrow seemed to have increased her devotion to Hal, and yet she hid her secret and made every effort to avoid seeing him. Peter knew Ruth felt guilty for loving her widowed brother-in-law. The need for him would not go away, and so Ruth strove to immerse herself in activities that would prevent their paths from crossing.

Through the summer Ruth worked as a Red Cross volunteer, attended dances and parties, and took over the tasks of running the house to allow Christina the freedom to continue managing the hotel.

One day, while Ruth was alone at home, she decided to clean out her room. After emptying and sorting her closets and drawers, she took a load of old clothes and papers up to the attic. It was while she was in the attic that she discovered her grandmother Janeth's boxes. The boxes had lain in the attic since the summer they had been brought to Rock Falls from Pleasantview.

With a gasp of excitement, Ruth lifted the lids and stared once again at the wonder of the lovely creations of her grandmother's hands. The remainder of the week Ruth spent her time sorting her grandmother's papers and inspecting the shawls and fabric lengths for any damage.

Ruth wrote several letters to Boston and New York museums, and in each letter she enclosed a page from her grandmother's notes and drawings. She wrote a brief biography of her grandmother, telling of her early life in the royal court of Denmark, of her courageous journey to the new land, and of her pioneer trek across the American continent to Utah. She told about Janeth's difficult life as a second wife, about the mountain man who had trained her, and then she catalogued the complete list of notebooks and some of their findings.

In the letter she also described the shawls and fabrics that had been preserved from her grandmother's original weaving.

Within two weeks Ruth received responses from each of the museums. The letter that caught her interest was from the Metropolitan Museum in New York City. It said, in part, "We are developing a new collection which includes the craftsmen and artisans of America's past. The exhibit will tour the nation and then be brought to a permanent place of display in the Museum. We are most eager to see the body of your grandmother's work."

Ruth showed the letter to her mother, who snorted. "Everybody wove cloth in Mama's days. I think you have them excited over nothing."

When Ruth showed the letter to Peter, he suggested, "Why don't you crate Janeth's things and take them to New York? I think it would be a fine thing if they were preserved by such a great institution."

A month earlier than she had expected to leave, Ruth packed for her return to the East. She was taking her grandmother's notebooks and weavings to the museum curator for the American Heritage collection. Peter and Christina put Ruth on the train and watched with sad hearts until the caboose was out of sight. Then the two of them returned to their places of work. There was nothing else to do.

361

New York was crowded and exciting. The streets were crammed with ex-servicemen and visitors. Peter had made reservations for Ruth in a sedate women's hotel off Fifth Avenue. Ruth felt overwhelmed at being alone in the big city, but since she had visited there before she knew a little about it. Her first priority was her visit to the Metropolitan Museum. Promptly at ten o'clock on the morning following her arrival she walked into the vaulted main lobby. A young woman sat at a desk in the center of the huge foyer.

Christina was wearing a lavender silk suit, with a long jacket and a draped hobble skirt with a modest slit up the front. Her shapely ankles showed, and she was wearing matching lavender slippers. Her blouse had a fichu of white frothy lace that cascaded between the jacket lapels. On her head was a deep-lavender, broad-brimmed hat, worn dipping over one eye, with violets at the band. She looked fresh, wealthy, and sophisticated, but she felt like a country bumpkin, lost in the cool vastness of the stately marble lobby.

"Pardon me," she said to the young woman. "I have an appointment with Dr. Wellington. Could you please tell me where I might find his office?"

"Certainly!" the young woman replied. "Go up the small staircase to the left of the grand staircase. Dr. Wellington is down the first corridor as far as you can go, and then turn left."

Ruth had to ask directions twice more before she found Dr. Wellington. He was younger than she had expected. About forty, with a dark Vandyke beard, glasses, and a somber suit.

"Well, Miss Saunders," he said in a dry voice, "let us see what you have brought us!"

She handed him the sample packet with two of her grandmother's notebooks and one of the silk and mohair shawls.

Without comment he opened the package, raised a magnifying glass, and began to peruse the books. The room was silent and Ruth could hear the ticking of the watch that hung from a chain on her bosom. She watched Dr. Wellington carefully for some sign of reaction, but his face remained remote and composed. Frantically she began to wish she had never come. What foolishness to think that the work of an obscure weaver from Utah would have any value in this lofty and hallowed place! She would have liked to grab the books and run away rather than expose herself and her grandmother's memory to humiliation.

Dr. Wellington turned another page, and Ruth coughed nervously.

At last he looked up from the notebook, and for a moment he seemed surprised to see Ruth sitting there. His concentration was so profound that once he had started looking at Janeth's work he had totally forgotten she was sitting there.

"Well?" she asked nervously.

"What a treasure!" Dr. Wellington breathed, and Ruth could have sworn there were tears in the eyes of the dry academician.

"This grandmother of yours was a brilliant scientist and artist! Look at her portrayal of the mountains!" He opened a double page on which Janeth had sketched the mountains around the upper Virgin Valley to indicate where specific plants could be found. "A remarkable miniaturist!" Dr. Wellington effused.

Ruth's heart was pounding. "You mean, I wasn't mistaken?" she asked. "It's not just because she was my grandmother that I think them remarkable?"

Dr. Wellington gave her a thin smile. "Not at all! We have our share of that kind, I can assure you! People believe that their family treasure is something the world should see. Often they bring in quite nice things—good craftsmanship—but the spark of genius is not there. The originality! The intellect! The creativity! Call it what you will. It is the spark which your grandmother's work has in full measure."

He picked up a notebook and stared at the pages. "There are ten of these?" he asked, and Ruth could hear the excitement in his voice.

"Yes," she answered. "Ten small notebooks, and eight shawls and fabric pieces. There are also loose papers and notes."

"May we see them all?" Dr. Wellington asked. "Of course we will care for them most responsibly. You will have receipts for everything. I know my colleagues both here and in other museums will be most anxious to help me evaluate the work."

Ruth sent a telegram to her father, and he telegraphed back his instructions to give the museum the entire collection on loan. The family could decide whether or not to make a permanent donation later.

By the end of the summer Ruth was back at Wellesley, having left Janeth's legacy with the museum.

Hal knocked on Peter's office door one day in late August. The hay crop had been baled for the winter, the last cattle shipped out, and the summer's receipts for the homestead had been gratifying. "C'mon in. It's open," Peter called.

363

"Christina's giving Faith a bath," Hal said, "and I think they both wanted me out of the room."

Peter laughed. "Christina is a fierce woman, Hal, when it comes to her mother feelings. However, as a grandmother she is showing a tenderness which was hard for her to express with her own babies. I'm grateful to you, that you let her spend so much time with Faith."

Hal cleared his throat and looked uncomfortable. "That's what I've come to talk to you about, Peter," he said. "I'm thinking of going away and taking Faith."

"What!" Peter gasped. "You can't mean it, Hal. Why?" Peter looked appalled at the idea. "Is anything wrong at the homestead?"

"No, nothing like that," Hal replied pensively. "It's just that . . . I'm twenty-three years old, Peter, and I don't think I want to be a rancher all my life. I don't mean to sound ungrateful, but I don't want to live with that kind of isolation—and I don't want to raise Faith that way either. I want to do something with my life that really counts!"

"I understand what you mean, Hal," Peter answered with a sigh. "But you're so good with the animals—especially the sick ones. You have a natural gift for this work."

Hal shook his head. "Not for the ranching, I don't," he said. "I am good taking care of animals—but I'm better with people, and, well, I think I want to work where I can be with people more. There are too many memories at the homestead. I don't want to spend the winter alone with them."

"Then come work for me in the bank!" Peter exclaimed. "I could certainly use a second man. Work seems to tire me out these days."

"Thanks," Hal replied. "But I'm no good with numbers!"

Peter sat in silent thought for a moment.

"If you could do anything you wanted, Hal, if there were no other considerations—not money, or family, or age or anything—what would you want to do?"

Hal looked up, surprised at the question. He didn't answer immediately, and he went to the window and stood looking out with his hands clasped behind him. His voice, when he spoke, was soft. "Ever since I lifted Faith into life from Leah's womb I've known what I would like to do with my life. It's the reason I'm good with the cattle—I have a feel for taking care of living things. I think I should have been a doctor."

In Hal's mind he could see the burning, torpedoed ship and the sick, frightened men screaming in the water, and he felt once again the same intense yearning to be of help. He had wanted to be able to lift them up out of the oil and the flames, to heal their burns. Caught in the memory, he nodded his head and repeated softly to himself, "I would like to have been a physician."

Peter leaped to his feet. "Well, man! If that's what you want why on earth don't you do it? I'll send you to the finest university in the world! You're young—you have plenty of time!"

Hal looked at Peter in amazement. "How could I possibly do it?"

"If you want it enough you'll think of the 'hows,' " Peter said gruffly. "I'll help you in every way I can. Sleep on it! We'll talk more tomorrow."

The next morning Hal was walking in the garden pushing Faith in her pram when Peter approached him. "I've been thinking about what you said last night, Hal," he said without preamble. "And I have a solution for you. I will call Sam Ostler in Salt Lake. I know he will be able to expedite your acceptance into the university medical school and you could start this fall, I'm certain. For the time being let Faith stay here with us." Hal began to protest, but Peter forestalled him. "You are paying with a bit of her presence to buy her a long, happy future!" he cautioned.

"Medical school will take years!" Hal protested. "What do I live on in the meantime? Don't tell me you'll pay. I don't take charity!"

"I understand," Peter replied. "What I have in mind is very difficult for me to put into words, and yet I have thought and prayed about the matter and I think it is the best solution for everyone."

Hal frowned apprehensively.

"Marry Ruth," Peter said simply. "Marry Ruth, and make her happy. I do not want to die without knowing that Ruth is happy. What have Christina and I worked for all of these years if our only surviving child is . . ."

Fury suffused Hal's face. "What are you saying, Peter? Don't go any further!"

Peter could not be stopped. "Don't you see! Ruth would love Faith, raise her as her own daughter—you would become a doctor, and Christina and I could feel we had counted for something. . . . I'll settle part of Ruth's inheritance on her for a wedding present. You could attend school in comfort—"

"You can't sell Ruth!" Hal shouted. "You can't act as though

365

she were some kind of chattel, or a pawn in a chess game! I don't believe I am hearing this! What do you take me for!''

Peter was calm in the face of Hal's fury. "Don't you know she loves you?'' he asked quietly.

"And if she does?'' Hal retorted. "Isn't that her business? Do you think that by moving people into the right positions, and telling them what to say and do, you can make them happy?''

Peter flinched under his son-in-law's anger.

"It seemed logical,'' Peter said hopelessly. "I only wanted to find a way to help.'' He sighed. "You're right, Hal, of course. I don't know . . . my judgment doesn't seem to be what it used to be.'' His tone was deeply apologetic. "Forget what I said, please, Hal. It was unforgivable, I know.'' Peter suddenly looked very old and frail.

Hal would not be mollified. "Don't you know what you've done, Peter?'' he asked in a voice of despair. "If there was ever to be anything between Ruth and me, you've destroyed it! How could I ever marry her now?''

Peter would not accept Hal's evaluation. "Nonsense!'' he exploded. "This conversation will never go beyond the two of us. If you decide to marry Ruth, the things I have said will have no effect on that decision!''

Hal squinted into the sun. "Perhaps,'' he said solemnly. "Perhaps, Peter, but I shall find it hard to forget and it is bound to color my thinking.''

Peter grabbed Hal's arm. "Don't let it, Peter! Please! For my sake! Or I shall never forgive myself!''

By selling everything he owned and pooling all his savings, Hal was able to enter medical school in September. Faith remained with her grandparents to give Hal a year to settle into his studies.

The following spring, Christina received a copy of the *Atlantic Monthly* from Ruth. In the magazine there was a long article about Janeth. Christina read the words of praise for her mother with a look of incredulity on her face. The article made Janeth sound like an undiscovered genius—a woman of remarkable talent, creativity, and worth.

Other articles followed in national magazines. Drawings by Janeth and reproductions of her work were shown on the printed pages. Hal sent Christina a long article from a Salt Lake newspaper that claimed that Janeth was one of the great women of Utah.

Christina felt a rush of triumph when she thought that Mary must certainly have seen the article. "How would Mary feel when she read it?" she wondered. Mary, who had always been so sure that Janeth and her daughter were beneath her—beneath her station in life and beneath her notice! Christina thought how odd it was that her mother, who had seemed the most peculiar woman in Pleasantview, who had made Christina ashamed because she was not like other women, who had lived in a humble, backyard house, who had occupied the most unenviable position in the family, and who had spent her days in solitary pursuits, had suddenly become the one woman from her culture to obtain prominence and admiration!

Christina's heart was a jumble of emotion. She knew she had never understood her mother—had certainly never appreciated her— and yet, even now, when the world was proclaiming Janeth as some kind of a folk hero, Christina still could not define her feelings toward her mother. She felt pride, certainly, but also impatience at the terrible timing of Janeth's ascendancy, when it would do none of them any good. Perhaps she felt a tinge of envy, or pain, to know that her mother now belonged to the world. She was the world's to love, and Christina's no more—if, indeed, she had ever really belonged to her at all. For a moment she thought of the women of her line—the McElin women, by birth and marriage. How odd that out of all of them it was Janeth who had triumphed. "Why can't I just see my mother as another human being—understand, and forgive?" Christina asked herself furiously. The woman in her did forgive Janeth, but the child would not—could not.

Mary, her sister . . . Mary who had so many illusions about her place in life, her wealth, her dignity, her importance. How she must be galled by the fact that she could have no children of her own, that she was growing old and her beauty was fading. What an empty woman! "Why have I let my feelings toward her fill me with anger and fear?" Christina asked herself. "Why couldn't I simply lay our quarrel to rest, and forget her? Because," she answered herself, "the child in me still fears her—still envies her—still hates her!"

Her daughters—Leah and Ruth. She had never wanted daughters. She knew that now. She had never wanted to take on the pains and fears and uncertainties of any other women's lives. Her own had been enough—and she had not done all that well with them! How could the Lord expect her to do any better with her daughters?

And now, just Ruth was left—Ruth and little Faith. "Where does our legacy go?" Christina wondered. "How long before we find the way, like Janeth did, to take the pain, the anger, and the suffering, and turn it into something of beauty and meaning? Will Ruth? Will Faith?'' She didn't know, but she felt her heart grow warm at the thought.

In the spring Ruth came home from college. She was enchanted with little Faith, and the baby responded to Ruth with a natural love. Ruth's hair had grown out and she was wearing it in a new style, with a wave on the side and a low knot at the back of her neck. She wore light summer dresses with slim skirts and soft organdy collars. Her figure was slender and tall, with small breasts and long legs. The new styles showed her legs to great advantage, and she wore shining silk stockings and delicate, pointed high heels.

Hal came home from the university early in the summer. He was planning to work at the homestead to earn enough money for the following year, and he hoped to be able to afford a housekeeper to watch Faith so that he could take her back to Salt Lake with him when he returned to school.

The day he arrived home Ruth had spent the morning at a friend's house playing lawn tennis. She arrived home feeling hot and sticky with her hair curling damply on her forehead. She was wearing a white, sleeveless tennis dress with a dropped waist and the hemline just above her knees. She wore matching bloomers underneath and long white stockings and tennis shoes. Faith was in the garden playing, and Ruth, attracted by the child's laughter, ran out to play with her.

When Hal came in the front door, he hugged Christina and asked where Faith was.

"In the garden," Christina replied. Hal hurried out the back door to be greeted by the spectacle of Ruth and Faith rolling on the lawn together and laughing. Ruth was on all fours barking at Faith like a puppy dog, and the child clapped her hands and toddled over to hug her aunt. The sunlight bathed the young woman and the child in brilliant light, and their golden hair glowed in matching glory, like two crowns of light. Ruth's bloomers, peeping provocatively from the bottom of her skirt, had an innocent, flirtatious appeal, and Hal laughed.

Ruth turned at the sound of his laughter and her face broke into a joyful smile. "Hal!" she called. She stooped to pick up Faith and came running toward him. "It's your daddy!" she cried to Faith. "Your daddy's come home!"

Faith giggled and cooed and reached her arms toward Hal. "It's your daddy!" Ruth laughed again, and Faith looked at Hal, smiling her dimpled little smile.

"Da-da."

Hal was a changed man. His studies had opened worlds of thought and experience to him that he could not have imagined. Through the long afternoon he talked, and Ruth listened. She was the only one who could understand what he was experiencing as he studied and learned. For the first time since he and Ruth had met, they began a relationship that was based on reality—on the things they knew and felt, on the people they really were, on the ideas that were flaring in their young minds.

The changes in Ruth were subtle, but they were apparent to Hal. She had developed assurance and self-awareness that helped to balance the long years of living in Leah's shadow. Ruth had learned too that she was attractive—maybe not beautiful in the way that Leah had been, but, in her lovely bone structure and graceful features, she had a fine and enduring beauty that gave delight and peace to those who beheld her.

Perhaps it was inevitable that the two of them would be thrown together. So many things bound them to one another—family, Faith, their studies—and their minds were so similar. They found themselves with more things to say to each other than time in which to say them.

During long summer rides at the ranch, picnics with Faith, and quiet summer evenings of conversation, the days passed and they grew closer.

Hal thought he had forgotten how to laugh, but Ruth seemed to find humor in everyday things, and for the first time in almost two years he found himself waking with anticipation for the new day. He knew it was Ruth who had given his life this renewed sense of well-being.

With natural ease they were drawn into one another's lives and were scarcely aware of the rapid progression of their relationship until they realized they were spending most of every day in each other's company.

Between them a great warmth, friendship, and sense of mutual caring developed. But Hal had not spoken of love, and Ruth, who'd given him her heart years before, dared not speak of her secret for fear it might destroy their flowering affection.

Ruth prayed silently that the summer would not end before she could find the magic key to make him see her as a woman to be loved.

On an evening in late July Ruth was visiting Hal at the Broken Arrow ranch. They had spent the day on horseback riding fence, with Faith on the pommel of her father's saddle. The little girl had fallen asleep, and Ruth fixed a simple supper for the two of them.

They washed the dishes together, and Ruth hung up the checkered dishtowel. "Time to be on my way!" She yawned. "Or I'll fall asleep at the wheel. I'm as tired as Faith!"

Hal looked at Ruth with the lamp light shining on her golden hair. Her face was the color of sun-ripened peaches.

"Don't go," he said quietly.

"What!" Ruth laughed. "I have to go, Hal. Think what they'd say in Rock Falls if I stayed the night?"

Hal answered roughly. "I don't care. I want you to stay. We have things to talk about!"

"Hal," Ruth answered seriously. "You know I can't!"

"Hang what they'll say in Rock Falls!" Hal exploded. "There are so many things I want to talk to you about! Between Faith and the ranch and your folks, and all the driving back and forth—there's never enough time alone with you!"

"But Hal . . ." Ruth began, her heart beating crazily. "We can't change that."

"Look!" Hal exclaimed. "I'll go sleep in the bunkhouse with the men. It will be perfectly proper. Sit with me for a while with neither one of us having to hurry off . . ."

"My parents . . ." Ruth said sadly. "They'd be worried. Oh, Hal! You must know how much I want to stay!" Her voice trembled and she turned away so he could not see her eyes.

Just then Faith cried out in her sleep and Hal, with a helpless shrug of his shoulders, turned to go comfort her.

"I guess it wasn't meant to be, Hal. We both have things we must do." Ruth picked up her car keys, gave him a quick kiss on the cheek, and hurried out into the twilight.

The next day Hal drove down to Rock Falls to see Ruth. He invited her to walk with him in the rose garden, and stood facing her with his hands on her arms.

"Ruth, we both know these silly rules aren't working. We're too mature to be dating like a pair of teenagers. Our lives are too full of responsibilities to give us the time we want to be together.

370

"I'm tired of being alone. Tired of having no one to talk to. Tired of filling up the quiet hours with work and books!

"I've never known anyone I like being with more than you, Ruth—and Faith loves you. What I'm trying to say—and I'm not doing it very well—is, will you marry me?"

Without even pausing to think, Ruth nodded and her eyes brimmed with happy tears. It didn't matter that he had never once said he loved her. He needed her and wanted her and for now that was enough.

They were married quietly in August, and again, since it was the busy time of harvest, Hal could not leave the ranch. After kissing Faith and putting her to sleep at her grandparents' house, the newlyweds drove up to the ranch for their honeymoon.

When the bridal couple was alone in the bedroom, a stiffness descended on them. After the ease of their long summer's friendship, they could not seem to overcome the strangeness of being alone together in the quiet room.

Awkwardly Ruth walked over to Hal and kissed him, and he felt the sweet stirrings of desire after his long abstinence. They made love slowly and gently, but they both knew it had not been a success. Hal was haunted by the memory of his other wedding night. The bed in which he had lain with Leah seemed to shriek her name, and he could not help comparing the two women.

After their lovemaking he sat on the edge of the bed with his head in his hands. "This was a mistake!" he murmured, meaning it was a mistake to bring his new bride to the bedroom of his first honeymoon, but Ruth, lying in the darkness feeling a sense of failure, thought he meant it had been a mistake to marry her at all, and she turned her back to him and wept.

They were nevertheless happy together, and little Faith thrived under Ruth's tender care. Ruth cooked for the whole harvesting crew, and the ranch kitchen rang with the hearty good humor of the men. Hal whistled as he went about his work, and often in the afternoon Ruth and Faith would come to watch him at his final chores, or bring a lunch to share with him in the pasture.

He talked to Ruth about his dreams and rested in her quiet, intelligent, nurturing ways. At night their lovemaking improved and he felt an overwhelming gratitude and pleasure in her gifts. But the comfort and sweetness of the marriage troubled him. Was this really love, or had he simply chosen the easiest path? He didn't know.

Ruth was so different from her willful, sensual sister. Perhaps it was Leah's fire that he missed? But the thing he did not know was, could real love exist without the fire? And if he did not feel a flaming passion for Ruth, had he deceived her—and himself—by marrying her?

Over and over again he cursed Peter for having put the thought into his head that this marriage was the logical solution to his problem. It was such a pat answer, but he could not feel assured that, at some level, it hadn't been a part of his decision.

Chapter Twenty

Hal, Ruth, and Faith left for Salt Lake City in late August. Four days after that a load of cattle came into Rock Falls on the train from the Chicago stockyards. The animals were distributed among the ranchers who had bought them. A month later the first outbreak of hoof-and-mouth disease was reported out on the Nelsons' ranch. Within ten days, four more ranchers reported sick cattle. The government inspectors came into Rock Falls and began inspecting all the herds of the area. Nearly every herd was infected, and even Peter's herd, isolated in its narrow valley, finally succumbed.

It was an economic and emotional disaster of outrageous proportions. There was no cure for the epidemic, and the diseased cattle, as well as any cattle from the same herd, were forbidden by law to be butchered, shipped, or sold. Huge trenches were dug, and hundreds of animals were rounded up and stampeded into the holes. The ranchers lined the sides of the pits and shot the animals. Gasoline was poured on the carcasses, and the smell of burning hide was sickening. The once-beautiful herds were completely destroyed and covered with earth, and a deep silence of despair gripped the land and the men who lived from the cattle.

Not only was the loss of the animals distressing to the cattlemen, but the economic effects of the disease were disastrous. Most of the herds had been bought on loan from Peter's bank; when the herds were sold the bank would be paid off. Few of the farmers or ranchers had any assets other than the cattle with which to pay off their loans. Their land was now worthless because of the infestation of the disease and they had to find ways to wait out the quarantine period, or else pack up and declare bankruptcy. The smaller farmers simply gave Peter IOUs. "We'll pay when we can" was all they could say.

Peter knew there was no point in evicting men from their land. Their houses were of no significant market value, and he would be unable to realize any money from a landglut. Many of the large ranchers, whose debts were staggering, did simply declare bankruptcy. Peter begged them to reconsider, but they allowed the courts to take over their spreads, and Peter could recover nothing on the settlements as long as the properties remained tangled in court proceedings.

The large corresponding banks in Idaho Falls, Pocatello, and Boise from which Peter had borrowed the money to make the loans then began pressing him for payment. The tragic outbreak of hoof-and-mouth disease had spread through the state and it threatened to rock the region's economy. Under increasing pressure, the large banks insisted that Peter meet his obligations.

Night after night Peter slaved over his books, juggling his assets and the bank's position. Finally, late one night, he met Christina in her office at the hotel.

"Christina," he said quietly, "we have a very important decision to make." He paused. "I've been thinking about what all our work has been worth. I haven't worked for the money, Christina—that wasn't what I was after. I wanted the feeling that I had done something worthwhile. Of course, when our boys were alive, I wanted something to leave for them. But they were such fine men—even if I hadn't left them anything they would have gone out and made something of themselves. I just wanted to feel I had done something of value with my life!"

"I know," Christina said, nodding. "I think maybe that's what I felt about the hotel."

Peter nodded and took her hand. "Christina, I am going to lose all of it. Not just the money, but my reputation, the integrity of my business, our good name—I could lose it all. I don't care about the money—but the other things! That's all I ever wanted. I would hate to lose them!"

"How could you, Peter?" Christina asked indignantly. "After all you have done for other people, surely they will struggle to help you out of this—''

Peter laughed ruefully. "I'm afraid I've discovered, Christina, that in a crisis like this, memories are very short. No, if we are to save our reputation and behave responsibly, I must pay the bank's debts by myself. I will take the IOUs of all the men who owe me money and keep them. Maybe in a few years some of them will repay us—but, for now, it will take everything we own to repay the corresponding banks, satisfy my depositors, and close down with honor. Are you willing to give away the labors of twenty-five years to a tired old man, just so he can save his good name?''

Christina looked at Peter sitting beside her. His hair had turned sandy white and his face was seamed with furrows of concern and wisdom. His eyes were as blue as ever, but his body seemed frail and thin.

"It's my name too," Christina said crisply. "And if you are a tired old man, then we match—because I am a tired old lady! Maybe it will feel good to start over!''

He laughed and reached over and gave her a hearty kiss, and she pushed him away, but not too vigorously. "Don't do that!" she said. "Someone might see!''

They sold the businesses, the inventory, the house, the furnishings, their horses, cars, carriages, the bank building, the investment portfolio, and even the silver and few pieces of jewelry Christina had acquired over the years.

The only property Peter retained was the Broken Arrow homestead. "We can go there to live," he said. "In a year we can run cattle on the fields again. It will be a good life.''

Neither of them acknowledged to themselves or to one another how difficult it was to leave the home Peter had built with such personal care and the businesses that had been like an extension of their family. On their last day in Rock Falls they drove down Elm Street in the ranch truck, which they had kept. The vehicle was piled with personal belongings and luggage. "Just like leaving Pleasantview!" Peter said cheerfully, as he strapped the last chair into place.

Christina smiled. Her head was held high and she would not let the neighbors see so much as a hint of defeat or distress in her bearing. As the couple passed the school and turned down Main Street, Christina averted her eyes from the hotel and storefronts. The new owners were tearing down the old facades and replacing the old

'Saunders and Sons'' sign with a new one that proclaimed ''Rock Falls Market.''

''The old order changeth!'' Peter said with a grin, and they drove down the road out of Rock Falls, which had been widened and improved during the war. Later that night as they sat at the table in the kitchen at the homestead, Christina burst into a sudden angry tirade.

''After all these years no one stepped forward to help! None of those men who owed you money offered to sell a thing to help pay off the debts! They handed you their worthless IOUs and acted as though they had filled their obligation! And now you must repay their loans to the corresponding banks with your hard-earned money! Those banks wouldn't take an IOU—only you, Peter! You could have all those men thrown into jail! The loans are their obligations!''

''Now, Christina. Only their loans to me are their obligations! My loans from the other banks are mine! Besides, many of these men will honor their IOUs eventually—I promise you!''

''Well,'' Christina snapped, ''if we are counting on that for comfort in old age, we may just as well forget it! I don't ever expect to see a cent of their money! The thing that makes me furious is, why didn't they come to you and at least offer to help? Or express their gratitude that you didn't let the bank go under? Come to you like human beings to say they are sorry!''

''Because I wasn't their friend, Christina, I was their banker. They don't think I need their friendship—and they are too shy and diffident to offer it.''

''We pay the price for our years of independence and isolation, I suppose,'' Christina said ruefully. ''But it still makes me angry—it seems so unfair after all you have done!''

Peter laughed gently. ''Christina, are you still hoping for 'fair'? Have you learned nothing?''

She subsided and laughed with him. ''Well, I always said I didn't want the big house on Elm Street,'' she said ruefully. ''Maybe it's 'fair' that I've lost it!''

Two weeks later a demand for a final payment of twenty-five thousand dollars came from Idaho Falls First National Bank.

''I simply don't have it!'' Peter said, looking at the paper with a gray, exhausted look on his face. ''How could I have missed this in my accounting?''

He shook his head, dismayed by his error and sick at the amount of the deficit. Even if he sold the homestead from Broken Arrow, which he could not bring himself to do, and left himself and Christina homeless, he would not have enough money to meet the loan.

Peter spent the next day going from farm to farm, ranch to ranch, but everywhere the same answer: "We have nothing, Mr. Saunders. Not a nickel. We'll start paying you back next year. Please give us time."

He nodded. "Time!" If only someone would give him time! But the note was due, and if he forfeited on it he would have to declare bankruptcy. He simply could not face that alternative.

"I'm going to Idaho Falls to see what I can do," he lied to Christina and left on the train the next morning. He did not get off the train in Idaho Falls, but continued to Salt Lake City, where, after hours of pacing the sidewalks, he finally presented himself to Samuel Ostler at his offices. When he entered Sam's private office he noticed a large walnut door next to Sam's. It bore the words "Greg Ostler, Vice-President, Ostler Enterprises."

"What can I do for you, Peter?" Sam asked. His voice was thin, and he looked frail and stooped, but his eyes were as shrewd and warm as ever. "You look like you have been through a wringer."

"Do you remember when we met the first time in Pleasantview?" Peter asked with a reminiscent smile.

Sam nodded.

"You told me if you could ever do anything for me—" Peter didn't finish the sentence. He didn't need to.

Sam looked at him squarely. "I still mean it," Sam said.

Peter reached in his pocket and handed a paper to Sam. "This is between the two of us. No one else is to know. I promise you I will repay the loan in full as soon as possible."

Sam took the proffered paper. It was an informal, handwritten deed. "What is this?" Sam asked.

"I need to borrow twenty-five thousand dollars," Peter told him. "I am giving you the deed to the Arrow Valley as collateral. If I do not repay the money by June thirtieth, two years from today, the ranch is yours."

Sam was incensed. "For heaven's sake, Peter. I'll lend you the money on your word alone! You don't need this deed for security!"

Peter flinched. "I am not asking you for charity, Sam. I am asking for an honest and legal loan, backed with collateral. That is the only way I can take the money!"

"The McElin pride seems to have rubbed off on you!" Sam said with an attempt at humor.

Peter did not smile. "It is the Saunders pride, Sam, and I have always had it."

"I'm sorry, Peter. It was a poor joke. Of course I will lend the money to you, and I will keep the deed until the loan is quitted, if that is what you wish."

Suddenly Peter grinned, and the strain vanished. "I'll tell you, Sam, you have saved my life!" The two of them chuckled and parted as the friends they had always been.

Peter sent a telegram to Christina. "All is well. Home in two days." He did not go see Ruth, Hal, and little Faith because no one was to know he had been in Salt Lake; his visit was a secret.

Peter returned to the homestead, and he and Christina passed a quiet summer. The next spring they began working the timber stands up on Crowsnest Mountain, and brought in some new, hardy livestock. By the end of the summer the ranch was turning a profit, and some of the money from the IOUs began trickling in. Peter saved every possible dollar. In January a sizable loan payment came from one of the ranchers who had sold a large piece of his property to some railroad developers who were planning to build a winter ski resort in the area. For the first time Peter was certain he would be able to repay Sam. He planned to lease his timber rights in the spring and that would give him the last of the money. The second winter became pleasant to Peter as his worry diminished.

With each season's passing, Peter became more aware of the beauty of Broken Arrow's valley. He and Christina tramped in snowshoes following tracks of rabbits and paused to trace in wonder the spiraling flight of hawks above the white mountain vastness.

Between them, in the small, cozy cabin, there developed a sweet understanding that was like a soothing balm after their years of struggle and resistance to one another. The harshness of their lives had sanded them down like fine wood, and they fitted one another smoothly, but with just enough abrasion to keep their minds salty and their tongues clever.

One snowbound night they sat before the flames in contented silence. "I think perhaps this is what I have always wanted," Peter said suddenly, putting his arm around Christina's shoulders. "You

377

and me—alone with one another and the world far away. I've paid quite a price to get it—but it's been worth it!''

"Oh, pshaw!" Christina said, flushing with pleasure. "Peter, you can be a conniver when you want to be! I know what you want!''

"You!" he repeated, and kissed her.

Chapter Twenty-one

Hal was grim. He had begun his internship, and the hours were tortuous. Ruth never complained, even though when he was home he was so tired he could scarcely think. How long had it been since he had played with Faith? Or made love to Ruth? He didn't know! The days seemed to melt together—and the nights were endless and sleepless.

Now, to top it all off, a stupid nurse had fouled up his orders and an appendicitis patient had gotten out of bed and ripped his stitches! He would have to try to mend the damage. He hurried to the sick man's room and an hour later, with the patient neatly bandaged and resting comfortably, Hal went looking for the offending nurse. He found her in the chart room drinking a cup of tea.

"You!" he accused. "Are you Miss Hanover?''

"Yes," the girl answered, giving him a dazzling smile. "And you are Dr. Morgan?''

"Listen to me, Miss Hanover! This is not a social call. You let Mr. Cassio out of bed, strictly against written orders. He ripped his incision, and I have just spent an hour trying to undo your irresponsible damage.''

"There were no such orders on Mr. Cassio's chart!" Miss Hanover protested. "If you wish your patients to be given bedpans, then you should note it.''

"I did!" Hal hissed. "I wrote it in big, bold letters, which, if you could read, you might have noticed.''

The young woman's face was scarlet and her dark hair bounced with indignation. Even in his fury, Hal could not help noticing her full bosom as it heaved up and down in her tight, starched uniform. "There were no such orders!" Miss Hanover retorted. "I checked the chart myself!"

"Right here!" Hal shouted, pointing to the chart in his hand.

Miss Hanover looked at the chart in disbelief. "I know there were no orders on the chart I saw!" she faltered, continuing to study the chart. "Oh!" she exclaimed. "This is the chart for his private room. They just made this one up. I was working from the chart in the ward."

She ran to the files and, after a moment of hunting, found the other chart and showed it to Hal. He looked at it for a moment. No written orders were on the chart.

"Very well," Hal said. "It was an administrative error—but a mighty dangerous one. Mr. Cassio could have hurt himself! See that you use better judgment next time. If the written orders don't fit the situation, call and check with a doctor before you make a decision."

She smiled with relief. "Yes, Dr. Morgan. Of course I will."

From that evening on, it seemed to Hal Miss Hanover was on duty with him nearly every night. She passed him in the hallway, sauntered past his table in the cafeteria, came to fetch him when he was sleeping in the doctor's lounge, and followed him on early-morning rounds.

He knew the bold young nurse was chasing him outrageously, and yet he could not deny he was attracted to her. Her lips were full and red, and her small white teeth gleamed between them. She knew how to use her eyes, and Hal felt her reaching out to him, enticing him and leading him toward her.

Sometimes in the few hours of his broken sleep between patients he found himself dreaming of her, and he would wake up in a cold sweat. His feelings of guilt were real, but he did nothing to avoid his encounters with the provocative young nurse, and, in his exhaustion, he felt himself letting go of any pretense of control, simply sliding where his emotions led him.

Was this what he had missed in Ruth? This mysterious, exciting, tantalizing mystery? This rush of blood and desire that made him tingle with life, even when his body was filled with weariness and heavy concern? He had to admit his marriage to Ruth had always been comfortable, but she was so different from Leah! Did he miss the flame of passion that had been so much a part of Leah? He didn't know. He only knew that now he found himself wanting Miss Hanover.

And she grew bolder. When she handed him a chart, she would brush his hand accidentally, or passing beside him through a door brush her skirts against him, and smile her cool, enchanting smile. "Pardon me," she would whisper.

Juvenile and absurd though it was, he found himself infatuated like a callow youth, and his days passed in a blur of sleeplessness, frustration, guilt, and desire as he labored through the long hours in the hospital, struggling with something he felt must be a symptom of a deep problem in his marriage.

He turned his guilt upon Ruth and became sharp with her if she put any demands on him at home, recognizing, even as he did it, how unfair he was being. Ruth accepted his irritation with her usual equanimity even though she was busy and tired herself. His guilt was increased by his awareness of the staggering effort she had made to keep him in school.

Even though Ruth and Hal never intended to accept financial help from him, when Peter lost his money the young couple's financial situation became precarious since they then had no resources to fall back upon.

They watched in dismay as their savings dwindled away, and Hal began to think seriously about leaving medical school. Ruth was determined this should not happen. She could have gone to work in a bank, but she did not want to leave Faith to the care of strangers. The little girl, whom she loved as her own, had been passed from hand to hand so many times in the years of early childhood that Ruth felt it was extremely important to give Faith as much stability as possible. And caring for the beautiful child was the greatest joy in her life. She was determined to give this little girl all the love, care, and training she could.

One evening Hal and Ruth had some other medical students over for supper. Since their budget was tight, and Ruth was unable to afford a fancy menu, she decided to serve "crisp" potatoes—a recipe her mother had developed. Christina sliced potatoes paper thin, then fried them quickly in deep fat and sprinkled them with salt. Ruth and Leah, as little girls, had thought the crisp potatoes were the best treat their mother could make.

Ruth served the potatoes with hearty sandwiches and homemade soup. The guests raved about the food, particularly the potatoes.

"Will you give me the recipe?" one of the wives exclaimed. "I think these would be good hot or cold! Ted would love them in his lunch!"

The guests' enthusiasm gave Ruth an idea. She began making and packaging the potato crisps and selling them from a basket placed in the day room at the medical school. She soon found she could easily sell all the packages she could make, and so she organized several of the other wives, who were also struggling for funds, and began a small "cottage" industry. She was able to get several grocery and specialty stores in the city to buy the "crisps" too. With the help of an art student she designed and printed a white-and-red wax bag. "Ruth's Crisps" soon became a popular snack throughout Salt Lake.

In the two years that Ruth had her potato company she had made enough money to keep Hal in school, but the work was demanding. Her part-time workers often quit, or were undependable, and frequently, at midnight, Ruth would be standing at her stove, peeling, slicing, and frying the following day's orders.

One night she fell into bed with a groan. Hal, sleeping heavily beside her, rolled over and asked, "What time is it? Do I have to get back to the hospital?"

"No," she murmured. "Go back to sleep. It's only three."

"Three!" he exclaimed, horrified. "You mean you have been up working until this hour? Oh, Ruth! This is unfair to you!"

"Hush!" she said, and put her arms around him. "Don't think that way, Hal. You are working as hard as you can—and it makes me feel good to know I am working too. Don't feel guilty, or sorry for me. I want to do it! Really I do!"

He shook his head and sighed. There was so much he wanted to say, but he was too tired and under too much pressure. He turned over on his side.

They were both working hard and under so much strain that their sex life had dwindled to an occasional quick, exhausted encounter, more out of duty than passion. Ruth had grown thinner, and her blond hair had lost its luster, but she remained loving, sweet, and gentle. With Faith she was a perfect mother, disciplined and tender, and with Hal she was patient, understanding, and encouraging. Sometimes Hal could not help contrasting the humble quiet of their cramped apartment with the life-and-death vitality of the hospital. Unconsciously, he compared Ruth to the crisply uniformed nurses with their saucy smiles and authoritarian professional manners—self-assured and vibrant.

In early April Hal worked four straight days at the hospital without getting home. Catching what sleep he could on the hard cots in the dingy basement rooms where the interns slept between calls, wearing lab coats laundered by the hospital, and shaving with the razor he kept at the hospital, he had somehow made it through. On the fourth day, late in the evening, his rounds were finally completed and he took off his hospital jacket, shrugged on his coat, and prepared listlessly to go home.

"Hey, Hal!" a fellow student called. "There's a party going on over at the bio lab. Dancing, music, girls, and food! What more could a tired intern ask?"

"Yeah!" another of the interns called. "You are becoming a dull fellow! Nothing but work and home! C'mon, let us show you the bright side of life!"

"Yes," said Miss Hanover, stepping up to him wearing a fetching cloche hat and a smooth-fitting street dress that showed each of her luscious curves to considerable advantage. "Come just for a minute. Then you can toddle off home. You owe it to your fellow workers to let us see your human side. Who knows, we might even get a smile out of you!"

She was laughing at him, teasing him, challenging him, and, without ever consciously making a decision, he found himself in a battered open car, rattling across the campus toward the biology building. Miss Hanover was sitting on his lap and the car was filled with young nurses and interns. She was a solid weight, but her flesh was soft and where she leaned against him he felt himself burning with awareness of her.

When the group entered the lab the room already smelled of beer mingled with the tart scent of laboratory alcohol. The level of noise, confusion, laughter, and motion was disorienting. Hal, in his exhausted state, wandered around the party nodding at his acquaintances.

Someone grabbed his arm firmly. "You are not getting away from me, Dr. Morgan!" Miss Hanover laughed. "Not until we have had our dance!"

"I—I don't dance!" Hal mumbled, blinking at her attractive face with its dark, seductive eyes, and soft red lips laughing at him mischievously.

"In the darkness no one will know!" She giggled. She stepped close to him, took his arm, and put it around her shoulder, and reached for his hand and placed it firmly on her small rounded hip.

"There!" she murmured. "You can do that part just fine!"

"No," Hal said, taking his hands away. "I'm too tired for dancing, and all this noise is getting to me!"

She looked at him with concern.

"Hey!" she said. "You don't look well! Come with me!" She took his hand and led him through the frantic crush of bodies. They went out the front door and stood on the lawn by the side of the building. The cool night air cleared Hal's head and he took deep gulps of air.

"I'm not the party type," Hal said. "I think it's time I was getting home."

"But you don't want to!" Miss Hanover said softly. "I know you don't! I can see it in your eyes. I felt it in your hands. We don't need to stay at the party. I'll go with you—wherever you'd like to go." Her voice was light as air, and she came closer to him in the darkness.

"You're different from the others," she whispered. "I can see that! They're just boys—but you are a real man, someone a woman could give everything to. . . ."

She reached her arms up to him slowly, and he bent his head to her. Her face was so close he could feel her warmth on his own face and the motion of her lips as she spoke, almost touching his, but not quite, as though she challenged him to come to her, to reach out for that last agonizing fraction of distance to touch their moist softness.

"You want me. I know you do," she murmured, and he moved to her then and kissed the lips that were so tantalizingly close to his. Like a flashpoint of passion she was unleashed in his arms, and her mouth opened and her arms pressed him to her so he could feel the length of her body against his. She was too quick and too aggressive, however, and her response startled him. He dropped his arms and moved away from her with sudden repudiation. She was caught off guard.

"What are you doing?" she cried.

"Coming to my senses," Hal answered coolly. "I'm sorry, Miss Hanover. I am a married man, and I am truly ashamed of the way I have acted tonight. Will you forgive me if I have done anything to lead you on?"

She was furious. "Done anything!" she exclaimed. "No! You haven't done anything, not anything at all! Well, don't think that I need to throw myself at you! There are lots of others who are begging—who would stand in line—for what you are turning down!"

She whirled on her heel and flounced into the bio lab. Hal had the long walk back to the hospital and the slow drive home in his old car to think over the events of the evening. He was filled with disgust at the thought of Miss Hanover. Only at the last had he seen her for what she was—and yet her sexuality had almost undone him! Why had he been so vulnerable to her?

When Miss Hanover shouted there were many men who would welcome her favors, his attraction for her had vanished like a vapor, and left him cold and disgusted. He realized then that the thing that made a woman least appealing to him sexually was the feeling that all the mystery and complexity was lost in her—that what she had to give was equally available to any man. Was that why, in his deepest heart of hearts, he had always felt a small rind of dissatisfaction with Leah? Her body had been so easily and completely available to him! Her delights were straightforward and insistent. There was no mystery in her, no hesitation. She was so certain of her beauty and delighted with her own body, and she accepted the joys of marriage as simply and artlessly as a child accepts a gift from the confectionary shop. There had been no mountains or valleys in Leah. No uncharted peaks lost in the mist of desire.

"And Ruth?" he asked himself. "What of Ruth? What does she feel or think? What are her desires, or her hidden needs?"

Suddenly, driving down Fifth South, he realized he did not know. In the years of their marriage he and Ruth had never been alone. He had sworn to himself that he had married her for love and not convenience. But the love he felt for her didn't seem passionate. It had more to do with companionship and intellectual unity and respect. Since their marriage, with his studies, Ruth's business, and the press of raising Faith, he knew that he had never tried to unlock the quiet door of Ruth's inner self. There was no passion in his marriage because he had chosen not to search for it. He had let Ruth serve him as wife, mother, helpmate, and friend, but he had not let her become his lover. Was he secretly afraid of what he might discover? Did he struggle still with guilt over Leah and fear to search for the secrets of Ruth's heart? Whatever the reasons for his failure, he knew the time had come for him to give his marriage a better chance.

Exhausted as he was, he felt a flame of relentless curiosity forming within him. He felt as though he had discovered a new country and stood on the threshold waiting to explore it. He knew he would need to proceed with wisdom, tenderness, and caution. As he sought to open the door to Ruth's heart he must not do anything that would hurt or confuse her.

"I only hope it's not too late," he whispered to himself as he drove up to the door of their small apartment and let himself in.

When he walked into the house Faith ran to kiss him, but Ruth looked up without smiling. He crossed the small room and put his arms around her and kissed her warmly. It wasn't until he felt her stiffen in his arms and step back from him that he saw the wary look in her eyes.

"What's the matter?" he asked. "Can't a man kiss his wife when he feels like it?" He grinned at Ruth, willing her to smile back, but her eyes were dark with hurt—or was it anger?

"I suppose," she said coldly, "that a man can kiss anyone he feels like."

"What do you mean by that?" Hal asked, trying to keep his voice light, but a terrible constriction tightened his heart. She knew! He didn't know how, but she knew!

"Oh, Hal!" Ruth exclaimed in a pain-filled voice. "How could you? I didn't expect you to love me—not right away! You still had Leah to work out of your heart—and the way we were living—and your studies! You weren't ready! But I thought—I imagined—that someday, when you needed love, I would be here and you'd see me. Really see me! And you would love me!"

"I do love you, Ruth!" Hal protested, almost by reflex, but she cut him off. With a sinking heart he noticed her suitcases stacked by the front door.

"You don't love me, Hal," Ruth whispered and shook her head sadly. "You don't even know me!"

She turned to the small desk. "Here are the keys, the bankbook, and the bills. I think I've taken care of everything."

"Ruth!" Hal exploded. "This is ridiculous! What are you doing?"

"I'm leaving, Hal," she said calmly. "Faith and I are going back to the ranch to live with my parents until we work this out. I think we both need time. When you have finished your internship, if you want us, you know where we'll be!"

"Faith dear." Ruth turned to the little girl who was playing with her dolls. "Kiss Daddy good-bye and run out on the porch to wait for the taxi. I'll be right along." Faith, excited about the trip, did as she was told.

Hal grabbed Ruth by the shoulders and held her in an impassioned embrace. "I don't understand any of this, Ruth!" he exclaimed. "Nothing's happened—if that's what you think!"

Ruth pulled away from him again and his eyes were filled with her loveliness. How could he have forgotten how beautiful she was!

"Nothing has happened, Hal?" she said with a cross between a laugh and a sob. "You're right. Nothing! I've been a convenience, a friend—a nothing! But that's what you needed, so I didn't mind. I was happy to be what you needed! The only thing is—when you needed more, why didn't you come to me?" Her voice rose and he caught a glimpse of the power and fury of the passions behind her practiced composure.

"You should have remembered how loyal medical wives are to one another, Hal!" Her eyes were blazing. "I got not one, but two phone calls about your little episode with Miss Hanover!"

"All right," Hal answered. "I kissed a nurse! I shouldn't have—and I'm sorry! She doesn't mean anything to me! It shouldn't matter!"

"It doesn't," Ruth said. "What does matter is that never once in the years we have been married have you kissed me as though nothing mattered—as though the only thing in the world that you wanted to do at that moment was to kiss me!

"I would have waited, Hal, but now I feel that waiting won't make any difference. You can't see me, Hal. I'm invisible to you!"

"Ruth," Hal pleaded, "don't go! Stay with me and let me try to love you the way you want."

Ruth shook her head. "No, Hal, it wouldn't work. I can't come to you anymore. I want you to think this through, and then when you're sure—and only if you're sure—you will have to come for me."

Chapter Twenty-two

Two weeks later Mary died at her home in Salt Lake. Sam Ostler sent a telegram to Christina and Peter. Her obituary filled a large column in the Salt Lake newspaper. Peter read Sam's telegram and began to pack his things. "Her funeral is on Tuesday. If we leave on the afternoon train we can be there," he said to Christina.

"No!" Christina dissented. "I will not be guilty of hypocrisy! If I could not go and ask Mary's forgiveness in life, what right do I have to go in death? I will not stain her funeral with such a selfish act!''

"You're her sister!" Peter exclaimed. "Whatever was between you is passed!''

Christina nodded. "Yes, in my heart, it is passed. But I do not have the right to be at her funeral. I forfeited that right.''

She was adamant, and Peter went to the funeral alone. Hal also went to the services, to see Peter and ask for news about Ruth and Faith.

"They're getting along fine," Peter assured Hal. "We love having them." He looked at the younger man thoughtfully. "Want to talk to me about it?" he asked. Hal shook his head. "Thought so," said Peter. "Ruth won't talk about it either."

After the funeral Sam Ostler came up to Peter and Hal, and shook their hands. "Thank you for coming," he said. "It means a great deal to me." Peter began to speak. "You don't have to explain why Christina isn't here," Sam added with a smile. "I know how her mind would have worked. I knew she wouldn't feel it was right to come."

"She sends you her love, Sam," Peter said.

Sam beckoned to a young man who was just beginning to show the touches of soft living. Short, balding, with the trace of a self-indulgent waistline and a double chin, the man was dressed in impeccable mourning and was surrounded by people, shaking his hand and expressing sympathy.

"Greg," Sam said, as the young man came over, "I want you to meet some of your relatives. This is Peter Saunders and his son-in-law, Hal Morgan."

Greg looked as though he had been struck. He did not speak to Peter or Hal, instead he turned to his father with a look of shock and anger. "How dare they come to Mother's funeral?" he asked coldly. "How can you ask me to speak to people who gave my mother nothing but sorrow and hurt!''

Sam's face grew stern. "Greg! These are my guests! What was between Aunt Christina and your mother was personal between the two of them. They understood one another—and would have bridged their differences if they had not been so much alike. Your mother would not have wished this quarrel to extend beyond them!''

Greg turned to walk away. "I'm sorry, Father, I cannot change the way I feel."

With an apologetic gesture Sam turned back to Peter and Hal.

"Please forgive him. I'm afraid Mary spoiled him. They were very close and her death has been a terrible blow. Will you come over to the house?" Sam continued graciously.

Watching Greg stalk away, Peter answered, "Perhaps we had better not, Sam. This is not a day to bring discord into your home."

Hal bid Sam Ostler good-bye, and once more expressed his sympathy. "Before I leave, Sam," Peter said, "I want to tell you that I will be sending the twenty-five thousand in June as I promised—as soon as I get the payment for my timber lease."

"Let me return that deed, Peter," Sam urged. "I know you will pay as soon as you can."

Peter was adamant. "Keep the deed to the homestead. This is a business loan, and the deed becomes yours if I don't pay on time. Those are the terms of our agreement."

"Very well," Sam said, knowing the subject was closed. "Thank you for coming, Peter, old friend."

When Peter returned to the ranch, he felt a surge of joy as he drove down through the pass and came out into the valley. The house, nestled among the aspens and pines, looked warm and welcoming, and the river, filled with the spring runoff, cascaded through the green pastures. He thought of the fine herd he would reestablish there, and his eyes sought the high peaks where the rich stands of timber lay. For the first time he began to understand Christina's love for the mountains, and her feeling of joy and security in their midst. If it weren't for his concern about Hal and Ruth, he felt he would be one of the happiest men alive.

"Thank you!" Peter thought, with a rich flood of well-being flowing through his heart. "Thank you, Broken Arrow."

When he came into the house, Christina looked up in surprise. She had been crying, thinking of Mary, and her face was white and stained with tears.

"I have been repenting, Peter," she said. "And the thing I need to repent of the most is that I still cannot forgive Mary for asking for my baby, and telling me I could not care for him the right way. I cannot forgive her, because she has made me wonder all of my life if he might have lived if I had given him to her. How can a mother live with thoughts like that?"

"Still?" Peter asked.

Christina nodded. "Still. If I think about it, the years are stripped away and the pain and the questions are as real as though I were still in the Garden House! Age doesn't make us wiser, or stronger, or less vulnerable—it doesn't soften the past!''

"I know!" Peter affirmed. "I know. So let us live in the present. Let's be happy with Ruth and Faith and each other. And let's pray that Hal and Ruth come to their senses!"

With a smile, Christina patted his hand. "There's no hurry," she murmured. "It took us over thirty years!"

In June the timber lease was signed in Rock Falls. Peter went to the bank, which had been reopened as a branch of the bank in Idaho Falls, and purchased a cashier's check made out to Sam Ostler in the amount of twenty-five thousand dollars.

"You be mighty careful with that check, sir," said the bank clerk. "It's the same as cash money!"

Peter smiled. "Yes, I know," he said quietly. "I used to be something of a banker myself."

After he had finished his business, Peter walked out of the bank he had built and lost. He walked down the main street of the town he had helped found. Since that war many newcomers had moved to Rock Falls and the streets were crowded with strangers. Only one or two familiar faces greeted him. He thought with sadness of the days when he could walk the distance from the bank to the hotel and greet everyone he met by name.

The store, grain business, and hotel had been expanded, and many new stores and commercial establishments had been built during the war, pushing the business district far past Elm Street. Peter knew the inevitable pattern of the growth of towns, and he realized that in a few years the beautiful home he had built there would either be turned into a business or be torn down.

It was hard for him to remember why the house had meant so much to him at one time. Now he found he could hardly wait to leave the bustling little city and return to the peace and beauty of the valley ranch.

He climbed into his battered old car and drove carefully out of town toward the homestead. He felt very tired and old, which he knew was ridiculous. "After all," he thought, "I'm not even sixty years old yet! I am far from an old man!" But the nostalgic view of Rock Falls, and the many changes, had given him the feeling of having lived through a long period of history.

When Christina looked out the window and saw Peter walking

toward the house later that afternoon, she felt a stab of concern. He walked slowly, and his face looked tired and drawn.

"He must get more rest!" she thought.

Christina knew nothing of Peter's loan from Sam Ostler or of the agreement for repayment with the deed left as security. Peter was certain he could take care of the matter and he wanted to spare her any concern.

The following morning, Peter told Doug Whitman, the ranch foreman, to ride up to the timber lease area and check out a possible site for the lumbering crews that were to arrive in the next few weeks.

Doug left at the crack of dawn and rode toward the peak Broken Arrow called Crowsnest. The trail was extremely rugged, and at one point the tip of the snowpack, still unmelted, forced Doug to ride down a small ravine across a section of loose stones.

As Doug and his horse struggled to find their way back to the main trail, they moved down a canyon with a trickling stream that was unfamiliar to the man. After following the stream for a while, he headed his horse up a rocky bank, trying to break out of the canyon. The horse's hooves set off a small rock slide. Then Doug heard a terrible rumbling, cracking sound, and he barely had time to gallop downstream as a higher outcropping of stones broke away and roared down into the canyon bed. The sound of the crashing rocks and rumbling stones was deafening, and Doug trembled for fear he would be caught in the slide as the earth shook beneath him.

At last there was silence, and Doug stared at the heap of boulders and small rocks settling in a thick cloud of dust, damming the stream. It was the sun's rays that made the discovery.

Doug saw something shining in the heap of rocks, and, after checking to make sure that there were no more fissures or evidences of further avalanches, made his way carefully through the stones. He picked up a small rock and found it was veined with a gray-blue streak. In the streak were threads and crystals of dull gold. Doug gasped and picked up another rock. Again he found the odd pattern of minerals, only this time there was a large vein of gold—subtle and dull, but unmistakable! Shaking with disbelief, Doug carefully made his way up the canyon side where the shaft of rock had broken away, and there in the raw, exposed earth he could see a vein of gold, matted in blue-gray matrix. The rocks of the mountains, having withheld their secret for centuries, had been exposed to the probing light of the morning.

"Gold!" Doug whispered. "Gold!" He scrambled down the rocks, bringing a shower of small stones with him. Farther downstream he remounted his horse, which was quietly cropping on a small patch of grass, and, trembling with excitement, Doug stuffed the specimen rocks in his jacket pockets and worked his way downstream until he found a trail out of the canyon. He rode back up across a familiar ridge and down again into the valley.

Once on the grassland Doug smacked his horse with his hat, and the weary horse broke into a canter. They sped across the valley floor toward the ranch house.

Peter was in his bedroom writing a letter to Sam Ostler to accompany the loan payment check that was on his desk when he heard the clatter of a horse pulling up near the doorway and the frantic cries of his hired man. Not wanting Christina to see the letter or the cashier's check, Peter snatched up the documents, put them in his pocket, and ran out the door to see what the clamor was all about. Doug's news of the gold strike took Christina and Peter by total surprise. They found themselves shocked by the implications of his discovery as each turned the rocks over in their hands and stared at the blue-and-gold-veined stone.

At last Peter gave a sigh. "It certainly looks like gold ore, Doug," he said tiredly. Doug could not understand why Mr. Saunders looked as if he had just received bad news. Peter's face was grave.

"Will you take me to the place where you found these rocks?"

"Sure thing, Mr. Saunders," Doug answered eagerly. "But it's a far piece to go in the heat of the noon sun."

Christina begged to go with the men, but Peter dissuaded her. "I'll take you as soon as I'm sure it's something worth getting excited about," Peter promised.

The men took fresh mounts and headed toward the canyons. Doug was right. The noon sun pounded hotly on their backs, but once they got into the mountains a cool breeze began to blow and Peter felt better. He had not slept well the night before, thinking about getting the money into Sam's hands before the deadline, and Peter felt deeply weary in spite of the excitement over Doug's find.

By early afternoon the men were in the heart of the canyon. In front of him Peter could see the fresh mound of the rockslide and his heart raced with mixed emotion. The wind had picked up tempo and was whistling vigorously down the canyon. The sound of the rushing air and the racing waters seemed to heighten the strange wildness of the setting, giving it a feeling of unreality. A part of Peter was praying the strike was a mistake, and the blue and gold veins were not silver and gold as he believed but merely some similar geological phenomena.

The peacefulness and isolation of Arrow Valley had never been so precious to him. He recognized that this lode of gold, if it proved to be rich and minable, could shatter everything he and Christina had at last achieved. Peter stopped and got off his horse. Before riding off from the main building, he and Doug had packed supplies and tools, so he pulled out a metal pan and bent to the stream where he began sifting the pebbles and bits of soil. Within seconds he could see the grains of gold clinging to the bottom of the pan.

The mountain water was bitterly cold, pouring as it did from the snowpack, and his hands were freezing as he stood up from his labors. Perspiration was pouring from his head and the high altitude and cold wind made him shiver.

There *was* gold, probably a lot of it, in the mountain beside him. The stream was filled with the alluvial gold that had washed for centuries from the hidden veins. Some of the gold was certainly near the surface, but that was probably just the tip of a long deep vein flowing at the angle of the earth's fault into the heart of the mountains. It was not quartz gold but gold that was held in a combination of silver ore, and thus the two metals could be mined together. Peter felt himself trembling with exhilaration and apprehension.

"Don't you think we'd better head back, Mr. Saunders?" Doug asked. "You look a mite done-in, and I reckon you've seen all you need to for today."

Peter's mind still balked at the reality of what he had seen.

"A moment more, Doug!" he said. "Let's climb up and look at the exposed slide area for a minute. Maybe I'll get a clearer picture."

Doug shook his head. "You sure you're up to it, Mr. Saunders?"

Peter nodded and began the arduous climb up the fallen boulders. Pulling himself from handhold to handhold, he reached a ledge above the slide area. Doug followed and wedged himself beside Peter on the shelf. The wind tore down the canyon, and Peter shivered in the blast. His arms and legs felt heavy as lead, and he had the terrible sensation of not being able to get his breath. He tried to gasp for air, but a pain shot through his chest, and he felt as though he could not open his lungs.

"Doug!" he gasped.

Doug looked at Peter and his face went white with fear.

"Mr. Saunders, what's wrong?" he cried and reached his strong arms out to hold Peter as he slumped against the canyon wall.

Peter fought for breath and struggled to control his shivering, but his forehead was drenched with perspiration, and the cold air chilled his wet body to the bone.

"I'm all right, Doug," he gasped. "Cold!" Peter leaned over to inspect the rock formation, and there he saw the vein of mingled silver and gold running downward across the face. It was thick and solid, and rich-looking. Peter knew he was looking at vast wealth, and he wondered why he felt no joy or excitement, only an all-encompassing desire to climb down from the ledge, get on his horse, and return to the sweetness of the valley.

The second pain caught him unaware and he groaned out loud. This time the pain would not stop. He felt as though a beast were clawing and tearing at his breast, and something deep inside him seemed to twist and buck and fight for its life. In the moment before he lost consciousness he saw the blue patchwork sky above him and the wind-swept mountaintops, the shining creek below, and Doug's horrified face, filled with terror and concern.

"Doug!" he gasped. "Take this letter—mail to Sam Ostler. . . ." His voice was less than a whisper, and he could not know that the words he thought he was saying took no form on his lips.

"What is it, Mr. Saunders?" Doug was crying, struggling to prevent Peter from falling from the ledge. With his last ounce of life, Peter reached into his pocket and took out the envelope with the letter and check for twenty-five thousand dollars for Sam. He tried to give it to Doug, but Doug, battling for footing and fighting for their lives, could not release his hand to take the paper. A strong gust of capricious wind swept past them, and Peter's hand, lifeless and limp, let go of the letter. It was caught by the wind, twisting and dancing through the air. Doug, desperate for Peter's safety, scarcely noticed its passage. The frantic wind swept the scrap of paper upward through the rock peaks into its own timeless wilderness.

Late that night Doug rode back to the ranch site. Peter was lashed to his saddle horse, lying across the pommel. Christina, who had been waiting apprehensively for hours, came running out of the house toward the horse with its lifeless burden.

"Peter!" she wept. "Oh, Peter! You were worth more than all the gold in the world!" She would not allow the authorities to take him away. No one could touch the body. It was not until Hal arrived from Salt Lake that she finally seemed to come back to her reason and permitted the arrangements for his burial to be made. She refused to have him buried in the Rock Falls graveyard. "Not after the way the people of Rock Falls treated him!" she insisted adamantly. "He was too good for them! I shall bury him at the head of the pass, so that his grave will look out over Broken Arrow's valley forever. I think he was happier here than he has ever been any place in his life."

After the funeral, before Hal left to return to his studies, Christina sat down with Hal and Ruth and asked them if they wanted the gold. They shook their heads.

"Mama," Ruth murmured, "we are in no condition to think of such things now! Let the problem of the gold wait until we can stop thinking about Papa."

"And you, Hal?" Christina asked.

"I would do anything in this world to help you, Christina," Hal answered. "But for myself, I cannot think about the gold. I have worked hard to become a doctor. It's something I've wanted all my life, and, if I'm to be any good at it, I will need to pursue it singlemindedly. You do see that, don't you?"

"Yes, Hal dear," Christina answered with a sigh. "I think Ruth is right. We just won't think about it for a while."

Ruth and Faith had loved Peter with all their hearts. He had been the one constant in their lives. They mourned for him with tears and smiles. Ruth would take Faith in her lap and rock her gently.

"Remember how Grandpa would stomp into the house and call 'Where's my girl!' and you'd run to him and he'd swing you way up in his arms?" she asked.

Faith nodded her head and snuggled deeper into Ruth's arms. "I miss him," she said in a small voice, and Ruth hugged her tightly.

"I miss him too," she murmured. "But aren't we lucky to have so many wonderful things to remember about him! Let's always keep the good memories!"

Christina remained unapproachable in her grief. Neither Faith nor Ruth could get through to her. For weeks she roamed the fields, silent and lonely, or sat in the kitchen staring at the mountains. Ruth did the cooking and cleaning and Faith grew quiet and almost tiptoed around her grandmother, who had become so strange and absent.

However, the world would not stay at bay. Word of the gold strike had gotten out, and Rock Falls and the surrounding territory was filled with speculators, prospectors, and panners. Christina was able to control traffic into her valley since the passroad was a private throughway. She posted "no trespassing" signs, and the sheriff was supportive in helping her guard her property. She also had her ranchhands patrol the access road.

Christina engaged an engineer to assess the gold strike. He spent several days in the canyon and then informed her that the vein was rich and deep, and the quality of the mineral superb. If adequate roads and mining facilities were built, the costs of mining could be carefully controlled and the profits of the lode should be outstanding.

Christina thanked the man and put the report away in her desk.

One evening Ruth finished the dishes and stepped outside for a breath of fresh air. Her mother was in the yard planting petunias. It was the first thing Christina had done in weeks, and Ruth's face registered surprise.

Christina stood up. "Your father didn't feel this place looked like home without pink petunias by the walk," she said.

"Mama!" Ruth exclaimed. "That's the first time you've talked about Papa since the funeral!"

"I don't need to talk about him!" Christina answered crisply. "I heard you say to Faith 'remember the good things.' You're like your father—you can see the good things—but I can't. Never could! I remember the bad times too well—and there were lots of them. I don't like remembering."

"But, Mama," Ruth exclaimed, "you can't let the past go! You can't forget Papa!"

"I know," Christina answered soberly. Her face was lit with a lovely serenity. "But I didn't want to spend my life remembering either. Then it came to me. I don't need to! You see, Ruth, for me he is not gone! He is so much a part of me—his voice, his thoughts, his heart, his hands—that he is always here.

"When I plant the petunias, I know it is for him and it gives me pleasure. I ride in the fields and I feel his joy in the valley and it makes me happy. In my mind I know what he would be thinking—oh, I still argue with him, but that's a part of it too! Do you see what I mean, Ruth? Because I'm not altogether sure I do, myself!"

"I think so, Mama," Ruth answered. "I think you're saying that you loved him. That you still love him. That you will always love him."

Christina was still as the stars for a moment and then she looked at Ruth with a wondering smile. "Yes!" she breathed. "Yes! That is what I'm saying! Isn't that strange? I don't know if I ever told him! But I have a feeling he knew."

"But, Mama," Ruth said, "you used to fight against him so much!"

"Yes, dear," Christina said. "I know! It took me a long time. I couldn't trust love so I didn't dare acknowledge it. Your father knew me so well! Better than I knew myself. And he waited. He never doubted I loved him; he was simply waiting until I found out."

Ruth sighed. "What a waste."

Christina's voice was impatient. "Growing time is never wasted, Ruth!" she declared. "In most marriages there are times when one is growing and the other one must wait. There are things you can't force—you have to stand aside and give them time to struggle into place."

"Are you talking about you, or about me?" Ruth asked warily.

"Maybe both," Christina answered. "I made my peace with your father. When we came here to live alone, we brought all the mourning and joy of our lives and nothing else. This is where we found each other. Nothing can separate us again. Certainly nothing so puny as death!"

Ruth put her arms around her mother. "You're quite a lady, you know!" she said fondly.

Her mother, always uncomfortable with affection, nonetheless gave Ruth a quick embrace in return.

"Now it's your turn, Ruth," her mother said.

"And Hal's?" Ruth asked with a tinge of bitterness in her voice.

"You can't change Hal," Christina replied. "All you can do is believe in him—like your father did in me. Believe and keep loving and wait."

Christina did not want to confront the issue of the gold, or to let it take her over, and yet she could not ignore the fact that it was there, and that people were hovering around it like vultures.

Winter came as a benison. Christina remained at the ranch, with Ruth and Faith. Doug Whitman lived in the bunkhouse with two other hands. The men took care of the stock, kept the roads open, brought wood and supplies. Christina and Ruth cooked for them and spent their days sewing pretty clothes for Faith, snowshoeing through the fields, occasionally saddling a pony and riding to the mountains on the clear bright days, or greeting old friends and business associates who came to visit—some from curiosity, some out of sympathy, and many to repay the IOUs that they had given to her husband when Peter had singlehandedly saved the valley from financial ruin.

Ruth and Christina were staggered by the amount of money Peter had forwarded to protect the ranchers from bankruptcy. By spring Christina had collected enough from the old debts to insure she could live comfortably for the rest of her life.

In late March Christina received word that Sam Ostler had died of pneumonia. She was sad to hear of the death of her sister's husband, even though she had met him only once. She suspected Peter had maintained a relationship with Sam through the years because Peter had occasionally alluded to a conversation or letter from "Sam." The two men had been much alike—self-contained, dignified, and honorable. She wrote a kind note of condolence to Greg, the adopted nephew she had never seen. She did not receive a reply.

Chapter Twenty-three

In the month following Sam Ostler's death, his adopted son Greg became sole heir to the Ostler estate. He moved into his father's office and assumed control of the many business activities his father had owned. Greg began systematic perusal of his father's files and old correspondence, discovering few surprises, since in the years he had worked as Sam's vice-president he had made it his business to learn as much as possible about his father's private dealings.

One night long after the other office workers had departed Greg prepared to open the one drawer he had not yet sorted through. It was protected with a double lock, and since Greg could not find the second key he had finally broken the desk drawer with a heavy screwdriver in his eagerness to gain entrance to the last bastion of his father's privacy.

Greg was disappointed in the disclosed contents. Nothing was in the drawer except a faded daguerrotype of his mother as a young girl, a piece of blue satin ribbon, a second copy of Sam's will—identical to the one that had already been probated—and a few letters written in Mary's girlish hand. Disgusted at the waste of his efforts, and tired from the long day of close paperwork, Greg grabbed the motley assortment of mementos, preparing to cast them into the wastebasket, when another document fell from the pile.

The paper of the last item was newer than the others, and he opened it with listless curiosity. Immediately his eyes opened wide, and he sat up straight in his chair, rereading the document to which a legal, signed agreement was attached.

After reading it the second time he laughed out loud. Then he picked up the picture of Mary in his hand and smiled at her likeness. "We've got them now, Mother!" he whispered.

The snows were beginning to melt in the high pastures, but the roads were still foul with frozen mud. Christina opened the door when she heard a knock, surprised that anyone had made a journey to the ranch on such a nasty day. Ruth and Faith had gone to Idaho Falls for a few days of shopping. The wind was howling, bringing with it a dreary, cold rain.

The man on her front steps was not very tall. He was holding a black silk umbrella, and his hands were covered with fine calf-skin gloves. She noticed even in the mud and rain that his shoes were shining, the water beading on the smooth, dark leather.

"Mrs. Saunders?" he said. There was something vaguely familiar in the man's looks. He was wearing a dove-gray fedora, with a white silk scarf at the throat of his alpaca overcoat, but even the slim line of his coat could not disguise his pudgy waistline, or the indulgent roundness of his smooth face.

"Yes?" she said coolly.

"May I come in for a moment please?" he said. "I am your sister's son, Greg Ostler, and I believe we have something important to discuss."

Christina was overwhelmed by the sight of this young man. Was it possible? Would her handsome young boys, who were Greg Ostler's contemporaries, even now be showing the same signs of the relentless touch of time? For her, Russell and Cameron were forever in the golden flower of their manhood and, as she looked at this foppish man before her, for a brief moment she felt a raging

398

joy that they never had to be diminished by time, or live to see their manhood fade.

No wonder the man looked slightly familiar! She had seen pictures of him as a college student in her father's room, but he had changed quite dramatically since then.

"Come in," she said. He followed her into the main room, with its deep comfortable furniture, where the wide fireplace was burning brightly. Under the front window she had placed the plants that she nurtured in the house through the winter—the Jerusalem cherries, the geraniums, the ferns and ivy. They made a lovely spot of green, and the firelight relieved the gloom of the afternoon.

"I was sorry to hear about your father," Christina said in a formal voice. "He was a very fine man."

"Yes," Greg answered coldly, "I guess you and your husband counted on that fineness. Well, you are not dealing with him anymore! You are dealing with me!"

"What are you talking about?" Christina asked, puzzled and irritated. "I have not spoken to your father in years. Peter, I think, had some correspondence with him, but we certainly had no business dealings that I know of." She was indignant at the tone of his voice.

"Then perhaps you would like to explain these," Greg said, his voice hard as steel.

Frowning, Christina took the pieces of paper from his hands and read them carefully. The first was the deed to the Broken Arrow Homestead, copied exactly from the original deerskin document Peter had shown her so many years ago. The deed was signed by Peter and legally notarized. Clipped to it was a legal agreement stating that the deed would automatically revert to Samuel Ostler or his estate if the note for twenty-five thousand dollars had not been paid by the given date.

"You will note," Greg said as Christina lifted her eyes from reading, "the date on which the payment was due is long since passed, and no payment has been received."

"It's the gold, isn't it?" Christina whispered with dreadful intuition. "You wouldn't be here except for the gold."

"Partly the gold," Greg answered. "But partly for my mother."

"No," Christina said calmly, shaking her head. "Mary would never have wanted this—would never have done this! We fought and we were estranged, but we would never have deliberately tried to destroy one another! In an odd way we still loved each other—only

399

we were too much alike. We did not know how to forgive. But not this, Greg! Not spiteful revenge! Neither one of us would have done such a thing!''

"I am only doing what is legally right," Greg said coolly.

"Legally?" Christina snorted. "You know that my husband died one week before the date on this note! Obviously he and Sam were the only two who knew of the existence of this agreement!"

"You will have to prove that!" Greg answered. "I myself find it hard to imagine that your husband would sign away your home without even consulting you."

"He didn't sign away his home!" Christina rapped. "Don't be a fool, Greg! Surely you can see that it cost my husband an enormous amount of pride to go to your father to ask for this loan. He knew if I had known he was taking help from Mary's husband I would have chosen bankruptcy instead! I am equally sure that your father took the deed as surety with no intention of ever claiming it. But above all''—her voice rose with assurance—"I know that Peter would have repaid the loan on time!"

"The loan was not repaid!" Greg responded.

"I shall call my lawyers," Christina answered. "We will get to the bottom of this matter!"

Greg looked at the woman in front of him. As a child he had always imagined her as a wicked witch, someone who had quarreled with his mother and made her unhappy. Now, in Christina's fierce eyes, the tilt of her head, and her firm straight back, he saw the fiery independence and stubbornness of his own mother. Even her face, so unlike his mother's in youth, had somehow mellowed with the years, and the strong McElin resemblance showed through. For an eerie moment Greg had the feeling he was facing his own dead mother, come to life in all her dignity and intensity. He took a deep breath and strengthened his resolve.

"It is not my fault! The documents speak for themselves," he asserted. "The law will verify my claim."

"Very well," Christina answered. "If you insist on it, I will see you in court, Greg."

Christina telephoned Ruth to tell her what had happened. The long-distance wires and the awkward crank phone that she had had installed at the ranch popped and fizzed and gave her a very poor connection.

She also called Hal. Despite his rift with Ruth, he was the only man left in the small family, and Christina had come to depend on him.

He offered to leave Salt Lake for a few days to come up and help her, but she refused to let him jeopardize his schoolwork.

"You are too close to board reviews, Hal," she shouted. "I will get Peter's lawyers to look into it."

The next day Christina drove on the muddy roads down to Rock Falls. Raymond Esterbrooke had been Peter's lawyer for years, and Christina parked her car and walked across Main Street, now paved, with neat cement sidewalks on either side, into the new office building next to the bank.

"Will you please tell Mr. Esterbrooke that Mrs. Saunders is here to see him," she informed the neat young woman sitting at the front desk.

The girl went into one of the offices and a moment later Raymond Esterbrooke, in his neat, dark suit, hurried out to greet Christina.

"How nice to see you, Christina!" he exclaimed. "What brings you to town?"

Christina noted with humor that since the discovery of gold on her property, she had become something of a celebrity in Rock Falls. Everywhere she went she received the finest of courtesy. She was not cynical about it, knowing that people would probably have treated her well anyway, but she smiled at the extra warmth that the promise of wealth seemed to bring.

Only Raymond Esterbrooke knew she was already a wealthy woman in her own right. When the IOUs had been collected and carefully invested, she found that the interest alone provided her with an income that was more than adequate for her needs. She had established a trust fund for Faith and was planning to build a clinic for Hal, which she hoped to dedicate and name after Peter. She hadn't told Hal or Ruth about this though, and she was waiting for the young couple to settle their troubles and get back together before she did. However, these were dreams for the future, and now she had a battle on her hands.

How ironic it would be if, after all these years of struggle and sacrifice, Mary should finally take away the last remnant of all that Christina cared for. Mary had always wanted whatever Christina could wrest out of life for herself, and now, even after death, she seemed to be reaching out to take the thing that gave Christina a feeling of security—the homestead—the legacy that Broken Arrow and Peter had given to her. But Mary's son wasn't Mary, and he wasn't fighting with the shadows of childhood fears, loves, and hates as Mary and Christina had. She suspected Greg was using his mother's old feud as an excuse, that it was the gold he really wanted. Well, he wasn't going to get it. Not without a darn good fight!

Christina explained Greg's discovery of the deed and note to the lawyer. Mr. Esterbrooke sat with his hands in a tent under his chin and a faraway look of worry in his eyes. "We'll need to immediately research where and how the documents were registered," he told Christina. "And could you get Peter's bank records for the months preceding his death?" he added.

A week later Raymond called Christina into his office. He explained that Greg had filed suit against Peter's estate for the full deed, which, according to Broken Arrow's original wording, included all mineral and land rights.

"I must tell you, Christina, it doesn't look good," Raymond said with a worried frown. "The deed is valid and so is Peter's agreement. Apparently the loan was never repaid."

"But you saw the withdrawal record of the twenty-five thousand dollars the day before Peter's death!" Christina cried. "Surely any court of law would know the money was to repay the loan! He couldn't help it if he died before he could pay! I didn't know about the loan—or I would have repaid it. I'll repay it now, with interest. How can Greg or the legal system justify—"

"Now, now, Christina!" Raymond soothed. "If you could only find out what happened to the twenty-five thousand! It seems to have vanished without a trace!"

Christina shook her head in despair. "I have been through Peter's drawers a hundred times—all of his records—and there is nothing."

"It is very strange," Raymond mused.

"One thing," Christina said. "I remember that Doug mentioned when he told me about"—her voice faltered but then grew strong again—"about Peter's death. He said the last thing Peter did was try to hand him an envelope—but the wind blew it away. I've wondered if that could have had anything to do with the lost money."

"It wouldn't make any difference legally, anyway." Raymond sighed. "It doesn't prove intention to pay."

"Doesn't the withdrawal indicate intention?" Christina asked.

"Not in a court of law," Raymond answered. "I am afraid that Greg Ostler is the only one with documents which will stand up to legal scrutiny. Of course we will have character witnesses to testify that Peter would have made good on the loan. But the documents stand inviolate."

"Inviolate!" Christina said. "Why should something written on paper be more valid than the abstract total of a man's life!" She thought deeply for a moment.

"That's the law!" Raymond stated. "Documents are incontrovertible."

She stared at Raymond with triumphant eyes. "Then we will simply have to bring the documents into question!" she exclaimed.

"What?" Raymond looked astounded. Staring at Christina, he thought she looked years younger. The stimulation of the fight had brought vitality and sparkle back into her eyes. "You wouldn't seriously question Peter's legal agreements! You might damage his reputation. It wouldn't be worth that."

"Of course not!" Christina snapped. "I wouldn't question Peter's document! But what about the deed itself? Raymond—that is what we need to bring into question!"

"But, Christina!" Raymond exploded. "That's ridiculous. The original deed is in the historical society in Boise, for anyone to see! Peter registered the first deed legally years ago. It was surveyed and filed as required. That deed, unorthodox though it may have been, is unmovable. It's a historic document, for heaven's sake! Broken Arrow owned the land—it was not owned by the tribe, so there is no question of placing the deed into litigation with the Bureau of Indian Affairs over ownership."

"What happened to the rest of Broken Arrow's property?" Christina asked curiously. "He has been gone for long over seven years and is considered legally dead. Who owns the surrounding area now?"

"I believe it is held in trust by the Indian Bureau."

"Could the courts order the disposal of the income from the chief's property to be used in a specific way?"

"Yes, I believe so, as long as ownership is under the administration of the courts."

"How long would that be?" Christina asked.

"As long as the property is in dispute—years maybe."

Christina nodded. "I want you to free up your appointment calendar tomorrow, Raymond," she said. "You and I are going on a trip across the border into Montana."

"What are we looking for?" Raymond asked.

"The oldest living member of the Shoshoni tribe," Christina

answered. "In the meantime could you get your staff to try to locate every map of this territory they can find. The older, the more detailed, the better!"

On a golden day in late June Christina, her daughter, Ruth, and Raymond Esterbrooke prepared to enter the Rock Falls County Courthouse.

Hal, who had insisted on coming in from Salt Lake City the night before, was with them too. He had graduated three days earlier, and Christina was expressing her regret at not being able to attend the graduation ceremonies. Ruth had not attended the graduation either, but she had not expressed regret. Hal was staying at the Rock Falls Hotel, and he and Ruth had yet to be alone.

"That's all right, Christina," Hal assured her. "I'm sorry I couldn't have been in Rock Falls helping you!"

Christina smiled an enigmatic smile. "I think it is Greg Ostler who is going to need the help!" she said smugly.

They entered the crowded courtroom where people from all over the county had come to witness the proceedings. Many of the onlookers were curious to see the woman whose property held the richest gold strike in the state's history and who seemed to be sitting on the find. A lot of the courtroom observers were hoping Greg would win his case. Rumor was that Greg was a fine businessman and would develop the gold mine, which would mean work and money pouring into the region.

Others among the audience were old friends of the Saunders family. They were hoping Christina would be able to hold on to the ranch property because they understood how much she loved it.

The warm morning passed slowly. The courtroom was crowded and stuffy with flies buzzing in the stifling air. Ruth leaned over to Christina. "I'm glad I didn't bring Faith!" she whispered. Five-year-old Faith had been left at the farm with a responsible farmhand who doted on her. Faith loved the ranch. The hired men had saddle-broken a pony for her, and she was enchanted by the animals and the wide-open playing spaces. She also loved her grandma, Christina. The older woman and the young girl had developed a quiet, deep rapport that was a beautiful thing to see.

Sometimes Ruth watched her mother playing with Faith. Christina was endlessly patient and sweet with the little girl, laughing at her piquant comments and tenderly showing her the wonders of the world. The two of them seemed to shimmer in mutual affection.

Ruth thought, without bitterness, "Why couldn't Mother ever have been that way with Leah and me?" But then, if Ruth were totally honest, she knew she would have to admit that the twins had never given their mother a chance. They had never opened up their own private childhood world to their mother and invited her in.

The morning in the courtroom dragged on with the tedium of legal presentations. Exhibits were presented and depositions drawn. There would be no jury, so each of the lawyers made opening statements for the benefit of the judge as well as the crowd.

Greg could not believe Mr. Esterbrooke's presentation! None of his own lawyer's points were even disputed! Unchallenged, Greg's attorney presented the deed, Peter's loan agreement, the absence of evidence of payment, and the legal claim of Greg Ostler to the property. All was done in meticulous order by Greg's lawyer without question or objection from Esterbrooke.

When Greg's lawyer finished presenting his case, Raymond Esterbrooke stood up and stated that his client had no debate with any of the facts that had been submitted. He asked for permission to put Christina on the stand, where, clearly and succinctly, she testified that Peter had withdrawn the money to repay the loan and his untimely death had apparently prevented it. She freely admitted they had no proof of this other than the bank statement of the withdrawal.

Raymond Esterbrooke then placed before the court Christina's written offer to pay the amount of the twenty-five thousand dollar note plus interest. He also informed the judge that Greg Ostler had refused the offer. He placed before the judge a written offer to pay Greg Ostler the full amount of the value of the Broken Arrow property, appraised in any manner, as long as the appraisal did not include the value of the gold discovery. This was followed again by Greg's refusal—in writing.

The judge shook his head sadly. He was puzzled that Christina and her lawyer had not put up more of a fight, although, in keeping with the law, he was certain that, no matter what defense Christina offered, he would be required to award the settlement to that young smart-aleck sitting with a satisfied smirk on his face beside his citybred lawyer! Sometimes the judge disliked his profession thoroughly—and today was going to be one of those times! He felt a great sympathy for Christina and was extremely aware of the debt Rock Falls owed to her and her husband. "What a bitter way to repay her!" he thought.

"Your honor," Raymond was addressing the bench. "We do not

question the plaintiff's right to the deed on your bench. We feel his claim is not just—but it is legal. However, your honor, at this time we would like to bring into question the validity of the document— the original deed!''

The whole courthouse erupted in astonishment, and the judge pounded on his podium. ''Silence!'' the bailiff called. ''Silence in court!''

When order was restored, Raymond continued. ''I would like to place in evidence every existing map of the Rock Falls region, your honor. On these maps I have circled the mountains surrounding the Broken Arrow Valley with their established names written on them wherever they have been recorded.''

Puzzled, the judge took the sheaf of maps and began to glance through them.

''Your honor,'' Raymond continued, ''if you will note, not on one single official map do the names 'Coyote Pass,' 'Crowsnest Mountain,' or the 'Mountain of the Three Song Falls' appear. It is therefore assumed that the names of the mountains used to delineate the perimeters of the property deeded to Peter Saunders were known only to Broken Arrow. There is no way of legally establishing where those designated borders are located!''

The judge frowned. ''It is assumed that the names given on the deed were the common designations used by the Shoshoni tribe for the specific mountains.''

''Your honor,'' Raymond said. ''I would like to call a witness. Will Red Cloud please come forward?''

There was a stir in court as an aging Indian, wearing a flannel shirt with a long fringed vest and wrinkled work pants, came forward slowly. His feet were shod in heavily beaded moccasins, and his hair was twisted in two long plaits wrapped with black flannel on either side of his head.

His face was seamed with wrinkles and his hair was gray, but his eyes were as black as obsidian and intelligent.

After Red Cloud was sworn in, Raymond led him through a series of questions that established the fact that he was a member of the same Shoshoni tribe as Broken Arrow. Red Cloud had been a young brave in the band that Broken Arrow's father had led, and he had known Broken Arrow when he was a young man and Broken Arrow still a boy. The two of them had gone to the reservation in the same year.

"How old was Broken Arrow when he went to the reservation?" Raymond asked.

"About twelve summers," Red Cloud answered.

"Had he lived in the valley all of his life?" Raymond Esterbrooke inquired.

"No!" replied Red Cloud. "Our valley was not safe. We were hunted like animals by the authorities. Most of Arrow's young life was lived in hiding, or in retreat."

"Let me show you a picture of the valley in question," Raymond said. He held up a large drawing of the valley. It was a three-dimensional portrayal, intricately sketched, showing the outline of each mountain.

"This peak to the north," Raymond said, pointing to the northern perimeter mentioned in the deed as Moon Mountain. "What is the name of this peak?"

"Sun Journey," Red Cloud answered.

"Then can you show me Crowsnest?" Raymond asked.

Red Cloud took the pointer and pointed to a small mountain near the base of the other.

"And Mountain of the Three Song Falls?" Raymond asked.

"There is no such mountain," Red Cloud answered. "None of the mountains of our valley had that name. It was a name in a child's story which we told around the campfire. Broken Arrow must have remembered it from the story."

"I see." The lawyer looked at the judge.

"There are no written records which give us proof of any of the mountain names in the valley, your honor. Broken Arrow and Peter Saunders are both dead and cannot testify which mountains, in fact, Broken Arrow was indicating when he wrote the deed. I call into legal question every portion of the Broken Arrow deed which covers the mountains. Legally, the boundaries used in the deed applying to the mountainous areas simply do not exist. Therefore, until legal verification of those boundaries can be determined, I move that the deed in question remain in a state of probate, as a trust of the courts."

"I object!" shouted Greg's lawyer. "Such a determination could take years! How can records be found which do not exist!"

"That," the judge answered, "will be a problem for the courts to decide. Objection overruled."

The judge was in his chambers for a long time. Ruth fidgeted on her bench. "What could be taking so long?" she asked a dozen times.

Christina sat serenely silent beside Raymond Esterbrooke. She had fought the best fight she knew how, and now it was out of her hands. She would accept the decision, whoever won, but the thought of the valley being taken from her moved her with a sense of loss and impending sorrow.

The judge reentered the courtroom. Everyone rose at his coming, and, when the rustle of the audience resettling had quieted, the judge spoke in his deep, authoritative voice.

He recounted the legal facts of the case, and reviewed the documents as presented by each party.

"It seems to me that we are stuck with an irony," the judge continued. "If it were not for the extraordinary wealth enclosed in those mountains, the questionable nature of the deed's perimeters might be loosely accepted. However, the deed, always considered an unorthodox document, has been shown to be legally unsupportable and will require significant title search. I have been informed by Raymond Esterbrooke that Mrs. Saunders has formally relinquished all rights to any of the mountain property and has placed its disposal entirely at the discretion of the courts.

"I have also been informed by the Bureau of Indian Affairs and the United States Government that they both wish to make legal claims to the mountain area of the property. There will also be a legal search instigated for any known descendants or relatives of Chief Broken Arrow, to whom original title was given.

"It is my honest prediction that the disputed property could well be tied up in litigation for many years to come.

"Now, as to the floor of the valley itself. By any reading, it is immediately apparent that the deed legally covers all of the valley floor. This section of the property will not be involved in the claim dispute and will be considered legally bound by the original deed.

"Due to the rare and unusual circumstances in which the original loan agreement to Sam Ostler was made and terminated, I have, upon serious reflection and perusal of the property laws, decided for the defendant, Mrs. Peter Saunders.

"The floor of the property known as the Broken Arrow Valley, and all of the buildings, animals, and appurtenances thereunto, I award in title to Christina Saunders, upon the payment of the sum of thirty-seven thousand dollars to Greg Ostler, which reimburses him for the amount of the loan, full, compounded interest, and a subsidy which

408

brings the total payment to the approximate value of the real property, minus improvements, such as the ranch house and barns.''

Christina permitted herself a small smile, but Ruth laughed out loud. "She did it!" she cried. "She won!"

As soon as the court was dismissed, Greg came over to Christina. "I'm going to fight this in every appeals court in the country!" he warned her.

She looked at him quietly for a moment. "Don't, Greg," she said softly. "Can't you see, it's over. Don't waste your life on something that doesn't matter to anyone anymore. Please, Greg, if you want to do something to make your mother's memory count, go, get married, and raise a family of beautiful children. No one will see that gold in our lifetime. Your mother's and my quarrel is finished.''

To Greg's astonishment, his aunt, tiny and delicate, with an almost girlish grace, stood up and kissed him on the cheek. "You have your whole life ahead of you, Greg dear. Get out from under the shadow of my generation, and live!''

Greg shook his head, and his proud face broke out into a reluctant smile. "You McElin ladies!" he said. "You are all alike! No one can resist you when you set your minds to something.''

Christina's eyes were on Hal and Ruth, who were standing at the back of the courtroom waiting for her. They were standing carefully apart. Hal was searching the crowd for Christina, but Ruth's eyes were on him.

"I hope that's true, Greg," Christina answered with a smile. "I really hope that's true.''

"I intend to keep after the gold," Greg assured her. "I still have the deed and my lawyers will pursue it to the highest court.''

"Then fight it out with the government, Greg. If it's what you want I wish you luck. As for me, I've found that life is too short for unimportant things.''

She turned and walked toward Hal and Ruth.

"That's one eccentric lady!" his lawyer exclaimed, half in admiration.

"No," Greg replied. "Just a 'lady'!''

Chapter Twenty-four

Faith was standing beside her grandmother, laughing and talking on the lawn in front of the ranchhouse. Beyond them the meadows and the mountains shone against the bright blue sky. The two of them were going to be alone at the ranch while Hal and Ruth took a long-delayed trip together to try to work out their relationship.

"You'll have to do your chores every day," Christina was telling her little granddaughter in a mock-serious voice. "The eggs need to be brought from the hen house. . . ."

Faith was laughing. "I know, Grandma!" she said. "I like to get the eggs! The hens aren't afraid of me. They know I'll be soft with them."

"That's the secret," Christina assented. "You must be soft with them."

Ruth and Hal came out of the house. Ruth was wearing a short chemise dress in robin's-egg blue. It matched her eyes perfectly. Her hair was bobbed, shaped to the nape of her neck with a long sweep of bangs in the front that brushed her eyes. She had on a small fitted hat that matched the dress and sheer stockings with a tiny woven design that enhanced the lovely line of her legs. Christina thought she had never seen her daughter look more beautiful.

"Have a wonderful trip, my dear," Christina said, walking to her daughter. They embraced, a little stiffly, since mother and daughter could never quite overcome the rigid patterns of Ruth's childhood.

Ruth glanced around the large empty bowl of the valley. Nothing was moving within the range of her vision except the cattle in the far pasture and one lone rider, herding the cows.

"Are you sure you want to live out here on the ranch, Mother? When I get back from Yellowstone, don't you think we should look for a little place for you in town? Winters will be very long—what on earth will you do out here?"

Her mother gave her a funny, happy smile. "Raise sheep!" she said laconically.

"Oh, Mother!" Ruth said with a shake of her head. "I never know what to expect from you!"

"Neither did your father!" Christina said lightly, and there was a mischievous twinkle in her eye. "That was my secret. You might remember that with Hal!"

Suddenly Christina grew serious; she reached up and embraced Ruth a second time. "Be happy, dear daughter," she whispered.

Hal was in the car and Ruth hurried to climb in beside him. They drove away, heading for the pass road. Ruth looked back and saw Christina take Faith's little hand and start walking to the house. It was incredible from this distance how much they looked alike! Christina's white hair in the sunlight looked like Faith's blond curls, and they both walked with a straight, sprightly step which seemed to hurl a fearless challenge to the world.

"You know, Hal," Ruth said, "it's odd. All the death and sorrow Mother has had to deal with—and this awful court fight with Greg, and losing the gold—you'd think she would be battered—you know, defeated! But I can't ever remember seeing her so happy and complete."

Hal stopped the car at the entrance to the pass, and they both looked down over Broken Arrow's valley.

"That's because she's finally come home," Hal said. "She's found a place she loves—she knows she belongs!"

When the earth was formed the crust buckled and plunged and shrank and bulged as it cooled around its seething inner core. Sometimes, as the crust formed, it left fragile, thin-skinned areas, not deep enough or strong enough to contain the wild, untamed fury of the subterranean layers. Such a place was the Yellowstone region.

Almost eight thousand feet above sea level, the great Yellowstone plateau, framed by the Snowy Mountains on the north, the Absarokas on the east, the Tetons on the south, and the Gallatin range to the west, lay with its massive forests of lodgepole pine, spruce, Douglas fir, and aspens. The valleys, during the short season of its summer, were covered with thick growths of grass and wild flowers.

In the wilderness, the wildlife was protected, and the elk, deer, antelope, mountain sheep, buffalo, moose, and grizzly roamed without fear of men. The rivers and lakes teemed with waterfowl, and the forests sheltered the birds and smaller animals. The lakes and streams spawned the finest trout—cutthroat, black-spotted, rainbow, and brook.

Through the years, roads had been carefully built through the region, to take visitors to the most famous sites without spoiling the natural beauty of the landscape. In the 1920s it had become a favorite spot for honeymoons.

Hal and Ruth, married over four years now, had never really been alone together. The years of their marriage had been marked with the tension and pressure of Hal's schooling and Ruth's struggle to raise Faith and support his studies. When Ruth had left him to return to the ranch with Faith, Hal had begun to understand how completely he had grown to rely on her love and care—and how terribly he had taken her for granted. He understood why she had left him. The incident with the nurse had only been the trigger. The reason for their separation had been his failure to give her the love and understanding she needed and deserved. Under her sweet nature was the McElin pride, and she could not endure his indifference, so she had left. He knew she was right. But now he wanted her back desperately and he didn't quite know how to begin. She was so familiar to him—and yet so unfamiliar. Her kind nature, her lucid intelligence, the outward lines of her body—all those things he knew by heart—but her inner thoughts, the emotions that touched and motivated her—these things were as elusive and unknown to him as though they had just met.

Today she seemed different to him. Some subtle chemistry between them since his return made her seem fresh and new. Even her face had a changed look—a look of insouciance and mystery—as though she herself did not know exactly what to expect, or how to act with him.

"This is so fine!" Ruth exclaimed, leaning her head back against the seat. "So fine to be alone with you, and to be free of cares and worries—for a few days at least! I can't remember the last time I felt it was my time—my desires—my impulses that counted!"

"It is your time!" Hal said. "I want it to be."

"Good!" she exclaimed with a teasing lilt in her voice, and she looked at him out of the corners of her eyes with a hint of challenge and mischief that put him off stride. All of her familiar responses were gone—and her lighthearted independence was as unexpected as the way she held her body, delicately posing for him. He could

412

ense her preening in his aroused interest, and she stretched luxuriously
nd crossed her legs, so that her knees peeked fetchingly from under
er short skirt. She was enchanting, the more so because he could
ot tell if she knew her actions were seductive, or if they were
mply the natural outgrowth of her feelings of relaxation and freedom.
low much did Ruth know about men—or of the innuendo of motion
nd voice that could ensnare a man's desires? Certainly he had not
een any evidence of that awareness in the cramped and dingy
partment in which they had lived, or in the tense atmosphere of the
anch bedroom he had shared with Leah before he married Ruth. But
en, perhaps he had not been looking—too caught up in his past,
o burdened by studies.

Here, together on the road, free and triumphant, Ruth seemed to
e shedding the role of conscientious wife and mother, friend and
upporter. "I have given you those things already," she seemed to
e saying to him. "There is more here—much more. But the rest
ou must win!"

She sighed and ran her fingers through her hair so that the soft,
oose bangs fell over one eye. "Smell the fragrance of the mountain
ir!" she murmured. "It is so rich and soothing!"

He glanced at her. Her eyes were closed, and the fresh air, roaring
nrough her open window, caught her hair in its hands and she
eveled in the sensation.

They drove through the day and entered the park in the early
vening. In the blue glow of the long summer twilight they drove
ast the steaming formations of colored rock and bubbling pools.
he heated mist from the pools rose like the breath of angels in the
ir. Once, far to their left, they saw the giant plume of an erupting
eyser spewing across the sky.

They arrived at their lodge just as darkness descended and the
tars burst upon the sky like fireworks. Hal registered in the massive
obby with its arched, rustic log framework lifting high above their
eads, and an open staircase that led to their floor.

Their bed was made of brass and covered with a heavy hand-
vorked quilt. Already the evening had turned chilly, and Ruth was
egretting her short-sleeved dress and wishing she had worn a heavy
weater and slacks.

"You've got a great view of Old Faithful geyser out your window,"
heir attendant told them as he put down their bags.

"Thank you," Hal said, tipping him, and the man left, closing
he door behind him.

413

"Here we are!" Hal said, a trifle too heartily. He was surprised to find himself feeling awkward, as though he did not quite know how to proceed.

"I'm going to change," Ruth said and stepped into the bathroom.

Hal was exhausted from the long drive, and since the room was chilly, he quickly put on his pajamas and climbed under the warm covers. He turned off the small lamp beside the bed so that the room was in darkness.

"I'm freezing!" Ruth called. Hal propped himself up on his elbow as the bathroom door opened. The light from the other room was behind Ruth and he could not see her face, only the misty cloud of white silk she wore and, within it, the graceful beauty of her body outlined by the light shining through the sheer billow of her gown. Her body was like a statue, perfect in proportion and detail.

She said nothing, but reached behind her and switched off the light, and then he could see her face, the shining passion of her eyes and the delicate lace outlining her shoulders.

"Ruth!" he exclaimed hoarsely, wonderingly. "Who are you, Ruth? All the magic and mystery and loveliness I could ever imagine! How could I have been so blind!"

She came to him where he lay and pulled back the covers slowly and he raised his arms to receive her.

The clouds of silk around her were like a sweet, full tent. They billowed above them and below them, sliding across the secrets of her body, revealing and concealing and tantalizing Hal until he swept the robe away and loved this wondrous woman who had brought him, after all, more gifts than he could hold, with a deeper passion than he had ever known.

Afterward, they lay talking in the brass bed, their smooth bodies touching as they lay in one another's arms. "Ruth," Hal whispered against her hair, "I thought I knew you, and you have shown me yet another woman! Are you full of a thousand surprises?"

"All women are a hundred women, Hal," Ruth answered softly. "A hundred times a hundred! We're made up of bits and scraps and pieces of all the women that went before us. My mother, my mother's mother, my father's mother, their mothers—each one has handed down a bit of herself, some scrap of emotion, some unresolved problem or quirk of personality. We inherit them like the bones of our cheeks or the shape of our noses. Pride, passion, humor, stubborness, love—given to us like a string of beads to play with and arrange.

414